NATURE DETECTIVE

How To Solve Outdoor Mysteries

Eileen M. Docekal

Illustrated by David Eames

Sterling Publishing Co., Inc.   New York

To Jamie, With Gratitude

Edited by Timothy Nolan

Library of Congress Cataloging-in-Publication Data
Docekal, Eileen M.
    Nature detective : how to solve outdoor mysteries / by Eileen M.
Docekal ; illustrated by David Eames.
        p. cm.
    Includes index.
    Summary: Gives instructions for exploring different aspects of
nature by recognizing and interpreting a variety of clues and signs.
    ISBN 0-8069-6844-3
    1. Nature study—Juvenile literature.   [1. Nature study.]
I. Eames, David, 1965–   ill. II. Title.
QH53.D53   1989
574'.078—dc20
                                                            89-31387
                                                            CIP
                                                            AC

Copyright © 1989 by Eileen M. Docekal
Published by Sterling Publishing Co., Inc.
387 Park Avenue South, New York, N.Y. 10016
Distributed in Canada by Sterling Publishing
c/o Canadian Manda Group, P.O. Box 920, Station U
Toronto, Ontario, Canada M8Z 5P9
Distributed in Great Britain and Europe by Cassell PLC
Artillery House, Artillery Row, London SW1P 1RT, England
Distributed in Australia by Capricorn Ltd.
P.O. Box 665, Lane Cove, NSW 2066
Manufactured in the United States of America
All rights reserved
Sterling ISBN 0-8069-6844-3

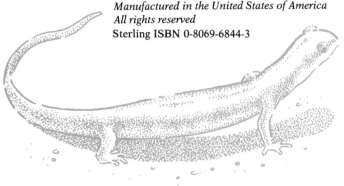

CONTENTS

INTRODUCTION

There are exciting things outside! A pile of fur and bones, footprints in the sand, an insect hidden under a leaf, or, if you are very lucky, a wild animal. Watching animals in the wild is a rare thrill, but many are very shy of people and nocturnal, coming out only at night.

Visitors to an area often leave behind clues or signs and searching for these clues is a lot like going on a treasure hunt, because finding these signs and figuring out what they mean can be as exciting as actually seeing the animals.

This book will help you be a nature detective. Nature detectives explore the world around them looking for clues and signs to solve the mysteries of nature. They figure out what each plant and animal needs to live in a certain area, how they are related to the other plants and animals nearby, and how they are part of the natural world.

Nature mysteries can be found anywhere: in your yard, the woods, even at the seashore. Some of the clues can only be found during a certain time of the year, while other signs can be found all year round. Note the time, date, place, and weather conditions when you go exploring, and you'll discover some patterns to the animals' activities. Finding more clues can point to or eliminate a suspect, can be used to reenact the crime, and, sometimes, may lead you to a wild animal.

Good nature detectives have a sense of adventure. They also remember to leave only footprints as clues to the wildlife that they have been in an area.

Primary Tools

Eyes • To closely inspect any find, and to search an area.

Ears • To listen for any sounds of animals moving or communicating.

Nose • To sniff out suspects. Just like police detectives use hound dogs, use your nose to track down a recent visit of a fox or to smell a flower.

Hands • To feel all the parts of a clue, to turn over logs and leaves, or to feel the shapes and textures of things outdoors.

Never touch poison ivy, poison oak, or poison sumac. Touching these plants creates an itchy rash on the skin, and burning the twigs of these poisonous plants can create poisonous smoke. Remember: "Leaves of three, let it be."

Many wild plants are good to eat, but during these investigations, *never* taste any wild plant. Only an expert can correctly identify edible plants, and many plants look alike. Eating the wrong plant can make you very ill and maybe even kill you.

Dress according to the season, and keep in mind that a good detective checks out all clues, and sometimes this means lying down on your belly, crawling on your hands and knees, and even stepping into water. So wear old clothes and comfortable shoes or sneakers.

Additional Tools

- **Binoculars**
- **Magnifying lens or bug box**
- **Aquarium fish net or tea strainer**
- **Empty cottage cheese container**
- **Camera**

·1·

MYSTERIOUS VISITORS

Forests, fields, beaches, and even your own backyard are home to many animals. Go outside and look around. The area may look quite deserted. Most wild animals are very shy and afraid of being seen by you or by other animals that may be looking for a snack. You may not be able to see them, but they're there.

You may not see many wild animals, but there's plenty of evidence that they were recently around. As you develop your detective skills, you'll be able to figure out exactly what creatures were visiting the area when you weren't around.

Illus. 1

Illus. 1. Animal tracks are often your best clues. Each animal's footprint is unique. Size, shape, and pattern can help you identify who and what passed through while you were not around. Look for tracks in mud, sand, or snow, especially next to a stream or lake. Tracks can reveal last night's chase between a fox and rabbit, show the path that a herd of deer travelled along, or lead you to a squirrel's hidden supply of acorns. Mammals leave tracks, but so do birds, insects, snakes, and even worms.

Suspects and Clues

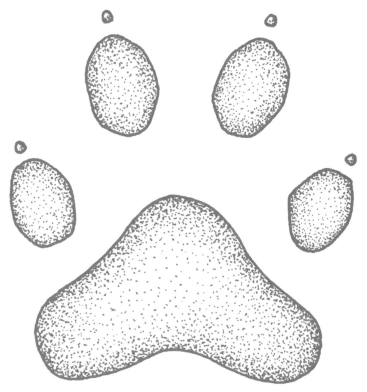

Illus. 2

Illus. 2. Make a track with your hand and foot next to the animal track. How large is the mystery track compared to your prints? Do you think you are larger or smaller than that animal? Gently touch the track. Is it fresh or old? Is there any smell around the track?

Follow the tracks to see if they lead anywhere. Look for other tracks in the area of the trail, and check if the other tracks cross this animal's path. Are there any signs of a chase?

Illus. 3a

Front

Hind

Illus. 3b

Front

Hind

Illus. 3c

Front

Illus. 3. The number of toes can also tell you a lot. Some animals have a different number of toes on their forefeet than they have on their hindfeet.

Mice and tree squirrels have four toes on the front foot and five toes on the hindfoot (Illus. 3a). As these animals bounce along, they land with their hindfeet ahead of their forefeet. Dogs, foxes, bobcats, and rabbits have four toes on all their feet (Illus. 3b). These animals are called *digitigrades*, because when they run, they only leave tracks with their toes.

Skunks, raccoons, opossums, and muskrats have feet with five toes (Illus. 3c). Animals that leave both heel and toe impressions on the ground are called *plantigrades*.

Cows, sheep, deer, antelope, and elk actually walk on specialized toenails, called hooves. Tracks from hooves leave two impressions that look like an upside-down heart (Illus. 3d). Horse tracks are easy to identify because they have horseshoes nailed onto their hooves. The iron rim of the horseshoe leaves an upside-down U-shaped outline.

Bird tracks have three or four finger-like markings. Perching birds (robins, sparrows) hop around on the ground and leave side by side, or paired, tracks. Game birds (doves, quail) and some ducks and gulls walk along as they feed and leave alternating tracks (Illus. 3e).

Illus. 3

Illus. 3d

Hind

Illus. 3e

10

Check for claw marks. Members of the dog family leave claw marks as they walk, while cats retract, or pull back, their claws when moving about, so that their tracks leave no claw marks.

Look for webbing. Ducks, gulls, and beavers all have webbing to help them swim.

There may be marks left by the animal's tail or wing—muskrats leave a curving tail mark between their prints, while mice leave a fairly straight-line mark. Birds often leave both tail and wing marks as they take off and fly. These marks are easiest to spot when the ground is covered with fresh snow.

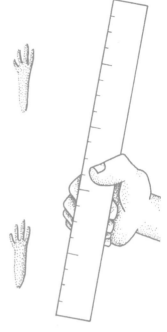

Illus. 4. The distances between the set of tracks can usually indicate if the animal was walking or galloping. Most wild animals don't run for very long distances. As you follow the tracks, see if the distances change to show a change in the gait of the animal. When a bobcat walks across a field, its tracks are spaced about 10 inches apart. When it's galloping, the spacing is anywhere from 4 to 8 feet apart.

Illus. 4

Illus. 5. The pattern of movement can also narrow down the list of suspects. Is it straight? Dogs, cats, foxes, and hooved animals move in a straight line when they walk. Cats walk so straight that they place their hindfeet in the impressions made by the front feet.

Do the tracks meander? Skunks and porcupines waddle along as they search out plants or grubs to feast on.

Not all animals leave a trail of footprints. Have you ever seen a trail that looks like a silver ribbon on your sidewalk in the morning? This is a snail's slime. The slime helps the snail to move easily over the ground.

Insects and snakes often leave tracks in sand or wet soil. A snake leaves curved lines as it moves its body over the earth. The small legs of insects leave fine tracings that are often in parallel rows. Sand dunes are a great place to look for snake and insect tracks.

Illus. 5

11

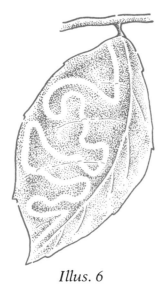

Illus. 6

Illus. 6. Other places to look for tracks are on leaves and tree trunks. Have you ever wondered about those lace-like trails on leaves or the fancy carvings on the surface of wood? They're footprints, too! Leaf miners are the larvae of insects that live within leaves and feed on the leaf's internal tissues. Leaf miners chew through the leaf along very small feeding tunnels, known as mines. These mines are so thin that they go through the middle of the leaf, and thus appear as light-colored trails from the outside of the leaf. These feeding tunnels widen as the larvae grow. Eventually, a newly hatched moth, fly, or beetle cuts a hole and flies out of the leaf. Each species of leaf miner creates distinctive mines. Some never backtrack, while others never cross the leaf's thick midrib.

Illus. 7. Bark beetles also leave tunnel tracks. Adult beetles carve out a tunnel, or nursery, under the bark of trees, then they lay their eggs. As the beetle larvae feed and grow, they create lines that radiate from the nursery. What do you think happens when the larvae reach the end of the radiating tunnels?

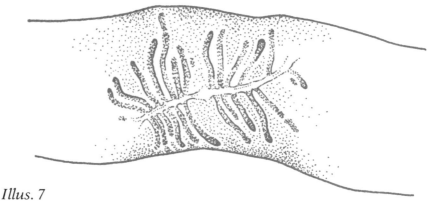

Illus. 7

If you find bark in the area, look for tiny holes. This is where the beetle emerges when it becomes an adult. It bores a hole to get out of the tree where it hatched and flies to a new host tree.

Take a look at the tracks you left behind while you were investigating an area. Would another nature detective be able to figure out what type of shoes you wore, how big you are, and how and where you moved?

Illus. 8

Illus. 8. While inspecting or following a footprint, make sure you have all your senses working to find other clues. Putting these together can create a picture of what an animal ate, where it moved, and how it behaved. Some of these clues can be found alone or together.

Feathers and fur • Look for a clump of hair or a pile of feathers. Is there any sign of blood or other evidence of a struggle?

Crushed leaves • Does the area look as if an animal bedded down for the night? Is it large enough for a herd of deer or only one rabbit?

Illus. 9. Check also for teeth marks on the trunks of nearby trees. Look for chips of wood below the chewed trunk. They are probably the work of nature's lumberjack, the beaver.

Look for beaver gnawings along creeks and ponds. Beavers are messy chewers. They take a few bites from the top, bottom, and center, scattering wood chips everywhere. If you find a chewed trunk, feel how smooth the grooves are. Beavers have two large incisors that are constantly growing,

Illus. 9

just like your fingernails. They must continually chew to wear these teeth down.

Termites and beetles also eat wood but only leave piles of sawdust after they dine.

Most animals are fussy eaters; they only eat particular plants and only certain parts of that plant. Like people, they often leave some food on their dinner plates.

If you find chewed plants, look at what part has been eaten. Deer and grasshoppers will eat whole leaves, while Mexican bean beetles favor only the soft leaf tissue. Tougher veins are left behind for other insects.

Illus. 10

Pay attention to how high the chewed area is. Would a rabbit have been able to reach that high, or would a deer?

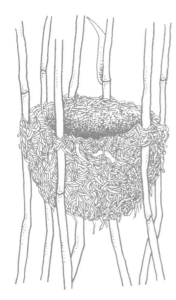

Illus. 10. Fall and winter are good times to look up in the treetops for abandoned nests. These nests were probably homes for eggs and baby birds during the spring and summer months. Look at the materials used to make the nest. They can tell you who lived there. Hummingbirds often weave their nests with spider webs and lichens, robins lay a groundfloor of mud, while goldfinches use fluff from cattails to line their nests.

Piles of leaves in treetops may belong to squirrels. They also use sticks for support, so watch for these as well. Crows and hawks also make fancy nests, using sticks and leaves to make a sturdy home for the babies.

Illus. 11–12. Search the ground for holes. What size animal could fit in it? Look for any clues that indicate if the animal was looking for food or for shelter. Squirrels and jays bury acorns during the fall and retrieve them throughout the winter. Skunks often paw the ground in search of grubs and earthworms.

Is the dirt piled to one side or is it scattered? Moles raise the ground as they move underground. When they emerge, the opening looks as if the ground exploded. Gophers, on the other hand, frequently come above ground and push the dirt to one side of their underground tunnel. Crayfish, (Illus. 11) use their front pincers to pile up mounds of wet mud in a circle around their tunnels.

Are the digging piles round and pinhead size? These are traces left by earthworms. As they tunnel along, the soil passes through their digestive system and is left behind as tiny round castings.

If you are near a stream or lake, look for a mud slide along the water's sloping banks. One of nature's most playful creatures, the river otter, leaves a slippery slide as a clue

Illus. 12

that it has been there. River otters are related to weasels and skunks and are expert swimmers. They slide and dive into fresh-water areas to feed on fish, snakes, frogs, and turtles. During the winter, they turn snow-covered banks into their own toboggan runs (Illus. 12.)

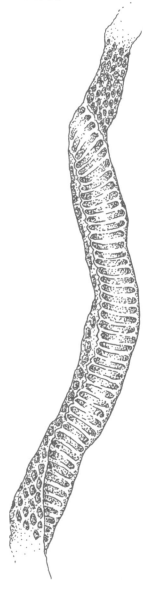

Illus. 13. In the spring and fall look for shed skins by rocks and tree roots. Snakes, of course, grow, but their outer skin stays the same size. They must shed these old skins, using rocks and roots to help remove the outer skin, pulling it off as you would remove a glove. If you find a shed snake skin, feel it. You'll probably be surprised to find that it's dry, not slimy.

Notice the belly of the skin. How do you think the snake used the scales to move over the ground? If you're wearing sneakers, take a look at the pattern on your soles. Many soles have overlapping scale patterns similar to the scales on snake skins. This pattern gives good traction and helps the snake move over dirt and logs. Cicadas, an insect, also discard their skins as they change from nymphs to adults.

Can animals use the discarded skins? A spider may curl up inside, and sometimes, birds will weave the skins into their nests.

Illus. 14. Many mammals and large birds cannot digest the hard seeds, or the fur, feathers, and bones of the other animals they eat. These items are passed out in their "scat" (feces) and deposited along on the trail as they travel. At first, inspecting scat may not seem very appealing, but it can reveal the diet of many animals. Use a stick to break the scat apart. Can you find any teeth or jaw bones? These can tell you exactly the what kind of animal a coyote or fox ate. For example, finding yellowish, curved, incisor teeth that have a long groove could indicate a gopher was eaten. Seeing a zig-zag pattern on the upper surface of a molar tooth suggests it's the remains of a woodrat.

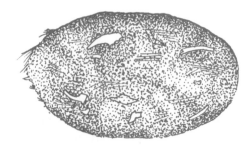

Illus. 14

Is the color of the fur in the scat the grey from a mouse that a hawk feasted on, or the white and silver from a rabbit that a fox ate? A hard, spoon-shaped persimmon seed may have been part of a raccoon's lunch, while a large pile of scat with berry seeds might be the remains of a bear's afternoon snack.

Owls and hawks cough up undigested pieces of fur and bone in the form of pellets. They usually feed each time from the same perch. If you discover some pellets, find a place to hide that gives you a good view of the perch. After a while, you may get to see a hawk returning with its next meal in its talons. Try returning at dusk and maybe you'll see an owl.

This list can help you identify what mysterious visitors came to your area.

Common Tracks and Signs

Deer *(Illus. 15)*

Walk on hooves, which are specialized toenails. Common in forest and brushy areas. Deer are best seen during early morning and late evening, when they come out to browse on vegetation. Males (bucks) have antlers, which are shed each year.

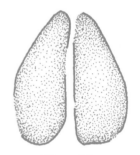

Illus. 15

Coyote *(Illus. 16)*

Similar to dog tracks. May appear almost anywhere. The best sign that they're in an area is hearing "yapping" during the late night. Eat mice, berries, rabbits, lizards. Tracks have claw marks and follow a straight line.

Illus. 16

Illus. 17

Red Fox *(Illus. 17)*

Prefer the forest. Change diet with the season, eating berries and insects when rodents are scarce. Very agile creatures. Look for claw marks and hair impressions in tracks.

Illus. 18

Bobcat *(Illus. 18)*

This secretive animal hunts chipmunks, squirrels, rabbits, and insects at night. Prefers rocky terrain. Small ear tufts and bobbed tail identify this cat. No claw marks. Look for a 2-lobed pad and double print from hindfeet stepping into front feet prints.

Illus. 19

Raccoon *(Illus. 19)*

This masked creature is often found raiding campsites. "Washes" food because it lacks enough saliva to moisten food before it can swallow it. Feeds on fish, grasshoppers, bird eggs, berries. Makes its home inside tree holes. Track resembles a tiny handprint.

Illus. 20

Opossum *(Illus. 20)*

Only North American marsupial (an animal that carries its young outside its body in a pouch on the abdomen). Slow moving, it eats almost anything—eggs, birds, garbage. Lives in wooded areas by streams. Notice the thumblike inner toe of rear foot in print. Curved tail markings between prints.

Adults weigh up to 300 pounds. During winter they enter a deep sleep, or hibernation, from which they periodically wake up. Feed on berries, insect larvae, squirrels, gophers. Live in the mountains. Large print is easily identified.

Black Bear *(Illus. 21)*

Illus. 21

Largest rodent in North America. Builds dams and bank burrows, or lodges, for shelter. Gnawed tree trunks are familiar signs of their activity. Eats bark, plant bulbs, and twigs. Its broad, flat tail aids in swimming, dam-building, and warning. Look for webbing between hind toes and large tail marks.

Beaver *(Illus. 22)*

Illus. 22

Very common but rarely seen because it feeds under the cover of darkness. Largely a seed eater. Look for tiny prints with a straight tail mark.

Deer Mouse *(Illus. 23)*

Illus. 23

Illus. 24

Tree Squirrel *(Illus. 24)*

Feeds on nuts, berries, mushrooms. Scurries from tree to tree, piling leaves and twigs for nest material between tree branches. Hindprints are in front of foreprints.

Illus. 25

Cottontail Rabbit *(Illus. 25)*

Frequently found under brush on the edges of meadows. Feeds on green plants and twigs. Breeds several times per year. As it bounds along, the hindfeet land in front of the forefeet, one foot slightly in front of the other.

Illus. 26

Mallard *(Illus. 26)*

This duck is common on lakes and ponds. Males have a distinct green head and white ring around the neck; females are brown with a violet patch on the wing. Webbed feet track. Leave an alternating pattern when walking.

Illus. 27

Robin *(Illus. 27)*

Its common red-breast and chunky size are familiar to most. Feeds on worms and insects. Paired tracks indicate it hops on the ground.

This harmless snake is common in meadows, marshes, and near water. Ribbon-like body with colorful stripes running down its entire length. Feeds on fish, frogs, earthworms. Notice the side "looping" of the track as they move through dirt.

Garter Snake (*Illus. 28*)

Illus. 28

A blackish, one-inch long beetle, common under stones and near water edges. Preys on caterpillars, other insects, and snails. Use a magnifying lens to help you see the fine markings left by the insect's legs.

Ground Beetle (*Illus. 29*)

Illus. 29

Treat your finds as clues that add up to solve the mystery of what animals were in an area when you weren't around. Putting the clues together can help you recreate what happened while you were not present.

Case #1: The Midnight Visitor

Here's how to find out what mysterious visitors came to your yard last night. Place a shallow box filled with sand or dirt in your backyard. Smooth out the surface and leave it out overnight.

The next morning check to see if there are any tracks in the box. If there are, make a cast of them so that you can identify your suspect. To make the cast, follow these simple steps:

• stand a cardboard collar around the track (Illus. 30);

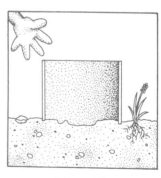

Illus. 30

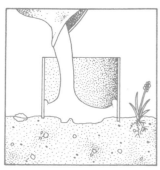

Illus. 31

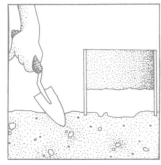

Illus. 32

Illus. 33

- mix plaster of paris with water until you get a slightly thick batter that can pour easily;

- pour the batter into the track to the top of the collar (Illus. 31);

- allow the plaster to stand and harden (about fifteen minutes);

- dig slightly under the dirt to loosen the collar; Pick it up, and you will have a raised cast of the footprint. Once it is completely dry, brush off any dirt (Illus. 32).

Now grease the first cast (shortening should do fine), fit a cardboard collar around it, and fill it with plaster, as before. And there's your track!

If the track is in the snow, spray a mist of water from a spray pump on the track. This will form a thin layer of ice over the track. Fill the collar with a cold batter of plaster of paris (Illus. 33) and you can make a cast from a winter track.

Case #2: The Chase

1. At the edge of a field you find four-fingered tracks with claw marks. You follow the tracks in a straight line down the field and find scat with rabbit and mouse fur and bones in it (Illus. 34). Who are your suspects?

Illus. 34

Answer: *A fox or a coyote (measuring the size of the actual tracks would then determine which one it was).*

22

2. The morning after a snowfall you find these tracks near the woods (Illus. 35). What happened last night?

Illus. 35

Answer: *While a coyote was chasing after a mouse, an owl swooped down on the mouse and coyote. Who ate the mouse?*

·2·

HIDDEN HAVENS

Illus. 36

There are many, many animals hiding or resting in secret homes very near yours. Animal homes, or shelters, come in a variety of shapes and materials. Some are complex, some are temporary, and some last forever. Some animals live in their dens alone (except during the mating season) and some, like the prairie dog and the bee, live in large groups.

Illus. 36. A good detective can usually find some of the homes that are hidden or camouflaged from your immediate view.

Suspects and Clues

One of the best ways to start the search for homes is to get down on your hands and knees and look around.

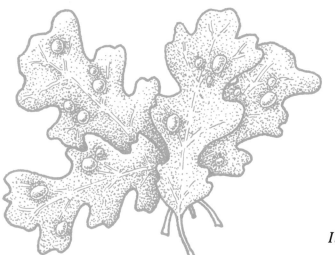

Illus. 37

Illus. 37. Look on the ground for some fallen leaves. Do any of the leaves have odd-shaped bumps that are bright-green, red, or yellow with red polka-dots on them? These colorful growths are called *galls*.

Galls are created when an insect (usually a wasp) lays its eggs. The leaf reacts to the eggs, forming this growth. The gall then becomes a home for the developing larva. The insect larvae feed on the soft tissues inside the gall. Try opening one up. Hard, aren't they? The gall encloses the egg with a tough case to protect the larvae growing inside. When the larvae become adults, they drill a hole in the side of the gall and fly away.

Illus. 38. A large pile of crushed-down leaves suggests that an animal has bedded down for the night. Scout around for chewings on nearby twigs and for bullet-shaped scat samples. If you find these clues, it's a good guess that deer have slept here. Deer and rabbits forage mostly in the early morning and evening hours. During the day, they simply find a cozy spot on the ground and curl up to rest.

Illus. 39. While searching among the leaves, you may find an animal that carries its home on its back—the turtle. Box turtles live in the woods; other turtles live at the seashore. Many other seashore creatures, like limpets, snails, clams, and whelks, move around with hard shells on their backs. If threatened, they pull their soft body parts into their shells; then they close the shell or clamp it down on a rock for protection.

Illus. 39

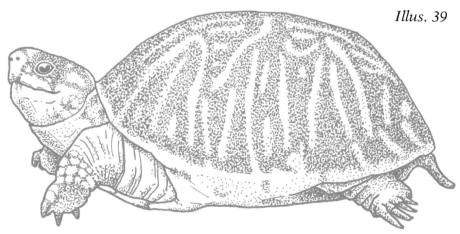

Illus. 40. The hermit crab, found in tidepools around the world, uses empty shells for its home. As the crab grows, it trades its home for a larger shell.

Illus. 40

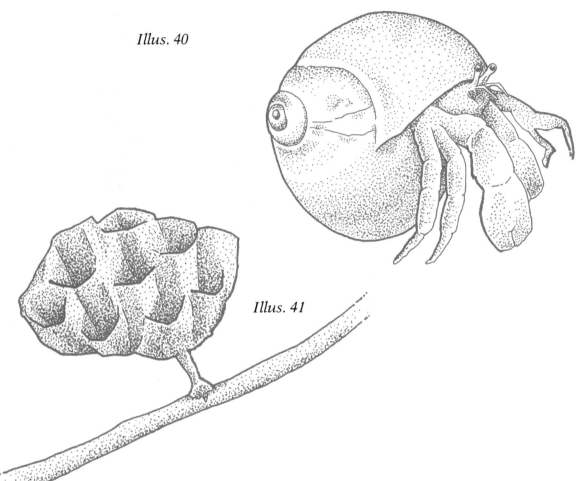

Illus. 41

Illus. 41. Carefully look for paper wasp nests among the leaves on the forest floor (winter is the best time for this). If you find a piece of the nest, pick it up. It feels like tissue paper. The female adult wasp mastered the art of paper-making long before people did. She makes the pulp by chewing plant and wood fibres and mixing them with saliva. She shapes the pulp into cylindrical columns and lays the eggs inside. The nest hangs by a single strand from a tree branch or under building eaves. When the nest is abandoned, the autumn winds blow it down.

Is there anyone inside the discarded nest? Hopefully not mama! But insect eggs and larvae sometimes spend the winter in paper wasp nests.

Illus. 42. While you're down on your knees, look for holes in the ground. Try to guess from its size who made the hole.

Are there any holes big enough to fit a snake? If it's a snake's hole, how did he dig it? Snakes simply don't have any body parts designed for digging (no hands or feet). Instead, snakes find homes in rocks and trees, or take over another animal's home. If you come upon a snake, don't harm it! The snake may be non-poisonous, but don't take chances. How big are you compared to the snake? What would you do if something large was poking at you? Snakes will try to run from you, but they'll attack if they have to defend themselves.

Illus. 43. You might find long, low, rounded ridges meandering along the ground. These are actually the outside of tunnels made by moles. Moles spend most of their time underground hunting for worms, insects, and bulbs. They use their broad forefeet with powerful claws to "swim" through the soil.

Illus. 43

29

Illus. 44. Chipmunks, ground hogs, prairie dogs, and badgers are just some of the other animals that dig underground homes. The chipmunk constructs a complex underground tunnel. Like your home, it has rooms for sleeping, food storage, and even a bathroom.

Illus. 44

Illus. 45. Having a home underground is a convenient getaway from aerial hunters and most large mammals that are looking for an easy meal. But being under the soil doesn't guarantee safety. Snakes can slither down most holes and badgers are notorious for digging out their prey. With their powerful forearms, badgers can dig a hole in a few seconds to capture rodents. They also dig to escape a dog looking for a quick bite. Badgers leave a telltale hole that's about 12-inches wide and shaped like a semi-circle to fit their flattened bodies. Badgers live in meadows and open dry areas and are fierce fighters. If you hear grunts and hisses coming from a large hole, stand back—a badger is probably inside.

Illus. 45

Illus. 46

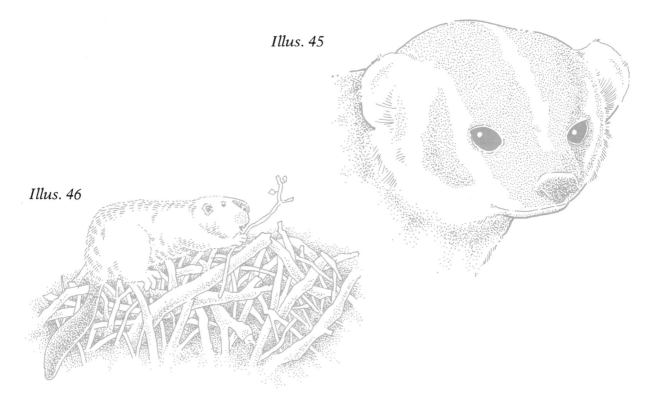

Illus. 46. While you're in the woods, you may come across a large pile of sticks and mud along the banks of a stream. This is a beaver's home, or lodge. The lodge can be at the shore, or in the deep water of a pond. Fresh mud piles around the lodge tell you that it's active. You may also find small openings for ventilation on the top of the mound, but none big enough for an entrance. As a means of protection, the entrances to the home are underwater.

Illus. 47. You may come upon caves in rocky areas. They can be just a shallow indentation under a rocky ledge or may extend for long distances into the earth. If you see a cave, don't go near it! Most animals have sharp ears and will quickly be alerted to your presence, and they know their caves better than you do. If the cave is in a forest, a bear, fox or skunk may be resting inside. In mountainous areas, rocky ledges are homes for bighorn sheep, coyotes, and mountain lions. The mountain lion, or cougar, is a large cat that can weigh up to 200 pounds and is often 8 feet or more in length

Illus. 47

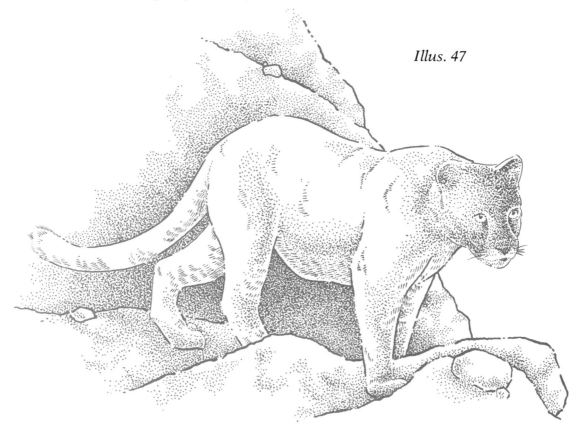

(including its tail). It preys on deer, rabbits, and foxes, but contrary to what many people believe, the cougar won't leap and attack if it spies you. Instead, it shies away from any contact with humans.

Lizards are also rock-goers. On a warm spring day you'll usually find them basking in the sun, though they will flee into rock crevices once they sense your presence. The chuckwalla, a desert inhabitant, will seek narrow crevices when alarmed and inflate its lungs to wedge itself tightly.

Illus. 48

Illus. 48. Try to find an old tree to uncover some more hidden havens. Fallen trees can serve as dens for skunks, weasels, or raccoons. Peer into the hollow—is there anything looking back at you?

You can tell if the den is occupied by looking for feathers, fur, grasses or pine needles on the floor. Just like you, wild animals make their homes comfortable and warm by lining them with soft materials. Keep an eye out for tracks around the hole to help you identify the inhabitant.

Illus. 49

Illus. 49. At the base of a standing dead tree (a *snag*) you can find some openings. It might be a hideaway for a weasel or an opossum. Opossums are poor fighters and will play dead ("play possum") to protect themselves, falling to the ground, closing their eyes and becoming limp.

Old tree trunks are often riddled with holes, sometimes going all the way into the tree. Bluebirds, nuthatches, and woodpeckers are a few of the birds that nest in tree holes. Sometimes if you tap a trunk, a bird will fly out, but don't disturb a bird if you suspect it's sitting on a nest with eggs.

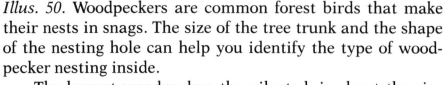

Illus. 50. Woodpeckers are common forest birds that make their nests in snags. The size of the tree trunk and the shape of the nesting hole can help you identify the type of woodpecker nesting inside.

The largest woodpecker, the pileated, is about the size of a crow and has a brilliant red crest. In large trees it excavates a nest that's rectangular- or triangular-shaped and about 7 inches across. The red-shafted flicker cuts a circular hole 2 inches in diameter; the acorn woodpecker carves out a circular nest 1⅗ inches across.

Woodpeckers have long, sharp bills that chisel away the wood. Bark beetles, carpenter ants, and their larvae live here under the bark where it's warm and secure from most predators. Woodpeckers, however, have specially designed tongues that "roll out" and probe deeply into the holes they drill in search of insects inside trees.

Knock on a dead tree, then on a live one. Which one would be easier to chisel for insects?

Illus. 51. Glance up into the treetops. Are there any holes high up on the tree trunk? Only animals that can fly (birds), climb (grey fox, squirrels), or soar (flying squirrels) could reach a high hole.

What might look like a branch or a clump of leaves at the top of a tree may be an owl looking down at you. Owls rest in trees during the daytime. Most have grey or brown mottled coloring to match the tree bark and camouflage them from view. The long-eared owl will even stretch its body to look like a long branch if it's startled.

Illus. 51

Illus. 52

Illus. 52. Owls and woodpeckers are not the only birds that make their homes in trees. During the spring, look for bird nests on all parts of trees.

In woodlands look for:

Red-tailed Hawk	• Builds a platform of twigs at the top of trees.
Northern Oriole	• Builds a deep, 9″ long pouch of woven plant fibres that hangs at the end of a limb.
Solitary Vireo	• Weaves bark, feathers, and moss. The nest hangs by its rim in a twiggy fork.
Robin	• Builds a cup of mud and grass that sits on a horizontal branch.
Brown Creeper	• Piles a bunch of grass inside a loose piece of tree bark.

Illus. 53. The branches of trees are also good places for insects to hide. Bagworms build a cocoon covered with bits of sticks to resemble a twig.

What may appear to be a randomly piled clump of leaves on a limb may be a well-disguised cocoon. When do you think those hidden, protected larvae will hatch out as adults? What season are you bothered by insects?

Look for tent-like webs in the forks of the branches. Get a close look at the inside of these webs with your magnifying lens. You'll find a large community of tent caterpillars. When they're hungry they leave their nest and crawl up the limbs to feed on the foliage. They can often completely strip a tree of its leaves.

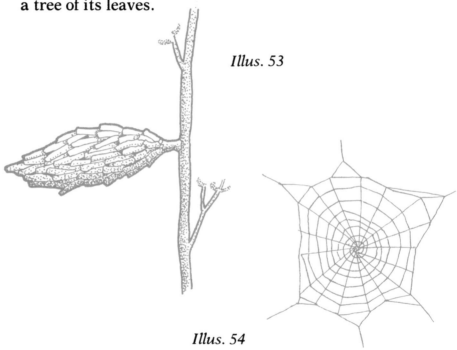

Illus. 53

Illus. 54

Illus. 54. Search between low limbs and grass clumps for webs. On a dewy morning, webs are easy to spot. Many spiders spin a web of silk to catch food. Look at the edge of the web for the spider. Some female spiders wait at the edge of a web with one foot on the strands. When an object lands on the web, she can determine the location and size of the catch from the vibrations on the web.

Check near the roots of a tree or your lawn for funnel-shaped webs. You'll find the spider hidden at the narrow end of the funnel.

Illus. 55. In a field, you may discover a hollow ball lined with dried grasses. This is a mouse house. If you see tiny trails that lead to the nest, your suspect is a meadow mouse. It snips grass blades as it moves in and out of its nest to feed, creating runways. If you find a mouse nest that's littered with seed hulls and food bits, the owner is probably a deer mouse. The deer mouse likes to eat in bed. When the nest gets too messy, instead of housecleaning, it moves out and builds another home.

As you find animal homes, you will begin to see that everything in nature has a use and that materials have to be recycled continually. An abandoned home of one animal can serve as a new home or nesting material for another member of the outdoor community. Nothing is wasted.

Illus. 55

Case #3: Shelter Search

Pretend you have to spend the night in the area you are investigating. Look around for a good spot to sleep. What spot would you pick? What would you use to build your shelter? Think about what materials were used in the construction of the animals' homes you found. Would your shelter protect you from the cold? the wind? the rain? the hot sun? from bears or other animals? What color clothes would best camouflage you from the wild animals?

Case #4: Material Match

Illus. 56. What would these animals use to build their homes? Match the animals with the correct materials.

Illus. 56

1. House Sparrow

2. Human

3. Blackbird

4. Red-tailed Hawk

5. Squirrel

6. Hummingbird

7. Beaver

A. Sticks

B. Mud

C. Cattails

D. Feathers

E. Leaves

F. Trash

G. Spider Web

H. Bricks & Mortar

·3·

CREATURES OF
THE DEEP

Ponds, creeks, lakes, and oceans are full of plant and animal life! Some animals just visit to feed or drink, while others make their homes in the water. Even puddles are teeming with life. Ponds and lakes provide rich wildlife habitats that supply us with fresh drinking water, not to mention a good fishing hole.

Fishing is just what we're going to do. But forget the bait and tackle because we're not looking for supper. Instead, a small aquarium fish net (or similar strainer) and an empty cottage cheese cup (not glass jars because they can break) are all you'll need to find these creatures of the deep.

Suspects and Clues

Illus. 57

Illus. 57. Approach the pond as quietly as possible. Walk slowly and keep your body low. When you get to the edge of the pond, sit quietly. Any animal you may have disturbed will resume its normal activities when it feels no more movements.

Close your eyes and listen for the different sounds, then open your eyes and look for ripples on the water's surface. Before long, you should see some animals surfacing. Why are they coming to the surface? Like you, turtles, snakes, and insects need oxygen to breathe. They come to the surface, take a gulp of air, then dive back under.

Illus. 58. See any birds? Ducks and wading birds (herons, coots, rails) come to fresh-water sites to feed and to nest. Look at the shape of the bird's bill. Does it tell you anything about its diet? Herons use their bills to spear fish, while

Illus. 58

mergansers have tiny projections, like hooks, on their bill to catch the fish. Pelicans scoop fish out of the water with their large pouches.

Ducks are classified either as divers or dabblers according to their method of feeding and how they take off and land on the water.

Illus. 59. Mallards, shovelers, and teal are dabblers. They take flight directly from the surface and "tip-up" their tails when feeding on submerged plants.

Illus. 59

Illus. 60. Mergansers, buffleheads, and ruddy ducks are divers. They "run" off the water's surface and dive into the water to feed on clams, fish and plants.

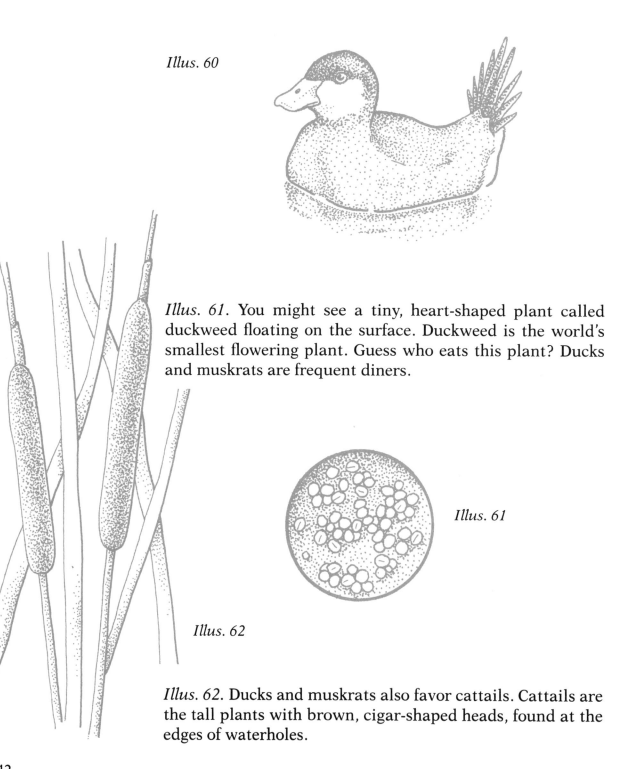

Illus. 60

Illus. 61. You might see a tiny, heart-shaped plant called duckweed floating on the surface. Duckweed is the world's smallest flowering plant. Guess who eats this plant? Ducks and muskrats are frequent diners.

Illus. 61

Illus. 62

Illus. 62. Ducks and muskrats also favor cattails. Cattails are the tall plants with brown, cigar-shaped heads, found at the edges of waterholes.

Illus. 63. Broken-off pieces of cattails are clues that muskrats are around. They prefer "take-out" meals, dragging the plants to their bank burrows before eating.

Illus. 63

Illus. 64. A loud, nasal call that sounds like "tee-urr" may come from the cattails. Sneak up on the source of this chatter, and you'll see a bird with scarlet shoulder patches—the male redwing blackbird. It balances on the cattail stems, calling out and displaying the red epaulets to defend its nesting site.

Illus. 64

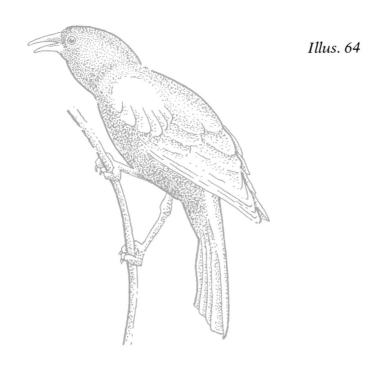

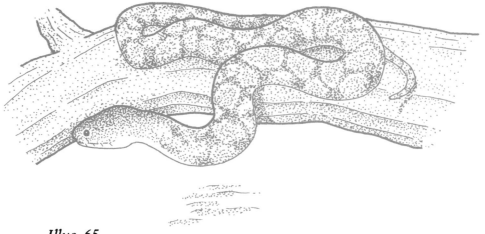

Illus. 65

Illus. 65. Look for exposed logs or rocks with turtles and snakes on them. Are they working on their tans? Sunning heats up their muscles so they can move around. Reptiles, amphibians, and insects are cold-blooded—their bodies are different temperatures, depending on the temperature outside. To warm up, they go into the sun, to cool down, they move into the shade.

Look for a place where you can fish from. If the water is shallow, the best way to experience the pond environment is to get into the water, but *never step into the water if you're alone*! If you have a buddy with you, then keep your sneakers on, roll up your pants, grab your fishing gear, and slowly step into the water.

Fill your cup up with water (everything you catch must stay in water in order to live) and scoop your net through the cup. Move slowly. Take a few dips, then look at your catch. There will probably be many aquatic insects and insect larvae swimming around.

Thousands of insects use ponds as nurseries. These young insects are *nymphs*. They bear little resemblance to the flying adults. Some nymphs look like worms, others look like grubs. After the eggs hatch, the nymphs go through a transformation process before they become adults, called *metamorphosis*.

If the animals stop moving for a minute, see if you can get a look at their mouths with a bug box or magnifying lens. Do the mouths give you any clues as to whether they are plant eaters (*herbivores*) or active predators?

When you catch an animal, think about what it eats and what might eat it. Generally, the size of an animal should tell you. For example, it would probably be a losing battle for a nymph to try to eat a giant water bug.

See if you can figure out how the insects breathe. Is there a shiny, silvery-coated appearance to any of them? Often, aquatic insects cover their bodies with a bubble of air. This lets them breathe underwater.

Illus. 66

Illus. 66. Whirligig beetles spin in circles. Their eyes are split into two parts. This enables them to keep a watch out for prey and predators from above and below the water at the same time. Whirligig beetles carry their air supply in their bubbles. As they hunt underwater for insect nymphs, they take their oxygen from this bubble.

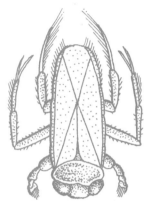

Illus. 67. Waterboatmen use their hind legs like oars to paddle.

Illus. 67

Illus. 68. The tiny water flea feeds on microscopic plants and detritus that sweep by with the water currents.

Illus. 69. Snails have a rasping tongue, called a *radula*, to graze on algae.

Illus. 68

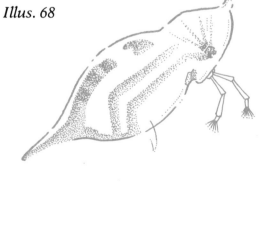

Illus. 69

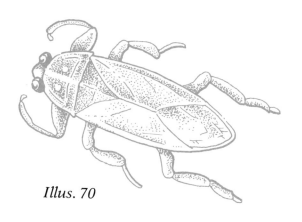

Illus. 70

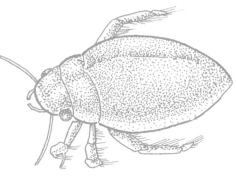

Illus. 71

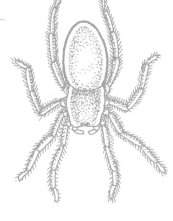

Illus. 72

Illus. 70. The giant water bug is 3-inches-long and preys on larvae, fish, and will even try for your toes. Its nickname is the "toe biter." It seizes prey with its front legs, thrusts its beak into the victim, and sucks it dry.

Illus. 71. Predaceous diving beetles have large "chompers" to catch a meal of other insects.

Illus. 72. Water spiders use the hairs on their legs to trap air, which gives them a silvery appearance. The trapped air spreads the spider's weight and keeps it afloat. Like all spiders, it has eight legs, as opposed to insects, which have six.

Illus. 73. If it's summer, look for dragonflies flying above the water's surface. They are harmless to you, but not to mosquitos! They're sometimes called "mosquito hawks." The adult dragonfly shapes its six legs into a basket to capture these insects while in flight.

Adult dragonflies drop the eggs onto plants in water (or right in the water itself). The eggs develop into nymphs which molt as they grow, until the time comes to emerge from the water, then crawls up on a piece of wood or plant, sheds its outer skin, and becomes an airborne adult.

Illus. 73

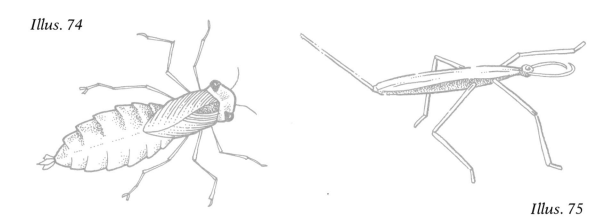

Illus. 74

Illus. 75

Illus. 74. Look for a broad, 1-inch-long, brown-colored nymph without gills. It has large chewing mouthparts and swims by propelling water out of its abdomen.

Illus. 75. A brown, stick-like insect, the water scorpion is equipped with its own snorkel. Two long filaments at the abdomen interlock to form a respiratory tube for air intake at the surface film.

Illus. 76. Mosquito larvae "wiggle" through the water.

Illus. 77. Fish have gills that take the oxygen directly from the water. Frogs and turtles, like you, have lungs. They fill their lungs with air before they submerge.

Illus. 76

Illus. 77

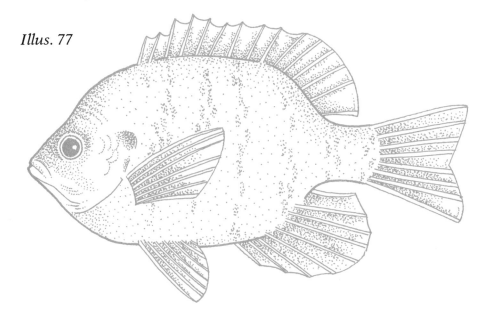

Illus. 78. If you spot a turtle, see how long it can hold its breath underwater.

Illus. 78

Illus. 79. If you're lucky and quick, you might catch some minnows or a frog. The small (2-inches-long) mosquito fish is one fish that you'll be glad to see in your cup. These minnows love to eat mosquito larvae, keeping down the number of mosquito bites you might get.

Place your net over the cup to keep any frogs you catch from jumping away. Try to avoid handling the animals. How would you like having some large stranger picking you up?

Illus. 79

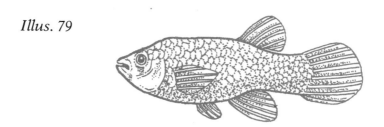

Illus. 80. Have you netted any tadpoles? A tadpole, or polliwog, looks like a fish with a long, flat tail propelling itself through the water. Tadpoles are herbivores and have internal gills for breathing.

Like insects, tadpoles go through metamorphosis, changing into either frogs or toads. Their hindlegs develop first, then their forelegs appear, and lungs develop in place of the gills. Eventually, the tail shrinks and disappears and the tadpole looks like a miniature copy of an adult. The change can take anywhere from a few weeks to two years, depending on the species.

Illus. 81. Do you know the difference between a frog and a toad? Frogs have smooth, moist skin and long, strong legs for jumping. Toads have dry, warty skin and short legs built for hopping. If you touch a toad, don't worry—you won't get warts. Toads do secrete a poisonous liquid from a gland behind their ears that may irritate your skin but that's all. Its foul taste discourages most predators.

Country people have all heard the chorus of frogs on a spring evening. When frogs come out after the winter, they begin trilling and croaking as part of their mating rituals. Visit the pond at dusk and see if you can identify any of these calls:

Chorus frog
- Like the sound made by running your fingernail along the teeth of a comb.

Leopard frog • A deep, low chuckle

Bullfrog • A low, deep "jug-o-rum"

Spring peeper • Like sleigh bells

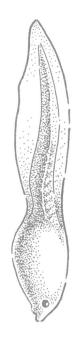

Illus. 80

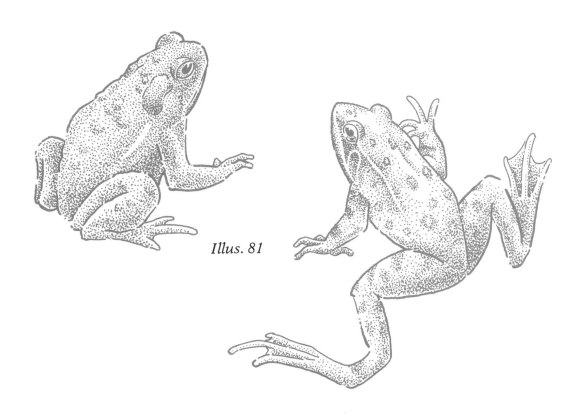

Illus. 81

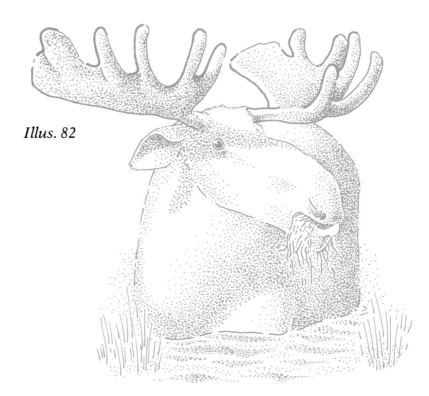

Illus. 82

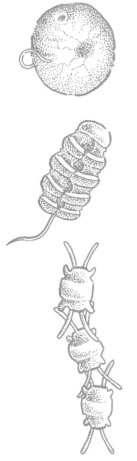

Illus. 83

Illus. 82. If you live in the Northern United States or in Canada, and if you're very lucky, you may see a moose feeding at your pond. The moose is the largest deer in the world and has massive antlers that are 4 to 5 feet apart. It usually feeds early in the morning or late in the evening, and is especially fond of eating the umbrella-sized leaves of water lilies.

Illus. 83. Besides everything you can see with your naked eye, pond water is full of tiny microscopic plants and animals. Collectively these plants and animals are called plankton. The plants (algae and diatoms) contain chlorophyll, the green pigment needed by plants to make food using the sun's energy. They are fed on by the microscopic animals.

Whenever you go fishing, notice where you caught different animals—under a rock, in the mud, on top of the water, or swimming freely. All plants and animals in a pond have special features that let them live in specific areas of the water. This is why the water environment can support so many life forms.

Case #5: The Missing Links

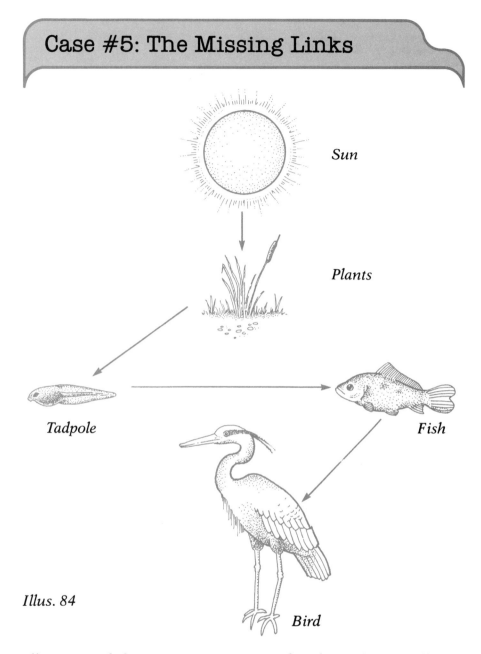

Illus. 84

Illus. 84. While you are sitting on the shore drying off and emptying the minnows and insects out of your sneakers, make a food chain of the different water life. A food chain is a chain of what eats what. The plants are the start of the food chain. They take the sun's energy to make food. Tadpoles feed on the plants, fish eat the tadpoles, and herons eat the fish.

How do other animals fit into this chain?

How are you part of this chain?

Case #6: Who's Who?

Illus. 85. Can you find these creatures of the deep? Check off the animals you find.

Illus. 85

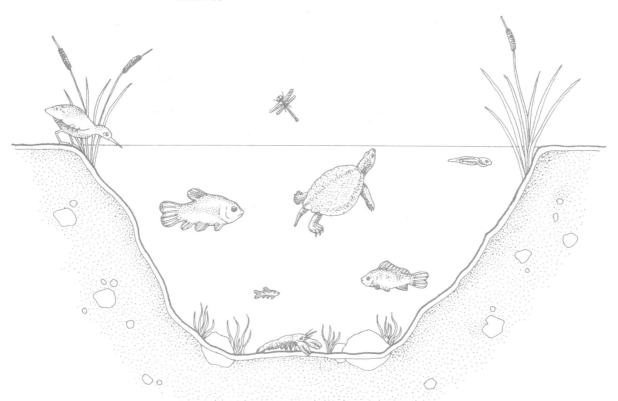

minnow_____ turtle _____ tadpole_____
dragonfly_____ sunfish _____ heron _____
crayfish _____

• 4 •

NAME THAT TUNE

Wherever you live, you're sure to hear some bird's song. Chirps, coos, whistles, rolling melodies, and other familiar sounds are not made simply for entertainment (though they are fun to listen to), but are the birds' form of communication. Through singing, birds attract mates, warn of danger, or mark off their territory.

Songs and calls are, of course, the easiest way to identify a particular species of bird. Birds are easy suspects to identify because they're quite vocal, not very shy, and most are diurnal, or active during the daytime.

Suspects and Clues

Illus. 86. Shortly after sunrise and before sunset are the best times to listen for songs. Try not to listen on windy days, because the noise of gusts through trees overwhelms other outdoor sounds.

Illus. 86

Illus. 87

Illus. 87. Bird calls and songs are used for communication and are distinctive for each species. A call is usually short, made up of one or two notes, while a song is a complex pattern of notes that's repeated. Just as you can recognize your friend's voice, you can identify a bird by its song even before you see it. Some bird's songs are:

Robin • Cheerio, cheerio
Chickadee • Dee-dee-dee-dee
Bobwhite • Ah-bobwhite
Killdeer • Kill-dee
Yellowthroat • Witchy-witchy
Nuthatch • A nasal ank-ank-ank

Make a note of the type of habitat you're investigating, and you'll narrow down your list of suspect singers. Some birds only live in the forest, some live in meadows, and others like the seashore. You can hear the yodel-like laugh of a loon along lakes and rivers, or the high-pitched scream of a red-tailed hawk over open country.

Illus. 88

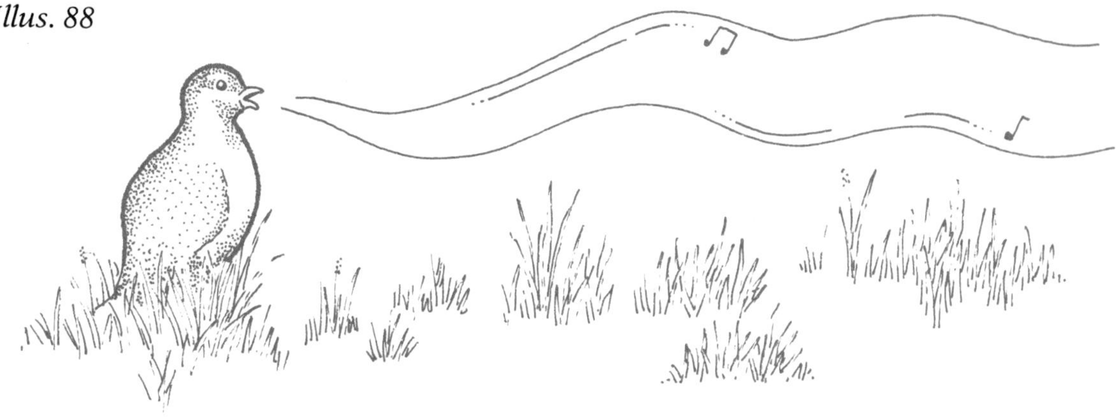

Illus. 88. Find a hidden spot to sit and listen to the outdoor melodies. Try to pick out one song or call, and pay attention to how high or low the note is.

Does the song appear to be coming from the treetops or from down on the ground? Most ground-dwelling birds, like the mourning dove, make low, drawn-out sounds. They're easier to hear because lower sounds travel farther.

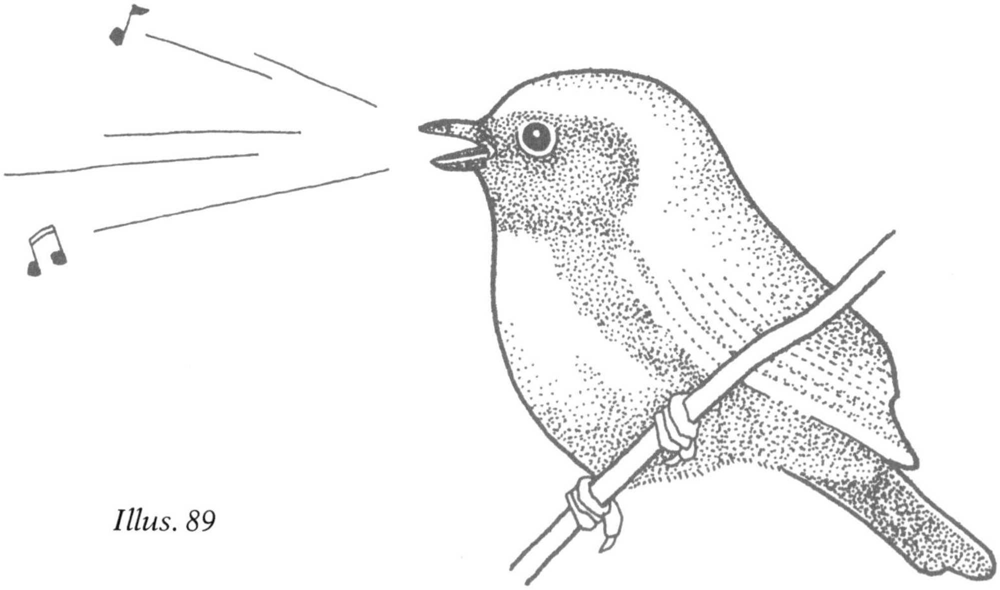

Illus. 89

Illus. 89. A warbler on a limb in the treetops sings a song with high, short notes. These sounds travel easily in the clear air, but not as far.

Illus. 90. One of the loudest sounds in the woods is the drumming of a woodpecker. Did you ever wonder why the woodpecker doesn't get a headache from all that pounding? A woodpecker's head has extra cushions of fatty tissues to protect it. Whenever you get a good view of a woodpecker drumming, watch how its head hits the tree trunk. By holding the neck very stiff and banging the wood straight on, the head jars less than if it was hit at an angle.

Listen to the speed of the drumming. The smaller the woodpecker, the faster the drumming. Woodpeckers chisel into old tree trunks in search of insects for food. During spring, woodpeckers also make drumming noises for courting purposes.

Correct

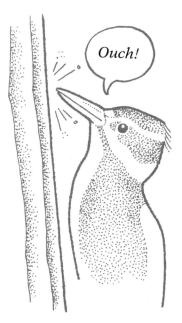

Illus. 90

Illus. 91. Woodpeckers also drum, and other birds sing, to stake claim to an area. Males set up territories and sing to chase out other birds of the same species that try to enter their domains. Songs also let the females know that a male is defending an area for nesting and raising babies, and that he is ready for mating.

Another reason that birds call is to alert others that someone is in the area (maybe that chickadee is making a racket to let other chickadees know that you're here). Birds that travel in flocks often call to keep track of each other, especially in a thick forest where it's hard to see.

Illus. 91

Incorrect

Illus. 92. Track down where a bird is by following its song. Try to find the bush, tree, or rock the bird is perched on; then figure out what particular bird made that song. Different species can be identified by various body features. Binoculars are handy for this task.

A bird's color is probably the first thing that'll catch your eye. Most land animals are shy, quiet, and inconspicuously colored. But birds can get away with being noisy and vividly colored because they're able to fly. Flying allows for fast and easy escape from predators and lets them build nests in sites that are difficult to reach. Even the most agile of predators have a difficult time raiding nests that are perched on the edge of a cliff or dangling from a tree limb.

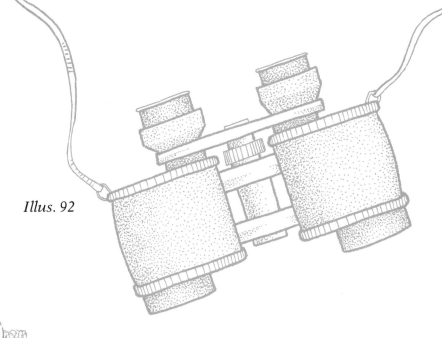

Illus. 92

Illus. 93

Illus. 93. Have you ever heard the begging calls of baby birds from a nest? This usually means they're hungry. If you discover a nest with eggs or chicks in it, be sure to leave it alone. The parents may abandon a nest if it's disturbed.

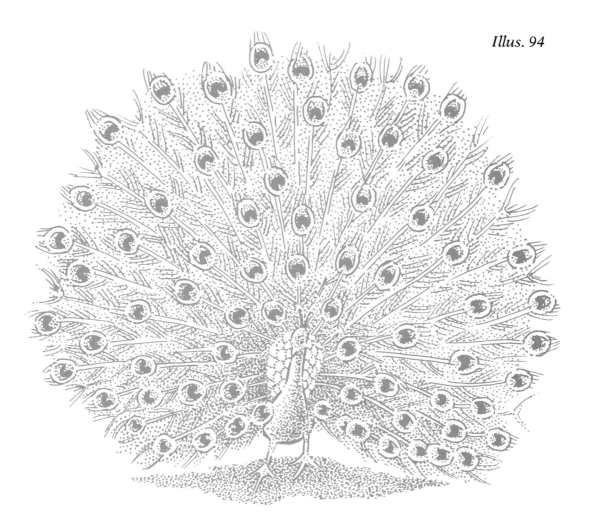

Illus. 94. Bright colors help birds recognize each other. Males are often more colorful. During the breeding season, they signal with their plumage that the courtship ceremonies are about to begin. They strut and dance, spreading their feathers to impress females. The male peacock puts on a dazzling display. He raises his crown and unfolds a shimmering fan of tail feathers patterned with indigo, aquamarine, yellow, and orange colors.

Once you have a bird in view, look at the shape and size of its body. You won't be able to measure it in feet and inches from a distance, so measure it by comparing it to other birds. Is it as big as a crow, about the size of a robin, or as tiny as a wren? See if the bird has any field marks, such as spots or stripes on the chest, a crest, or patches of color on the head.

Illus. 95. Field marks are other clues. The meadowlark is a common grassland bird that feeds on grasshoppers and other insects. It's about the size of a robin and has a black crescent mark on its bright yellow chest. Meadowlarks perch on fence posts, filling the air with a lovely, melodious song. When they fly, their outer tail feathers flash white.

Illus. 95

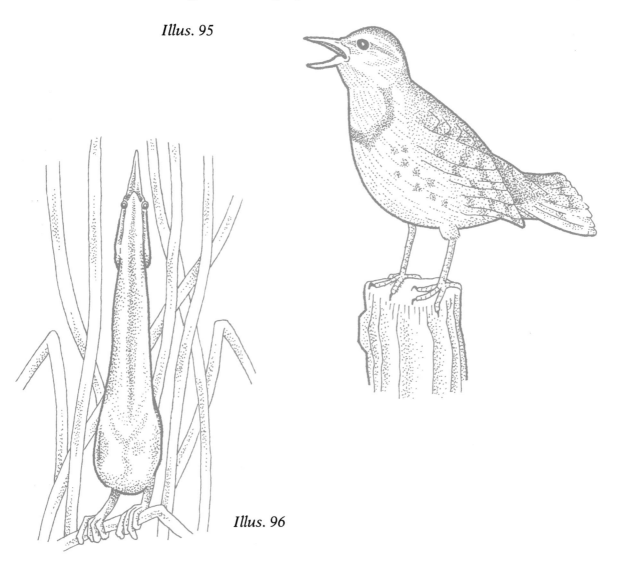

Illus. 96

Illus. 96. Sometimes field marks help a bird live in a certain area. The bittern, which lives among reeds and cattails, has a brown and white striped breast. When threatened by an enemy, it stretches its neck and head and points its bill towards the sky. This helps the bittern blend in and look just like a reed.

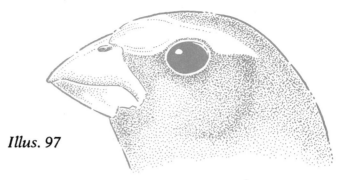

Illus. 97

Illus. 97. Another clue to help you identify a bird is its beak shape, or bill. The bill is really just hard skin. It has two parts, the upper and lower *mandible*. Birds use their bills for eating, to preen their feathers, for protection, and for nest building. Bills are adapted for catching different types of food. Some are very long, while others are curved up, down or sideways. The black skimmer, a gull-like black and white seabird, has an unusually large red bill. As it flies along just above the water's surface, it skims the surface with its long lower mandible to pick up fish.

Illus. 98

Illus. 98. The feet, like the bill, reflects a bird's lifestyle. Birds' feet have many designs because their feet do lots of jobs. Besides running and hopping, their feet catch food, paddle in water, and build nests.

Birds usually have three toes pointing forward and one pointing backwards. This alignment is good for perching. When a bluebird rests on a branch, its leg muscles tighten and cause the toes to curl around the branch and lock tight. This prevents the bluebird from falling over when sleeping.

Birds of prey, like hawks, ospreys, and owls, have extremely strong, curved feet. They make high-speed dives from up in the air to catch food with razor-sharp claws called *talons*.

Ducks have webbing between their toes for paddling. Wading birds have long toes for walking on mud.

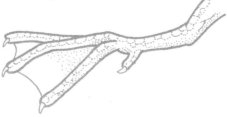

Illus. 99

Illus. 99. Climbers have two toes in front and two toes in back. If the bird you're looking at is climbing a tree, watch how it moves. Nuthatches climb down a trunk head-first, while creepers spiral up a trunk. Woodpeckers use their stiff tails as a supporting brace as they move up a tree.

Illus. 100

Illus. 100. When a bird becomes aware of your presence, it'll sound the alarm to other birds. If the bird is near or on a nest, it'll fly away to attempt to distract you from finding the nest's location. As the bird flies, observe how it moves through the air. Certain birds have distinctive flight patterns.

Woodpeckers often fly in an undulating path (they dip up and down like they're on a roller coaster), ducks and doves fly in a straight line, kingfishers hover before they dive, and hawks and gulls soar and glide. Check to see how the bird flies, beating its wings rapidly like a sparrow or slowly like an egret.

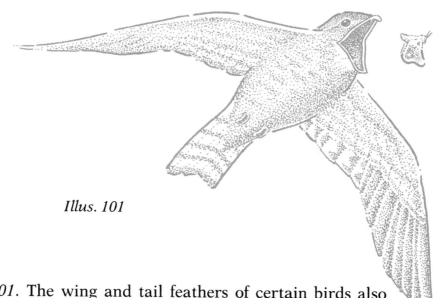

Illus. 101

Illus. 101. The wing and tail feathers of certain birds also produce sounds during flight. Mourning doves and woodcocks "whistle" as they move through the air. Nighthawks are also called boomers because of the booming noise the wings make as the bird dives.

Illus. 102. The male Anna's hummingbird puts on a dramatic aerial display during courtship. He climbs up to about 150 feet, facing the sun to flash his iridescent rose-colored throat at a prospective female or at an intruder to his territory. Then, he dives down at high speeds and arcs back up again. An explosive popping sound is made by the wing and tail feathers as the bird comes out of the powerful dive.

Whenever you go out to listen, take along a pencil and note pad. It's easy to forget what you hear and see. It's also helpful to have a pocket bird guide to aid your identification. Pretty soon, you'll be able to name that tune.

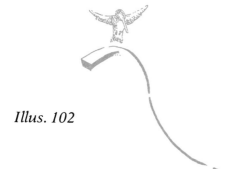

Illus. 102

Case #7: Mix and Match

Illus. 103. Try to match the bird beaks with right type of feet.

Beaks:

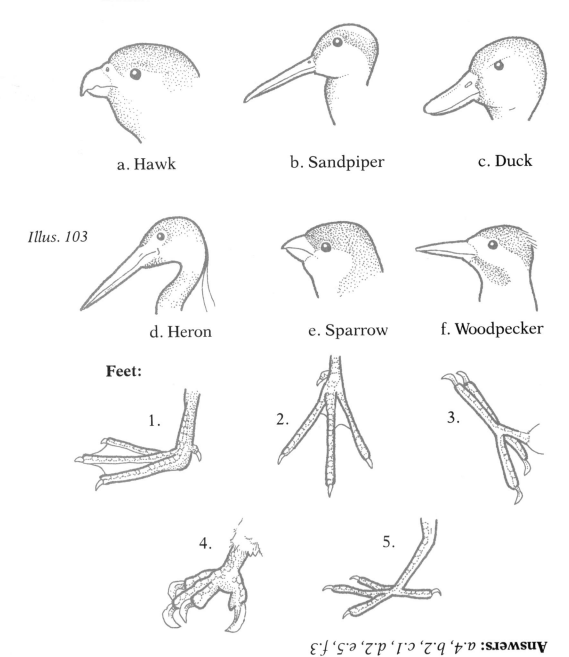

a. Hawk   b. Sandpiper   c. Duck

Illus. 103

d. Heron   e. Sparrow   f. Woodpecker

Feet:

1.   2.   3.

4.   5.

Answers: *a.4, b.2, c.1, d.5, e.2, f.3*

64

Case #8: Who Gets the Bill?

Illus. 104. Try to match these beak shapes with the following tools:

1. chisel
2. bucket
3. spear
4. nutcracker
5. strainer

a. heron

b. duck

Illus. 104

c. woodpecker

d. jay

e. pelican

Answers: *1.c, 2.e, 3.a, 4.d, 5.b*

Case #9: The Return of the Tracks

Illus. 105. You are walking across an open field that's bordered by a thicket of bushes and vines. On the dusty ground, you find a series of finger-like tracks about 1½ inches long. The tracks are paired and are 4 inches apart. A splashing of white stains on the plants leads you to a cup-like nest in the bushes. The nest is 3 inches across and woven out of grasses and plant stems. On the ground below the nest are hulls of seeds and some scat that is stained blue.

What can you deduct about this animal from these clues?

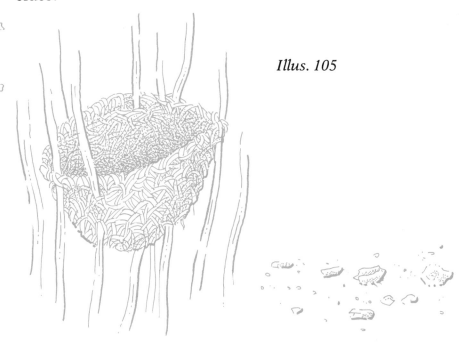

Illus. 105

Answer: *The size and shape of the tracks, as well as the nest, suggest the animal is a small bird. The shape of the tracks and the fact that they're paired indicate a perching bird that hops when foraging on the ground. The bird probably has a stout bill that it uses to crack open seeds. The blue stains mean it also eats berries. Since the clues were found in a field, the bird is probably some type of sparrow or finch, both common to this habitat. To positively identify the bird, keep spying on the area to hear its call or see it.*

·5·

FOLLOW THAT SCENT

If you move around in the dark, live in a place covered with plants taller than you, or live in murky waters, your nose would be more helpful to you than your eyes. Odors carry a great distance, so they can warn you of danger before you get too close. Smells can attract you or send you running the other way, so they are messages that plants and animals use frequently. Plants lure insects and birds to fertilize their flowers with sweet perfumes. Animals use scent for warning, to mark territories, for courtship and mating, and for finding food. Odors are handy messages because they can be left behind after an animal is gone. And, unlike taste, you don't have to make contact with something in order to smell it.

Illus. 106

Illus. 106. Most wild animals are very sensitive to scent, especially human odors. Whenever you go outside, your personal scent is carried into the air. If you are quietly stalking an animal, it may detect and run from your scent even if it can't see or hear you. Try to be downwind when you approach an unsuspecting animal. When you go out investigating in the summer, you'll probably put on insect repellent. Have you ever wondered why the best repellents don't smell very pleasant?

Suspects and Clues

When you step outside, sniff the air. Do you smell anything? Try to track the scent to its owner.

If there's an odor on the ground or on tree trunks, is it in only one area? Can you smell it along the trail?

Illus. 107

Illus. 107. A red fox marks it territory or home area by making a "scent fence." At certain intervals, it leaves fenceposts by urinating on bushes and on the dirt. Lots of animals let others know where their property is by scenting.

Illus. 108

Illus. 108. Male rabbits rub their chins on twigs.

Illus. 109. Bears plaster mud on trees; then rub their backs against the mud. This rubs some of their hairs off, leaving the bear's smell behind.

Territorial markings can be detailed messages. Animals can tell from odors who lives in an area, whether it's male or female, and whether or not they still live there.

Illus. 109

Illus. 110. If the odor is concentrated in just one spot, does the smell make you hold your nose? This bad smell might be from a skunk. Skunks shoot a foul-smelling spray to defend themselves, but only as a last resort. Look for signs of a struggle near the skunk's odor.

Illus. 110

70

Illus. 111. Some animals release odors to warn of danger. The pronghorn, North America's fastest wild animal, travels in groups on the open plains. When this lightning-swift animal senses danger, it flashes its white rump patch to alert the other members. It also releases a scent that can be smelled up to 100 yards away to warn those that may not be able to see the rear patch.

Illus. 112

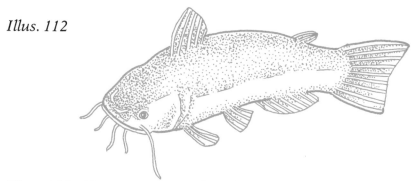

Illus. 112. Since vision is often limited in murky waters, fish rely on scent to communicate. Fish travel in groups, called schools. Catfish live in the dark, muddy bottoms of lakes and rivers. They're nearly blind, but they can recognize and identify each other by scent. When one member of the school is hurt, it releases a scent to notify others of danger. This odor is picked up by the nearby fish, and causes them to flee. Catfish also use their sense of smell to hunt out snails, insects, and crayfish.

Illus. 113. Mussels and clams are able to pick up on the odor of one of their predators, the starfish. When they smell the starfish coming, they hide by burrowing down in the sand. But they have to dig deeply because starfish can sniff out prey buried up to 4″ deep.

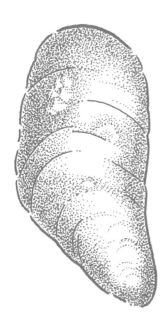

Illus. 113

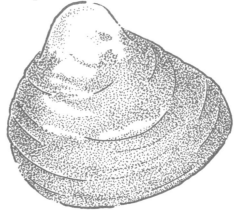

Illus. 114. While some scents are warnings, many odors serve the purpose of attracting mates. If you visit certain swamps in the spring, you won't be able to miss the rotten smell that fills the air. This terrible odor comes from the bull alligator. He produces a strong scent from glands under his lower jaw to woo a mate. If you don't think this smell is attractive, remember the bull alligator is not interested in attracting you.

Illus. 115

Illus. 114

Illus. 115. Like alligators, salamanders use their sense of smell to locate a suitable mate. Salamanders hide in damp spots under rocks and logs and travel to streams and ponds to mate during the spring. Each species of salamander produces a unique scent, so that others can recognize their own kind.

Illus. 116

Illus. 116. If you're near the banks of a pond or creek, you might notice a musty odor in the air. This is the male beaver announcing his desire for a female partner.

Do you have an older brother or sister? Why do you think they put on perfume or cologne before going out on a date?

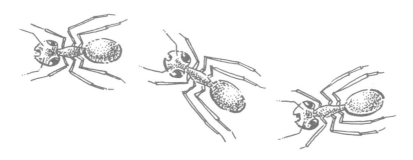

Illus. 117

Illus. 117. While you're searching for insects, you might come across an ant trail, a line of ants marching in single file. Ants leave a narrow ribbon of scent to lead other ants to food.

What leads you to someone baking cookies?

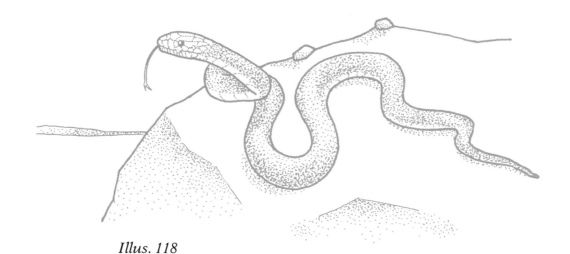

Illus. 118

Illus. 118. A sunny day is good for finding snakes and lizards basking on rocks and logs. If you spot a snake, keep a good distance from it and watch what it does with its tongue. When snakes flick their tongues in and out they're not getting ready to strike. They're smelling and tasting the air. Snakes rely almost entirely on their sense of smell to find food. The tongue picks up odor particles and carries them to two small openings (*Jacobson's organs*) inside their heads. A nerve then takes the smell to the snake's brain.

Illus. 119

Illus. 119. Many outdoor smells will lead you to a flower. Plants often depend on odors to attract animals that will help in their reproductive cycle.

Get close to the flower (watch out for bees) and get a deep whiff of the flower's aroma. What you smell is the flower's *nectar*. The nectar is inside the flower. Bees, as well as birds and other insects, like to eat it. *Pollen* is also inside the flower. When the bee comes to the plant for the nectar, it picks up pollen from the plant's stamens (the male part of the flower). When the bee travels to another flower for more nectar, some of this pollen drops off onto the *pistil* (the female part of the flower). The flower's scent draws the bee, the bee feeds and transfers the pollen, and a fertilized seed (which will become a new flower) is created.

74

Illus. 120. Once a bee "follows its nose" to the flower, it finds the nectar like a plane following runway lights at the airport. Flowers have dots or lines, called *nectar guides*, to lead the bee.

While you're looking at the petals, notice the general shape of the flower. Some flowers have one petal larger, like a landing platform. Others have all the petals form a landing "saucer". Flowers in the pea family, like vetch, lupines, and wisteria, usually have the two lower petals connected. When a bee lands on these petals, its weight causes the stamens to swing down and dust the bee with pollen as it feeds. The bee then carries the pollen to the next flower it visits.

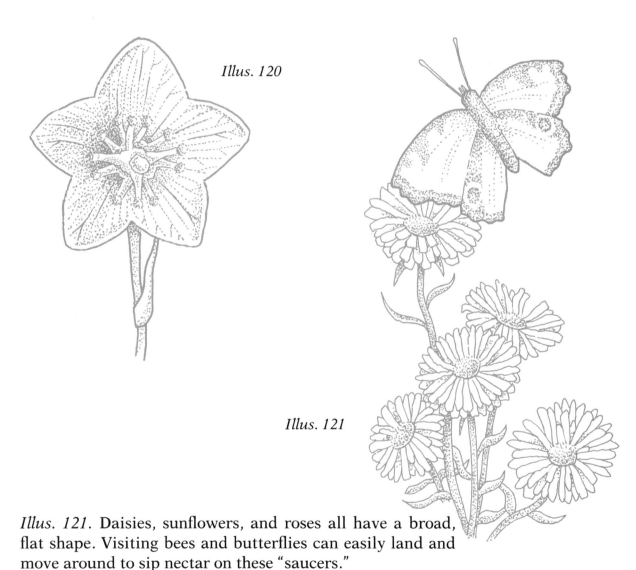

Illus. 120

Illus. 121

Illus. 121. Daisies, sunflowers, and roses all have a broad, flat shape. Visiting bees and butterflies can easily land and move around to sip nectar on these "saucers."

Illus. 122

Illus. 122. Only animals with long tongues or bills, such as hummingbirds, can reach the nectar at the base of tubular flowers. The length of the trumpet creeper flower is perfectly designed to match the length of a ruby-throated hummingbird's bill.

Hummingbirds also feed while hovering. That's why they don't need a place to land, and how they got their nickname of "flower kisser."

Smells are all around us. A bouquet of roses can make you smile and the beach at low tide can make you gag. Although you're not as sensitive to scent messages as most wildlife is, make a habit of periodically smelling the air. Who knows what aromatic treasure chest you'll sniff out?

Case #10: The Scented Trail

Illus. 123. This is another way to play hide and seek with your friends.

1. Get an empty spray bottle or soap bottle and fill it up with water.
2. Add a few drops of old perfume or cologne (ask your parents). Add enough so you can easily smell the odor.
3. One person gets to run and hide while everyone else closes their eyes and counts to 100. The runner must spray or squirt the path every time he or she takes five steps.

Illus. 123

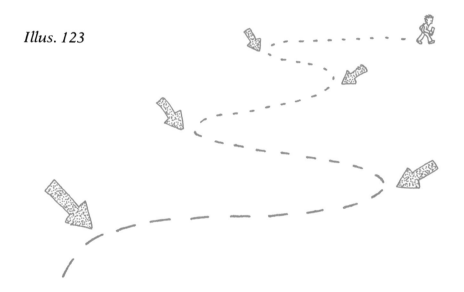

4. Everyone else tracks the runner by following the scent trail that was sprayed. The first person who catches him (or her) wins.

This can also be played using teams. Each team must have a bottle scented with a different odor. One member from each team runs and hides, spraying along the way. Then each team has to find the other team's runner.

·6·

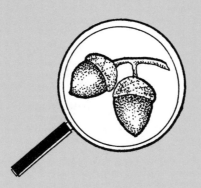

THE TRAVELLING SEED

Throughout spring and summer, wildflowers paint fields, roadsides, and gardens with rainbow colors. This is the beginning of the process of reproduction for the plants.

Illus. 124. A flower's job is to make seeds. A seed develops from the *ovule*. The ovule gets fertilized when the flower blooms in spring or summer, with the help of pollinating insects. The fertilized ovule gradually becomes a seed. Seeds are enclosed in fruits, nuts, or pods, and contain all the parts necessary to begin a new plant. But before sprouting into new plants, the seeds must leave the old one.

Plants send out seeds throughout the year, but mostly in the fall and winter. Long after the flowers have faded and the leaves have fallen, many seeds are beginning their journeys.

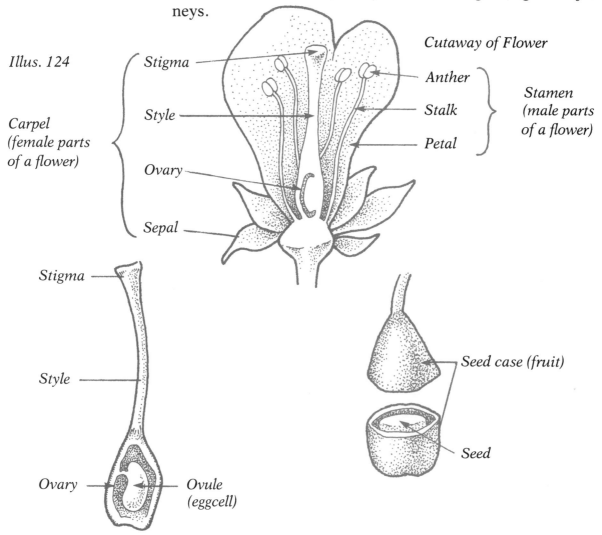

Illus. 124

Carpel (female parts of a flower)

Stigma

Style

Ovary

Sepal

Cutaway of Flower

Anther

Stalk

Petal

Stamen (male parts of a flower)

Stigma

Style

Ovary

Ovule (eggcell)

Seed case (fruit)

Seed

80

Suspects and Clues

Your front lawn is a good place to start looking for the "runaway seeds."

Illus. 125

Illus. 126

Illus. 125. Lawns are often covered with white, ball-shaped dandelion heads. Blow one into the air. Catch some heads and inspect them closely. Attached to the hairs are brown specks. Inside these hard coats are the dandelion's seeds. The silky hairs act like parachutes that carry the seeds far away from their starting place to spread the seeds.

Illus. 126. Each dandelion flower releases hundreds of tiny, light seeds to the wind. For a seed to grow, it needs to land in an area with the right soil, enough moisture, and plenty of sunlight. How many seeds from one dandelion plant are likely to land in a spot that's good for growth? Probably very few.

Illus. 127. Have you ever taken a walk through some weeds and come home with your socks and sneakers (and maybe your dog) covered with stickers and burrs? The next time this happens, peel off some of these "hitchhikers" and examine them. These are seed cases. The seeds are inside.

If you look closely at these seed cases with a bug box or

magnifying lens, you'll see that they are covered with hooks, barbs, or spines. Some of them are as sharp as fishhooks and may even stick to your fingers.

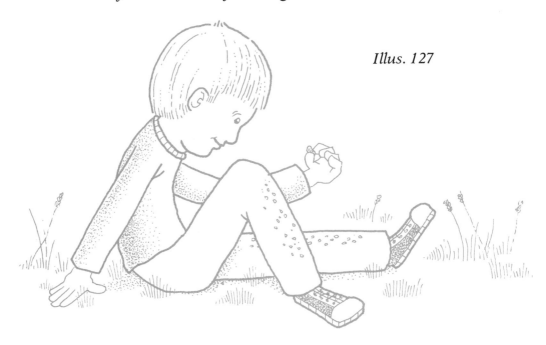

Illus. 127

Illus. 128. Tickseed, teasel, and cockleburs are some of the common seeds that hitch to your pants or to the fur of animals. These prickles are timed to fasten to a passerby only

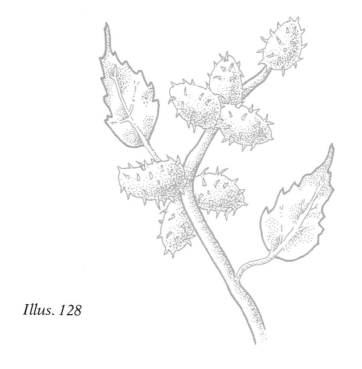

Illus. 128

when the seed is ripe. Until then, the hooks, barbs, and needles are covered with shields. (George de Nestral noticed how seeds hooked onto animal fur. He took this design from nature and invented Velcro®.) When you brush the seeds off your clothes you are doing an important job for nature—spreading seeds.

Illus. 129. What would happen if all the seeds simply fell from the parent plant to the ground below? There wouldn't be enough light, soil, and water for all the seeds to survive, so the seeds have a better chance of surviving if they travel to less crowded areas.

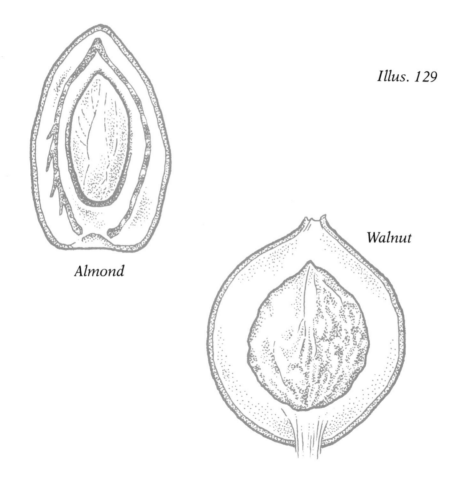

Illus. 129

Walnut

Almond

Illus. 130. Crack open one of the seeds. Inside the hard shell is the embryo and food to keep it alive until it can exist on its own. The embryo will sprout all the parts of a new plant

—the roots, stems, flowers, and leaves. The shell protects the embryo from being eaten by animals and from drought.

Deserts have long droughts. Desert seeds survive these harsh times by hiding in the soil. The shells of desert seeds are coated with a "growth inhibitor." The only time you'll ever see the desert covered with wildflowers is after a great deal of rain seeps down into the soil. The heavy rains wash away the growth inhibitor, letting the seeds sprout into wildflowers.

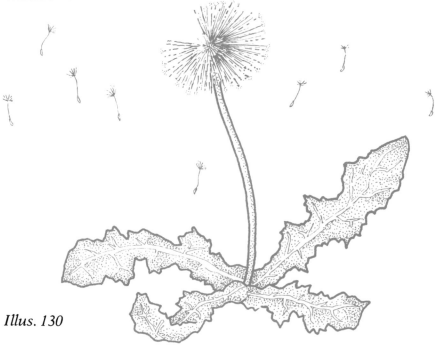

Illus. 130

Illus. 131. On a pleasant spring day, you may rest under a clump of trees in your neighborhood park or woods when something falls out of the treetops.

Maple, ash, and elm trees send out their seeds using "helicopters." If you pick up some of these winged seeds and twirl them into the air, you can see how they travel with the breeze.

Illus. 131

A tree's branches reach high into the air, where the breezes are stronger. With their wings, the heavier seeds catch these gusts and sail far away to new soil.

84

Illus. 132. If there are pine trees around, look for a pine cone on the ground and peel it apart. The papery pieces inside are the seeds. Throw some of the seeds into the air and watch them fly away.

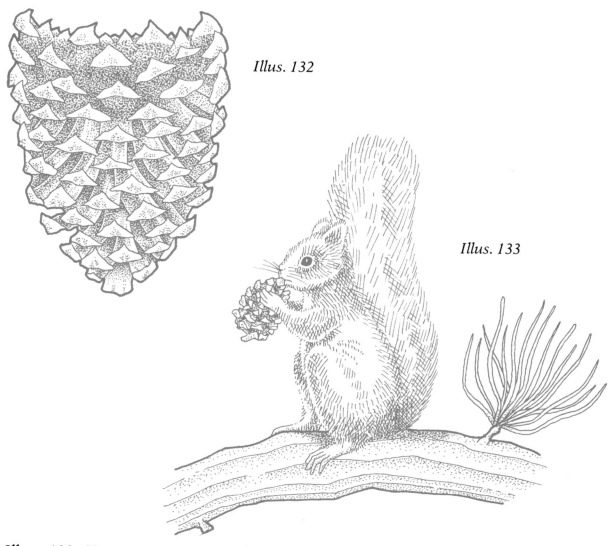

Illus. 132

Illus. 133

Illus. 133. You may see squirrels around the pine cones. Squirrels commonly eat their seeds. However, they don't get all the seeds as they feed, and many escape into the wind.

If there are any oak or nut trees in your area, hide and spy on the squirrels that visit the trees.

Squirrels play an important role as replanters of the forest. They bury nuts and acorns as food supplies for the winter and often forget to dig some of them up. When the conditions are right, these seeds will sprout into new trees.

Illus. 134

Illus. 135

Illus. 134. Bears feast on apples. If a bear finds an apple grove, it will spend hours popping whole apples into its mouth. The bear can't digest the small seeds inside the core and passes them out later in scat. Some of the seeds may now sprout and grow into apple trees. Feel how smooth the seeds inside the apple core are. This smooth surface helps the seeds easily pass through an animal's digestive system.

When you toss the apple-core pits into the field, you may be helping these seeds to find a suitable place to grow. If you can remember where you tossed the seeds, come back next year and see if they sprouted.

Illus. 135. When you bite into raspberries and blackberries, the tiny gritty pieces inside the juicy pulp are its seeds. Many wild fruits advertise their location to raccoons, birds, and foxes by their bright colors. Most birds have a very poor sense of smell, but they do have keen eyesight. The brilliant red berries of the Carolina snailseed and deciduous holly ripen in the winter, and animals can spot them easily against the winter landscape.

Illus. 136

Illus. 136. Biting into an unripe persimmon will make your face pucker. Fruits are timed to be sweet only when the seeds are mature. The animals that eat the fruits and berries scatter the seeds with their scat, the same way the bear spreads apple seeds.

Illus. 137. If you live by tropical waters, look for the world's largest seed, the coconut, washed up on the beach. The coconut can float long distances. If you find one (or see one in your grocery store) pick it up and feel how light it is. The thick husk is water repellent, yet light enough to float.

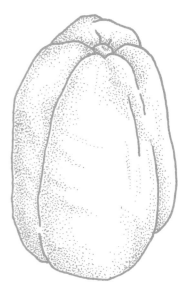

Illus. 137

Illus. 138. If you touch the seed pod of the jewelweed flower, watch out! The pod violently snaps open with a popping noise, shooting the seeds out like a slingshot. How do you think it got its nickname "touch-me-not"?

Beans, peas, geraniums, and violets are some other seeds that are "spring-loaded" to scatter with a toss.

These are just some of the ways seeds spread. The plants

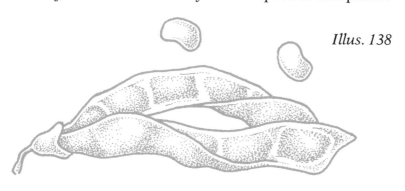

Illus. 138

that develop from these seeds are vital to all living things on earth. Many animals get their entire food supply directly from seeds and plants. Your peanut butter and jam sandwich and your cup of hot cocoa are made from seeds. Your jeans are spun from the fleecy hairs on the cottonseed. See, seeds really are everywhere.

Case #11: The Runaway Hitchhiker

Illus. 139

Illus. 139. Make a small grid of tape. Attach strips of masking tape (sticky side up) to a sheet of cardboard. Take the grid to a field, anchor the ends with rocks, and leave it out overnight.

Pin some pieces of flannel material to your pant legs, then walk through a field or clump of weeds.

The next day, see what hitchhikers you "arrested" on the board and your pants. If you caught any airborne or clinging seeds, inspect them to discover what designs they have for travelling.

Illus. 140

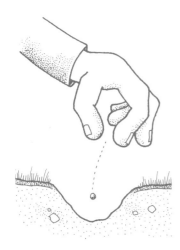

Illus. 140. Now find a home for the runaways by planting some of the seeds you caught to discover what plants they came from. Find a place where they won't be disturbed, trampled, or washed away, and cover the seeds with a thin layer of soil. Most seeds will only sprout in the spring to early summer, so be patient.

·7·

THE FAIRY RINGS

Last night, heavy rains fell from the sky. This morning your lawn is covered with toadstools. What are these magical eruptions? Are they the homes of fairies, meeting places for leprechauns, or just resting spots for passing trolls? We do know that these umbrella-shaped plants are mushrooms. Mushrooms belong to a primitive group of plants called fungi. Fungi also includes yeasts, mildews, and molds. Mushrooms come in rainbow colors and are shaped like parasols, horns, jelly beans, buns, and hats.

A search along any forest trail, especially after a spring or fall rain shower, will reveal a treasure chest of mushrooms on the ground and on tree trunks. Mushrooms are an important part of nature's recycling team, because they decompose the dead wood they live on. This process releases the nutrients in the wood, so they can fall into the earth and make fresh soil.

Suspects and Clues

Illus. 141. Of all the creatures living in dead trees, the most important decomposers are fungi and bacteria. If there are

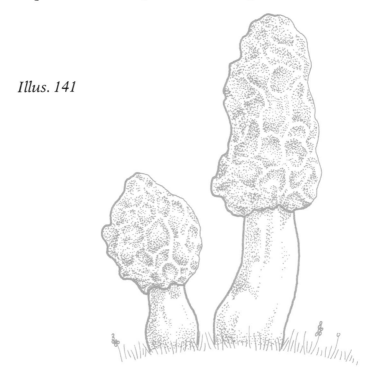

Illus. 141

any umbrella-shaped growths on the bark or on the ground, these are mushrooms or fungi. What you see isn't all of the mushroom. Part of it grows underground or within the dead wood.

Illus. 142. If the mushroom is growing on a log, gently lift a piece of the bark. Look for fine white threads underneath. These threads, called *hyphae*, are the main body of the mushroom. The whole tangled mass of threads is called the *mycelium*. The mycelium is the feeding stage of the mushroom.

The part you see above ground is the *cap* and *stalk*. This is the *fruiting body* of the mushroom. It develops from the mycelium. The fruiting body starts as a button underground and pushes up through the bark or soil. The fruiting body needs warmth and moisture to grow. That's why mushrooms appear suddenly on your lawn after a spring rainstorm.

The fruiting body is the reproducing stage of the mushroom. Its job is to produce spores. Spores are like microscopic seeds and will grow into new fungi plants.

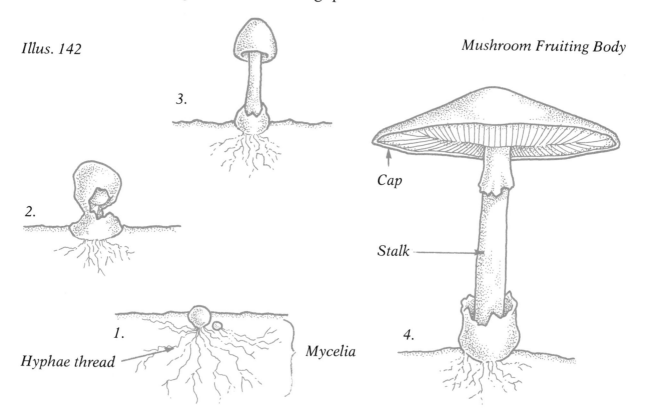

Illus. 142

Mushroom Fruiting Body

3.

2.

Cap

Stalk

1.

4.

Hyphae thread

Mycelia

Gills

Illus. 143

Illus. 143. Look under the mushroom cap. The plate-like things you see are gills. Stroke your finger along the gills. Is there a fine dark powder on your finger? The powder is made up of millions of spores. If you see holes under the cap, look for spores there, too.

Illus. 144. The stalk lifts the cap into air currents. When the time is right, the spores are released to spread with the wind. Some fungi, like this stinkhorn, use animals to scatter the spores. There is a sticky slime in the slim green stalk of the stinkhorn, and while you may find its odor horrible, insects love it. The stinkhorn keeps its spores in the slime, so when insects come to the slime, they carry the spores.

Very few spores land in an area suitable for growth. That's why mushrooms produce millions of spores.

Illus. 145. If there are any brown balls pushing up through the piles of fallen leaves or spongy white balls in a meadow, gently touch their tops. You'll find out why these mushrooms are called puffballs. The puff of "smoke" that shoots out is actually a blizzard of spores.

Illus. 144

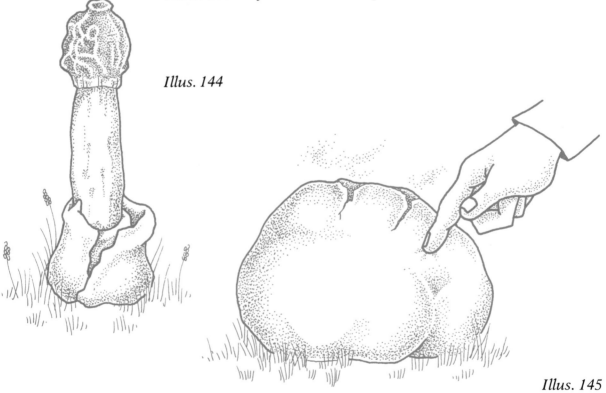

Illus. 145

Illus. 146–147. Look for other common fungi—

- On forest floors: orange peel and witch's butter
- On tree limbs: tree-ear fungus (Illus. 146).
- On tree trunks: shelf or bracket fungi
- In fields: inky caps (Illus 147) and fairy rings

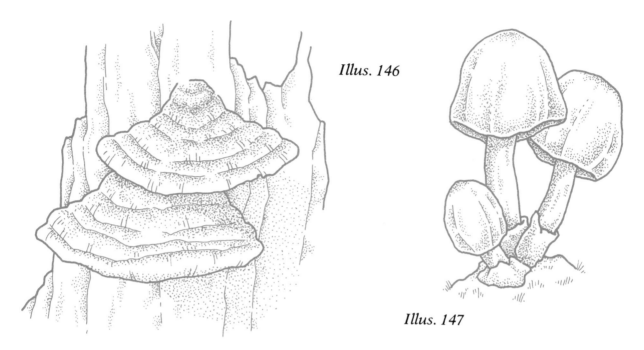

Illus. 146

Illus. 147

Illus. 148. Fairy rings are usually in meadows. These circles of light-colored grass surrounded by mushrooms were once believed to be where fairies lived and danced in the night. Fairy rings form when the mushroom mycelia spread out in a circular pattern under the earth. As the food supply is used up, the hyphae in the center die off. The ring of growth increases outward. At the edge of the ring, mushrooms pop up, drop spores, and new growth spreads out from the center again. In England there are fairy rings that are several miles wide.

Illus. 148

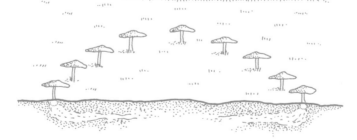

Illus. 149. Fungi don't have chlorophyll (the green pigment other plants use to make food from sunlight) and can't make their own food. So how do they eat? Most mushrooms get their food from dead and dying plants, such as fallen logs. The hyphae release chemicals which digest the wood. As mushrooms "eat" the log, the wood breaks down.

Illus. 150

Illus. 150. Crush the wood where mushrooms are feeding and growing, and feel how mushy the log is.

With the help of bacteria, the fungi are breaking down the dead wood, and recycling nutrients. Eventually, the tree completely crumbles and mixes in with the soil, making *humus*. If a seedling from a nearby tree lands on the humus, you'll find a new tree sprouting soon.

Illus. 151. Sometimes you see a crusty green layer growing on the tree bark, lettuce-like clumps hanging from limbs, or small colored plants on the surface of nearby rocks. These are *lichens*. Lichens are unusual because they are really two plants that cannot live apart from each other. Lichens consist of a fungus body and colonies of microscopic algae. These plants are an example of *symbiosis*. Symbiosis is when two things live together and each gets something from the other. The fungus part of the lichen can't make its own food. Algae are green plants. They use the sun's energy to make food for themselves and for the fungus. In return, the fungus anchors the plant with the minute hairs that make up its body. The fungus also absorbs moisture from the air and minerals from the rock or bark. These are all things that the algae must have in order to survive. So, the algae feeds the fungus and the fungus provides support, minerals, and water for the algae.

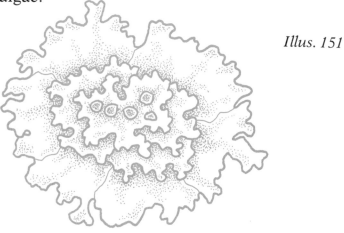

Illus. 151

Illus. 152. With your fingernail, scrape up an edge of the lichen. It is very gritty because lichens are another soil-

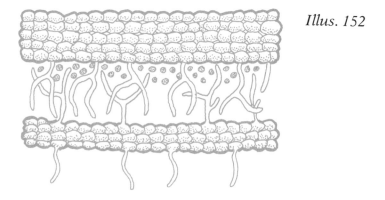

Illus. 152

making plant. Lichens produce a weak acid which dissolves the surface they grow on. This helps to break bark and rocks up into tiny bits. Look for seeds that have settled in these soil pockets.

Lichens are called pioneer plants because they settle on bare rock, sand, or soil. Sun-loving, they can be found in the desert, on the coast, and atop mountain peaks. They come in colors that range from pastel greens to burnt orange and bright purple.

Illus. 153–155 Lichens come in three main forms. Crustose (*Illus. 153*) make a crusty layer on rocks or soil. Fruticose (*Illus. 154*) are shrubby. They hang from branches. Foliose (*Illus. 155*) are leafy. They live on tree trunks and dead logs.

Illus. 153

Illus. 154

Illus. 155

Illus. 156 The tree bark may also have soft, dark green patches growing along with the lichens and mushrooms. This primitive plant is *moss*. Mosses like to grow in wet areas. Feel how spongy the moss is.

Illus. 156

What happens if you walk across a carpet with muddy shoes (besides getting yelled at)? The dirt settles in the carpet threads. Like a carpet, moss traps dust and dirt that blow by with the wind.

Illus. 157. If you use a hand lens, inspect the moss. You'll probably find a layer of soil building up in its leaves. When a seed landed on this bed of moss, there will be a new plant.

Look for thin, reddish stalks with capsules growing on the moss. These are the *fruiting bodies*. Inside the capsules are the spores, which spread with the wind and the rain. When they land, some will grow into new moss plants.

Illus. 157

Illus. 158. While the death of a beautiful tree may sadden you, remember this is the beginning of the tree's journey back to the soil. From this death, life in the forest endures. What would happen to all the logs and limbs that fall in the forest if there weren't any decomposers?

Illus. 158

*NEVER EAT ANY MUSHROOMS IN THE WILD WHEN YOU'RE OUT EXPLORING. EATING EVEN ONLY A BIT OF A POISONOUS ONE CAN KILL YOU. ONLY AN EXPERT CAN IDENTIFY WHICH MUSHROOMS ARE SAFE TO EAT.

Case #12: The Mushroom's Fingerprints

Illus. 159. Spores come in many colors and their prints are an important tool for identifying the type of mushroom you find.

Illus. 159

To make a mushroom fingerprint:

• Cut the mushroom off at the stem

• Place the cap, gills facing down, on a piece of white paper.

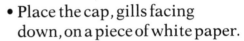

• Place a damp cotton ball on the top of the cap to keep it from drying out. Cover the mushroom cap with a bowl or cup and let sit overnight.

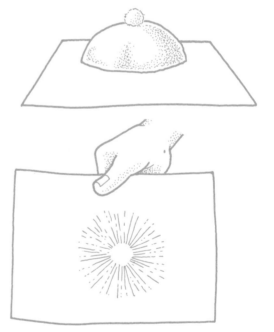

• The next morning, lift the bowl and carefully remove the cap from the paper. You'll have a finished print of the spores that fall from the gills. To preserve the print, coat the paper with gum arabic (ask someone at your local hobby store for some) before you lay the mushroom cap down on the paper.

·8·

SKY WATCH

Illus. 160. Clouds can be fun to watch because their shapes always change as they drift across the sky. Early navigators and farmers looked to the clouds for clues to help them predict the weather. You can use the clouds to tell you what the weather will be later that day or tomorrow.

Illus. 160

Illus. 161. Clouds are formed by water vapor that rises up into the atmosphere. Water vapor comes from all over: oceans, lakes, plants, and animals. You can't see the water vapor until it cools enough and condenses, then it changes into tiny water droplets or ice crystals and attaches to dust or smoke particles in the air. This mass of visible droplets of water or ice is the cloud. By a careful watch of the sky, you can decide whether to pack rain gear or suntan lotion when you go out investigating.

Illus. 161

Suspects and Clues

Illus. 162. If it's a cold day, step outside and let out a big puff of air. You just made a cloud. Your breath has moisture in it and since your body is warmer than the air, when you blow out, some of the moisture condenses into water droplets and a steamy cloud forms.

Illus. 163. If the sky is cloudless and a deep blue, the air is too dry for clouds to form. Take out your sunglasses—clear days are in store. Be careful not to look directly at the sun because this can severely damage your eyes.

Illus. 164. If you've ever taken a walk on a foggy day, you've walked through a *stratus* cloud. If the fog burns off by noon, expect the rest of the day to be fair. Otherwise, it'll be a day of drizzle.

Illus. 162

Illus. 163

Illus. 164

Illus. 165. Wispy, white clouds that look like cobwebs or brush strokes are *cirrus* clouds. Cirrus clouds are the highest clouds in the sky, about 20,000 to 45,000 feet up. A few cirrus here and there usually indicate fair weather ahead.

However, if the cirrus begin to fill the sky and develop into long streaks, they can be the early warning that a storm is approaching. Increasing amounts of cirrus clouds take on shapes of angel's hair or mare's tails.

Illus. 165

Illus. 166. The high cirro-form clouds may also look like fish scales. These "mackerel skies" or *cirrocumulus* mean the upper air is unstable and also hint at poor weather ahead.

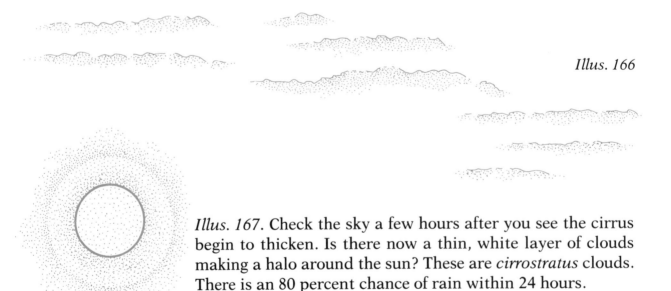

Illus. 166

Illus. 167. Check the sky a few hours after you see the cirrus begin to thicken. Is there now a thin, white layer of clouds making a halo around the sun? These are *cirrostratus* clouds. There is an 80 percent chance of rain within 24 hours.

Illus. 167

Illus. 168. Cirrostratus following cirrus is the first sign of an approaching *warm front*. When air masses meet they do not blend. Rather, a boundary or front is formed. Along a warm front, warm, moist air moves up and over a colder air mass. Clouds form by condensation along the boundary between the warm and cold air masses. These clouds progressively thicken, lower, and eventually produce *precipitation* (rain or snow).

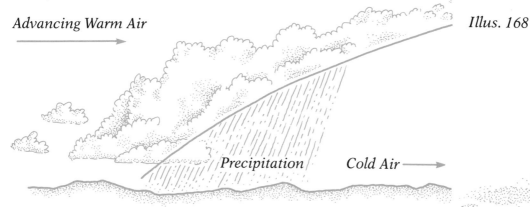

Advancing Warm Air

Precipitation   *Cold Air* →

Illus. 168

Illus. 169

Illus. 169. When you see the sky filling up with a grey or bluish sheet of clouds that look like a frosted pane of glass, these are the *altostratus*. Alto clouds are a middle-level layer, and replace the higher cirro clouds as the warm front nears.

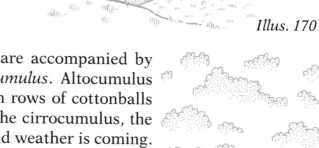

Illus. 170

Illus. 170. Sometimes the altostratus are accompanied by another middle-level cloud, the *altocumulus*. Altocumulus make the sky look like it's packed with rows of cottonballs and is called "wool-packed sky." Like the cirrocumulus, the altocumulus sometimes suggest that bad weather is coming. The saying, "Red sky at morning, Sailors take warning, Red at night, Sailors delight" comes from the sun's morning rays reflecting off the alto and cirrus clouds coming in from the west. This is where most storms in North America come from.

Illus. 171

Illus. 171. If you look up and see the sky covered with grey flannel sheets that don't let the sun shine through, better get your umbrella.

These are the low-level *nimbostratus*. Nimbostratus are the last arrivals of the warm front and bring with them the long-awaited precipitation. Constant rain or snowshowers that last 12–24 hours fall from these gloomy clouds.

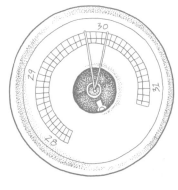

Illus. 172

Illus. 172. When you expect a storm, pay attention to the wind and air pressure (use a barometer to measure the pressure). As the storm system gets closer, pressure drops, and winds pick up and change directions. When air pressure drops, the force the weight of air exerts on the earth's surface is less.

104

Illus. 173. Wildlife can provide clues that the weather is changing. Animals feel and react strongly to pressure changes. Fish swim deeper, insects swarm and bite more, and low air pressure makes it hard for geese and ducks to take off. Frogs and toads, though, like the increase in humidity that precedes a storm, and emerge from ponds, croaking loudly.

Illus. 173

Illus. 174. Look for rainbows when the sun breaks through the clouds and rain. You must have the sun behind you and the rain in front of you to see a rainbow. Look for rainbows mostly in the early morning or late afternoon, when the sun isn't too high in the sky.

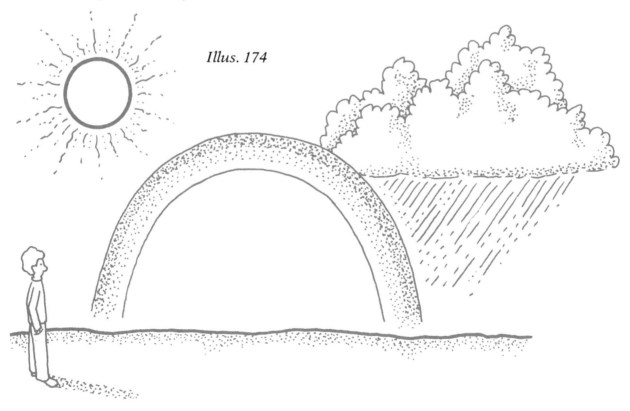

Illus. 174

Illus. 175. When a ray of sunlight shines on a raindrop, it bends, and separates the light into different colors. When it does this, it acts like a *prism.*

Sometimes you can see a double rainbow. When the sunlight that enters the raindrops is refracted, or bent, twice before passing, you get a double rainbow. One bow is usually fainter than the other, with the colors in reversed order for the darker rainbow.

When the warm front passes, expect mild weather and gentle winds.

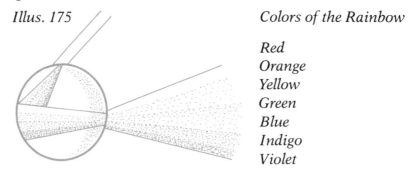

Illus. 175

Colors of the Rainbow

Red
Orange
Yellow
Green
Blue
Indigo
Violet

Illus. 176. If you are looking up into sunny skies, on a summer's day, there's a good chance you'll see puffy white clouds with flat bottoms. These are the *cumulus.* Like a hot air balloon, bubbles of warm air rise through the denser, colder air above, expand and cool to form clouds. They disappear towards evening as the ground surface cools.

But if these innocent-looking clouds start climbing vertically, you better keep an eye on them. If *towering cumulus* begin to build up on a hot muggy morning, thunderstorms are a real possibility by late afternoon.

Illus. 176

106

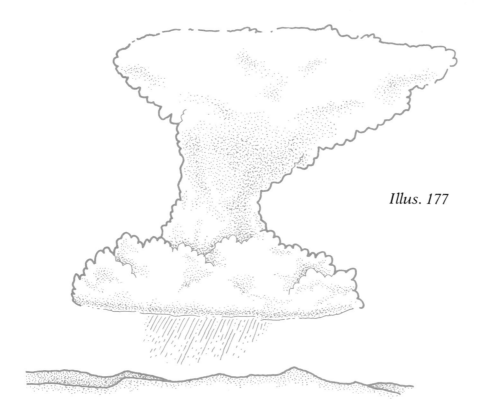

Illus. 177

Illus. 177. Cumulus can build to tremendous heights, up to 50,000 feet, mushrooming into the most dramatic clouds, the *cumulonimbus*, or thunderheads. You can usually see the high anvil-shaped tops of thunderheads only when they're on the distant horizon. As they move closer, only their dark bases are visible. If you look up and see these huge clouds with black bottoms, take cover immediately. Cumulonimbus can unleash their fury with high winds, heavy rains, thunder, lightning, and sometimes hail.

Illus. 178. The scariest part of a storm is the thunder and lightning. During a thunderstorm violent air currents blow up and down inside the cumulonimbus clouds. This causes friction, which produces electrical charges on any particles inside the cloud. The charges separate within the cloud—the lighter, positive charges rising to the top, and the heavier, negative charges gathering at the base. These negative charges, or ions, are drawn from the cloud base to the positively charged ground below like a magnet. This attraction is the lightning. The lightning discharges from the cloud

107

with a negatively charged stroke. Before it reaches the ground, a positively-charged ground stroke meets it. When they meet, a lightning flash is created. This is the flash you see.

The air along the path of the lightning bolt becomes so hot that it explodes in the sky. Molecules of air move very rapidly outward from the lightning bolt and produce a strong, loud sound wave. This is the thunder you hear. Thunder and lightning happen at the same time, but because light travels faster than sound, you see lightning before you hear thunder.

To tell how far away in miles the storm is from you, count the seconds between the lightning flash and the thunder and divide by five.

Illus. 178

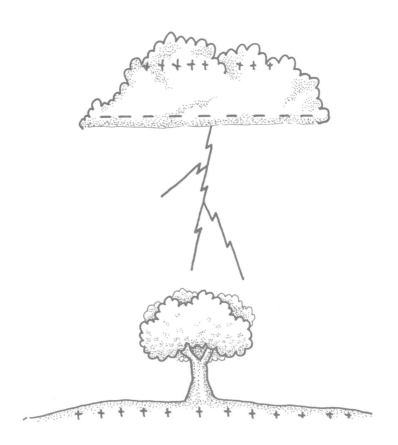

Illus. 179. Lightning always takes the shortest path from a cloud to the ground, striking the tallest object. If you are caught out in the open during a thunderstorm, *get away from any water*, and keep away from isolated trees. Crouch if you can't get to a safe spot immediately.

Illus. 179

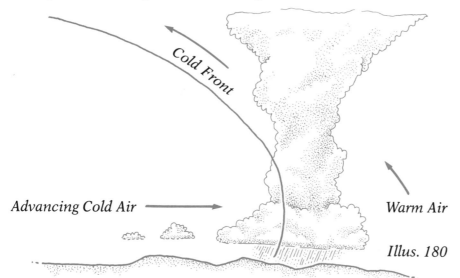

Cold Front

Advancing Cold Air

Warm Air

Illus. 180

Illus. 180. Cumulonimbus also develop along an advancing cold front. If the sky to the west is dark with a bank of thunderheads, and the wind is strong, gusty, and from the south, a cold front is coming. Unlike the gentle approach of the warm front, a cold front travels rapidly and produces severe weather. Heavy rains, hail, or snow falls, temperatures drop 20 to 30 °F (11 to 17 °C) in a few minutes, and winds of 50 mph are not uncommon with cold fronts. However, they pass rapidly leaving behind clear skies and cooler temperatures.

Illus. 181

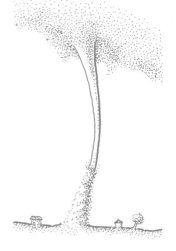

Illus. 181. Do you live in the midwest section of the United States? Cold fronts in the springtime can mean *tornadoes*. Tornadoes form mainly in North America, and *Tornadoes* are funnel-shaped clouds that descend from thunderheads, whirling at speeds up to 300 mph. The air spins so fast that it sucks things up like a vacuum cleaner. Most tornadoes just skip along the ground for a few minutes.

The largest tornado ever tracked was two miles wide, stayed on the ground for three hours and eighteen minutes, and travelled 219 miles from western Missouri to central Indiana in 1925.

Illus. 182. Hurricanes are another type of fierce storm. While tornadoes form over land, hurricanes form over the ocean in tropical regions. They occur mostly in the late summer and early autumn. The summer sun heats up large masses of warm, moist ocean air. A disturbance causes the warm air in the middle to rise as cooler air streams in from the sides. A whirlpool forms, with winds spiraling upwards, counter-clockwise in the Northern Hemisphere and clockwise in the Southern Hemisphere. Hurricanes batter coastlines with torrential rains, surging seas, and destructive winds of speeds from 75 to 150 mph. The most unusual feature of a hurricane is the center, known as the *eye*. The eye is an area of calm about 25 miles wide, and is sunny and dry while the storm rages around it.

Our weather is so changeable because the air on earth is never still. The clouds, though, are your messengers for whether cold polar air or warm tropical air is moving into your area. When you look up at clouds, let their shapes stir your imagination, but also remember that they have a lot to tell you.

Illus. 182

Case #13: Sky Surveillance

Illus. 183. When you get up in the morning, look out your window and check the condition of the sky. Look at the sky later on in the day, and just before the sun sets.

Use this chart to keep a record of the weather. Compare your weather predictions against the predictions made on radio or TV.

Day	Time	Wind Direction	Cloud Shapes	Cloud Cover	Forecast
3/30	7AM	NE		1	Clear & Sunny
4/3	12 NOON	N	cumulus	2	partly sunny
4/12	8AM	SE	cumulonimbus	3	shower
4/15	7AM	S		1	sunny & clear

Illus. 183

*Cloud Cover Scale: 1—no clouds in sky
2—a few scattered clouds
3—sky ½ or more covered
4—sky totally covered*

*Wind Direction: Winds are named for the direction from which they come;
a west wind blows from the west.*

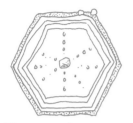

Illus. 184

Hexagonal

Hexagonal Columns

Stellar

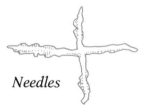

Spatial Dendrite

Needles

Irregular Crystals

Cupped Columns

112

Case #14: The Falling Stars

Snowflakes	Shape	Air Temp	Seen?
2/2	Stellar	0°F	Yes
2/3	Needles	10°F	

Illus. 184–185. Snowflakes are made up of ice crystals joined together. Different shapes of snowflakes form in different cloud layers. Their shape depends on the temperature and humidity of the air in which the crystal is formed. As snowflakes fall from the clouds, they continually form new shapes as they melt, collide, and refreeze. Snowflakes are always six-sided, and though their shapes follow patterns, no two snowflakes are alike.

Put some black construction paper in the freezer. The next day, when the snow begins to fall, take the frozen construction paper outside and catch some falling snowflakes on it. They won't melt on the frozen paper. Use a magnifying lens to look at their delicate and beautiful designs.

What shapes can you find? Put a check next to the general shapes listed in Illus. 184. Also, jot down the air temperature. Do certain shapes form only when it's bitter cold or when the air is just at the freezing point? Star-like crystals usually form between −5 °F (−21 °C) to 0 °F (−17 °C), while hexagonal plates form between 27 °F (−3 °C) and 32 °F (0 °C).

·9·

EVENING SPOOKS

Suspects and Clues

Illus. 186

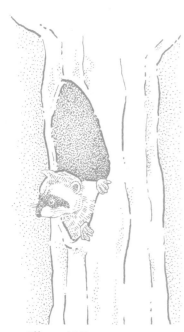

Illus. 187

Illus. 186. Dark covers the earth. Piercing screams, scratches, hisses, and roars surround you. Something darts by overhead. Gigantic shapes hover in the distance. Something furry brushes your leg. Frozen with fear, you imagine all sorts of creatures from the underworld roaming the land.

Nighttime is scary and full of mystery. Our senses don't work well at night, so we can't tell what's going on around us. Because you can't see very well, simple shadows turn into werewolves, goblins, and witches.

Illus. 187. Some nocturnal (awake at night) critters have eyes well-suited for low light. Many others don't, but have fine-tuned their other senses to help them carry out their chores. Like daytime creatures, nocturnal animals spend most of their time looking for food, finding mates, and setting up territories.

Illus. 188. Being active at night has its advantages. Animals can move about more secretly than during daylight. They're less likely to be attacked by the predators that hunt in the daytime. Night is also cooler and more moist, so scorpions, pack rats, and other desert dwellers have an easier time.

Illus. 188

Illus. 189. Darkness also gives protection to those that molt. Arthropods (insects, spiders, and crabs) have a hard outside skeleton. As the animals grow, they molt this *exoskeleton.* When dragonfly nymphs change into adults, they can't fly until their wings dry, which takes about an hour. By molting at night, they are less visible to predators and have a better chance of surviving.

Illus. 189

Illus. 190

Illus. 190. Predators that eat the same food their daylight friends eat can avoid competition by hunting at night. Hawks hunt for mice in the daytime while most owls prey on mice after the sun goes down.

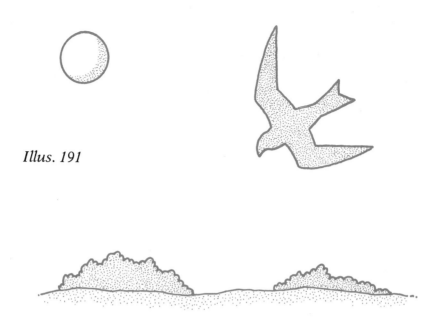

Illus. 191

Illus. 191. When you go out at night, take along a flashlight and if you're going near roads wear reflective clothing. Stay in areas that you know well so that you won't get lost in the dark. Start out just after sunset when the sky fills with a soft purple light. Deer, rabbits, and nighthawks are some of the animals you might see moving around. The dim light of dusk gives these animals some protection from predators, yet allows them to see where they're going. Animals that are active at dusk and dawn are called *crepuscular*.

Illus. 192. Can you see details and color as well at dusk as you can in daylight? Probably not. Your eyes are designed to work best in good light. Do nocturnal animals need to see color? No, and many, like opossums and bats, are color blind. Instead, their eyes are very sensitive to the low light at night.

Illus. 192

Illus. 193. Scan the forest floor for pale, yellow-green lights. These lights are made by a glowworm, a type of flightless female beetle. When she lifts her tail, the light attracts flying males for mating purposes. A special chemical reaction in the glowworm's body called *bioluminescence* produces the light. Pick up a glowworm and feel how cool it is. The light gives off little heat.

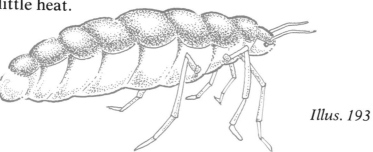

Illus. 193

Illus. 194. Many organisms luminesce. Fireflies are another type of beetle that send mating signals with blinking greenish yellow tailights.

Illus. 194

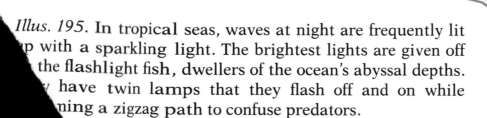

Illus. 195. In tropical seas, waves at night are frequently lit up with a sparkling light. The brightest lights are given off the flashlight fish, dwellers of the ocean's abyssal depths. have twin lamps that they flash off and on while ning a zigzag path to confuse predators.

Illus. 195

Illus. 196

Illus. 196. One of the eeriest green glows comes from certain mushrooms. After picking the jack-o'-lantern mushroom, the gills light up in the dark. One type of honey mushroom found in the rain forests of Sumatra can be seen glowing from over 40 feet away. These fungal lights don't seem to have any function. They occur when the hyphae are exposed to the air after the wood the mushroom is growing on breaks open.

Illus. 197. Try standing at the edge of a field, or if you're feeling pretty brave, near a cemetery at night. You'll hear rasping hisses, deep hoots, and screeches, but don't be afraid. Stay in place and try to locate where these sounds are coming from. Most likely, you'll find owls, the creatures responsible for these noises, up in trees or in church steeples.

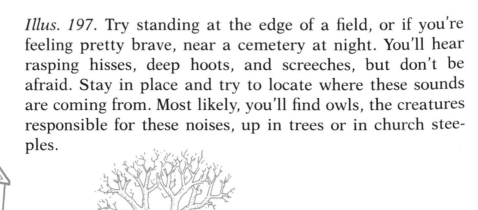

Illus. 197

Illus. 198

Illus. 198. The owl is wonderfully adapted to nighttime. Look at the size of its eyes. They're huge in comparison to the size of its head. An owl's eyes are designed to pick up all the light that's available. As you might expect, owls have eyes that are 100 times more light sensitive than your eyes. That's why they don't crash into trees while flying in the dark. Hold your head still and look up, down, and sideways. Notice how freely your eyes move in their sockets. Owls can't do this. To compensate, owls swivel their heads at least 180 degrees, and can even turn upside down to see around and directly behind them. Like you, owls have good binocular vision, meaning they can see an object with both eyes. They move their heads to precisely judge how far away a mouse or rabbit (their next meal) is from them. They also have keen ears. Owls can hear extremely faint noises inaudible to our ears because of the shape of their faces.

Illus. 199. Barn owls have heart-shaped faces ringed with a densely packed wall of curving feathers. These feathers funnel sound to the eardrum. Like other owls, the ears of barn owls are long slits placed at slightly different positions on each side of the head. This helps them to fine-tune locations of sound. Sound coming in from below eye level will sound louder in the left ear and sounds coming in above eye level sound louder in the right ear.

Illus. 199

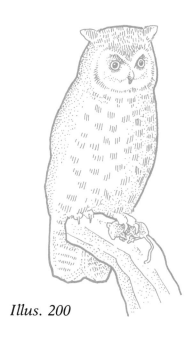

Illus. 200

Illus. 200. Using its sharp eyes and ears, the barn owl pinpoints exactly where a toad or mouse is on the ground. It is as silent as possible, flying to its prey with its large wings open wide. The velvety soft feathers on the wings have a soft fringe to muffle the whistling sound of the wind. If you're lucky, you might get to see the ghostly white barn owl drop from the church tower, its talons extended as it swoops down and grabs a mouse.

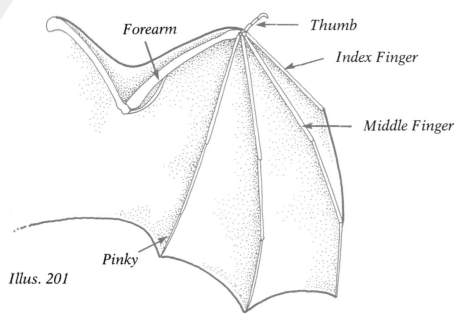

Forearm

Thumb

Index Finger

Middle Finger

Pinky

Illus. 201

Illus. 201. While listening and watching for owls, you may see something dart by overhead. Another creature that dwells in the belfry (as well as in caves and attics) is the bat. Bats are the only mammal that can fly. The wing of a bat is simply a membrane that's attached to the animal's side and to its fingers. If all your fingers, except your thumb, could stretch down to where your feet are, and the spaces between your fingers and ankles were connected by a flap of skin, you'd have a "bat's wing."

Illus. 202. Most bats scoop up insects as they fly, using their wings much like a baseball mitt. Bats are nearly blind. They use their ears instead of their eyes, because they have a natural sonar system. Bats fly with their mouths open and send out little clicking sounds so high-pitched that you can rarely hear them. When the sound hits an object in its path, it's reflected back to the bat as an echo. The bat's large, upright ears then go into action. They listen for the echoes to tell how near or far away an object is. The louder the sound is to the bat, the nearer the object. This way a bat can tell whether an insect is flying towards or away from it.

By varying the pulse, duration, and pitch of the sounds, and listening to the echoes, bats can determine the exact location, size, motion, and speed of its prey. This is called *echolocation*, and it allows bats to fly around in totally dark caves.

120

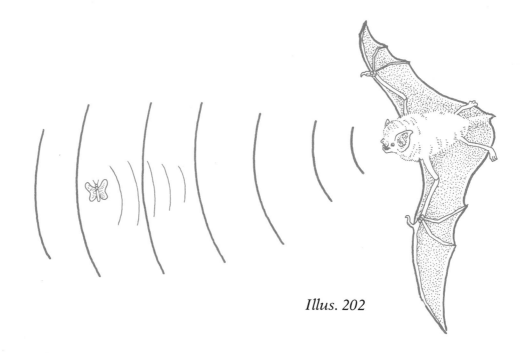

Illus. 202

Illus. 203. In the dark, what do you depend on to move around? Without a flashlight, your hands would probably be most important. Many small nocturnal critters scurry around by feel. Weasels, for example, have modified hairs that are touch-sensitive organs called *vibrissae.* Skunks and foxes also have these organs.

Illus. 203

Illus. 204. An acute sense of smell also helps animals hunt at night. Since there is less wind at night, odors remain in the air longer. Many nocturnal moths have sensitive scent

Illus. 204

organs on their antennae. They find their mates in the dark by smell alone. One bird that can't fly, the kiwi of New Zealand, waits for the cover of darkness before it comes out to feed. Unlike most birds, they have a sense of smell. Their nostrils are at the tip of their long, curved beak. They walk along with the tip of the bill close to the ground, sniffing loudly to hunt out earthworms.

Illus. 205

Illus. 205. Take out your flashlight and scan the area around you for night creatures. If you shine your light over a swamp during springtime, hundreds of ruby-red eyes will glow back at you. Although this sight will probably raise goosebumps on your flesh, these are not goblins. Rather, what you're seeing is the *eyeshine* from the alligators. Eyeshine is caused by a reflective layer in the eye called the *tapetum*. The tapetum lies behind the retina. Not all light that enters the eye is absorbed by the cells in the retina. The tapetum acts like a mirror to reflect stray light back through the retina. This increases the eye's ability to see at night.

Different kinds of tapetums reflect different colors. The eyeshine color can help you to identify the animal.

eyeshine color	animal
bright orange	*bear*
bright yellow	*raccoon*
yellowish-white	*bobcat*
bright white	*porcupine*
cloudy green	*bullfrog*
pale green	*domestic cat*
green	*fox*
red	*hare, rabbit*
ruby red	*alligator*

The more you go out at night, the more comfortable you'll be seeing strange lights and hearing eerie noises. Don't be afraid to explore the world of darkness for the fun of the unexpected.

Case #15: The Eyes Have It

You're up in the mountains and decide to take a stroll in the woods at night. You hear a snort and see a large, dark shadow move between the trees. When you shine your flashlight, the animal flees. You're not certain if the glow was red or orange because you only got a quick glimpse of the eyeshine.

The next day you return to the area and find pieces of fur and scratch marks on the trunk of a pine tree. Further down the trail, you find a large mound of scat that contains lots of berry seeds. What animal did you spook last night?

Answer. Bear—*a red glow would be a hare, or rabbit, or an alligator. Since alligators don't live in the mountains, and rabbits and hares leave small, bullet-shaped scat, you probably saw the orange eyeshine from a bear. The tree rubbings are a common territorial marking for bears and the scat further confirms the bear's existence.*

123

Case #16: Is Anyone Home?

Along a creek you find a series of footprints that wander up and down the creek banks. The tracks look like tiny hand-prints that show both the heel and the toe impressions. There are no tail markings. As you follow the tracks, they lead to a hole at the base of a large cottonwood tree. You decide to return at night and stalk out this tree to spy on its occupant. If you shine your flashlight into the hole when you return, what color eyes may glow back at you?

Answer: Bright yellow. The habitat and pattern and movement of the tracks point to a raccoon.

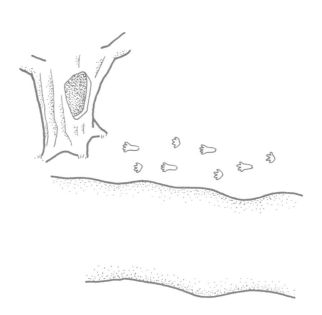

124

INDEX

127

METRIC EQUIVALENCY CHART

MM—MILLIMETRES   CM—CENTIMETRES

INCHES TO MILLIMETRES AND CENTIMETRES

INCHES	MM	CM	INCHES	CM	INCHES	CM
1/8	3	0.3	9	22.9	30	76.2
1/4	6	0.6	10	25.4	31	78.7
3/8	10	1.0	11	27.9	32	81.3
1/2	13	1.3	12	30.5	33	83.8
5/8	16	1.6	13	33.0	34	86.4
3/4	19	1.9	14	35.6	35	88.9
7/8	22	2.2	15	38.1	36	91.4
1	25	2.5	16	40.6	37	94.0
1 1/4	32	3.2	17	43.2	38	96.5
1 1/2	38	3.8	18	45.7	39	99.1
1 3/4	44	4.4	19	48.3	40	101.6
2	51	5.1	20	50.8	41	104.1
2 1/2	64	6.4	21	53.3	42	106.7
3	76	7.6	22	55.9	43	109.2
3 1/2	89	8.9	23	58.4	44	111.8
4	102	10.2	24	61.0	45	114.3
4 1/2	114	11.4	25	63.5	46	116.8
5	127	12.7	26	66.0	47	119.4
6	152	15.2	27	68.6	48	121.9
7	178	17.8	28	71.1	49	124.5
8	203	20.3	29	73.7	50	127.0

YARDS TO METRES

YARDS	METRES	YARDS	METRES	YARDS	METRES	YARDS	METRES	YARDS	METRES
1/8	0.11	2 1/8	1.94	4 1/8	3.77	6 1/8	5.60	8 1/8	7.43
1/4	0.23	2 1/4	2.06	4 1/4	3.89	6 1/4	5.72	8 1/4	7.54
3/8	0.34	2 3/8	2.17	4 3/8	4.00	6 3/8	5.83	8 3/8	7.66
1/2	0.46	2 1/2	2.29	4 1/2	4.11	6 1/2	5.94	8 1/2	7.77
5/8	0.57	2 5/8	2.40	4 5/8	4.23	6 5/8	6.06	8 5/8	7.89
3/4	0.69	2 3/4	2.51	4 3/4	4.34	6 3/4	6.17	8 3/4	8.00
7/8	0.80	2 7/8	2.63	4 7/8	4.46	6 7/8	6.29	8 7/8	8.12
1	0.91	3	2.74	5	4.57	7	6.40	9	8.23
1 1/8	1.03	3 1/8	2.86	5 1/8	4.69	7 1/8	6.52	9 1/8	8.34
1 1/4	1.14	3 1/4	2.97	5 1/4	4.80	7 1/4	6.63	9 1/4	8.46
1 3/8	1.26	3 3/8	3.09	5 3/8	4.91	7 3/8	6.74	9 3/8	8.57
1 1/2	1.37	3 1/2	3.20	5 1/2	5.03	7 1/2	6.86	9 1/2	8.69
1 5/8	1.49	3 5/8	3.31	5 5/8	5.14	7 5/8	6.97	9 5/8	8.80
1 3/4	1.60	3 3/4	3.43	5 3/4	5.26	7 3/4	7.09	9 3/4	8.92
1 7/8	1.71	3 7/8	3.54	5 7/8	5.37	7 7/8	7.20	9 7/8	9.03
2	1.83	4	3.66	6	5.49	8	7.32	10	9.14

What Your Colleagues Are Saying . . .

Throughout *A Fresh Look at Phonics*, readers will hear and be reassured by the voice of a master teacher who has been where they have been and understands their challenges and their questions. In this excellent and timely volume, Wiley Blevins brings foundational instruction to life. He engagingly addresses the content, terminology, and scope and sequence of phonics instruction specifically and word study more broadly. He shows teachers how to knowledgeably support children's understanding and acquisition of the ways in which the relationship between sound and print operates. Wiley demonstrates how to balance the role of teachers' direct explanations with children's explorations, including word sort activities. Importantly, he addresses the all-too-often overlooked role that *discussion* plays in acquiring and deepening understanding of foundational knowledge.

—SHANE TEMPLETON
Foundation Professor Emeritus of Literacy Studies
University of Nevada, Reno

When Wiley Blevins wrote his first book on teaching phonics 20 years ago, I thought that it was one of the most practical approaches to teaching this foundational reading competency. It may seem like a cliché, but Wiley has outdone himself with this book! In *A Fresh Look at Phonics* he provides teachers and others interested in effective phonics instruction with a comprehensive and practical guide to making phonics instruction work for all students, all year. Just as the title promises, Wiley provides us with a truly *fresh* way of thinking about how phonics plays out in classrooms.

—TIMOTHY Rasinski
Professor of Literacy Education
Kent State University

Wiley combines the latest research and his own years of trusted know-how to provide educators with a timely trove of high impact tools they can readily use to deliver world-class phonics instruction. *A Fresh Look at Phonics* is sure to be another must-have, well-worn classic.

—JANIEL WAGSTAFF
Literacy Coach and Author of
The Common Core Companion: Booster Lessons, Grades K–2

(Continued)

(Continued)

I devoured this book! Who would have thought that a book on phonics would be a page-turner? It's quick, practical, and teacher friendly and yet comprehensive enough to be a refresher course for experienced teachers and the needed foundation for teachers new to teaching beginning readers. I can't wait to share this with teachers with whom I work in professional development—they are going to love the clear links to reading, writing, and spelling. My favorite feature? The broad scope and sequence that pairs with guided reading instruction and provides links back to phonics lessons.

—JUDY LYNCH
Teacher and Author of *Easy Lessons for Teaching Word Families*

Wiley Blevins' fresh take on phonics is a must-read for anyone looking to improve phonics instruction. He boils phonics down into critical ingredients and supports teachers in the ever-important process of reflection. The book gives professional learning communities the tools needed to turn common instructional failures into effective, timeless practices.

—CAROLYN BANUELOS, DANIELLE JAMES, AND ELISE LUND
Literacy Coaches and Authors of *Puzzle Piece Phonics*

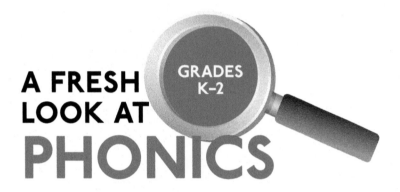

A FRESH
LOOK AT
PHONICS

GRADES
K-2

A FRESH LOOK AT
PHONICS

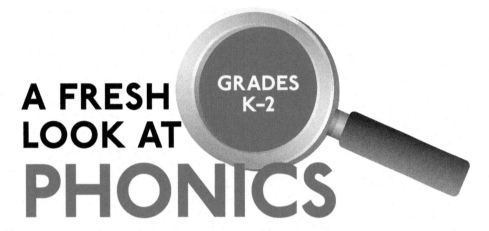

GRADES
K–2

Common Causes of **FAILURE** *and*
7 Ingredients for **SUCCESS**

WILEY BLEVINS

Foreword by Douglas Fisher

http://resources.corwin.com/blevinsphonics

CL CORWIN
LITERACY

FOR INFORMATION:

Corwin

A SAGE Company

2455 Teller Road

Thousand Oaks, California 91320

(800) 233-9936

www.corwin.com

SAGE Publications Ltd.

1 Oliver's Yard

55 City Road

London EC1Y 1SP

United Kingdom

SAGE Publications India Pvt. Ltd.

B 1/I 1 Mohan Cooperative Industrial Area

Mathura Road, New Delhi 110 044

India

SAGE Publications Asia-Pacific Pte. Ltd.

3 Church Street

#10-04 Samsung Hub

Singapore 049483

Publisher: Lisa Luedeke

Editor: Wendy Murray

Editorial Development Manager: Julie Nemer

Editorial Assistant: Nicole Shade

Production Editor: Melanie Birdsall

Copy Editor: Melinda Masson

Typesetter: C&M Digitals (P) Ltd.

Proofreader: Theresa Kay

Indexer: Molly Hall

Cover Designer: Rose Storey

Marketing Manager: Rebecca Eaton

Library of Congress Cataloging-in-Publication Data

Names: Blevins, Wiley, author.

Title: A fresh look at phonics, grades K–2 : common causes of failure and 7 ingredients for success / Wiley Blevins.

Description: Thousand Oaks, California : Corwin, a SAGE Company, [2017] | Includes bibliographical references and index.

Identifiers: LCCN 2016011377 | ISBN 9781506326887 (pbk. : alk. paper)

Subjects: LCSH: Reading—Phonetic method—United States. | English language—Orthography and spelling.

Classification: LCC LB1050.34 .B54 2017 | DDC 372.46/5—dc23 LC record available at https://lccn.loc.gov/2016011377

This book is printed on acid-free paper.

16 17 18 19 20 10 9 8 7 6 5 4 3 2 1

Contents

SECTION I

The Key Ingredients for Phonics Success
and Next Steps to Improve Your Instruction
Once You Have Them in Place   I

Rick Harrington

Rick Harrington

Rick Harrington

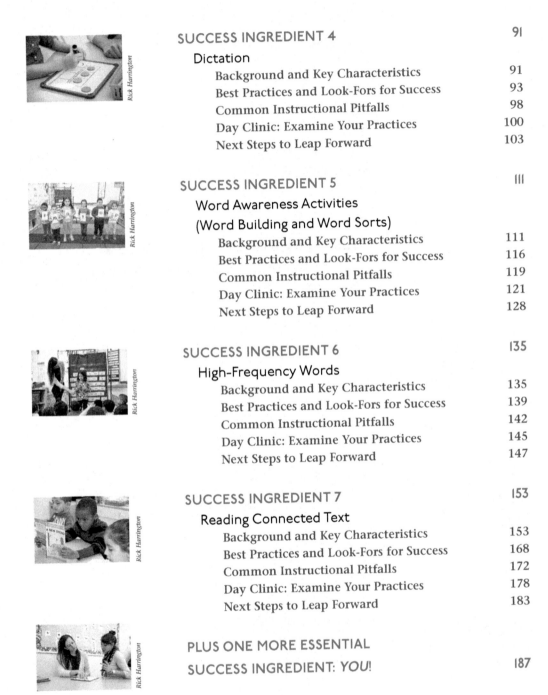
Rick Harrington

SECTION 2

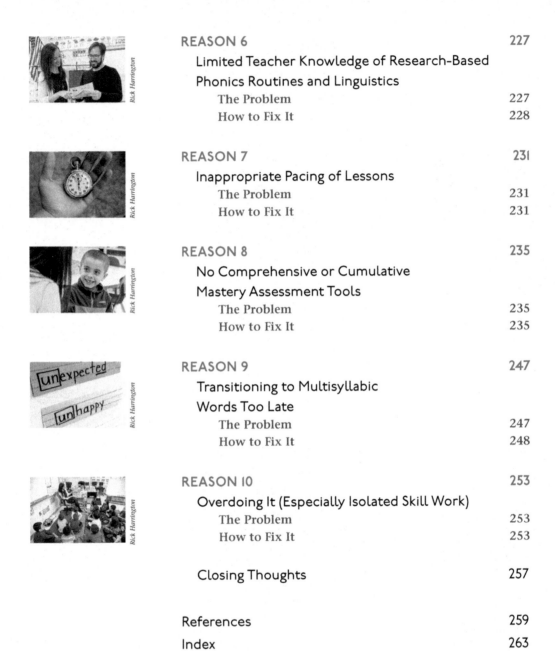

Visit the companion website at
http://resources.corwin.com/blevinsphonics
for downloadable resources.

Foreword

Not too long ago, there was some "research" circulating the Internet about reading, specifically on how letter order did not matter for comprehension. According to the "study," the human mind does not read every letter by itself but rather sees the word as a whole. Here's a quote that circulated about this investigation:

> Aoccdrnig to rsearch at Cmabrigde Uinervtisy, it deosn't mttaer in waht oredr the ltteers in a wrod are, the olny iprmoetnt tihng is taht the frist and lsat ltteer be at the rghit pclae. The rset can be a toatl mses and you can sitll raed it wouthit a porbelm. Tihs is bcuseae the huamn mnid deos not raed ervey lteter by istlef, but the wrod as a wlohe.

As far as I can tell, there never was a Cambridge University study. But that didn't seem to stop people from making claims that students did not need phonics instruction. What? That didn't seem logical to me. I believe that your brain can read the paragraph above, with all of the mixed-up letters in the words, because you have a very sophisticated knowledge of letter-sound combinations, and you were able to rearrange the letters into patterns that you recognize. In other words, it was your phonics and comprehension knowledge, together, that allowed you to make sense of this paragraph.

The premise we can read because we have been explicitly taught a sound and letter system is what this book is based upon. At the height of the whole-language approach, Wiley Blevins advocated for systematic phonics instruction, and he's stayed the course ever since. In this new book, he teaches us how to help students break the code so that words make sense to them.

Blevins also shares the "how nots" of phonics instruction and makes the case that knowing common instructional missteps and misunderstandings can be as important as knowing what's effective. In fact, before I share more convincing evidence for the efficacy of the ideas of this book, let's make sure we are operating with a shared definition of phonics and phonics instruction. I have adopted the definition forwarded by Ehri, Nunes, Stahl, and Willows (2001), which reads:

> Phonics instruction teaches beginning readers the alphabetic code and how to use this knowledge to read words. In systematic phonics programs, a planned set of phonics elements is taught sequentially. The

set includes the major correspondences between consonant letters and sounds, short and long vowel letters and sounds, and vowel and consonant digraphs . . . It also may include blends of letter-sounds that form larger sub-units in words. (p. 394)

There are so many aspects of this definition that I appreciate. First, the authors are clear that we are focused on beginning readers. That doesn't mean that they are always young children, but many of them are. We also have beginning English readers who speak another language. We also have beginning readers who have been under-taught and simply did not gain a deep understanding of the English language.

In addition, this definition makes it clear that we are focused on an alphabetic code, meaning that we need to teach students how to map sounds onto the letters they see. Most important, this has to become a habit. Proficient readers do not slowly decode each word (and some words are not decodable). Rather, with practice and feedback, students develop automaticity, and their brains become rather automatic at the process of mapping ideas onto strings of letters. That takes time and effort, which is why I appreciate Blevins's focus on the fact that phonics instruction should be systematic and planned. Hope is not a plan. We don't hope students will learn to read; we teach them to read. Thankfully, *A Fresh Look at Phonics* provides great ideas, and a solid review of evidence, for systematically teaching students.

The evidence is clear. As an example, let's review the work of John Hattie (2009). He has collected thousands of meta-analyses from research conducted around the world. Meta-analyses are studies of studies that aggregate information into larger units so that we can determine "what works." Using these meta-analyses, Hattie used a statistic called *effect size* to determine the impact that a given teacher action had on students' learning. Effect sizes demonstrate the amount of learning expected. They measure the magnitude of the impact, or how much growth can be expected. The meta-analyses that Hattie collected now include data from 300 million students. That's an impressive collection of evidence. From this data set, Hattie determined that an effect size of 0.40 equated to one year of growth for a year of school, which seems to me to be the minimum we should expect from schools. Hattie also noted that there are some influences or teacher actions that exceeded a year of learning for a year of school and identified these as being in the zone of desired effects.

When he examined phonics instruction, the evidence was compelling, with an effect size of 0.60. At the time of his writing, there were 14 different meta-analyses conducted that included 425 different studies with 12,124 students. To my thinking, that's pretty big data and clearly establishes phonics instruction as a necessary component of an effective literacy instructional effort. Hattie also noted that phonics instruction was more effective for younger students and that the effect sizes decreased as students got older, meaning that we need to be sure that students receive this type of instruction as part of their early literacy learning.

I could go on, but I think that the point has been made: students deserve instruction, planned and purposeful instruction, that includes relevant and interesting instruction in the way that language works. I'm not suggesting, nor does *A Fresh Look at Phonics*, that we only teach students how to sound out words, but learning the basics of language is important. And that learning has to be combined with oral language development, fluency, vocabulary learning, and comprehension. It's a concerted effort that is required to teach every child to read. You see, there is no reading gene that students inherit from their ancestors. We have to teach every brain to read all over again, and Wiley Blevins has provided us with a valuable resource for getting students started on the path to literacy.

—Douglas Fisher

Welcome and Overview

Twenty years ago, I wrote my first book on phonics, *Phonics From A to Z*. When it was published, the field of education was at the height of the "phonics versus whole language" debate. This debate led to an all-out reading war pitting teachers who favored a strong skills instructional approach for beginning readers against those who believed children learn to read primarily through exposure to great trade books, a love of and interest in reading, and some lighter skills work. Of course, this is an oversimplification, but the battle lines were drawn, and teachers were forced to take sides. As a young educator and recent Harvard graduate, I understood why whole language gained in popularity. Following years of skill-and-drill phonics work, teachers craved something fresh and exciting. Along came whole language with its promise that by reading great books to children and getting them interested in reading again, we would solve the reading crisis. Teachers were hungry for an approach that seemed to promise greater student engagement, authenticity of reading and writing experiences, and independence.

Whole language ultimately failed to be the magic bullet that transformed all students into readers. But while it was having its day in the sun, those of us who carefully examined the research that supported explicit, systematic teaching of phonics kept practicing, kept publishing, and endured being pilloried in the media, who loved to present this debate in terms of either–or extremes.

Flash forward to the present: The media, and some in the education field, still continue to pit phonics against other practices within balanced literacy as if it is an all-or-nothing proposition, but the overwhelming research support for phonics turns any media buzz into white noise. More importantly, teachers today are levelheaded and savvy about media spin. They realize that phonics helps students gain access to words, which in turn helps them gain access to meaning. And that is the point of reading—to comprehend the information, to learn something new, to enjoy escaping into the world of a story. Phonics is just a tool to gain that access. Most teachers also understand that students need to be immersed in great literature from the beginning—books that inspire their curiosity about words, expose them to new vocabulary and ideas, and delight them. Effective instruction in the primary grades involves reading hundreds of picture books to, with, and by children along with an explicit phonics program.

I'm not a political person. I don't enjoy the art of the argument. I like facts. Data. Solid research. Truth. My goal with this book is to provide evidence-based solutions and options to help you become more efficient at meeting the decoding needs of your early readers. This book is a reflection on decades of my work on phonics—how students break the code and develop a deep understanding of how English words work. I've looked at which instructional practices and materials have stood the test of time, which have failed, which need fine-tuning to maximize their potential for helping students achieve greater success, and which are missing from most classrooms.

I understand that education, for complex reasons, is always particularly vulnerable as a profession to all-or-nothing thinking and neck-bending pendulum swings, and as I work in schools providing professional development, I see that phonics can't shake this skill-and-drill reputation, this notion that it's going to somehow be damaging to children if they are subjected to weeks and months (even years) of decodable texts and rote instruction. However, the reality is that explicit phonics instruction, when done effectively (i.e., not rote, but active and thought-provoking, instruction), is a transitory phase of learning to read, and never keeps students from reading and engaging with high-quality trade books. In fact, research shows students who received explicit phonics instruction are better able to select and read trade books independently than those who didn't receive systematic instruction, but more on that later.

So, at its heart, this book is designed to show how phonics and great literature easily and naturally coexist in K–2 classrooms. And beyond that, I want to show you how to best use phonics instruction to meet the decoding needs of your early readers. Some of the things in this book might make a big impact on your teaching; others might not. I offer them only as things to try—things that have worked in other schools and classrooms. My hope is that they will encourage you to think about your phonics instruction in a fresh way. The best teachers I've worked with over the years are never satisfied. They are always questioning, always searching, always striving to improve their practices. That is why, I believe, you are reading this book. Hopefully, the ideas presented will create a conversation within your district and among your grade-based teacher teams to challenge everyone who comes in contact with your early readers to push their instruction to its highest level. All of our students deserve that.

One common thread throughout the book is this need to constantly take a step back from our practices and reevaluate them objectively. We have a habit in education of taking an idea, falling in love with it, and digging in our heels even when there is evidence that our original idea needs some modifications. Sometimes we even apply the ideas in ways that were never intended. It's like falling in love with bell-bottom pants (you know who you are) and continuing to wear them even when the world has moved on to skinny jeans. It is a look, just not the right one for today.

I also feel strongly that we shouldn't stake our professional identity on any one particular idea, philosophy, or method. Rather, we should stake our identity on the pursuit of being the best teacher, literacy coach, principal, or administrator we can be. That requires us to be open and flexible in our understanding as new information presents itself, but having a strong enough foundation in early reading that we can process that information, filtering out what isn't strong or useful, ignoring hype, and demanding data. A teacher with a strong foundation is less likely to sway with the pendulum.

If you are a new teacher, or perhaps one who was trained in the No Child Left Behind era, and currently working with a curriculum that comes with intense pressure to get students to Common Core State Standards grade-level bench-marks, then I want this book to provide you with the basics to build the strongest phonics foundation possible and filter through the activities and routines provided in your curriculum to select the best, toss out those that are ineffective, and modify those that aren't working to capacity.

If you are a veteran teacher, and perhaps one who feels forced to use a phonics program that isn't meeting the needs of your students, then this book will be a benefit because it reiterates what you know about strong instruction and prompts you to explore ways you can fine-tune that expertise, giving you the data to modify faulty instructional materials and practices with confidence.

If you are a principal, either looking at K–2 student test data that concern you or ready to upgrade professional development for teachers around phonics and early reading, then this book will be an aid because it's organized to facilitate collegial conversations focusing on the seven distinct and essential aspects of successful phonics instruction and the 10 common reasons instruction sometimes fails. The book also provides brief, succinct overviews of phonics background research and key instructional routines for you to refer to when evaluating teachers' instructional effectiveness.

If you are a coach, I encourage you to use this book to organize differentiated support for your teachers. Throughout the book, you'll find Day Clinic pages that facilitate teacher self-reflection and provide in-class activities for teachers to try, examine, and reflect on.

For all readers, I hope that this book provides the answers you've been looking for as to why your students in Grades K–2 are not meeting and/or exceeding expectations despite your efforts and resources. These answers have deep roots in the research of others but, perhaps more importantly, in my own professional experiences in the field. For me, the three words that best describe quality phonics instruction are *active, engaging,* and *thought-provoking.* I hope that these three words can also be used to describe this book and your exploration of phonics instruction.

IMPORTANT NEW BRAIN RESEARCH

We should always put our stake in the firmest ground possible (i.e., a deep understanding of what works as evidenced by solid research and classroom application), remembering that this stake is not in cement. An exciting aspect of being teachers is that we are always learning. New research continually provides insights into how to best meet our students' needs. For example, in the past several years, brain research has been providing exciting insights into how we learn and has forced us to reexamine our practices in light of these new understandings. A recent brain research study out of Stanford revealed that "beginning readers who focus on letter-sound relationships, or phonics, instead of trying to learn whole words, increase activity in the area of their brains best wired for reading" (Wong, 2015). That is, words learned using letter sounds activate the left side of the brain. This is where the visual and language regions of the brain reside. Words learned using a whole-word method activate the right side of the brain. This is significant because left-brain activation during reading is characteristic of skilled readers and is generally lacking in both children and adults who struggle with reading. The researchers described it as "changing gears" while reading. When you focus your attention on different aspects of a word, you activate, or amplify, different parts of your brain. So cool! And it is fascinating that we can now map the brain activity when students read and learn using different teaching methods and practices. Brain research is also suggesting that the learning pathways can be altered with specific methods. This has remarkable potential for teaching and learning.

HOW THIS BOOK IS ORGANIZED

I've organized *A Fresh Look at Phonics* into two major sections. **In the first section,** I examine the key characteristics of strong phonics instruction. While most teachers have some or all of these in place, I offer guidance in fine-tuning that instruction to take it to the next level and increase student reading growth. The characteristics I explore include

1. **Readiness skills:** I examine the two best predictors of early reading success—phonemic awareness and alphabet recognition—and their role in beginning phonics instruction.

2. **Scope and sequence:** I examine the characteristics of a strong scope and sequence that builds from the simple to the complex in a way that works best for student learning.

3. **Blending:** I examine the main strategy for teaching students how to sound out words, its various forms, and how to enhance blending work to provide deeper, richer, more differentiated decoding practice.

4. **Dictation:** I examine how to best transition students' growing reading skills to writing through all-important guided spelling activities.

5. **Word awareness:** I examine two key aspects of word awareness for early readers—word sorts and word building—and how they solidify and consolidate students' understanding of how English words work.

6. **High-frequency words:** I examine how best to teach those high-utility words that are irregular based on common sound-spelling patterns or need to be taught before students have all the phonics skills to access them through sounding out.

7. **Reading connected text:** I examine the power of the types of text we use in early reading instruction and the impact decodable text has on early reading and writing growth, as well as motivation to read.

8. **You, the teacher:** I point out how the power and impact of the above characteristics depend on them being implemented by a skilled, informed teacher and explain how to build teacher capacity through differentiated professional development.

In this first section, each characteristic of strong phonics instruction is examined from several vantage points. Some of you will encounter this information fresh (e.g., preservice teachers, beginning teachers, or experienced teachers new to the primary grades); others will have years of experience using some or all of these instructional routines, procedures, and techniques in their classrooms. Therefore, each characteristic will be explored by

1. Examining the background information associated with each characteristic so you have a solid understanding of its research base

2. Looking at best practices associated with each characteristic and ways to identify if you have these in place in your classroom

3. Exploring key issues and pitfalls associated with each characteristic that often stand in the way of its effectiveness as a teaching tool

4. Giving you an opportunity to engage in activities associated with each characteristic to identify ways in which it might assist you in your teaching and deepen your understanding of its instructional benefits

5. Providing you with ways to take each characteristic to the next level if you already have the basics in place and want to fine-tune your instruction to maximize student learning

In the second section, I examine the 10 most common causes of phonics instructional failure. These causes are based on my observations and work with school districts in which I have been asked to compare test data with instructional materials and practices when there is a disconnect. That is, I delve in to find the root causes of failure when schools have what they believe are strong instructional materials teachers are routinely implementing, yet the test scores associated with phonics skills and early reading show students are not making adequate progress. This can be perplexing for a teacher, school, or district because, on paper, it doesn't make sense. What I've discovered is that, in most instances, there isn't one main cause of this systematic breakdown. Rather, a combination of these causes can create a perfect storm of failure to the great disappointment of caring, committed teachers. To avoid this, I've outlined the 10 major causes and ways to avoid or fix them:

1. Inadequate or nonexistent review and repetition

2. Lack of application to real reading and writing experiences

3. Inappropriate reading materials to practice skills

4. Ineffective use of the gradual release model

5. Too much time lost during transitions

6. Limited teacher knowledge of research-based phonics routines and linguistics

7. Inappropriate pacing of lessons

8. No comprehensive or cumulative mastery assessment tools

9. Transitioning to multisyllabic words too late

10. Overdoing it (especially isolated skill work)

In this section, I draw from some of the material in the first section and review it as needed. In fact, you will find a fair amount of repeated information in this book. That is because I know the book will be the kind of resource you dip into to explore specific areas of interest. Plus, it never hurts to hear the same thing multiple times!

This second section requires a great deal of reflection on your classroom practices and an intense examination of your classroom materials. It's the kind of challenging thinking that can really affect teaching and learning, and I applaud you for jumping in and taking that challenge. Our students deserve us to be at our best, deserve the strongest materials and instructional practices, and deserve all this delivered by someone who deeply cares about giving them the tools to be successful readers, writers, and lifelong learners. That defines a teacher. It is a responsibility we've all accepted. And we are proud to do so!

I wish you the best of luck as you continue to transform your classroom practices and hope that this book will spark discussion and thought.

Enjoy.

Wiley Blevins

Acknowledgments

Corwin gratefully acknowledges the contributions of the following reviewers:

Melissa J. Black
Elementary Teacher
Harlem Village Academy
New York, NY

Jill Gildea
Superintendent of Schools
Fremont 79
Mundelein, IL

Kendra Hanzlik
Instructional Coach
Prairie Hill Elementary, College Community School District
Cedar Rapids, IA

Janiel Wagstaff
English Language Arts Coordinator/Literacy Coach
Davis School District, UT

Introduction to Phonics

Because I graduated from Harvard, no one would expect what happened on my first day of elementary school, as it was anything but predictive. When my parents threw on their best clothes and marched me down to the tall brick schoolhouse to enroll me in kindergarten, they had one concern—did I have a learning issue? You see, I struggled with communicating properly as a young child. People couldn't understand me well, and as a result, I spoke little. No one had any idea what I was learning or if I had learned. My parents believed I should be in a special setting for children with learning difficulties. So, they suggested to the school that I be tested.

Luckily, at this time, kindergarten was primarily focused on social–emotional development. We weren't expected to know the alphabet until Grade 1, so if I was behind, my parents hoped I wouldn't be that far behind. After a series of tests, it was discovered that I didn't have an intelligence issue; I had a speech issue. In fact (as odd as this might sound), the string underneath my tongue that attaches it to the bottom of my mouth was too long. My tongue was literally getting in the way of me speaking correctly. A couple weeks later, I had the string clipped and retied to the appropriate length, and as my mom says, I haven't shut up since.

Those first years in school are so important for getting students started on the right track to academic success and building a solid foundation in early reading. Phonics plays one of the key roles in creating that foundation. In the Common Core State Standards, these skills are highlighted in a special section called "Reading: Foundational Skills." They really are the building blocks on which reading is formed—not the only building blocks, but key pieces of the structure. Should the CCSS fade, the skills will remain, evergreen, incontestable.

So, what role has phonics played in early reading? The purpose of this book is not to provide a comprehensive history of phonics. However, I want to highlight key research books and documents that have tackled this topic, such as the following, as they are good resources for further exploration and study of the topic:

1. ***Learning to Read: The Great Debate*** by Jeanne Chall (1967): This book, by my beloved former professor, reflects a balanced and scientific approach

to how children learn to read. In it, Chall outlines the stages of reading development and advocates including phonics instruction in the early grades. She talks about how it is critical for students with limited literacy backgrounds or who struggle with reading. She also talks about how it benefits advanced learners, many of whom intuit aspects of English sound spellings through exposure to print and limited instruction, because it helps them systematize that learning and accelerate their growth.

2. ***Becoming a Nation of Readers: The Report of the Commission on Reading*** by Richard Anderson, Elfrieda Hiebert, Judith Scott, and Ian Wilkinson (1985): This survey of all the research on early reading focuses on the role of phonics in the context of a more balanced and comprehensive approach to reading instruction. In it, the authors outline the key characteristics of decodable text, an important teaching tool associated with phonics.

3. ***Beginning to Read: Thinking and Learning About Print*** by Marilyn Adams (1990): I had the good fortune of working with Adams after the release of her now classic book. It is a thorough and academic look at how children learn to read and includes new research since the release of the previous books and documents on the topic. It highlights the essential role of systematic and explicit phonics instruction in early reading. It also brings to national attention the key role of phonemic awareness in learning to read and offers support for teachers and publishers in designing phonemic awareness curriculum.

4. ***Report of the National Reading Panel: Teaching Children to Read: An Evidence-Based Assessment of the Scientific Literature on Reading and Its Implications for Reading Instruction*** by the National Institute of Child Health and Human Development (2000) and ***Preventing Reading Difficulties in Young Children*** by Catherine Snow, M. Susan Burns, and Peg Griffin (1998): These texts started the 21st century with a solid body of research on early reading that confirmed what Chall, Anderson et al., and Adams had previously written and added new understandings. Following these books, teachers began being trained intensively on the five key areas of reading instruction—phonemic awareness, phonics, vocabulary, comprehension, and fluency. Much of that training continues today.

5. **Visible Learning** (2009) and **Visible Learning for Teachers** (2012) by John Hattie: Both books offer an important new contribution to our look at phonics instruction (and reading instruction in general). As Hattie asserts, teachers need to understand the strategies and instructional practices that are most useful and in which situations they should and should not be used. To date, Hattie has examined over 1,200 meta-analyses conducted by educational researchers all over the world. These have included over 70,000 studies with 300 million students. With visible teaching, a teacher must continually evaluate the impact of instructional practices and materials on each student (not falling in love with specific practices and thereby ignoring their effects). When growth is not occurring, the instruction must change—not the child.

What is interesting about all this research over the past 50–60 years is its consistency. The researchers have all documented that learning the alphabetic principle is essential to learning to read, and phonics is best taught when it is systematic and explicit. *Systematic* means that this instruction builds from easy to more complex skills with built-in review and repetition to ensure mastery, and *explicit* means that sound-spelling correspondences are initially taught directly to students, rather than using a discovery, or implicit, method. That is, students are taught, for example, that the /s/ sound can be spelled with the letter *s*. A discovery method is less effective for initial teaching because it relies on students having prerequisite skills that some do not have (e.g., sophisticated phonemic awareness skills). As a result, the implicit method can leave some students behind—either not learning the new content or having difficulties and confusion (Adams, 1990).

The research has also been clear about the connection between phonics and comprehension. The simple flowchart that follows shows that connection. What is interesting to me is that when I visit their classrooms, I can easily tell whether or not the teachers I'm observing are aware of this connection. When they are, I see strong phonics instruction in which the bulk of the lesson is devoted to applying those skills to real reading and writing experiences (where learning occurs and is consolidated). When they aren't, I often see the bulk of the lesson devoted to isolated skill-and-drill exercises. Without larger amounts of application to authentic reading and writing experiences (at least 50% of each day's phonics lessons), these students run the risk of falling behind or not mastering the content.

PHONICS-COMPREHENSION FLOWCHART

Phonics instruction teaches students how to map sounds onto letters and spellings.

The more phonics skills students learn, the better able they are to **decode**, or sound out, words.

The more opportunities students get to decode words (including repeated exposure to the same words), the stronger their **word recognition** skills become.

When students begin to recognize many words automatically (through repeated exposure), the better their reading **fluency** becomes. This refers to the ease with which they can read (accuracy and speed). Students' store of sight words increases, thereby lessening the amount of mental energy required to work through words while reading.

Reading fluency improves reading **comprehension**. As sentences become longer and more complex, students need to get through enough words fast enough to make a meaningful chunk. If they don't, their understanding breaks down. If students have to devote too much time to decoding, their reading will be slow and labored. This is characteristic of many struggling readers.

The other thing this body of research has shown us is that English is more regular than its reputation. Because some of the most frequent words in English (e.g., *said*, *was*, *they*) don't follow typical sound-spelling patterns, English is perceived as highly irregular. However, the truth is that 84%–87% of English words follow common and consistent sound-spelling patterns. That is, one letter stands for a sound (e.g., the letter *s* stands for the sound /s/), or a combination of letters stands for a sound (e.g., the spelling *oa* stands for the long *o* sound, and the spelling *sh* stands for the /sh/ sound) (Anderson et al., 1985). Why does this matter? Because if we teach students these regularities, they will have access to the majority of words they will encounter in printed English. I often ask the teachers I work with, "If you had an 87% chance of winning the lottery, would you buy a ticket?" It'd probably take a wheelbarrow to hold all of my tickets!

So, if the research has been consistent, what hasn't been as predictable? What has prevented us from taking advantage of this large, solid body of knowledge? Well, it's the way we've interpreted and applied this research to our classroom practices, school policies, and instructional materials that has sometimes fallen short. And that's what the rest of this book addresses.

Phonics

The Key Ingredients for Phonics Success

and Next Steps to Improve Your Instruction Once You Have Them in Place

Courtesy of Rick Harrington Photography

Background and Key Characteristics

The two best predictors of early reading success are alphabet recognition and phonemic awareness (Adams, 1990; Beck & Juel, 1995; Chall, 1996; Stanovich, 1992). These skills open the gate for reading. Without a deep knowledge of the English letters and an awareness that words are made up of sounds, students cannot learn to read. Also important in early reading instruction are other foundational skills (e.g., concepts of print) and a basic understanding of story structure, vocabulary, and the language of instruction.

Students who recognize letters with accuracy and speed have an easier time learning the sounds associated with them.

English is an alphabetic language. To read in English, students need to understand the alphabetic principle (that our letters stand for sounds) and recognize these letters in various contexts and forms (e.g., uppercase, lowercase, manuscript, cursive, different fonts). Students also have to be skilled at distinguishing visually similar letters (e.g., *E* and *F*, *b* and *d*). Letters can be distinguished by their position on a line; their length; their size; whether

4 BEST EFFECT

"The Alphabet Song"

- Sing the song as a warm-up to daily instruction.
- Sing the song as a transition between activities.
- Slow down when singing the letters *L*, *M*, *N*, *O*, and *P*.
- Point to an alphabet chart while singing the song, and sing parts softly to listen for how well students know the letters.

they contain horizontal, vertical, diagonal, or curving lines; whether they have descenders (parts that extend below the line); and their orientation.

Learning the alphabet begins with "The Alphabet Song." Many students enter school knowing this song and recognizing some letters, such as those in their name. The goal, however, is to get students to rapidly name all the letters. Students who recognize letters with accuracy and speed have an easier time learning the sounds associated with them (Adams, 1990).

Students learn the alphabet best through "active exploration of the relationships between letter names, the sounds of the letter names, their visual characteristics, and the motor movement involved in their formation" (Bear, Templeton, Invernizzi, & Johnston, 1996). This results from direct instruction and multiple exposures to print, including the wide use of alphabet books.

Phonemic awareness is the understanding that words are made up of a series of discrete sounds (phonemes). A student who is phonemically aware is able to pick out and manipulate sounds in spoken words. A related term is *phonological awareness*. It is an umbrella term that includes both awareness of words at the phoneme (sound) level and awareness of larger word units, such as syllables and onset and rime.

Research shows that the combination of letter work and phonemic awareness is quite powerful, especially for more sophisticated skills like phoneme substitution, addition, and deletion.

Phonemic awareness deals with sounds in spoken words, whereas phonics involves the relationship between sounds and written letters or spellings. As a result, phonemic awareness is most commonly associated with oral activities, and phonics is associated with print. However, research shows that the combination of letter work and phonemic awareness is quite powerful, especially for more sophisticated skills like phoneme substitution, addition, and deletion. These skills are generally addressed after students have begun reading, and the use of print in these activities helps students (Adams, 1990). When students begin learning letter–sound relationships, combining phonemic awareness and phonics can accelerate students' progress (Ehri & Roberts, 2006). Prior to that, the activities are oral.

There are five basic types of phonemic awareness activities, all designed to increase student understanding of how sounds work in words. See the following. Note that the individual activities in Activity Types 2–4 are presented in a progression from easy to complex.

FIVE BASIC TYPES OF ACTIVITIES

Activity Type I: Rhyme and Alliteration

1. Rhyme (Begin by having students identify rhyming words, then progress to having them generate rhyming words.)

2. Alliteration (Say aloud a sentence containing words that mostly begin with the same sound, as in "Six seals sell sandwiches at the seashore," and have students identify the repeated sound.)

3. Assonance (Say aloud a sentence containing words that mostly have the same vowel sound, as in "The leaf, the bean, and the peach are all within reach," and have students identify the repeated sound.)

Activity Type 2: Oddity Tasks (phoneme categorization)

1. Rhyme (e.g., "Which word does not rhyme—*sat, mat,* or *pan*?")

2. Beginning consonants (e.g., "Which two words begin with the same sound?")

3. Ending consonants (e.g., "Which two words end with the same sound?")

4. Medial sounds (long vowels—e.g., "Which word does not have the same middle sound?")

5. Medial sounds (short vowels—e.g., "Which two words have the same middle sound?")

6. Medial sounds (consonants, as in words like *kitten* or *lesson*)

Activity Type 3: Oral Blending

1. Syllables (Say the syllables in a word and have students put them together, as in "*ta . . . ble.*")

2. Onset and rime (Say the onset and rime in a word and have students put the sounds together, as in "/s/ . . . *at.*")

3. Phoneme by phoneme (Say a word sound by sound and have students string together the sounds, as in "/s/ . . . /a/ . . . /t/.")

Activity Type 4: Oral Segmentation (including counting sounds)

1. Syllables (Say or clap a word by syllables—explain that each syllable has one vowel sound or "chin drop.")

2. Onset and rime (Say a word by onset and rime. The *rime* is the vowel and everything after it in a syllable. The rime in *sat* is *at*. A word with more than one syllable has more than one rime. The *onset* is the consonant, consonant blend, or consonant digraph that precedes the rime. The onset in *sat* is *s*.)

3. Phoneme by phoneme (Say a word sound by sound and/or count sounds.)

Activity Type 5: Phoneme Manipulation

1. Initial sound substitution (Replace the first sound in *man* with /p/.)

2. Final sound substitution (Replace the last sound in *bad* with /g/.)

3. Vowel substitution (Replace the middle sound in *hat* with /o/.)

4. Syllable deletion (Say *noble* without *no*.)

5. Initial sound deletion (Say *sat* without /s/.)

6. Final sound deletion (Say *make* without /k/.)

7. Initial phoneme in a blend deletion (Say *slip* without /s/.)

8. Final phoneme in a blend deletion (Say *nest* without /t/.)

9. Second phoneme in a blend deletion (Say *slip* without /l/.)

10. Initial sound addition (Add /s/ to the beginning of *at*.)

11. Final sound addition (Add /t/ to the end of *res*.)

Why is phonemic awareness so important? Many students struggle with phonics because they don't have the prerequisite phonemic awareness skills other

Phonemic Awareness Terms

- *Rime* = the vowel and everything after it in a syllable
- *Onset* = the consonant, consonant blend, or consonant digraph that precedes the rime in a syllable
- *Phoneme* = sound
- *Initial* = beginning, *medial* = middle, *final* = ending

children acquire through years of being read to, singing nursery rhymes, and playing with sounds through songs. Research shows that approximately 20% of students lack phonemic awareness (Shankweiler & Liberman, 1989). Without early preventive measures, many of these students will fall behind their peers in reading and/or be diagnosed with a learning disability. These readers tend to read less, have fewer exposures to print, and are less likely to memorize large numbers of words, further falling behind their peers.

However, phonemic awareness can be taught. And, it doesn't take a great deal of time to bring many students' phonemic awareness skills up to a level at which phonics instruction begins to make sense. In some studies (Honig, 1995), as few as 11–15 hours of intensive phonemic awareness training spread out over an appropriate time period produced results. "The purpose of training is to help children respond to reading instruction more effectively. Specifically, it helps children understand how spoken language is represented by the alphabetic system" (Torgeson & Bryant, 1994). The goal of this instruction is understanding how words work.

As few as 11–15 hours of intensive phonemic awareness training spread out over an appropriate time period produced results.

Best Practices and Look-Fors for Success

Source: Images courtesy of Pixabay (cat: Elisabeth Rijsken; hat: PublicDomainPictures; pan: Walter Bichler).

The most important aspects of teaching readiness skills include the following:

1. For phonemic awareness, focus on the "power skills" of oral blending and oral segmentation. I call these the power skills because they are directly linked to early reading and writing success in the most powerful way. For example, if a student can't orally blend the sounds to form a word (e.g., you say three sounds like /s/, /a/, /t/, and the student can't string them together to make *sat*), then that student won't be able to sound out the word *sat* when he sees it in print. Why? Because what the student must do is attach a sound to each letter and orally string together those sounds to make a real word.

Likewise, if a student can't orally segment a word (e.g., you say *sat*, and the student can't break it apart into its three constituent sounds—/s/, /a/, /t/), then that student will struggle writing words. Why? When we first learned to write words, we said the word in our minds, then thought about each sound in the word and attached a letter or spelling to that sound.

2. Teach the phonemic awareness skills in progression from the easiest to the most complex. For example, teach students how to blend syllables before you teach them how to blend onset and rime. You can teach activities from multiple activity types simultaneously. That is, students can be clapping syllables and identifying rhyming words in the same instructional cycle. It is not essential to master one activity in one activity type before moving on. Your goal is to create an overall awareness of how words work. Use your state standards (e.g., the Common Core State Standards) as a guideline for which skills should be taught at each grade level.

3. Provide supports for students during phonemic awareness activities. For example, initial exercises might include picture cards to help students remember the words being compared (e.g., pictures of a *cat*, *hat*, and *pan* in a rhyme activity). Limit the number of items in an exercise (e.g., two to start) and slowly increase the number as students become more proficient or as a challenge for advanced learners (up to four or five). Also, use manipulatives to make the activities concrete where applicable. One classic example of this is the use of Sound Boxes and counters during oral segmentation exercises, as shown below.

4. Many software and training programs exist to help students who struggle with phonemic awareness. I recommend finding those based on the most current research and that have a body of data to support their effectiveness. Use them with your struggling readers during small group differentiated instruction time.

5. Below are examples of strong instructional routines for both oral blending and oral segmentation.

Oral Blending Routine

Step 1: Introduce

Tell students the purpose of the activity. Say, "We will be blending, or putting together, sounds to make words."

Step 2: Model (I Do)

Say each sound in a word. Model how to blend the sounds to make the whole word. Start with two-letter words (e.g., *am*, *is*), progress to consonant–vowel–consonant (CVC) words (*sat*, *man*) starting with continuous sounds that can be stretched (e.g., /f/, /l/, /m/, /n/, /r/, /s/, /v/, /z/), progress to words that begin with stop sounds (e.g., *bad*), then

(Continued)

(Continued)

progress to words beginning with consonant blends (e.g., *slip*). You will progress as students begin showing consistent success with the current level of activity. For some students, this may occur quickly, within a few weeks. For others, it will take much longer. The goal is to continually and gradually stretch students by introducing activities of slightly more complex skill demands. Say, "I am going to put sounds together to make a word. I'll say each sound in the word. Then I will blend the sounds together to say the word. Listen: /s/, /a/, /t/, /sssaaat/, *sat*. The word is *sat*."

Step 3: Guided Practice/Practice (We Do/You Do)

Provide a word sound by sound for students to practice putting together (blending the sounds) to form a whole word. Say, "Listen to the sounds. Blend, or put together, the sounds to say the whole word: /f/, /i/, /sh/."

Corrective Feedback

When students make mistakes, stretch together (or sing) the sounds. Move your hands from right to left as you move from sound to sound to emphasize the changing sounds. Repeat the routine using the same word, asking students to respond without you.

Oral Segmentation Routine

Step 1: Introduce

Tell students the purpose of the activity. Say, "Today we will be segmenting, or taking apart, a word sound by sound."

Note: It is ideal to use Sound Boxes (or Elkonin boxes—named after the Russian researcher who created them) to help students see and feel each sound in the word. Other tactile approaches include modeling how to stretch the sounds (like a rubber band) before students segment the word, or moving your hands from right to left (or down your arm) as you move from sound to sound.

Step 2: Model (I Do)

Model how to segment the sounds in a word. Start with two-letter words (e.g., *am*, *is*), progress to CVC words (*sat, man*) starting with continuous sounds that can be stretched (e.g., /f/, /l/, /m/, /n/, /r/, /s/, /v/, /z/), progress to words that begin with stop sounds (e.g., *bad*), then progress to words beginning with consonant blends (e.g., *slip*). Say, "I am going to say a word, then I will say it sound by sound. As I say each sound, I will place one counter in each box. Listen: *sat*. Now I will say *sat* sound by sound [stretch each sound three seconds so students can hear each discrete sound]: /s/ [place counter in first box], /a/ [place counter in second box], /t/ [place counter in third box]. The word *sat* has three sounds: /s/, /a/, and /t/ [point to each box as you say the sound]."

Step 3: Guided Practice/Practice (We Do/You Do)

State words (at least 6–10) for students to segment phoneme by phoneme, or sound by sound. Do the first word with students. Say, "Listen to the word. Segment, or break apart, the word sound by sound." (Use Elkonin boxes, or Sound Boxes, as a support early on. You can use Sound Boxes for CVC words, short-vowel words with consonant blends and digraphs, and even some simple long-vowel words. However, as spellings become more complex, such as words with a final *e*, the boxes will be less useful, and students should have enough experience segmenting words to not need them.)

Corrective Feedback

When students make mistakes, stretch the word using the rubber band technique. Have students repeat. Then use the Sound Boxes to model how to place one counter on each box as you stretch the word and move from sound to sound. Repeat the routine using the same word, asking students to respond without you.

Connect to Spelling

Use segmentation and the Sound Boxes to help students transition to spelling words. After students have segmented a word, have them

(Continued)

(Continued)

replace each counter with a letter (or letters) to spell the word. This breaking apart and then putting together of words with print will accelerate students' understanding of how words work. Say, "What is the first sound in the word *sat*? /s/. What letter do we write for the /s/ sound? *s*. Write that letter in the first box." Continue with the rest of the word.

6. **For alphabet recognition, focus on a sensible sequence** (I'll address this in detail in the next section); separate confusing letters and sounds; teach the name, shape, and sound of each letter to mastery; assess for both accuracy and speed in recognition; connect handwriting to letter sounds; use mnemonics and action rhymes as appropriate; include multisensory activities (including sorts) to distinguish similar letters; adjust the pace based on student needs; and read tons of alphabet books.

Courtesy of Rick Harrington Photography

Common Instructional Pitfalls

Many common pitfalls regarding teaching readiness skills exist. These include the following:

1. There is an overfocus on rhyme, instead of the power skills of oral blending and oral segmentation, which have stronger reading and writing payoff. Recent research states that "focusing early phonemic awareness instruction on blending, segmenting, and manipulating phonemes has been shown to produce greater improvements in phonemic awareness and future reading achievement in young children than time spent on rhyming and alliteration" (Reutzel, 2015). Although rhyme and alliteration activities and associated books are plentiful and loads of fun, the instructional benefit isn't as strong as devoting the majority of your instructional time to working with words at the phoneme, or sound, level.

Although rhyme and alliteration activities and associated books are plentiful and loads of fun, the instructional benefit isn't as strong as devoting the majority of your instructional time to working with words at the phoneme, or sound, level.

2. The language of instruction used by some teachers causes confusion or isn't specific enough to positively affect learning. For example, when teaching rhyme, I often hear teachers say, "Two words rhyme because they sound the same at the end." To us—skilled readers and writers—we know what that means. When we see the words *mat* and *sat*, we know instantly that they rhyme. However, a beginning reader who learns the above definition of rhyme might think that *mat* and *bit* rhyme since they both "sound the same at the end." That is, both end in the /t/ sound. So, why do words *really* rhyme? That's what we need our students to understand deeply. Let's look at *mat* and *sat* again. They rhyme because they both end in /at/. In order for a teacher to explain rhyme in a way that avoids possible student confusion, the language of instruction has to change and be more explicit. As a result, the teacher might say something like this: "The words *mat* and *sat* rhyme because they both end in /at/. Listen, /m/ . . . /at/, *mat*. /s/ . . . /at/, *sat*. Do you hear /at/ at the end of *mat* and *sat*? Yes. The two words rhyme because they both end in the /at/ sounds."

3. There is a lack of support during phonemic awareness exercises, such as not stretching sounds using hand signals or not using manipulatives (e.g., Sound Boxes, picture cards) during exercises to concretize the activity and support memory of sounds. These supports aid in student learning and should be included as scaffolds early on, then slowly removed to check student growth.

4. Not including letters in more sophisticated activities like phonemic manipulation because teachers have been taught that phonemic awareness activities that are only oral can slow or impede learning. Yes, early phonemic awareness activities are purely oral. Also, there was an emphasis on separating phonemic awareness from phonics when it hit prominence in our national conversation in the early 1990s. Many teachers were taught the mantra "you can do phonemic awareness activities in the dark (because you only need to hear), but you need the lights on for phonics activities (to see the print)." However, the research is clear that when students begin learning letter sounds, slowly incorporating them into phonemic awareness tasks is beneficial. For example, doing an oral segmentation exercise with the Sound Boxes and counters, and following it up by having students write or place letter cards in each box to connect the sound to a spelling, is beneficial. Or, modeling how to do a phonemic substitution task using letter cards before students do it orally can help them better understand and visualize the activity. For example, if you want students to substitute the first sound in *mat* with /s/ to make a new word, begin by having them form the word *mat* with letter cards. Then ask them what the first sound in *mat* (that they will be replacing) is. Ask them to point to the letter that stands for that sound. Have them physically remove that letter card. Then ask them what sound they will replace the /m/ sound with (/s/). Ask them what letter stands for that sound (*s*) and prompt them to place the *s* letter card in the same position that the *m* card was in. Ask them to read the new word formed (*sat*). This is a very concrete way to introduce a complex phonemic awareness task. We are missing opportunities to accelerate learning when we don't slowly incorporate letters into phonemic awareness activities as students progress through the skills.

5. Doing phonemic awareness well past the time students need it is another issue. In many reading programs, phonemic awareness activities are part of daily instruction in Grade 2 and sometimes Grade 3. The reality is that once students get a basic understanding of how words work, these activities become less useful. Plus, some of the phonics activities, such as word building in which students are building a series of words that vary by only one sound spelling, have built-in phonemic awareness practice (students must think about the sounds in words, which sound is different, what spelling stands for that sound, and in which position of the word to make the change). Thankfully, the Common Core State Standards end phonemic awareness work in Grade 1, which will help to raise awareness of when these activities should cease for most early learners.

6. Improper sequencing of activities is another common issue. The list of phonemic awareness activity types presented earlier provides some guidance in proper sequencing. Remember that students don't have to master one activity type before progressing to a different activity type (e.g., rhyme before initial sound identification). Rather, a mix of activities at approximately the same level should be done during the same time period (e.g., several weeks of instruction), then should progress to slightly more difficult tasks as students begin showing competence with the existing activities. Take stock of the range of skills you must cover throughout the year and make sure all are introduced by the time you have completed two-thirds of your curriculum (school year). That will ensure enough time for students to practice the later-introduced skills to mastery. Reserving more complex skills for the final weeks or months of the school year will not give students enough practice opportunities to achieve mastery.

7. Lacking cumulative assessment with respect to alphabet recognition and not testing both accuracy and speed cause some teachers to miss valuable opportunities to fine-tune their instruction and meet the diverse needs of their students. That is, we need to monitor student growth in identifying letters and their sounds over a longer period of time to check mastery. Therefore, assessments should be cumulative and become longer as the year progresses. We should also assess whether or not students can identify the letter and sound (an accuracy check) as well as whether or not they can do

The accuracy score tells you which letters are and are not being learned, and the speed score tells you which letters and sounds do and do not need more instruction and practice because of mastery issues.

so automatically (a speed check). You might want to check each letter and sound identified correctly on an assessment and circle all those that were identified rapidly to get two scores for the assessment. Each provides you different and useful information. The accuracy score tells you which letters are and are not being learned, and the speed score tells you which letters and sounds do and do not need more instruction and practice because of mastery issues. If one student can identify all the letters accurately in 30 seconds and another can identify all of them accurately in two minutes, are these students at the same level with the same instructional needs? No. That is why adding a speed check is so vital to differentiating and planning future instruction.

8. Some curriculum doesn't take into account confusing letters, separate instruction adequately, or provide supports to help students distinguish these letters. My favorite trick to distinguish *b* and *d* is to ask students what letter comes after *b*. I write the letter *c* on the board. I then draw a straight line down the right side of *c* to make the letter *d* as I say, "You have to go through *c* to get to *d*." It works every time! Remember that letters differ in the direction of their extension (e.g., *b* and *p*, *d* and *g*, *q* and *d*), their left–right orientation (e.g., *b* and *d*, *q* and *p*, *g* and *p*), their top–bottom orientation (e.g., *m* and *w*, *n* and *u*, *M* and *W*), and their line–curve features (e.g., *u* and *v*, *U* and *V*). The letters that confuse students the most are those with reversible parts (e.g., *b* and *d*, *p* and *d*, *q* and *b*, *h* and *u*, *i* and *l*) (Popp, 1964). Recent research has also shown that letters that go in the opposite direction of writing, such as *d*, are particularly challenging for young readers and writers and will require more attention. The following four letter groups are especially difficult for students and should not be taught at or near the same time—*e*, *a*, *s*, *c*, and *o*; *b*, *d*, *p*, *o*, *g*, and *h*; *f*, *l*, *t*, *k*, *i*, and *h*; and *n*, *m*, *u*, *h*, and *r* (Manzo & Manzo, 1993).

DAY CLINIC

Examine Your Practices

Now it's your turn. Ask yourself the following questions to consider your instructional practices and materials as they relate to readiness skills.

1. What sequence am I using to teach the alphabet? Are confusing letters and sounds taught far enough apart so students can master one before the other is introduced?

2. Am I focusing my alphabet instruction on the letter's name, shape, and sound in ways that are interactive and multisensory?

3. Do I have mnemonics to help students remember letter sounds or distinguish those that are confusing?

4. Do I teach handwriting? Do I have my students say the sound each time they write the letter to reinforce the letter–sound relationship, connect it to the physical act of writing the letter, and accelerate learning?

5. Which phonemic awareness activities am I spending the bulk of my time on? Do I include enough oral blending and oral segmentation tasks weekly? Am I careful not to overfocus on rhyme?

6. Am I sequencing my phonemic awareness tasks from easiest to most complex?

7. Am I using manipulatives and other supports in my activities to scaffold the practice as long as students need these supports, but taking them away over time?

List three ways you can modify your alphabet recognition and phonemic awareness instruction over the next month. Record the results of these changes in the chart that follows, then progress to other changes as needed.

Change	Effect on Student Learning
Change 1	Outcome
	Future Modification
Change 2	Outcome
	Future Modification
Change 3	Outcome
	Future Modification

4 BEST EFFECT

My Favorite Manipulatives

- Sound Boxes for oral segmentation exercises

- Oversized letter cards for word-building activities (e.g., Living Words, in which students hold the cards in the front of the classroom and line up to spell a word)

- Magnetic letters for a host of phonics activities (also available as an app)

- Interactive whiteboard activities with spinners, spinning cubes, and movable letters and pictures for high engagement

Select your favorite (or strongest) alphabet recognition and phonemic awareness lessons. I suggest selecting a week's worth of lessons for one letter (alphabet recognition) and an oral blending and/or oral segmentation lesson (phonemic awareness). You might also wish to write a sample lesson for each yourself—taking an existing lesson and modifying it. Meet with your grade-level teachers and share these lessons. Evaluate their effectiveness and brainstorm ways to fine-tune them to accelerate students' mastery.

Available for download at **http://resources.corwin.com/blevinsphonics**

Next Steps to Leap Forward

If you have fairly strong readiness skills instruction in place, there are several ways to take that instruction to the next level and ensure all students are benefiting from it.

1. **Analyze specific instructional moments and compare them to your overall instructional goals.** Ask yourself, "Can I accomplish more with this activity? Can I accelerate my students' learning?" A simple example of this occurred when I was working on handwriting with a group of Grade 1 students. I noticed that they were dutifully forming the letter on each line of their page, writing the letter 20 or more times. However, my students didn't seem to have full focus on the activity. Some were even chatting quietly with classmates while writing their letters. So, I asked myself, "What am I *really* trying to accomplish with this activity?" Sure, I wanted my students to correctly form the target letter, but when I thought about how that connects to early reading and writing growth, I realized that what I *really* wanted my students to acquire was a series of things: forming the letter properly and efficiently, connecting the letter to its associated sound, and creating a motor-skill link between the action of writing that letter and its sound. As a result, I asked my students to start saying the sound of the letter each time they wrote it. We were working on the letter *s*. So a chorus of "/s/, /s/, /s/, /s/" rang throughout the classroom as students wrote. At the end of the short activity, my students had practiced writing the letter about 20 times, and I had reinforced the letter–sound connection, thereby accelerating their mastery. This is the kind of thinking we need to do with all our phonics-related activities. If we consider how each activity connects to actual reading and writing, then ways to amplify the activity to move closer and faster to those goals can change what students do during the activity.

2. **Build in daily fluency work for mastery learning.** There often isn't enough cumulative review of letter sounds in most curricula. This can be corrected using some simple exercises. For example, keep a letter card set for all the letters and spellings you have taught so far in the year. This can be a simple stack of cards (the letters and spellings written on individual index cards), a set of cards on a ring for easy storage, or a set of alphabet/spelling cards provided by the publisher of your reading or phonics program. Each morning, as a warm-up to the day's activities, quickly flip through those cards as students chorally say the letter name and/ or sound (depending on what you are focusing on). This should take no more than a minute or so. No more! This daily warm-up is a regular review and reminder of past learning. It also serves as a great formative assessment tool. Observe students

throughout the activity. If the volume decreases for a letter sound, that might indicate a lack of mastery. Also keep an eye out for those students who respond *after* they hear other students respond, or don't respond at all. Take note of those students and the letter sounds causing the most difficulties. Use this information to adjust instruction and form small groups for extended teaching and learning.

3. Use instructional transitions to review skills. Many readiness skill lessons require materials, such as big books, letter cards, photo cards, magnetic letters, or other manipulatives. Often too much time is lost during a lesson distributing, organizing, and collecting these materials. To avoid this, list skills you want to review for the week (e.g., previously taught letter sounds, a lower-level phonemic awareness skill). Then, during these transition times, use these activities. Keep in mind that every minute of your day is instructional. These in-between times are ideal for singing "The Alphabet Song," doing a quick phonemic awareness task (e.g., First Sound—say a word and ask students to chorally say the first sound), or reviewing action rhymes associated with each letter. These activities not only provide important review; they also focus students' attention (increasing time on task) and decrease behavioral issues common to these transitional times.

4. Add articulation work for students who struggle with letter sounds or for English learners in whose native language the sound isn't used. Focus on the position of the lips, teeth, and tongue. For example, ask students to put their hand in front of their mouth as they make the /p/ sound. Ask them if

Especially for
**ENGLISH
LEARNERS**

---

4 BEST EFFECT

Quick Daily Letter-Sound Review

- Use a cumulative set of letter cards (containing all the letter sounds taught to date) and flip through them quickly as a 30- to 60-second lesson warm-up.

- Create a letter path on the floor. Have students walk the path as they say the letter name. Repeat with the letter sound.

- Point to letters on the alphabet chart or alphabet wall frieze in random order as students say the letter name and sound.

- Show a letter card to each student before lining up. The student must give the letter name, the sound, and a word beginning with that sound.

they feel a puff of air. (They should.) Then ask them to repeat the sound as they put their hand on their throat. Ask them if they feel a vibration, or shaking. (They should not.) Repeat with the /b/ sound. Point out that both sounds are made in the same way (the lips start out together, followed by a puff of air), but they differ because the /b/ sound causes the throat to vibrate or shake. Another example is to have students make two similar sounds, like /a/ and /e/, and focus on how their mouth "feels" when they make each sound (the position of the lips, jaw, etc.). You might even have students watch as a partner makes the sound or watch as they make the sound while looking in a small mirror. Then connect the feeling of each sound (/a/ or /e/) to the letter that stands for the sound. The goal is for students to become so accustomed to how each sound "feels" when they form it and how this "feeling" is different for each sound that when they go to write a word with a short *a* or short *e*, they will connect the way their mouth feels with the correct letter.

5. Include apps and whiteboard activities during whole group and small group instruction. These activities also make for great independent and partner activities for students to complete when you are meeting with other students during small group differentiation time. Below are some examples.

The following activity is from *Teaching the Alphabet* by Wiley Blevins (2011a). Similar sound sort whiteboard activities are easy to create yourself. You need a few pictures of items with the target sounds and two containers in which to sort the pictures.

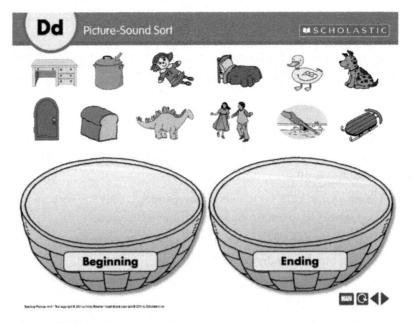

Source: Blevins (2011a).

Reading Raven (www.readingraven.com) has a range of activities and levels. To make purchasing apps worth your while, I recommend looking for those with the widest range of activity levels so they can be used for the majority of your students and over an extended period of time.

Source: Courtesy of Reading Raven.

Starfall ABCs is one of the most popular alphabet apps. The associated website, www.starfall.com, has loads of great resources for teachers.

Source: Starfall ABCs retrieved from Starfall.com, © 2016 Starfall Education, reprinted by permission.

iLearn With Boing: Ice Land Adventures! (www.ilearnwith.com/our-apps/literacy) provides a wide range of fun and easy games for letter identification. Students respond well to interactive games like these that have enough practice to make them worth students' time and effort.

BugbrainED (http://bugbrained.com) is one of those rare apps that models for students how to segment and blend words. I always look for apps that provide the kind of teaching—albeit probably brief—or corrective feedback that is of a quality similar to what they might receive by a teacher or well-informed parent.

Success Ingredient I: Readiness Skills

Background and Key Characteristics	Best Practices and Look-Fors for Success	Common Instructional Pitfalls	Day Clinic: Examine Your Practices	Next Steps to Leap Forward
• Phonemic awareness and alphabet recognition are the two best predictors of early reading success and must be addressed for phonics instruction to "work." • Students need to learn letter names, sounds, visual characteristics, and how to write them (motor movement). • There are five major phonemic awareness activity types: rhyme and alliteration, oddity tasks, oral blending, oral segmentation, and phoneme manipulation.	• Focus on oral blending and oral segmentation—the two phonemic awareness skills most closely connected to reading and writing growth. • Teach the phonemic awareness skills in progression from easiest to most complex. • Teach alphabet recognition from high-utility to low-utility letters and sounds and separate those that are visually or auditorily confusing. • Provide lesson supports such as picture cards and manipulatives. • Use software training programs for students needing extra support.	• Overfocus on rhyme, instead of the power skills of oral blending and oral segmentation • Weak language of instruction, causing learning confusion • Lack of supports during phonemic awareness exercises • Not including letters in more sophisticated phonemic awareness tasks (e.g., phoneme manipulation) • Doing phonemic awareness well past the time students need it • Improper sequencing of activities • No cumulative assessment tool • Not separating confusing or similar letters and sounds	Ask yourself: • What sequence am I using to teach the alphabet? Are confusing letters and sounds taught far enough apart so students can master one before the other is introduced? • Am I focusing my alphabet instruction on the letter's name, shape, and sound in ways that are interactive and multisensory? • Do I have mnemonics to help students remember letter sounds or distinguish those that are confusing? • Do I teach handwriting? Do I have my students say the sound each time they write the letter to reinforce the letter–sound relationship, connect it to the physical act of writing the letter, and accelerate learning? • Which phonemic awareness activities am I spending the bulk of my time on? Do I include enough oral blending and oral segmentation tasks weekly? Am I careful not to overfocus on rhyme? • Am I sequencing my phonemic awareness tasks from easiest to most complex? • Am I using manipulatives and other supports in my activities to scaffold the practice as long as students need these supports, but taking them away over time? **Try it!** • List three ways to modify your instruction. • Meet in grade-level teams and evaluate weekly lessons.	• Fine-tune instruction by analyzing specific instructional moments and compare to instructional goals. • Build in daily fluency work for mastery. • Use review skills for instructional transitions. • Add articulation work for struggling students and English learners. • Include technology (apps and whiteboard activities).

Courtesy of Rick Harrington Photography

Background and Key Characteristics

One of the most common questions I am asked by teachers, district coordinators, and publishers is "What is the right phonics scope and sequence?" The truth is there isn't a "right" or "perfect" scope and sequence. However, there are scopes and sequences that are better than others. Far better. These sequences assist the student in learning how English words work in the easiest possible way. They share the following characteristics:

• **They build from the simplest to the most complex skills in a way that takes advantage of previous learning.** For example, after teaching students how to read simple short-vowel consonant–vowel–consonant (CVC) words like *hat* and *bit*, it is beneficial to proceed to consonant–vowel–consonant–silent-*e* (CVCe) words (often referred to as final-*e* or silent-*e* words) like *hate* and *bite*. In that way, you can easily contrast a known set of words with new words (e.g., *hat* and *hate*, *bit* and *bite*) while easily highlighting the new learning goal—the fact that the final *e* is silent and works with the preceding vowel to say the vowel's name. This "vowel team" is a new concept for students that will be important to establish as they move on to learn other long-vowel sounds and spellings.

I recommend the following simple-to-complex sequence for the primary grades. This sequence takes advantage of these minimal contrasts, uses previous learning, and highlights new skills in a way that is obvious to the young learner. You will progress from one skill to the next based on the skills you must cover for your grade level (see your state and local standards to place skills in your yearly schedule) and student progress (ensuring enough time for mastery and monitoring student skill needs). Keep in mind that all skills must be introduced before two-thirds of the school year has been completed so that students have enough time to master the later-introduced skills before the end of the year. Introducing new skills in the final weeks or months of the school year too often results in decayed learning over the summer. Mastery must occur before students go on summer break.

1. Short-vowel vowel–consonant (VC) and CVC words (e.g., *at*, *sat*)

2. Short-vowel words with blends and digraphs (e.g., *flat*, *chat*); contrast *fat* and *flat*, *hat* and *chat*

3. Long-vowel CVCe words (e.g., *bite*, *hate*); contrast *bit* and *bite*, *hat* and *hate*

4. Long-vowel words representing multiple spellings (e.g., *maid*, *stay*, *coat*, *grow*); contrast *mad* and *maid*; *cot*, *cat*, and *coat*

5. Words with *r*-controlled vowels, complex vowels, and diphthongs (e.g., *part*, *spoil*, *mouth*, *bird*); contrast *pat* and *part*, *spill* and *spoil*, *moth* and *mouth*, *bid* and *bird*

6. Simple multisyllabic words containing common prefixes and suffixes (e.g., *reread*, *trusted*); contrast *read* and *reread*, *trust* and *trusted*

7. More complex multisyllabic words using common syllable types (e.g., *candle*, *napkin*); contrast *can* and *candle*, *nap* and *napkin*

• **They are created so that many words can be formed as early as possible.** The goal of phonics is to give students access to a wealth of words for reading and writing. Therefore, a strong scope and sequence allows for maximum, useful words to be formed. Imagine if you are a five-year-old eager to learn to read. Now imagine if this was the phonics scope and sequence for the first month in your reading program: *s, m, t, d, l.* Using *only* those letters, how many words can you make? That's right, zero. Now imagine if these were the phonics skills you learned in that first month: *s, m, a, t, d.* Now how many words can you potentially read and write? That's right—a lot! These include *at, am, sat, mat, sad, mad, Sam,* and others. This quick generation of useful words is not only more efficient; it's also highly motivating for young readers. As a result, teaching consonants and vowels in combination is the best way to begin instead of marching through the alphabet in order or teaching the easier consonants first before the vowels as some programs do.

- **They teach high-utility skills before less useful sound spellings.** Not all letters and spellings are created equal. Quite simply, some are utilized more in English than others. A scope and sequence that spends the same amount of time on the letter *x* as it does on the letter *m* is not efficient. Also, a scope and sequence that introduces less common sound spellings early on isn't benefiting the young reader and writer in the most powerful way.

Following is a chart listing the sounds in English and the most common spelling or spellings for each. This chart can help you decide which sound spellings to teach earlier and on which to focus more instructional time and practice. Some of the lesser used sound spellings can be reserved for later grades or addressed incidentally as needed; that is, they can be taught when students encounter a word or two containing that sound spelling. For example, since the short-*e* sound spelled *ea* isn't as common as the *e* spelling (10% vs. 70% of words), this spelling would be introduced later in the sequence or introduced incidentally when needed (i.e., when students read words like *head* and *dead*).

Hanna, Hodges, Hanna, and Rudolph (1966) created this list after reviewing the 17,000 most common words in English. Since some of these words are multisyllabic, which won't be addressed to any great degree in kindergarten or Grade 1, consider this when making decisions using the chart. Use your knowledge of the words most appropriate for the age and grade of the students you are teaching to go beyond a simple reading of the chart. For example, the *sh* spelling for the /sh/ sound is actually less common than the *ti* spelling (as in *nation*). However, you would never teach the *ti* spelling to early readers and writers as the types of words they will encounter in texts written for this level rarely contain those words. This is a skill best reserved for Grade 2 or later.

The Most Frequent Spellings of the 44 Sounds in English

Sound	Common Spellings
1. /b/	b (97%), bb
2. /d/	d (98%), dd, ed
3. /f/	f (78%), ff, ph, lf
4. /g/	g (88%), gg, gh
5. /h/	h (98%), wh
6. /j/	g (66%), j (22%), dg
7. /k/	c (73%), cc, k (13%), ck, lk, q
8. /l/	l (91%), ll
9. /m/	m (94%), mm
10. /n/	n (97%), nn, kn, gn
11. /p/	p (96%), pp
12. /r/	r (97%), rr, wr
13. /s/	s (73%), c (17%), ss
14. /t/	t (97%), tt, ed
15. /v/	v (99.5%), f (e.g., in of)
16. /w/	w (92%)
17. /y/	y (44%), i (55%)
18. /z/	z (23%), zz, s (64%)
19. /ch/	ch (55%), t (31%)
20. /sh/	sh (26%), ti (53%), ssi, s, si, sci
21. /zh/	si (49%), s (33%), ss, z
22. /th/	th (100%)
23. /th̶/	th (100%)
24. /hw/	wh (100%)
25. /ng/	n (41%), ng (59%)
26. /ā/	a (45%), a_e (35%), ai, ay, ea
27. /ē/	e (70%), y, ea (10%), ee (10%), ie, e_e, ey, i, ei

Sound	Common Spellings
28. /ī/	i_e (37%), i (37%), igh, y (14%), ie, y_e
29. /ō/	o (73%), o_e (14%), ow, oa, oe
30. /yōō/	u (69%), u_e (22%), ew, ue
31. /a/	a (96%)
32. /e/	e (91%), ea, e_e (15%)
33. /i/	i (66%), y (23%)
34. /o/	o (79%)
35. /u/	u (86%), o, ou
36. /ə/	a (24%), e (13%), i (22%), o (27%), u
37. /â/	a (29%), are (23%), air (21%)
38. /û/	er (40%), ir (13%), ur (26%)
39. /ä/	a (89%)
40. /ô/	o, oa, au, aw, ough, augh
41. /oi/	oi (62%), oy (32%)
42. /ou/	ou (56%), ow (29%)
43. /ōō/	oo (38%), u (21%), o, ou, u_e, ew, ue
44. /ŏŏ/	oo (31%), u (54%), ou, o (8%), ould

Source: Hanna, Hodges, Hanna, & Rudolph (1966).

- **They separate easily confused letters and sounds to avoid potential difficulties.** As a result, one sound spelling is mastered before the potentially confusing sound spelling is introduced. This minimizes the chance of learning interference. Letters can be confusing because of their orientation and visual similarity to other letters (e.g., *b* and *d*, *p* and *q*). Sounds can be confusing when they are formed in similar ways in the mouth to other sounds (e.g., /a/, /e/).

Look at the following illustration. It shows how the various vowel sounds in English are formed by the mouth and which are the most similar. For example, look at the placement on the chart of the /a/ sound and the /e/ sound. They are side by side, which means that they are formed in very similar ways. We would never teach these two letter sounds beside each other in a scope and sequence as that would cause potential learning interference and confusion.

Say /a/. Notice how your mouth feels. Then say /e/. Notice again how your mouth feels when forming this sound. Do you notice a slight difference? Yes. Doing exercises like these can help students "feel" sounds differently, which can help them make better decisions when selecting a letter or spelling to represent

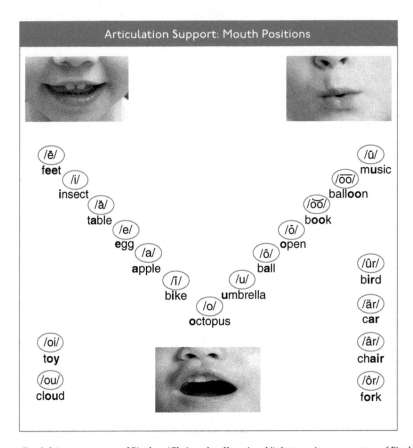

Source: Top left image courtesy of Pixabay (Christopher Kuszajewski); bottom image courtesy of Pixabay (tookapic); top right image courtesy of iStock.com/jaroon.

that sound. That is, when a student wants to spell the word *red*, he must say each sound in the word and think about which letter represents that sound. If the student "feels" /e/ differently than /a/ through repeated classroom practice and associates that mouth feeling or position with the letter *e*, then the student is more likely to correctly spell the word.

• **They adopt a scope and sequence (including the pace of instruction) that works for the majority of students, with built-in differentiation.** Test any group of first graders at the beginning of the school year, and you will quickly see the wide range of skill levels in one classroom. Below is a five-word spelling test I gave a group of students in New York City on Week 1 of first grade.

Test Words: sad, big, rake, coat, flower	
Student 1	1. sad 2. big 3. rakce 4. cote 5. flower
Student 2	1. sad 2. bag 3. rak 4. kot 5. flar
Student 3	1. sd 2. bg 3. lk 4. kt 5. fw
Student 4	1. Seivrne 2. Bog 3. Rigvet 4. Tetvai 5. Levneia
Student 5	1. ePraH 2. PEBL 3. eHPLn 4. sieHgt 5. cSeph

Differentiate From the Get-Go

- Don't miss a beat.
- Test your students on the first day of school.
- Plan to form groups based on the results *on the second day of school.*
- But don't forget the power of whole group instruction. You can differentiate very successfully during whole group time, too.

Notice the wide range of student abilities. I administered this test on the first day of school so I could begin differentiating instruction on the second day. For example, some students needed to start later in the scope and sequence during small group time. Some needed to receive additional work with phonics and phonemic awareness skills that had been taught in kindergarten because they hadn't mastered them. Other students needed targeted work on specific issues, such as Student 3 who was what I call a vowel avoider. I did a lot of minimal contrast work with these students (reading words like *hat, hot, hit,* and *hut* together to focus on the vowel) and loads of segmentation work using Sound Boxes and counters.

a. Student 1 can spell short-vowel CVC words and has a beginning understanding of the use of final-*e* or silent-*e* words. This student also uses more letters for words with more sounds, displaying a highly developed sense of phonemic awareness.

b. Student 3 has a basic understanding of beginning and ending sounds, but avoids the more complex medial vowel sound due to a lack of knowledge or confidence in spelling these sounds.

c. Student 5 displays no knowledge of letter sounds or phonemic awareness. This student has primarily used the letters in her name (Stephanie) in random and varied order in an attempt to form words.

This range of abilities is typical of most Grade 1 classrooms I visit. What this means is that those students below (e.g., Students 4 and 5) or above (e.g., Student 1) the standard scope, sequence, and pacing will need additional and targeted support. The good news is that there are fairly simple ways to differentiate phonics instruction both in whole group and in small group lessons. We will explore those ways in the next section. The goal is to challenge those students who already know the phonics skills you might be introducing to the whole group and to provide successful and purposeful learning for those students whose skill level is lacking. This is much more easily accomplished during small group time, but we must not forget the many ways to assist these students during whole group lessons. Not only will it maximize their learning time; it will also keep them engaged and on task during whole group lessons with the additional payoff of reduced behavioral issues.

Every time I talk about this issue of differentiating during whole group lessons, I have a flashback (and not the good kind) to my first day of student teaching. My cooperating teacher assigned me the spelling lesson for the day. Desperate to impress her and win over the students, I pulled out all the stops! I taught the lesson provided but added my special flair. The lesson was a huge success. In my mind, fireworks were going off, and the kids seemed to love me. My cooperating teacher was feverishly taking notes during the lesson, and at one point, I wondered, "Wow. How many ways can she write *great*?" After the lesson, she asked me to stay after school to discuss her observations. I was eager to do so. When the students left for the day, we sat at the back of the room. Her first words to me were "I don't know what you were doing in the front of my classroom, but it wasn't teaching."

This is much more easily accomplished during small group time, but we must not forget the many ways to assist these students during whole group lessons.

I quickly reminded myself that "there's no crying in student teaching" and took a deep breath. (It was actually quite hard for me to breathe at this point.) My cooperating teacher began to list all the students I had failed during the lesson. There were the above-level students who, as she said, "already knew the material, and my wasting of their instructional time was not going to help accelerate their learning and achieve all that was possible for them." In short, I had failed them. Then she listed the below-level students and how I had failed them. As she said, "I am responsible for getting them on grade level. I can't do that if you continue to ignore their instructional needs during the lessons." And finally, she listed the English learners. We had a new girl from China in the classroom, and as my cooperating teacher said, "She could have learned more if she was sitting in Beijing during my lesson." (Ouch!)

While all this might seem harsh (and it certainly shook me to my core), it was the best thing that could have happened to me on my first day of student teaching. From that day forward, I had to write detailed lessons for her review before I taught. In each lesson, I had to explain how I was going to meet the needs of my above-level, below-level, and English learners *during* the whole group lesson. I also listed additional small group support, such as preteaching to frontload content prior to the lesson and quick follow-up after the lesson. Even my practice exercises and assessments were reviewed for possible differentiation opportunities (e.g., I read aloud social studies and science tests to assess content knowledge of my struggling

The one-room-schoolhouse approach to whole group lessons is one I recommend.

readers). What she accomplished by tearing me down was the slow rebuilding of a preservice teacher who thought in multiple ways and about multiple things during each and every lesson. It was the greatest gift she could have given me. She said on that day she had the responsibility of helping me become not a good teacher, but a great one who would affect the lives and learning of hundreds, maybe thousands, of students. Thank you, Ms. Yon!

ONE-ROOM SCHOOLHOUSE

This one-room-schoolhouse approach to whole group lessons is one I recommend. Adapting each lesson and activity with a range of entry points and places to gather formative assessment information is critical. I will detail some ways to accomplish this in the upcoming sections.

Courtesy of Rick Harrington Photography

Best Practices and Look-Fors for Success

The most important best practice is to have a solid scope and sequence in place and literature that builds around it or supports it (i.e., literature that highlights words containing the phonics skills taught to date so students have ample practice applying their skills in authentic contexts). If you don't have this, below are my suggested scopes and sequences for kindergarten through Grade 2. In these grades, the basic phonics skills are taught, and that learning is consolidated. That means students can fluently read connected text containing words with these phonics patterns at an appropriate speed for their grade level and with the proper intonation. In Grades 3 and up, phonics instruction is still needed, but its look and feel changes. In these grades, there is more focus on word study, multisyllabic words, and using Greek and Latin roots, and the connection between phonics and vocabulary is (or should be) highlighted.

Jeanne Chall (1983) provides an easy framework for thinking about this if you're teaching the primary grades. She created a framework of stages that details how children learn to read. Teachers of primary-level students should focus their attention on Stages 0–2. The goals of each stage and time frame are clearly defined and provide strong guideposts for phonics instruction.

Stage 0: Prereading

This stage begins at birth and ends around the time the child enters school. During this stage, the child develops his or her vocabulary, gains some knowledge of how print works, and recognizes some letters and words (e.g., his or her name, environmental print).

Stage I: Initial Reading or Decoding

This stage generally begins in kindergarten and lasts through Grade I or early Grade 2 when the student learns the basic sound spellings needed to decode, or sound out, words. Much of the phonics

(Continued)

(Continued)

instruction in these grades is focused on teaching those high-utility phonics skills and applying them to reading connected text.

Stage 2: Confirmation, Fluency, and Ungluing From Print

The stage is typical of students in Grades 2 and 3. In these grades, students have enough practice reading words with basic phonics skills that they can apply those skills to new words and can read most words containing these skills fluently. These students also increase their ability to use context clues to determine or confirm word meanings and pronunciations while reading.

Stage 3: Learning the New

The stage generally begins in Grade 3 or 4. Students are exposed to texts that contain a lot of new words and concepts—not already in students' speaking and listening vocabularies or general knowledge base. Students need fluency with basic decoding skills in order to use the majority of their mental energies to access and comprehend this new information. Students who have decoding proficiency plus wide background knowledge and vocabulary (e.g., through rich read-alouds in the primary grades) are best prepared to tackle the challenges in this stage.

Stage 4: Multiple Viewpoints

This stage usually lasts throughout high school. Students read more conceptually complex text with increasing vocabulary demands, learn about multiple viewpoints on issues, and analyze texts critically.

Stage 5: Construction and Reconstruction

This stage lasts from college and beyond. Readers develop a worldview, use texts as needed (complete or in parts), and construct their own understanding based on their individual analysis and synthesis of information. Not all readers progress to this stage.

So, how do you know your scope and sequence is working? If students progress from skill to skill in small stairstep ways, with previous skills building to new skills, then your sequence is strong. Taking big leaps in skill complexity or a haphazard approach to teaching skills (ignoring those that are related or jumping around from one skill type to another) represents a sequence that isn't as effective.

Here are sample scopes and sequences for kindergarten, Grade 1, and Grade 2. They can be used as a starting point to create your own scope and sequence or to make modifications to an existing one. These are model sequences, not designed to be "written in stone." Adjust as needed for your students' needs. However, the basic progression should flow like this:

a. Short vowels and consonants to make VC and CVC words (e.g., *am, sat*)

b. Short vowels and blends (e.g., *step, flip*)

c. Short vowels and digraphs (e.g., *ship, chop, with*)

d. Final *e* (e.g., *like, make, hope*)

e. Long vowels (e.g., *train, play, road, snow, read, see*)

f. *r*-Controlled vowels, variant (complex) vowels, and diphthongs (e.g., *park, hurt, moon, boy, sound*)

g. Multisyllabic words (compounds, prefixes, suffixes—although some of this can be incorporated earlier)

h. Multisyllabic words (syllable types)

On the next page, I provide a staircase graphic to help you remember the progression of skills.

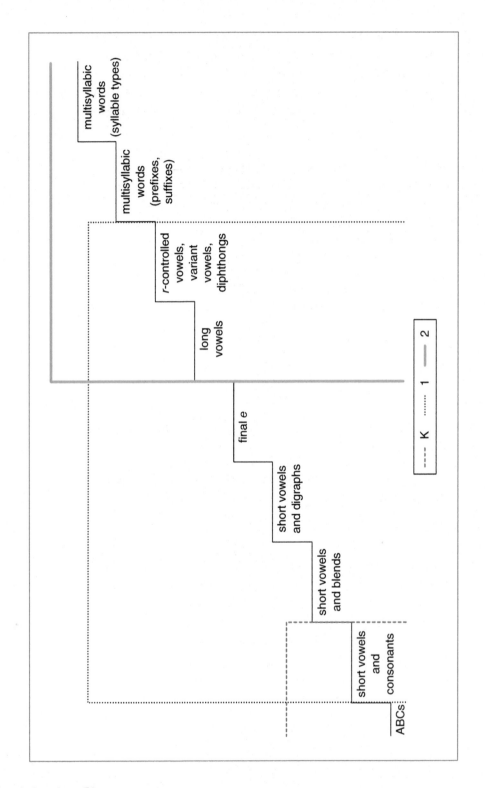

multisyllabic words (syllable types)

multisyllabic words (prefixes, suffixes)

r-controlled vowels, variant vowels, diphthongs

long vowels

final *e*

short vowels and digraphs

short vowels and blends

short vowels and consonants

ABCs

- - - K
······· 1
—— 2

Kindergarten

Skill Category	Skill Sequence	Word Study
Short Vowels and High-Utility Consonants	m a s p t i n b c	Plurals (inflectional ending -s for nouns) Inflectional ending -s (verbs)
Short Vowels and Mid-Utility Consonants	o f h d r g e l k	Include *ck* for /k/ Double final consonants
Short Vowels and Low-Utility Consonants	u w j x v qu y z	

* Common Core State Standards, Foundational Skills for Kindergarten, Standard K.3.B states: "Associate the long and short sounds with common spellings (graphemes) for the five major vowels." In Grade 1 (Standard 1.3.c), the CCSS state: "Know final–*e* and common vowel team conventions for representing long vowel sounds." So, *mastery* of long-vowel spellings is expected in Grade 1. I strongly believe that students in kindergarten should be focused on mastering the reading of CVC short-vowel words *only*. The inclusion of long-vowel spellings in kindergarten is not appropriate, unless students are above level.

Note that the California Department of Education, when adopting the CCSS, added the caveat that in kindergarten students are expected to know that vowels have two major sounds—long and short—but are only required to learn the spellings for the short-vowel sounds. I think this is a sensible solution, and we should not push down the phonics curriculum any more into kindergarten. We must give our students time to build a strong foundation without rushing it.

Grade 1

Skill Category	Skill Sequence	Word Study
Short Vowels With Single Consonants Notes: Students will read VC and CVC words such as *am* and *hop*. They will also review all the consonant sounds from kindergarten. Include work with *ck* for /k/ in this section.	Short *a* Short *i* Short *o* Short *u* Short *e*	Plurals (inflectional ending *-s* for nouns) Inflectional ending *-s* for verbs Double final consonants
Short Vowels With Blends and Digraphs Notes: Some scopes and sequences teach consonant digraphs before consonant blends. That's fine, but I choose to teach blends first because (1) it's just adding one sound to a word and blending it like students are used to and (2) digraphs represent a new concept—that "two letters" can stand for one sound. This is more complex.	*l* blends *s* blends *r* blends final blends Three-letter blends Digraph *sh* Digraph *ch, tch* Digraph *th* (both sounds) Digraph *wh* Digraph *ng* (also cover *nk*)	Inflectional ending *-ing* (no spelling changes) Inflectional ending *-ed* (no spelling changes) Possessives Contractions
Final e Notes: There are few one-syllable words with *e_e*, so you will need to use some multisyllabic words like *compete* or *complete*. The *u_e* spelling has two sounds: long *u* as in *cute* and *huge* and long /$\overline{oo}$/ as in *rule* and *June*.	*a_e* *i_e* *o_e* *u_e* *e_e*	Inflectional ending *-ing* (spelling changes) Inflectional ending *-ed* (spelling changes) Soft *c* and *g*
Long Vowels Notes: There are multiple spellings for each long-vowel sound. I recommend teaching only two to three per week or instructional cycle. Base the spellings you teach on frequency and utility. Delay less common spellings for later in the sequence or teach them in Grade 2.	Single-Letter Long Vowels *e, i, o* (open syllables) (*we, me, he, she, hi, no, go, so*) Long *a* (*ai, ay*) Long *e* (*ee, ea*) Long *o* (*oa, ow*) Long *i* (*y, igh*) Long *u* (*u, ew, ue*)	Common prefixes Common suffixes Compound words Comparatives and superlatives (*er, est*) Address *ea* as /e/ (*head*)

Skill Category	Skill Sequence	Word Study
r-Controlled Vowels, Complex Vowels, and Diphthongs Notes: *r*-Controlled vowel spellings have high utility. Some of them—such as *er*, *ir*, and *ur*—require students to have loads of exposure to words with the spellings to remember which to use when writing the words as there are no "tricks" like for other spellings. Diphthongs are also called "glide sounds." The mouth moves when making these sounds, and they are therefore more complex for students to spell. Try it. Say the /oi/ sound. Feel how your mouth moves from one place to another. Now say a long-vowel sound. Notice how your mouth remains in one spot as you make the sound.	*r*-Controlled *ar* *r*-Controlled *er, ir, ur* *r*-Controlled *or, ore, oar* Short *oo* (*book*) Long *oo* (*oo, ou, ew, ue, u_e*) (*room, group, new, glue, tune*) Diphthong /ou/ (*ou, ow*) Diphthong /oi/ (*oi, oy*) Complex vowel /ô/ [*au, aw, a*(*lk*), *a*(*lt*), *a*(*ll*)] *r*-Controlled *are, air, ear*	Common prefixes Common suffixes Begin transitions to multisyllabic words
Less Common Long-Vowel Spellings Notes: These lower-utility spellings for the long vowels can be introduced at the end of Grade I and reinforced for mastery in Grade 2 (or even taught then). There is no need to force every spelling for every phonics skill into the Grade I curriculum, and some of these spellings appear in so few Grade I words that they can be addressed informally at point of need.	Long *i* and *o* [*i*(*ld*), *i*(*nd*), *o*(*ld*)] Long *i* and *o* (*ie, oe*) Long *e* (*y, ey, ie, ei*)	

Skill Category	Skill Sequence	Word Study
Review Short Vowels Transition to Longer Words	Short vowels a, e, i, o, u Closed syllables (napkin) Consonant + le syllables (cattle)	Inflectional endings with no spelling changes (-s, -ing, -ed)
Review Final e Review Blends and Digraphs Transition to Longer Words	Final e (a_e, i_e, o_e, u_e, e_e) Final e syllables (reptile) Consonant blends (l-, s-, r-) Final blends Consonant digraphs (sh, ch, tch, th, wh, ph, ng/nk)	Soft c and g Suffixes -er, -est Prefixes Inflectional endings with spelling changes Silent letters
Review Long Vowels Transition to Longer Words	Long a, e, i, o, u (all spellings covered in Grade 1; add any not covered) Open syllables (going) Consonant + le syllables (table) Vowel team syllables (remain)	Prefixes Suffixes Compound words Contractions
Review r-Controlled Vowels Transition to Longer Words	r-Controlled ar r-Controlled er, ir, ur r-Controlled or, ore, oar r-Controlled are, air, ear (all spellings covered in Grade 1; add any not covered) r-Controlled vowel syllables (marker) Consonant + le syllables (marble)	Prefixes Suffixes
Review Complex Vowels and Diphthongs Transition to Longer Words	Short oo Long oo (oo, ou, ew, ue, u_e) Diphthong /ou/ (ou, ow) Diphthong /oi/ (oi, oy) Complex vowel /ô/ [au, aw, a(lk), a(lt), a(ll)] (all spellings covered in Grade 1; add any not covered) Vowel team syllables (cloudless)	Prefixes Suffixes
Syllable Types	Review all syllable types Add other final stable syllables (-ture, -sure, -ion, -tion, -sion)	Prefixes Suffixes

Recommended Phonics Sequence for Guided Reading

So, how do you dovetail your phonics instruction if you're using guided reading levels (or some other leveling system) instead of a basal series in which the stories were created or selected to more closely match the phonics scope and sequence?

I had the opportunity to create a guided reading program years ago when I worked for one of the major publishers. The levels are not based on the phonics elements present in the words in the books. Rather, a more complex and sophisticated look at the text layout and reading demands is considered. Several years ago, I examined the guided reading levels and sample books students read at each level. I then compared the words in the books to a typical phonics scope and sequence at each grade level or the one the teachers I was working with were using. My goal was to provide a phonics scope and sequence that more closely matched the decoding needs of students at each level and progressed in a sequence from simple to complex skills. While there is no perfect fit and a teacher can use a much wider variety of books at each level than I examined, I think a general phonics sequence can assist teachers in choosing books in which they can better reinforce the phonics skills they are teaching and books that more closely match their instruction in small group differentiated lessons. As I will discuss later, the disconnect I see between phonics skills taught and the actual words students read in books can be a major cause of reading difficulties or slow reading growth.

A general phonics sequence can assist teachers in choosing books in which they can better reinforce the phonics skills they are teaching and books that more closely match their instruction in small group differentiated lessons.

Below I have provided a possible scope and sequence that can help you focus your phonics instruction. This sequence highlights skills student need in a more natural progression and can assist you in selecting books at each level (although the decoding needs aren't your primary selection criteria).

Guided Reading Level	Recommended Phonics Skill	Notes
A	Alphabet (basic letter sounds)	Children read patterned text.
B	Alphabet (basic letter sounds)	Children read patterned text.
C	Alphabet (basic letter sounds)	Children read patterned text with a few short-vowel VC and CVC words.
D	Short vowels *a, i*	Children begin reading texts that contain larger numbers of decodable words. Instruction can also include inflectional endings, consonant blends, and plurals.

(Continued)

(Continued)

Guided Reading Level	Recommended Phonics Skill	Notes
E	Short vowels *o, u, e*	Instruction can also include consonant digraphs.
F	Final *e*	
G	Long vowels *a, e*	
H	Long vowels *o, i, u*	Instruction can also focus on introducing simple multisyllabic words.
I	*r*-Controlled vowels *er, ir, ur, ar, or, ore* Diphthongs *oi, oy, ou, ow* Variant vowels *oo, au, aw*	
J	Two- and three-syllable words	Review one-syllable words with short vowels, final *e*, blends, and digraphs to ensure mastery.
K	Two- and three-syllable words	Review one-syllable words with long vowels, inflectional endings, and plurals to ensure mastery.
L	Two- and three-syllable words	Review one-syllable words with long vowels to ensure mastery. Instruction can also include silent letters and soft *c* and *g*.
M	Two- and three-syllable words	Review one-syllable words with *r*-controlled vowels, variant vowels, and diphthongs to ensure mastery.
N	Syllabication	Instruction should include open syllables, closed syllables, consonant + *le* syllables, and prefixes.
O	Syllabication	Instruction should include vowel-team syllables, final-*e* syllables, *r*-controlled vowel syllables, and suffixes.
P	Syllabication	Instruction should include inflectional endings with spelling changes, prefixes, suffixes, and homophones.

Kindergarten: Levels A–C/D

Grade 1: Levels C/D–I

Grade 2: Levels I–M

If you focus primarily on a small set of skills (carefully sequenced) at each guided reading level, then you will better assist your students. Gay Su Pinnell and Irene C. Fountas (e.g., 2003) have provided a wealth of resources to assist the teaching of phonics for those teachers using their guided reading levels.

Just a couple things to consider:

1. You still can teach a whole class phonics lesson on skills that are the focus of your grade level and provide differentiated reading and spelling practice through the leveled books and activities. You can highlight those skills during the small group reading of leveled books throughout the week and add additional skills based on the needs of the book.

2. You will need decodable texts as part of your whole group phonics lessons to provide enough practice decoding words with the target skill because it's doubtful the texts you select will provide enough practice. I view this as great scaffolding. If you've encountered decodable texts of an inferior quality in the past (and many exist), then seek out better texts or create your own mini-passages for students to read. In this way, you teach a phonics lesson that corresponds to a strong scope and sequence and provide a short decodable text or passage as follow-up reading during that lesson. This tightly controlled practice tool allows your students time and opportunity to practice the skill. Then you select a guided reading book at the desired level, taking care to find books with a closer match to your phonics scope and sequence. During the guided reading lesson, you highlight any examples of the target skill in the book. Since these books are not created or selected based on decodability, the connection between the phonics skills and high-frequency words you have taught will be less. Therefore, this book will be more challenging than the decodable text (hopefully not too much, though). In this way, you provide students with a stairstep experience in reading where the supports and controls slowly lessen, but are still within the students' grasp.

3. You can provide differentiated support during small group guided reading time on any phonics skills with which students need support. For example, one group might need lots of blending, word building, and word sort practice while another group might need a quick review of the skill and a slight challenge (e.g., harder, more complex words with that skill).

I've had discussions with numerous guided reading teachers about phonics and its role in their instruction. The most common refrain I hear is "We are focused

> *If you focus primarily on a small set of skills (carefully sequenced) at each guided reading level, then you will better assist your students.*

on teaching all the cueing systems—graphophonic cues, syntactic cues, and semantic cues. We don't overemphasize one." That is terrific. Recent research reveals that students who use multiple cues when confronted with word reading challenges are more successful and more likely to be on grade level (McGee, Kim, Nelson, & Fried, 2015). This study examined which cues students receiving Reading Recovery training in Grade 1 used. The students who ended the year below level did not take advantage of multiple cues when confronted with reading difficulties. In contrast, when a student who ended the year *on* grade level arrived at a word that was new or challenging, he might first attempt to sound it out, then reread the sentence to see if the word made sense. These "action chains" employed multiple cues. Struggling readers often over-relied on one cue to the detriment of the others.

But that's not what concerns me the most. When these teachers say they want to equally develop all cueing systems and I compare the books their students are reading to the phonics skills they are teaching and less than 10% of the words can be sounded out using these phonics skills (which is generally the case), are they really developing all three cueing systems? If the texts we give students to read have few words that can be sounded out using the phonics skills we teach them, then they won't develop the strong and efficient habit of using the graphophonic cues to attack words—skills that will become even more essential as the texts grow in complexity and the text-to-illustration match decreases. It is an important thing to consider when selecting texts for your guided reading lessons.

Whole Group Lesson: Short Vowel a

Below Level (Extra Support)	Above Level (Advanced Learners)	English Learners
If students are still struggling with alphabet recognition and basic phonemic awareness skills, *then* continue to work on lower-level skills to build a strong reading foundation. Repeat some of the whole group instruction, selecting a subset of the words or text to focus on, as students are able to handle that content.	*If* students have already mastered the skill, *then* select skills from further in the phonics scope and sequence (as determined by a comprehensive phonics survey) and provide systematic instruction. Add differentiation to whole group lessons through addition of higher-level words in blending and dictation exercises, and in texts read.	*If* students' home language is something other than English or they have had limited language experiences prior to starting school, *then* focus on the vocabulary of words used during instruction, articulation of the target sound, and using words and text to build oral language.

Below Level (Extra Support)	Above Level (Advanced Learners)	English Learners
Day 1 • Based on your cumulative phonics and phonemic awareness assessments, select a starting point for instruction (e.g., their lowest-level skill deficit) to rebuild students' foundation. • Provide a mini-lesson on the lower-level skills, including follow-up decodable text reading. Do not limit these students' instruction to isolated skill work. Application is critical for them—both reading and writing—and lots of it.	**Day 1** • Add a line of more sophisticated words to the day's blending and dictation work during the whole group lesson. • Provide a mini-lesson on a skill further in the scope and sequence and follow it up with decodable text reading.	**Day 1** • Focus on articulation (how the sound is formed in the mouth). • Review the meanings of three to five words in blending lines (use gestures, pictures, simple definitions). • Preview the week's first decodable text (point to items in the illustrations and name them, page through the book and provide a sentence to summarize, have students repeat, etc.).
Day 2 • Review the skills you taught on the previous day by repeating the mini-lessons. • Have students reread the decodable text to build fluency. Add dictation and writing work. Provide sentence frames for support. • Address vocabulary needs by addressing three to five words in the decodable text and/ or adding two or three words about the story that will build more sophisticated vocabulary. Use the pictures as support.	**Day 2** • Reinforce the skill further in the scope and sequence while below- and on-level students partner reread the week's first decodable text. • Students partner reread their decodable text from the day before during independent work time. Add a writing extension.	**Day 2** • Review the meanings of three to five words in blending lines (use gestures, pictures, simple definitions). • Reread the decodable text (first for the week). Ask basic yes-or-no questions about the text and provide sentence frames for students to orally respond.
Day 3 • Review the skills for the week by providing additional mini-lessons. Increase the number of words in blending lines for the target skill. Continue to address a subset of the whole class lessons, as students are able to handle that content. • Have students read a second decodable text on the skill.	**Day 3** • Add a line of more sophisticated words to the day's blending and dictation work during the whole group lesson. • Provide a mini-lesson on the skill further in the scope and sequence and follow it up with decodable text reading.	**Day 3** • Review the meanings of three to five words in blending lines (use gestures, pictures, simple definitions). • Preview the week's second decodable text (point to items in the illustrations and name them, page through the book and provide a sentence to summarize, have students repeat, etc.).

(Continued)

(Continued)

Below Level (Extra Support)	Above Level (Advanced Learners)	English Learners
Day 4 • Review the skills for the week by providing additional mini-lessons. Increase the number of words in dictation lines for the target skill. • Have students reread the second decodable text on the skill to build fluency.	**Day 4** • Reinforce the skill further in the scope and sequence while below- and on-level students partner reread the decodable text. • Students partner reread their decodable text from the day before during independent work time. Add a writing extension.	**Day 4** • Review the meanings of three to five words in blending lines (use gestures, pictures, simple definitions). • Reread the decodable text (second for the week). Ask basic yes-or-no questions about the text and provide sentence frames for children to orally respond.
Day 5 • Have children write about the decodable texts read during the week (a longer exercise than providing a simple sentence frame, such as writing a summary or two or three facts learned). Students can use words and sentences from the books for support. Allow students time to verbalize their thoughts before writing, and to share their completed works.	**Day 5** • Provide higher-level trade books for students to read independently and with partners to further practice their developing phonics skills.	**Day 5** • Review the meanings of three to five words in blending lines (use gestures, pictures, simple definitions). • Have students write about the decodable texts read. Provide sentence frames for writing support. Allow students time to verbalize their thoughts before writing and share them after writing.

Common Instructional Pitfalls

Many common pitfalls regarding scope and sequence exist. These include the following:

- **Just because you have a scope and sequence in place does not mean that your instruction is systematic.** *Systematic* is a word commonly cited in phonics research. It refers not only to the sequence of phonics skills progressing from the simplest to the most complex, but also to the internalized review and repetition built into that scope and sequence. I will discuss this in greater detail later in the book when I write about the need for a purposeful and systematic review and repetition cycle of instruction for your students to achieve mastery. The bottom line is that it takes far more time for many students to master basic phonics skills than our curriculum allows. We teach so much so fast that our reading programs have turned into instruction that is "exposure" focused rather than "mastery" focused. In many curricula, only one week is spent focusing on a new skill, yet it takes the typical student four to six weeks to master the skill. That's four to six weeks of regular, meaty, intense practice.

The bottom line is that it takes far more time for many students to master basic phonics skills than our curriculum allows.

So what do you do? Realistically, so many phonics skills are now required to be covered at each primary grade. The only way to ensure mastery, then, is to create a formal review and repetition cycle (which I will show you in a later section). Without this formal review and repetition cycle, too many students lack the time needed to master skills, and the phonics foundation we build for them is too weak to sustain later learning.

- **Most published materials lack the review and repetition needed for students to achieve mastery.** I have reviewed most programs currently available and have even worked on several. It has been one of the most surprising and disappointing findings in my research. In the section "Next Steps to Leap Forward," I will outline ways in which you can evaluate your materials and make any necessary modifications to correct this issue.

- **Believing that your published materials, with their "research" support, have the amount of repetition, review, and reading practice needed to master skills is another common mistake.** I have worked with educators in many districts who have adopted materials they believe are strong. They have been told by the publisher to use the materials with "fidelity." What that means is that you follow the instructional sequence and coverage with great care and detail—not deviating in any substantial way. This is desired by publishers because they want to report your success with their materials in order to sell these materials to other school districts. This is important for district administrators because they have invested a great deal of time and money into purchasing and training these materials. They have chosen these materials because of their perceived strength. They want their teachers to follow the materials closely because they believe the materials will work (and they might). Since district administrators are responsible for increasing student gains, to them, if you dramatically modify the materials they have selected, then they have no control over what they think will be a success. I get all of that. But the major problem is that we have become so addicted to the term *fidelity* that we ignore common sense and the necessary adjustments needed to meet specific student needs. There must be some leeway. For example, one district I worked with was using a published program with fidelity—and I mean fidelity with a capital *F*. This program had several studies conducted by the publisher to prove its efficacy. However, when I reviewed the materials, the scope of the program did not cover the basic skills as required by the district's standards (at the time these were the Common Core State Standards foundational skills). In addition, the program had virtually no connected text reading for students to apply the skill, something essential for success. All the program provided was a short story each unit and some lists of possible isolated sentences to use periodically. Even given the obvious weaknesses and deficiencies in this program, the district administrators and teachers were committed to following it with fidelity because the publisher had research saying it would work. And to compound the issue, the test scores related to students' phonics growth revealed major weaknesses. That is, the students were *not* making the progress needed each year to become skilled, fluent, on-grade-level readers. Yet, the program continued to be used with fidelity, and the blame continued to be placed elsewhere. The problem wasn't the students! My point is that fidelity can be blinding, and we need to be more critical consumers of products—testing them ourselves with our students before purchasing, thoroughly evaluating them, and making modifications and course corrections as needed.

- **Far too many teachers received their teaching certificates at universities that did not provide them adequate information on linguistics,** the type of information that would assist them in making more-informed decisions about how phonics skills are related in the scope and sequence, which influence each other, which cause challenges, how they manifest themselves in reading and writing, the basic facts about sound spellings that would help students better understand how English words work to improve their reading and writing, and so on. I will provide some of this information later in the

> *The major problem is that we have become so addicted to the term* fidelity *that we ignore common sense and the necessary adjustments needed to meet specific student needs.*

book (see pages 227–229). In addition, teacher-friendly books and trainings are available that will assist you if you want or need to know more (see my bibliography and my online support at http://resources.corwin.com/blevinsphonics). I have found that the speech therapists in most schools have a strong foundation in linguistics. Enlist the help of your district's speech therapist. Have him or her provide training and insights into English sounds and spellings that will improve your teaching. The more we all increase our knowledge of linguistics, the stronger our teaching of phonics will be.

- **Another issue with a phonics scope and sequence is that it is not always tightly linked to the readings students do as follow-up work.** I will address this in great detail later in this book (see pages 247–251). However, I find the greatest discrepancies in Grade 2. If you look at the stories students read in this grade, they often contain many multisyllabic words. Now compare that to the scope and sequence at this grade. What you often find is an emphasis on reading one-syllable words. Why? Well, in Grade 2, most scopes and sequences review the numerous skills taught in Grade 1 to consolidate and solidify that learning before moving on. This is essential. What we need to *also* do is use that review as an opportunity to assist students in transitioning those one-syllable phonics skills to longer, more complex words. In the "Next Steps to Leap Forward" section, I will provide some ideas about how to best achieve this.

Fidelity can be blinding, and we need to be more critical consumers of products—testing them ourselves with our students before purchasing, thoroughly evaluating them, and making modifications and course corrections as needed.

- **There is a need in most curriculum for a strong comprehensive phonics mastery assessment** (as well as weekly, cumulative mastery checks) matched to the scope and sequence not only to monitor progress over time, but also to place students into the scope and sequence at the most appropriate place.

- **Another common issue is "overdoing it."** Sometimes there is such a focus on phonics instruction, especially with struggling readers, that their vocabulary, background knowledge, and general comprehension needs are not met. I have worked with districts in which their Response-to-Intervention (RTI) time for struggling readers is solely devoted to phonics. I get it. Students lack these skills. They are easily measured, and progress can be shown more readily. However, these students all need *tons* of vocabulary and background-knowledge building. This work is what plants and waters the seeds of comprehension, especially in the later grades. To not have a more balanced approach with these students is a serious flaw that will perpetuate many of the reading issues they face. But balance can be achieved with slight modifications to existing practices and a global understanding of this critical need. The vocabulary and background knowledge deficits might not be as evident until students reach

Grades 3 and beyond, but what we've done is lost three years (kindergarten through Grade 2) in which we could be aggressively building those skills to avoid the issues we know they will otherwise face in these upper grades. To overemphasize phonics in the early grades at the detriment of other critical skills is very shortsighted.

• **With English learners, we need to devote additional time to non-transferable or challenging sound spellings.** For example, with native Spanish-speaking students, many sound spellings are the same in both Spanish and English (e.g., *d, p, t*). So, if a student has knowledge of reading and writing in Spanish (or we are first teaching the student in his or her native language, then transitioning to English), it's as simple as letting him or her know these skills function in the same basic way in both languages. We don't need to waste students' time reteaching these skills. Rather, we focus on those skills that do not transfer, such as the short-vowel sounds or the sound for the consonant *j*, as examples. This is an efficient way to accelerate their growth in English reading and writing as it relates to basic decoding and spelling of words.

No English-to-Spanish Sound-Spelling Transfer	Positive English-to-Spanish Sound-Spelling Transfer
a (short *a*)	*b*
e (short *e*)	*c*
h	*d*
i (short *i*)	*f*
j	*g*
o (short *o*)	*k*
r (In Spanish, the /r/ in initial position is trilled; in English, the /r/ in initial position is soft.)	*l*
	m
u	*n*
v (Voiced /v/ is not used in Spanish. In Spanish, we do not bite our lips with our top teeth when pronouncing this letter.)	*p*
	q (but not *qu*)
x	*s*
	t
z (The /z/ in English is a voiced fricative. The /s/—like at the end of English plurals—in Spanish is an unvoiced fricative.)	*w* (All the *w* words that appear in Spanish text come from other languages, but they are pronounced /w/ and are spelled with a *w*.)
Long *a* spellings	*y*
Long *e* spellings	*ch*
Long *i* spellings	

No English-to-Spanish Sound-Spelling Transfer	Positive English-to-Spanish Sound-Spelling Transfer
Long *o* spellings	*ng*
Long *u* spellings	*r*-controlled vowel /är/
Diphthong /ou/	*l* blends
Diphthong /oi/	*r* blends
Complex vowel /o͝o/	
Complex vowel / o͞o /	
Complex vowel /ô/	
sh	
ch, *tch*	
wh	
r-Controlled vowel /ûr/	
r-Controlled vowel /ôr/	
r-Controlled vowel /âr/	
s blends	
Three-letter blends	
Silent-*e* (final-*e*) spellings	
Silent letters	
Schwa ə	

Examine Your Practices

Now it's your turn. Ask yourself the following questions to examine your instructional practices and materials as they relate to scope and sequence.

1. Do I know my basic phonics scope and sequence without looking? (I should always have the big picture in mind—the prerequisite skills taught, what is coming next, etc.)

2. Does my instruction have a formal scope and sequence, or am I selecting skills based on each week's readings? If so, on what am I basing my decisions? How am I keeping track of which skills have been taught, when, and how many times to ensure ample review and repetition?

3. Have I noticed specific skills with which my students struggle? Where are they in the scope and sequence? What has been taught before these skills? Is there a relation between this new skill and a previously taught skill? How much time am I spending on this skill? Is it at least four to six weeks? What support pieces do I have for students to practice this skill?

Try these activities to test the effectiveness of your scope and sequence.

1. Take one of the books students are reading this week. Make a copy of a few pages. Then compare the words to your phonics scope and sequence. Focus first on the phonics skill taught this week. Circle all the words containing this skill. Can all these words be sounded out using the new skill and all previously taught skills? If so, leave the word circled. Then put a box around all the words that can be sounded out using previously taught skills. If a word contains even one sound spelling not taught, it doesn't count (e.g., students can sound out *sat* because they have learned all the consonants and the short vowel *a*, but can't read *chat* because they haven't learned consonant digraphs like *ch* yet). Then put an X through all the high-frequency or sight words you have formally taught students. What's left? Is it a large number of words? Do these words have anything in common (that you could base a phonics mini-lesson on)? Is the percentage of words that students can't read based on what

you've taught larger than 30% or 40%? If so, how are your students accessing these words (guessing, context, picture clues)? Is this book a good fit for this point in your phonics scope and sequence?

2. Create a path for acceleration for students who enter your grade above level . Administer a comprehensive phonics survey that is linked to your curriculum's scope and sequence. Place the students into that scope and sequence and, if necessary, continue on to the next grade level's skills. Marching through these skills and standards in an organized

> Especially for **ADVANCED LEARNERS**

and systematized way will benefit your students and make the teaching and planning easier. For example, some students enter Grade I having mastered reading words with short vowels (e.g., *ran*, *hop*). I do a quick check to see if they can read short-vowel words with blends and digraphs (e.g., *slip*, *shop*), and if they can, I start them in the scope and sequence at final *e* (e.g., *take*, *like*, *hope*). This instruction occurs primarily during small group time, but you can fold what students are learning into whole class work through the blending work (I'll discuss in depth later), modeling of words while reading, and small targeted lessons while other students are engaged in easier practice activities (e.g., rereading a simple decodable text that above-level students don't need to reread).

3. Note "bumps in the road" in your current sequence. Are there places where students slow down or seem to have challenges grasping the new skills? Perhaps too much is taught too fast (e.g., more than a couple spellings for a given sound), or there is a big cognitive leap in understanding the new principle (e.g., jumping from one letter standing for a sound to letter combinations

4 BEST EFFECT

Writing Is a Window Into Phonics Growth

- Each week, check the writing of a subset of your students (four to six) to note transfer of previously taught phonics skills. *Are they using them consistently in writing?*

- Provide more whole and small group instruction and practice on previously taught skills that aren't transferring to writing.

- Each month, meet with your grade-level teacher teams and evaluate students' writing for phonics mastery.

- Add more dictation work for sound spellings not transferring rapidly or consistently enough.

standing for a sound). It might also be that the new skill is causing confusion because of its similarity to a previous skill that has not yet been mastered. Keep in mind that some skills require longer to teach, practice, and apply. Make adjustments to your curriculum's scope and sequence based on your students' needs. Separate confusing letter sounds and teach the first letter sound to mastery before introducing the second. Also, stretch out the instruction of sounds with multiple spellings (e.g., long vowels, complex vowels). Many of your students might only be able to handle two new spellings for the sound each week of instruction.

4. Look at students' writing to see evidence of transfer from reading to writing. Ask yourself, "Which previously taught skills aren't transferring?" Adjust your scope and sequence to include more work with these skills. Regularly evaluating students' writing for evidence of phonics knowledge and for what skills need reinforcing is a great monthly practice. I recommend doing this with grade-level teachers. Often a fresh eye on your students' work can provide valuable insights.

Next Steps to Leap Forward

If you have a fairly strong scope and sequence in place, there are several ways to take it to the next level and ensure all students are benefiting from it.

Teach to Mastery, Rather Than Just Exposure

As I mentioned earlier, the biggest flaw in most curriculum is the lack of time and practice spent on a phonics skill. Generally, four to six weeks of robust instruction and practice is needed for most students to achieve mastery on any given phonics skill. Select places in the weekly instructional plan in which review and repetition can naturally be added. These places can include (1) blending work, when you list words to model and practice blending before reading a story; (2) dictation, when you help students transfer their new phonics skills in reading to writing; (3) rereading decodable stories to extend practice opportunities and build fluency; and (4) word building and word sorts, when you provide activities to get students actively noticing discrete differences in words and improving their understanding of how words work. Let me show you an example of each.

Generally, four to six weeks of robust instruction and practice is needed for most students to achieve mastery on any given phonics skill.

1. Blending work: During blending, you list words with the new target phonics skill. Some of these words you will model how to blend, or sound out. For others, you will guide students through the blending process, providing corrective feedback.

Here is a sample blending list (which I call "blending lines") for a typical lesson in most programs. The target skill is short *u*. Previously, the teacher has taught all the consonants and the short vowels *a*, *e*, *i*, and *o*.

Words for Blending: *up, cut, cup, mug, but, duck, gum*

This list contains a small set of words, all focusing on the short *u* sound.

Now look at the list I revised to make the instruction more robust. It contains many more words, organized around word similarities. In addition, lines were added (Lines 5 and 6) with words containing review skills (the previously taught short vowels). In this way, the teacher can continue to provide guided practice in reading these words for an extended period of time (many weeks after the skill's initial introduction). The teacher has also repeated words across the blending lines for purposes of minimal contrast.

Blending Lines

up	*cup*	*pup*	*but*	*cut*	*hut* (vary by beginning sound)
cup	*cut*	*bug*	*bun*	*hug*	*hum* (vary by ending sound)
cap	*cup*	*pop*	*pup*	*bug*	*bag* (vary by medial sound)
map	*led*	*hip*	*rock*	*dot*	*rip* (mixed review sets)
fell	*tap*	*fog*	*beg*	*tan*	*lid* (mixed review sets)

2. Dictation: During dictation, you model how to transfer phonics skills to spelling, then provide practice for students to apply the skill. This can be done using Sound Boxes (Elkonin boxes) and counters, or simple hand gestures (e.g., moving your hand from right to left as you move from sound to sound while saying and stretching the sounds in a word).

Here are some sample words for dictation for a typical lesson in most programs.

Words for Dictation: *cup*, *bug*, *fun*

This list contains a small set of words all focusing on the short *u* sound.

Now look at the list I revised. It is only slightly longer, but contains a few words with previously taught short vowels. It is also organized so that it starts with a word beginning with a continuous sound (making it much easier to stretch the sounds). In addition, the list contains words with different numbers of sounds to give varied oral segmentation practice (a critical phonemic awareness skill linked to writing).

Dictation List: *up* (two sounds), *fun* (three sounds), *rub* (three sounds), *cut* (three sounds), *bugs* (four sounds), *map* (three sounds), *fix* (four sounds), *lock* (three sounds)

(Note: The letter *x* stands for the sounds /ks/. That's two sounds.)

3. Rereading decodable stories: The rereading of previously read books and stories is a great way to build fluency. It is also ideal for extending practice of skills over multiple weeks. Most programs have students revisit books read only during the initial instructional cycle, which is generally one week. However, to ensure practice with skills previously taught, I work with teachers to create a system in which students systematically reread stories. This can be accomplished in many ways. In one school district I visited, once students read a decodable story, they were given a one-page story sheet (just the text of the story—not the pictures) to put in their reading folder, which students kept at their desks. These stories were numbered in sequence. The reason the teachers gave a story sheet was that distributing and managing a large number of little books (e.g., all those decodable stories from the reading program) was difficult. So, the teacher typed in the text of each story read (two per week) and made copies for the students. Most stories fit on one page. Then, during small group instructional time when students were working independently or with partners (i.e., not meeting with the teacher), the students were assigned specific stories to reread each day. The teacher would list on the board the number or numbers of the stories to reread. So, for example, on Monday, the students might reread Story Sheets 4 and 5. On Tuesday, they might reread Story Sheets 6 and 7, and so on. In this way, the teacher could easily cycle through the stories from the previous four to six weeks.

Reading with partners during independent work time is far better than doing worksheets or other similar types of activities.

To hold students accountable for the rereadings, the students had to reread the stories to a partner. The partner followed along, then signed and dated the story on the back (which the teacher periodically checked). Not only did students have extended practice reading stories with review skills, but reading with partners during independent work time is far better than doing worksheets or other similar types of activities. The students interacted with, supported, and assisted their partner in any way necessary. Some teachers also send these story sheets home for students to reread with families. This helps parents see their child's growing reading skills.

Teachers with a wider range of resources created story sheets for *new* stories focusing on each previously taught skill instead of having students reread the same story so many times. Other teachers added follow-up discussion questions and prompts for the partners to use following the rereading, including retelling the story in their own words, answering basic comprehension questions, finding details in the story, extending the story through writing, circling all the words with a specific phonics pattern, and so on.

4. Word building and word sorts: In word building, the teacher has students use a limited set of letter

4 BEST EFFECT

Decodable Text Follow-Ups

- Have students retell the story (orally and in writing).

- Answer *who, what, where, when,* and *why* questions. Find and read aloud text evidence to support answers.

- Extend the text through writing. Change the ending. Write what happens next. If informational, write a summary and then create a list of questions about the topic.

- Circle words with specific phonics patterns, create a list, and sort the words.

cards to build a series of words that generally vary by only one or two letters. For example, a word building set for short *u* might include the following letter cards (*u*, *b*, *c*, *g*, *p*, *r*, and *t*) and series of words to be built in this sequence (*up*, *cup*, *cut*, *but*, *bug*, and *rug*). To build in review and repetition, a teacher would modify the sequence of words to include a few with review skills, such as *up*, *cup*, *cap*, *cat*, *cut*, *but*, *bat*, *bag*, *bug*, *big*, *rig*, *rag*, and *rug*. The new set of letter cards only adds the short vowels *a* and *i*.

In word sorts, students are given word cards and asked to sort them by related sounds or spellings. For example, for short *u*, students might be given the following word cards: *but*, *cut*, *hut*, *bug*, *dug*, and *rug*. They would then sort the words by phonogram -*ut* and -*ug*. To build in review and repetition, the words *bag*, *tag*, and *rag* or *big*, *dig*, and *rig* could be added. In this way, words with previously taught skills could be included. These words also require students to fully analyze and carefully distinguish them from the -*ut* and -*ug* words as they are quite similar in spelling (*ug*, *ag*, *ig*).

Word-building and word-sort sets are available for download at http://resources .corwin.com/blevinsphonics.

In these and other ways, you can easily add a systematic and purposeful review and repetition cycle to your basic instruction where it might be lacking *without* significantly increasing instructional time. In addition to these simple fixes, make sure you have at your fingertips review lessons and small group activities for the skills taught during the previous four to six weeks so you can pull over a group of students at any time to work on these skills as you notice needs based on their reading and writing progress. Keep a running folder with these resources "at your ready." If your reading program has print or online resources with mini-lessons for each skill, collect these lessons and put them in individual folders (e.g., by individual skill like *Dd*, or by a cluster of skills like short vowels). Add other resources such as short reading passages and links to whiteboard and online activities.

ONE-ROOM SCHOOLHOUSE | ## Differentiate Instruction During Small and Whole Group Time

Most teachers are accustomed to providing small group instruction based on student needs. This can occur as a result of

1. Noticing students who struggle during the whole class lesson, thereby needing an immediate reteaching or additional time to practice

2. Noticing students who are struggling with a skill over time and have yet to master it as evidenced by their misreading of words containing that phonics element or their lack of correctly using that phonics skill when writing

3. Using a comprehensive phonics survey to place students within a phonics scope and sequence and providing targeted small group work to move them from that point on in the scope and sequence

4. Using weekly, unit, or standardized test results to target skills not yet mastered

What is more challenging, and less often seen, is the incorporation of review skills in whole group instruction. Our classrooms are filled with a diverse range of abilities and needs. Each year, these gaps feel like they are widening. Certainly, principals could assist in limiting the range of abilities in any given classroom to assist teachers (and some do). But, because of the stigma of tracking and its often-cited negative effects, this isn't common. However, decreasing the range of abilities in a classroom can be accomplished in ways that are effective and limit the problems associated with tracking. For example, in one school where I taught, each teacher was given two to three basic groups of students. I was given two groups: a large group of below-level students and a small group of on-level students. These on-level students were shy students who the principal felt would blossom if they were the "stars" in my classroom. As such, they would help their less-capable classmates and develop a stronger sense of their abilities.

Now, to many, this smacks of tracking. However, what made this situation different was that my goal (as stated by my principal) was to work so hard in developing the skills of my students that they moved out of my classroom. That's right. The students' placement in my classroom could be temporary based on student growth. Plus, there was great pride and motivation in getting students back on track to the point that they could function successfully in higher-performing groups. This setup ensured that students in lower-performing groups weren't written off or given watered-down curriculum. Just the opposite. All efforts were made to get

4 BEST EFFECT

Advanced Learners During Whole Group Lessons

- Add specific blending and dictation lines for these students. It only takes an extra 30–60 seconds to address these words.

- Provide lessons on advanced phonics skills while other students are rereading their decodable stories with partners. There's no need to form small groups. Just direct these students' attention to the front of the room.

- Introduce and highlight multisyllabic words, syllable patterns, and words with affixes that appear in whole group readings. Select one to three words from each story to briefly address.

- Provide more advanced reading selections related to the story's topic or theme for students to read independently and use as basis for whole group writing and research exercises.

these students up to grade level and beyond. While it was sad to lose a student (when we would periodically reassess his or her placement and adjust accordingly), it was a great feeling of success to see a student move on to another classroom. Unfortunately, what I see in most schools is each classroom filled with four to five (or more) levels and many students not getting the time and attention they need because teachers are spread too thin. Above-level students are often ignored. I have yet to see another school use the system we used at my old school. Hopefully, someday I will.

ONE-ROOM SCHOOLHOUSE

But that's only part of providing differentiated whole group instruction. Regardless of what classroom I step into, I treat it like a one-room schoolhouse. Remember the old days—a time when students of all levels and grades were in the same classroom? Teachers taught targeted lessons toward specific grades (which students at other levels overheard and sometimes learned from) and wider lessons that all students benefited from. This same principle can be applied to our daily phonics lessons. How? Let's take one aspect of the lesson—the blending of words—as an example. Look at the words chosen for blending below. I have expanded on the previous blending lines a bit.

How does this list aid in differentiating instruction? It does in several ways. First, the organization of the blending lines goes from the easiest skills (Line 1, words that vary only by the first letter sound) to the most complex (Line 4, words that vary by all letter sounds). In this way, I can call on my struggling students (and/or listen more closely to them during choral readings of the blending lines) during Line 1, and so on. After the review lines (Lines 5 and 6), I have added a more challenging line of words for my above-level students. This takes the skill and applies it to more complex words (e.g., those with inflectional endings) or multisyllabic words. I only call on my above-level students to read these words. It takes less than a minute of everyone's time, but it pushes these students further in their phonics development. If the other students pick up these skills from listening, that's terrific and an added benefit, but they are not held responsible for this content.

Especially for
ADVANCED LEARNERS

Blending Lines

up	*cup*	*pup*	*but*	*cut*	*hut* (vary by beginning sound)
cup	*cut*	*bug*	*bun*	*hug*	*hum* (vary by ending sound)

cap	cup	pop	pup	bug	bag (vary by medial sound)
sun	rub	dug	fun	gum	jug (mixed set, target skill)
map	led	hip	rock	dot	rip (mixed review sets)
fell	tap	fog	beg	tan	lid (mixed review sets)
cups	hugs	buns	bugs	(challenge lines)	
cutting	hugging	bugging	humming	(challenge lines)	

Another example relates to the reading of decodable stories during phonics lessons. Most programs nowadays have more than one story per skill per week, due to the requirement for adoption in the California public schools. Since publishers have created these multiple stories (the state requires two per skill), schools in other states benefit from this. In these programs, generally the first story is read on one day, then reread on the next day. The second story follows on the subsequent day and is also reread on the day after that. While this practice is ideal for your on-level students and can benefit your below-level students (who might also need easier texts or texts with earlier skills during small group differentiation time), it is a waste of time for your above-level students. So what do you do? I generally have my above-level students read the book on the first day. It's a simple review, it confirms for me that they have mastered the skill, and they can assist in listening to other (lower-level) students read. However, to have them reread it on the second day is not a good use of their time. So, while the on-level and below-level students are rereading the story in pairs (to provide feedback and support) on the second day, I ask the above-level students to *stay* in their seats and face me. I then proceed to deliver a lesson on an advanced phonics skill—a skill further in the scope and sequence that they need instruction on. This is classic one-room schoolhouse. The other students are actively engaged in their whisper reading with their partners, I don't waste any time in moving students to another part of the classroom, and I simply and efficiently teach the lesson to those few students who need it. These types of one-room schoolhouse activities can be planned and implemented into whole group lessons far more regularly than they are.

Especially for
ADVANCED LEARNERS

ONE-ROOM SCHOOLHOUSE

Adaptive Technology

The burden of creating and maintaining a phonics scope and sequence that meets the daily needs of all your students is greatly lessened with the use of an

Courtesy of Rick Harrington Photography

adaptive technology phonics program. Adaptive technology holds the promise of future instruction. Companies are beginning to create phonics adaptive programs that can be used as stand-alone supports for classroom instruction (especially in the area of differentiation with ease) or with digital teaching and learning platforms. Although these programs have yet to meet their full promise, they are improving each year and hopefully will become a mainstay of phonics instruction in classrooms within the next 5–10 years. It is an area of instruction in which I have great interest, having designed a couple adaptive systems for publishers. Why? These programs create an individualized learning pathway for each student based on his or her strengths and weaknesses. Also, the stronger programs provide graduated levels of support based on students' responses as they complete the activities. Students receive just what they need when they need it— no more and no less. Plus, the better programs have loads of practice activities and built-in review to ensure mastery. It is a tool that can greatly assist you in providing all your students the differentiated support they need.

Success Ingredient 2: Scope and Sequence

Background and Key Characteristics	Best Practices and Look-Fors for Success	Common Instructional Pitfalls	Day Clinic: Examine Your Practices	Next Steps to Leap Forward
A strong scope and sequence • Starts with high-utility vowels and consonants • Focuses on making words as early as possible so students see the utility of the system • Uses a sequence that works for the majority of students, but has built-in differentiation • Recognizes that not all skills are equal	• Examine your scope and sequence with respect to the stages of reading development. • Examine the sample scopes and sequences provided, including one for guided reading levels.	• The fact that just because you have a sequence in place doesn't mean it's systematic • Lack of a significant review and repetition cycle in your curriculum (Most students need four to six weeks after initial introduction to achieve mastery.) • Following materials with fidelity without regard to your students' needs • Weak teacher knowledge of linguistics to make more-informed instructional decisions about how skills are related in the sequence and how they manifest themselves in reading and writing	Ask yourself: • Do you know your basic phonics scope and sequence without looking? (You should always have the big picture in mind—the prerequisite skills taught, what is coming next, etc.) • Does your instruction have a formal scope and sequence, or are you selecting skills based on each week's readings? If so, on what are you basing your decisions? How are you keeping track of which skills have been taught, when, and how many times to ensure ample review and repetition? • Have you noticed specific skills your students struggle with? Where are they in the scope and sequence? What has been taught before these skills? Is there a relation between this new skill and a previously taught skill? How much time are you spending on this skill? Is it at least four to six weeks? What support pieces do you have for students to practice this skill?	• Teach to mastery, rather than just exposure—which requires adjustments to your daily lessons. • Add a review and repetition cycle to current curriculum where it is lacking. • Differentiate instruction during small group and whole group lessons. • Use adaptive technology to create individualized learning pathways for all students.

(Continued)

(Continued)

Background and Key Characteristics	Best Practices and Look-Fors for Success	Common Instructional Pitfalls	Day Clinic: Examine Your Practices	Next Steps to Leap Forward
		• Lack of a match between phonics and connected text reading • Need for comprehensive phonics mastery assessment matched to scope and sequence to monitor progress over time • Overdoing it • Not devoting more time to nontransferable or challenging sound spellings for English learners	**Try it!** • Evaluate the books students are reading for one week as compared to the skills they're learning and previously taught skills. • Create an acceleration path for above-level students. • Note "bumps in the road" in the sequence and compare to related skills, adjusting as needed. • Regularly evaluate student writing for evidence of transfer.	

Courtesy of Rick Harrington Photography

Background and Key Characteristics

Blending is the main strategy we teach students to decode, or sound out, words (Resnick & Beck, 1976). It is simply the stringing together of letter sounds to read a word. For example, if a student sees the word *sat*, he will say the sound for each letter or spelling (/s/, /a/, /t/) and string or sing together the sounds (/sat/). Blending is a strategy that must be frequently modeled and applied in phonics instruction to have the maximum benefit for students. Research shows that teachers who spend larger than average amounts of time on blending— modeling blending and providing loads of practice blending words in isolation and in context (e.g., daily in early reading instruction and practice)—achieve greater student gains (Haddock, 1978; Rosenshine & Stevens, 1984).

When beginning to teach students how to blend words, it is best to use words that start with continuous sounds. These are sounds that can be stretched without distortion. These sounds include the vowel sounds and several of the consonant sounds (/f/, /l/, /m/, /n/, /r/, /s/, /v/, /z/). In this way, you can more easily model how to move from one sound to the next, blending them to form a word, as in /sssaaat/ to make /sat/. As a result, words like *am*, *sad*, and *fan* are great words for beginning blending models. If, for example, you chose the word *bat* instead to introduce how to blend words, there is a great likelihood you would add a vocalization to the end of the /b/ sound since it is a stop sound and very difficult to pronounce purely in isolation. What would result would sound like /buh/ to your students. Now imagine you ask students to string together the sounds in *bat* that you just pronounced individually (/buh/, /a/, /t). The resulting word would be /buh-at/, instead of /bat/. Once students understand the principle of blending, you don't need to worry about this as much. And, when sounding out words beginning with stop sounds like /b/, /k/, and /d/, you can move quickly from the first to the second sound in the word with no or minimal pause between them to avoid the vocalized "uh."

Two types of blending are common: *final blending* and *successive blending*. Each has its place in phonics instruction. In final blending, you blend one sound at a time as you work through the word. It looks like this for the word *sat*.

Final Blending

- The teacher writes the letter *s* (or displays a letter card), points to it, and says the sound /s/.

- The teacher writes the letter *a* (or displays a letter card), points to it, and says /a/.

- Then the teacher slowly slides her finger under the two letters as she blends the sounds to form /sssaaa/.

- The teacher repeats, but this time slides her finger under the letters and blends more quickly, /sa/.

- The teacher writes the letter *t* (or displays a letter card), points to it, and says /t/.

- The teacher slowly slides her finger under all three letters in the word, stringing together the sounds to form /sssaaat/.

- The teacher then repeats at a faster pace and says, "The word is *sat*."

This is the type of blending I recommend when first introducing the principle of blending to your students. It allows you to slowly work through the process of sounding out a word while reinforcing each letter sound. However, this is not the most efficient form of blending, and I wouldn't continue it past the first few weeks—after students understand the principle behind blending and have had some practice doing it on their own.

Extending the Use of Final Blending for Struggling Readers

The only time I recommend going back to final blending is when working with struggling readers during small group differentiation time. Why? If you notice that some of your students are struggling to blend words, it is helpful to work through the word sound by sound to identify if a specific sound spelling (e.g., the vowel letter sound) is standing in the way. That is, are there specific letters and sounds that the student hasn't mastered or is confusing with other letter sounds? This information will assist you in meeting that student's specific phonics needs. As a result, you might need to reteach certain skills and provide extended practice with them. If your student does know each letter and sound in the word, but cannot blend the word, then the issue might be related to phonemic awareness. That is, the student might struggle with oral blending or retaining the sounds long enough in working memory to blend them together.

Successive blending is a more efficient form of blending that you will use for the bulk of your phonics instruction. In successive blending, you run your fingers under the letters in a word and string them together. It looks like this for the word *sat*.

Successive Blending

- Write the word on the board (or display it using letter cards).
- Put your finger at the beginning of the word. Slowly run your finger under the letters in order as you string together the sounds, /sssaaat/. Do not pause between sounds. Each sound must "melt" into the next sound.
- Slowly compress the word. Therefore, go from /sssaaat/ at a slow pace to /ssaat/ a bit faster to /sat/ at a normal speed. Tell students that the word is *sat*.

Best Practices and Look-Fors for Success

The most important aspects of a successful blending strategy include

- Modeling and applying blending frequently (every day for early readers until they can do it with ease)
- Ensuring that the blending work you do with students prior to reading stories contains enough words to provide adequate practice and helps frontload words students will need in reading the stories for the day or week (e.g., minimum of 20 in Grades 1 and up)
- Selecting blending lines that contain minimal contrasts so students practice fully analyzing words
- Creating blending lines in such a way that they provide formative assessment information
- Ensuring that the blending lines contain differentiated practice to meet all students' needs
- Ensuring that the blending lines also contain sentences to provide connected text reading practice

I discussed blending lines a bit in the chapter on scope and sequence. Let me review and expand on that information. Following are example lines for a variety of skill types. Use these samples as a model for the number and types of words necessary for effective blending practice. They vary slightly based on the goal of the instruction. But what they all have in common is that they progress from easiest to most complex to provide differentiated student practice and ample opportunities for you to informally assess students. I recommend that the words you choose contain some from the stories students will read to frontload decoding these words. In addition, the sentences in the blending lines should be from or about these stories.

I recommend that the words you choose contain some from the stories students will read to frontload decoding these words.

When using these lines in your daily instruction, remember the following:

- **Model only one or two words at the beginning of the word set.** Let students do the work of decoding the remaining words. Provide corrective feedback as needed.

Sample Corrective Feedback Routine

Say, "My turn." Make the sound that students missed. Have them repeat the sound. Tap under the letter and say, "What's the sound?" Students chorally respond. Return to the beginning of the word. Say, "Let's start over." Blend the word with students again.

- **Have students read the words chorally the first time through.** Take note of words read softly (meaning a lack of confidence in reading the words or fewer students capable of reading them) and students who "fall out" as the lines get progressively more difficult.

- **Revisit the blending lines quickly by pointing to words in random order and calling on students to read each one.** Call on struggling readers for the early lines and more advanced readers for the challenge lines. Use a signal such as thumbs-up to engage all students in the activity (e.g., after one student reads the word, all other students give a thumbs-up to indicate whether or not the student is correct).

- **Use the blending lines for multiple days of instruction (e.g., the week) as a quick review or warm-up.** They can also be used during small group work for more in-depth modeling and practice.

- **Make copies of each week's blending lines or have students record them on a sheet of paper during independent work time to take home** for nightly reading with their families.

- **These "enhanced" blending lines should be a quick-paced activity** lasting no more than five minutes of instructional time. Do not belabor this activity.

- **The sentences can be drawn from upcoming stories, based on upcoming stories, and written in a way that builds meaningful chunks** to help students see related sentence parts (as in the examples below).

The frog hops.

The frog hops into the pond.

The dog barks.

The dog barks at the car.

Short-Vowel Example: Short *u*

Line 1 (vary initial sound)	*up*	*cup*	*pup*	*but*	*cut*	*hut*
Line 2 (vary final sound)	*cup*	*cut*	*bug*	*bun*	*hug*	*hum*
Line 3 (vary medial sound)	*cap*	*cup*	*pop*	*pup*	*bug*	*bag*
Line 4 (mixed set, target skill)	*bus*	*dug*	*fun*	*gum*	*jug*	*nut*
Line 5 (review words for mastery)	*map*	*led*	*hip*	*rock*	*dot*	*rip*
Line 6 (review words for mastery)	*fell*	*tap*	*fog*	*beg*	*tan*	*lid*
Line 7 (challenge words)	*truck*	*stuck*	*struck*	*fluff*	*stuff*	*plug*
Line 8 (connected text)	*The big red bug hid.*					
Line 9 (connected text)	*The big red bug hid under the rug.*					

Final-e Vowel Example: Long *a* (spelled *a_e*)

Note: Use minimal contrasts in the first line—previously taught skill compared to new skill—to go from "the known to the new" and emphasize the target skill.

Line 1 (minimal contrasts—new to known)	*hat*	*hate*	*tap*	*tape*	*cap*	*cape*
Line 2 (vary initial sound)	*bake*	*take*	*lake*	*came*	*same*	*name*
Line 3 (vary final sound)	*cake*	*came*	*brake*	*brave*	*made*	*make*
Line 4 (mixed set, target skill)	*late*	*game*	*Dave*	*fake*	*wave*	*vase*
Line 5 (review words for mastery)	*slip*	*trap*	*stick*	*flop*	*grass*	*clock*
Line 6 (review words for mastery)	*chip*	*shut*	*when*	*that*	*fish*	*with*
Line 7 (challenge words)	*tapping*	*taping*	*backing*	*baking*	*shaking*	*skating*
Line 8 (connected text)	*Dave can bake the cake for us.*					
Line 9 (connected text)	*Jane came over to skate with us.*					

Long-Vowel Example: Long o (spelled *oa*, *ow*)

Line 1 (minimal contrasts—new to known)	bat	boat	cot	coat	go	grow
Line 2 (vary initial sound, one spelling)	road	toad	goat	throat	coast	toast
Line 3 (vary initial sound, other spelling)	low	flow	glow	grow	snow	slow
Line 4 (mixed set, target skill)	foam	show	toad	float	blow	row
Line 5 (review words for mastery)	train	stay	plate	bike	main	cute
Line 6 (review words for mastery)	hope	tray	mile	paint	taking	baking
Line 7 (challenge words)	soaking	floating	showing	snowing	unloading	regrowing
Line 8 (connected text)	The slow boat floated down the river.					
Line 9 (connected text)	Did you hear that toad croak?					

r-Controlled Vowel Example: ar

Line 1 (minimal contrasts—new to known)	cat	car	cart	chat	chart
Line 2 (vary initial sound)	far	jar	card	yard	smart	start
Line 3 (vary final sound)	barn	bark	arm	art	part	park
Line 4 (mixed set, target skill)	scar	dark	chart	star	hard	farm
Line 5 (review words for mastery)	bird	girl	fort	more	verb	hurt
Line 6 (review words for mastery)	float	might	wheat	breeze	speed	few
Line 7 (challenge words)	market	marble	marker	target	farmer	smartest
Line 8 (connected text)	Where can I park my car?
Line 9 (connected text)	The farmer had a large, red barn.

Diphthong Vowel Example: *ou, ow*

Line 1 (minimal contrasts— new to known)	*shot*	*shout*	*moth*	*mouth*	*fund*	*found*		
Line 2 (focus on one spelling)	*cow*	*now*	*down*	*town*	*brown*	*drown*	*clown*	*crown*
Line 3 (focus on other spelling)	*out*	*round*	*sound*	*south*	*mouth*	*mouse*	*house*	
Line 4 (mixed set, target skill)	*couch*	*ground*	*how*	*frown*	*about*	*growl*		
Line 5 (review words for mastery)	*stir*	*verb*	*born*	*burn*	*sports*	*serve*		
Line 6 (review words for mastery)	*roar*	*porch*	*third*	*thorn*	*thirst*	*fork*		
Line 7 (challenge words)	*downtown*	*campground*	*doghouse*	*dropout*	*somehow*	*thundercloud*		
Line 8 (connected text)	*How do I drive to the next town?*							
Line 9 (connected text)	*My house is south of this town.*							

Common Instructional Pitfalls

Reading in context is like "putting the pedal to the metal" when it comes to phonics. It is when real learning occurs and is confirmed.

Many common pitfalls regarding blending exist. These include the following:

1. **Too much time is spent on decoding words in isolation instead of decoding words in connected text (e.g., through a decodable book or story).** The modeling of blending and the inclusion of blending lines is a *small* portion of the phonics lesson. Keep in mind that modeling how to blend words can also occur while students read simple stories via your corrective feedback. The blending lines provide an ideal way to practice blending words with the target skill before these words are included with lots of other words in a story or informational text. Because the focus of these connected texts is not solely on words with the target skill, students must use all they know about letters and sounds to read the words and make sense of the text. This is cognitively more demanding than reading isolated word lists and is therefore a more difficult task. The blending lines provide the necessary practice and scaffolding to help students successfully tackle these texts and take on that challenge. If too much instructional time is spent on isolated skill work, students won't have the necessary opportunities to apply these skills in real reading and writing situations—the kinds of application that students need to achieve mastery and accelerate learning. Reading in context is like "putting the pedal to the metal" when it comes to phonics. It is when real learning occurs and is confirmed. Far too many phonics programs have far too limited connected text reading. It should occur daily. In addition, struggling readers are often given more skill-and-drill work instead of application exercises, when in fact this model should be flipped for these students. They need even *more* reading practice.

2. **We need to work in our teacher teams to improve teacher knowledge of research-based blending routines and when to use each one.** For example, knowing the two types of blending (*final* and *successive*) and when to best use each is critical. (Use final blending with beginning readers and struggling readers to check knowledge of specific letter sounds. Use successive blending for most of your

4 BEST EFFECT

Blending Lines

- Provide robust blending lines after introducing a new phonics skill.

- Scaffold the blending lines so they provide differentiated practice that can be used as formative assessment.

- Reread the lines each day as a warm-up and send home the blending lines for at-home practice.

- Have students apply the blending work to connected text *every* day—do not limit phonics work to these isolated word lists.

blending instruction as it is more efficient.) In addition, having strong models of corrective feedback when students struggle with blending will provide the necessary instructional supports.

3. Often the words used to practice blending (in published programs) are low utility or have little relationship to the stories students will read in the upcoming lessons. The majority of the words in the blending lines should be high-utility words. That is, they should be words that students will likely encounter in their readings or use in their writings. For example, for short *a*, you could choose to have students practice blending words like *sat*, *cat*, *man*, and *bad* or words like *lab*, *tab*, *ad*, and *fad*. The first set of words has much higher utility and should be used. Keep in mind that you have limited instructional time. Take advantage of that time by selecting power words—words with the greatest use for your students. Also, scanning upcoming stories in your curricular materials and selecting words with the target phonics skill from those stories not only is a great way to

Courtesy of Rick Harrington Photography

frontload the decoding of some of those words, but gives you an opportunity to discuss their meanings with your English learners prior to reading.

It is important to include vocabulary work with your blending lines for your English learners. While the initial use of the lines should be fast-paced and brief, these valuable word lists can be used during small group time to review decoding *and* focus on meaning. For example, you might choose a few words each day from the blending lines to discuss meaning. Provide brief definitions, have students act out words, or offer synonyms and antonyms to highlight meaning. Here's an example using the blending lines below.

Especially for
**ENGLISH
LEARNERS**

Line 1	*up*	*cup*	*pup*	*but*	*cut*	*hut*
Line 2	*cup*	*cut*	*bug*	*bun*	*hug*	*hum*
Line 3	*cap*	*cup*	*pop*	*pup*	*bug*	*bag*

a. Provide photos of a *cup*, *hut*, *bun*, *cap*, and *bug*. Name each picture and have students repeat. Point out that a *cap* is a type of hat. Tell students that a *bug* is also called an insect.

b. Explain that *up* is the opposite of *down*, using hand signals.

c. Point out that a *pup* is a baby dog; it is short for *puppy*.

d. Demonstrate or act out how to *hug, hum,* and *cut* something. Have students repeat the actions as they say the words.

4. Don't overdo the modeling. Model only a word or two in the blending lines, then have the students do the heavy lifting by sounding out the remaining words. As the old saying goes, "Whoever does the thinking does the learning." If you model how to sound out each word, then have students repeat because you want to provide extra support for your struggling readers, you are actually doing them a disservice. These parrot activities do not increase learning. Sometimes early learning tasks are difficult and require effort. Allow students time to make the effort and trust that you will be there to provide the needed support after they have worked through the word giving their best effort. It is natural for us to want to protect our struggling readers from being overly frustrated. That is a good thing. However, we can't go overboard by not allowing them to do the essential work (thinking) important to learning.

Use final blending with beginning readers and struggling readers to check knowledge of specific letter sounds. Use successive blending for most of your blending instruction as it is more efficient.

Examine Your Practices

Now it's your turn. Ask yourself the following questions to examine your instructional practices and materials as they relate to blending.

1. Do I have enough words in my blending lines prior to reading a story?

2. Are some of the words linked to what students will read to prepare them for, or frontload, the decoding work with connected text?

3. Are the lists organized in a way that helps me assess students and engage them in full analysis of words? Am I able to use my lines to get formative assessment information regarding which students need more work with specific skills?

4. Are my lines differentiated enough to provide support for struggling readers, ample practice for on-level readers, and a challenge for advanced readers?

5. Are they read chorally first, then revisited multiple times (not calling on individual students first)?

6. Am I letting my students do the blending (limiting the modeling to only one or two words)? Am I letting my students decode the words first, without jumping in too quickly?

7. Do I have a corrective feedback routine that I regularly use to support my students?

8. Are my students noticing similarities and differences between minimal contrast words? Am I having conversations about words that help my students understand how words work?

(Note: Practice with minimal contrast sets helps students learn the importance of fully analyzing words when reading and become flexible in their understanding and use of a wide range of phonics patterns.)

Create blending lines for the following skills.

Focus Skill: Short *e*

Review Skills: All consonants; short vowels *a*, *o*, and *i*

Line 1   _____   _____   _____   _____   _____   _____   _____

Line 2   _____   _____   _____   _____   _____   _____   _____

Line 3   _____   _____   _____   _____   _____   _____   _____

Line 4   _____   _____   _____   _____   _____   _____   _____

Line 5   _____   _____   _____   _____   _____   _____   _____

Line 6   _____   _____   _____   _____   _____   _____   _____

Line 7   _____   _____   _____   _____   _____   _____   _____

Line 8   _____

Line 9   _____

Focus Skill: Long *a* (spelled *ai*, *ay*)

Review Skills: All consonants, digraphs, blends; all short vowels; final *e* (*a_e*, *i_e*, *o_e*, *e_e*, *u_e*)

Line 1   _____   _____   _____   _____   _____   _____   _____

Line 2   _____   _____   _____   _____   _____   _____   _____

Line 3   _____   _____   _____   _____   _____   _____   _____

Line 4   _____   _____   _____   _____   _____   _____   _____

Line 5   _____   _____   _____   _____   _____   _____   _____

Line 6   _____   _____   _____   _____   _____   _____   _____

Line 7   _____   _____   _____   _____   _____   _____   _____

Line 8   _____

Line 9   _____

Focus Skill: *r*-Controlled vowel *or, ore*

Review Skills: All consonants, digraphs, blends; all short vowels; all final *e*; all long vowels

Line 1   _____   _____   _____   _____   _____   _____

Line 2   _____   _____   _____   _____   _____   _____

Line 3   _____   _____   _____   _____   _____   _____

Line 4   _____   _____   _____   _____   _____   _____

Line 5   _____   _____   _____   _____   _____   _____

Line 6   _____   _____   _____   _____   _____   _____

Line 7   _____   _____   _____   _____   _____   _____

Line 8   _____

Line 9   _____

Now take a look at this sample text. What words would you focus on for your phonics lesson? What blending lines would you create?

Sample Text

On the Farm

Mr. Clark is a farmer. He has a large farm. On it is a big red barn.

Mr. Clark plants a garden each March. He grows corn and beans.

Mr. Clark has lots of chores each morning. He rides a tractor to do some of his work.

Mr. Clark feeds the animals, too. He has a black horse and four little pigs. When it is dark or stormy, the animals stay in the barn. That way, no harm can come to them.

Mr. Clark loves being a farmer.

Source: Blevins (2011b).

Focus Skill: _____

Review Skills: _____

Line 1   _____   _____   _____   _____   _____   _____   _____

Line 2   _____   _____   _____   _____   _____   _____   _____

Line 3   _____   _____   _____   _____   _____   _____   _____

Line 4   _____   _____   _____   _____   _____   _____   _____

Line 5   _____   _____   _____   _____   _____   _____   _____

Line 6   _____   _____   _____   _____   _____   _____   _____

Line 7   _____   _____   _____   _____   _____   _____   _____

Line 8   _____

Line 9   _____

Next Steps to Leap Forward

If you have a fairly strong blending routine in place, there are several ways to take it to the next level to ensure all students are benefiting from it.

1. Add review skills to your current blending word lists each day to extend the review cycle for previously taught skills. I recommend that you include words for at least four to six weeks after initial instruction. Vary the words you choose each week and don't select the most common words. For example, students will quickly learn *cat* and *big* because of their frequency in texts. So, to review previous skills, use important words that might not be already committed to memory by students, thereby requiring them to sound them out.

Include words for at least four to six weeks after initial instruction.

2. Add challenge words in your blending lines for all grades (kindergarten and up) to meet the needs of your above-level students. One good way to select these words is to consider a more complex application of your target skill.

For example, in kindergarten, you might be working on short-vowel *a* consonant–vowel–consonant (CVC) words such as *cat* and *fat*. You can upgrade these skills for advanced learners by adding words that begin with consonant blends or digraphs instead of single consonants. As a result, you might include words such as *flat* and *chat*. You would connect this work to small group lessons you are providing these students and texts you are giving them to read.

In Grade 1, if your focus is on short-vowel *a* CVC words and your above-level students are reading words with blends and digraphs, you can upgrade these skills for advanced learners by focusing on the next related skill in the scope and sequence—final *e*. As a result, you would include words such as *hat*, *hate*, *tap*, and *tape*. Or, you could include words with simple inflectional endings, such as *hats*, *bats*, and *bags* (focusing on plurals) or *batting*, *tapping*, and *slapping* (focusing on doubling the final consonant when adding *-ing*). Choose the skill to focus on based on your scope and sequence and the students' reading needs.

Especially for **ADVANCED LEARNERS**

In Grade 2, students need to transition to multisyllabic words at a much faster rate than is provided in most curriculum because they will encounter these words in increasing numbers in the books and stories they read. So, if you are reviewing short-vowel CVC words at the beginning of the year, then I recommend adding challenge words for *all* students that focus on a multisyllabic skill, such as

All whiteboard activities below are from *Teaching Phonics* by Wiley Blevins (2011b).

Source: Blevins (2011b).

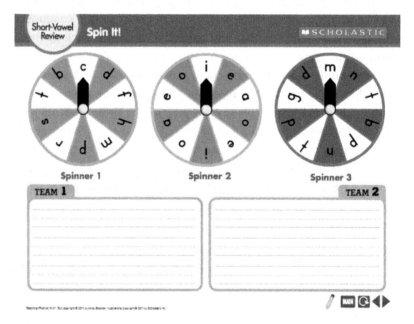

Source: Blevins (2011b).

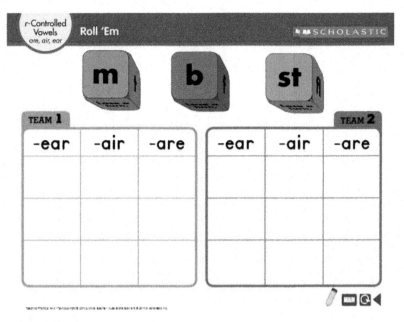

Source: Blevins (2011b).

Success Ingredient 3: Blending

Background and Key Characteristics	Best Practices and Look-Fors for Success	Common Instructional Pitfalls	Day Clinic: Examine Your Practices	Next Steps to Leap Forward
Blending is a primary decoding strategy and must be frequently modeled and applied.	• Use strategic blending lines (including minimal contrasts and differentiation for all students) and create them so they provide valuable formative assessment information. • Know the two types of blending (continuous and successive), each used at different times and for different purposes.	• Make sure the focus is applying skills to real reading and writing—not isolated skill work—in order for students to achieve mastery and accelerate learning. • Improve teacher knowledge of research-based blending routines and when to use each one (e.g., which is best for beginners and struggling readers). • Focus on high-utility words in lessons and words related to readings to frontload. • Include vocabulary work (especially for English learners). • Make sure the gradual release model is used (and the teacher isn't doing all the work/thinking).	Ask yourself: • Do I have enough words in my blending lines prior to reading a story? • Are some of the words linked to what students will read to prepare them for, or frontload, the decoding work? • Are the lists organized in a way that helps me assess students and engage them in full analysis of words? Am I able to use my lines to get formative assessment information regarding which students need more work with specific skills? • Are my lines differentiated enough to provide support for struggling readers, ample practice for on-level readers, and a challenge for advanced readers? • Are they read chorally first, then revisited multiple times (not calling on individual students first)? • Am I letting my students do the blending (limiting the modeling to only one or two words)? Am I letting my students decode the words first, without jumping in too quickly? • Do I have a corrective feedback routine that I regularly use to support my students? • Are my students noticing similarities and differences between minimal contrast words? Am I having conversations about words that help my students understand how words work? **Try it!** • Create differentiated blending lines using the skills listed. • Evaluate texts for blending skill focus and opportunities.	• Add review skills to blending word lists each day to extend the review cycle. • Add challenge skills for students above level. • Add "transition to longer words" work early on (beginning in late Grade 1 and all of Grade 2). • Add word pattern sorts (untimed and timed) to "train" students' eyes to see larger word patterns to make the transition to multisyllabic words easier. • Reconstruct blending lines so that they also serve as a formative assessment tool (going from easier to more complex skills). • Include technology (apps and whiteboard activities).

Background and Key Characteristics

Dictation is guided spelling practice. It is your way of modeling and providing supported practice for a student in how to transfer phonics skills from reading to writing. In the primary grades, students' spelling ability generally lags behind their reading ability. That is, students can read words by applying specific phonics skills before they can consistently write words accessing those same skills. This is beneficial for us to know. For example, if we see students correctly and consistently using consonant digraphs like *ch* or *sh* in their writing, then we know they can read words with these same sound spellings.

The great benefit of dictation is that it can accelerate students' use of taught phonics skills in their writing.

The great benefit of dictation is that it can accelerate students' use of taught phonics skills in their writing. That is one of the reasons some educators recommend connecting phonics reading skills to spelling skills in the early grades, and some states (e.g., California) have required this in their literacy standards. So, for example, you will often see in published programs phonics lessons on short *a* and spelling lessons that same week on a small set of short-*a* word families. Other educators have chosen to separate their phonics lessons from their spelling lessons and have created a spelling scope and sequence that is dictated solely by developmental appropriateness (see Bear, Templeton, Invernizzi, & Johnston, 2016; Moats, 2000). Whichever side of the debate you sit on, dictation can and should be a part of your weekly phonics instruction (at least twice a week) as it is a systematic way for you to show your students how to use their growing phonics skills in their writing, whether or not you expect mastery at that point in the school year, and no matter where the student is on the spelling developmental continuum.

The more opportunities students have to write and "try out" their developing skills, the better.

Courtesy of Rick Harrington Photography

Dictation is the primary way in which you will connect the skills you are teaching in reading to student writing. In addition to weekly dictation exercises, word-building activities (with letter cards) and both structured and unstructured writing experiences will provide opportunities for students to use their growing knowledge of how words work to express themselves in writing. The more opportunities students have to write and "try out" their developing skills, the better. In the early grades, this "invented spelling" or "phonic spelling" will provide you valuable formative assessment information on each student and assist you as you tailor your instruction, providing appropriate differentiated support.

Best Practices and Look-Fors for Success

It is ideal to incorporate a dictation (encoding) routine into your weekly instructional sequence—at least twice per week. Research and classroom practice show that students learn letter–sound relationships and spellings as they write. The formal, sequential dictation practice each week provides students with structured opportunities to develop their writing and spelling skills, with your guided support and corrective feedback.

Dictation is meant to be used *not* as an assessment tool, but rather as guided practice in writing words and checking students' understanding of sound–spelling correspondences. Since many of the words in the dictation exercises contain the new, target sound spelling introduced, students are not expected to have mastered the sound spelling. Below is an example dictation list for early Grade 1. It contains both words with the target sound spelling and at least one sentence using words with the new skill in context (and also incorporating any high-frequency words taught).

Dictation List (Focus Skill: Short a)

am   at   sat

Sam is sad.

Dictation Routine

- State aloud the first word in the dictation line, and have students repeat it. For those who have difficulty hearing the sounds in the words, you can provide two levels of support. One level involves saying the sounds more slowly while moving your hands from right to left while facing the class to illustrate beginning, middle, and end. A second level of assistance involves modeling the blending for each sound in the word. In effect, students are helped to hear and write one sound at a time.

(Continued)

(Continued)

- Then have students write the word. Walk around the room, and give help as necessary. This may include showing students the correct stroke procedure for writing letters or directing them to the correct spelling on the alphabet wall chart or frieze. In the case of multiple spellings for a single sound (such as *c*, *k*, and *ck*), tell students which spelling is correct and briefly explain why. For example, the *ck* spelling for /k/ appears at the end of a word and is preceded by a short vowel sound (e.g., *sick, back, rock, luck, deck*). Continue this procedure for each word in the dictation line. For the dictation sentence, read the entire sentence aloud and then focus on one word at a time. For multisyllabic words, do one syllable at a time.
- As each word is completed, provide feedback by writing the answer on the board so that students can correct their work. A key component of dictation is self-correction, in which students begin to notice and correct their errors.

This is what the routine would sound like in a classroom.

Dictation is meant to be used not as an assessment tool, but rather as guided practice in writing words.

- "This time, I want you to write a word that can be sounded out. The word is *sat*. Say *sat*." The students chorally say *sat*.

- "Sound *sat*." Here you slowly say the sounds in *sat* without any break and again showing beginning, middle, and end with right to left hand motions.

- Then you move your hand back to the beginning position and ask, "What's the beginning sound?" The students should say /sss/. "Write /sss/." Wait for the students to finish. Then ask, "What word are you writing?" *Sat*. "The beginning sound was . . .?" /sss/. "Next sound?" /aaa/. "Write /aaa/." Wait for students to finish. "What word are you writing? *Sat*. What do you have so far? /sssaaa/. Last sound? /t/. Write /t/."

- When students finish, ask them to chorally tell you the sounds in *sat* as you write the word on the board.

Follow the same procedure for all the words. While students are writing, around and monitor their work, paying more attention to those who are to experience difficulty. (Note: This teacher-assisted sound-by-sound pro critical for students who cannot segment sounds. Don't take shortcuts giving students the word, waiting for them to finish, and then writing the on the board. Some students will wait and copy what is on the board not learn to become independent. This is their time to try, to explore, their best attempts.)

- For the sentence, say, "Now you will write a sentence with [three] words. The sentence is *Sam is sad*. Repeat it. *Sam is sad*. What is the first word? *Sam*. How do we start a sentence? With a capital letter. Is *Sam* a word we can sound out or a word on our Sight Word Wall? Sound *Sam*." Use hand motions as before. "First sound?" Students say the first sound. "Write it. What word are you writing? What do you have so far? Next sound?" The students respond. "Write it." Continue in a similar manner until the word is done.

- "What sentence are you writing? *Sam is sad*. What have you written so far? *Sam*. What is the next word? *Is*. This is a word on the Sight Word Wall. If you know how to spell it, go ahead and write it. If you are not sure, check the Sight Word Wall."

- Repeat the above procedure with *sad*, treating it as a word that can be sounded out.

In order for dictation to be successful, consider the following:

1. Begin dictation as early as kindergarten. Oftentimes, I see dictation started too late in the instructional sequence. In early kindergarten, dictation might consist of you saying a sound and students writing the letter. You can then ask students to orally name any words that begin (or end) with that sound. As a result, the student's paper might look like this:

s   t   a

As students learn to sound out simple two- and three-letter short-vowel words, the dictation can progress to include both the writing of letters for sounds they hear and the writing of simple words. So, the student's paper might look like this:

s   t   a

at   sat

Finally, as students begin reading simple stories, the dictation can include writing simple sentences. The student's paper might look like this:

s   t   a

at   sat

I sat.

2. **When using Sound Boxes and counters to segment words by sound during phonemic awareness work (see earlier section on phonemic awareness), extend the work by having students replace each counter with a letter to form the word in print.** For example, imagine that the students have segmented the word *sat* using counters and their Sound Boxes. They would have three counters—one on each box. Their papers would look like this:

You would then ask the students, "What is the first sound in *sat*? Listen . . . /sssaaat/." Students answer /s/. Then ask, "What letter do we write for the /s/ sound?" Students answer *s*. "Replace the first counter with the letter *s*." Students write the letter *s* in the first box. Continue working through the word in this manner. This slow breaking apart of a word by sounds, then rebuilding it letter by letter, is a huge *aha* for many students and, if done consistently, teaches them to carefully think about the component sounds in a word when writing.

3. **If you notice students applying recently taught phonics skills in their writing, especially their freewriting in their journals, then dictation is having a positive impact.** Also, seeing students segment words—either by whispering each sound while writing or by using hand motions to break apart the word—shows that students are thinking hard about how words work, how to construct them, and how to use all they know about letters and sounds to form them in writing. I recommend periodically checking students' writing samples and journal entries for evidence of this transfer, then adjusting instruction accordingly, including forming small groups for additional dictation practice when transfer isn't evident.

Steps for Monitoring Student Writing

- Begin by making a checklist of the previous skills you have taught your students.

- Scan several pieces of their writing for words using those skills. Note on your checklist which students are not correctly using the skill in writing consistently.

- If it's a lot of students, continue to address this skill in whole and small group blending and dictation lessons.

- If it's only a few students, form small groups for differentiated instruction and practice with the skill.

Take a look at the student sample below. Which sound spellings do you think the student has mastered? Which sound spellings (or high-frequency words) might you focus on next for this student?

I no abowt pepl. Thay can hav pets. Thay can hav dogs. Thay can hav cats. That is rilley speshll. I like cats and dogs. I hav cats and dogs. Thay eat evrething.

Common Instructional Pitfalls

Many common pitfalls regarding dictation exist. These include the following:

1. While spelling instruction is common in Grade 1 and up, it generally consists of administering a pretest, providing a series of brief activities (e.g., word sort, using words in context sentences), and a posttest. **Often no attention is given to actual modeling of how to write words using the new skill and thinking aloud about that process.** That is the benefit of dictation and should be a key aspect of each week's encoding instruction. Instead of administering a pretest, use that time to do dictation (guided spelling) for a portion of the words. Choose sample words that show each spelling pattern in the week's spelling list (e.g., -at, -an). Then the complete list of words can be given to students to study and practice throughout the week. This will require you to reorganize the weekly spelling instruction in your current curriculum and/or replace specific activities. If you don't have a spelling curriculum (either built into your reading program or a separate spelling program), create one using your phonics scope and sequence as a guide.

It is through writing that all of a student's phonics knowledge is tested, confirmed, and consolidated. It is application at the highest level.

2. **Too often, spelling is treated in a haphazard manner.** Lists are created in which the words have no spelling connection (e.g., science or social studies words, theme words), which doesn't assist students in better understanding how words work because they don't see enough of any one pattern to generalize that information. Dictation is designed to formalize your approach to spelling and accelerate students' transitioning of phonics skills into writing. Without it, far too many students will struggle or delay that transition.

3. **Students need increased opportunities to write words.** It is through writing that all of a student's phonics knowledge is tested, confirmed, and consolidated. It is application at the highest level. Students do far too little writing in the early grades around their phonics skills. This includes dictation, but must be extended to writing about the stories they are reading. I recommend that students engage in this at least twice a week (e.g., after revisiting a book read the day before). This not only helps them express what they understood and learned from the stories, but because they are writing about stories containing many words with the target phonics skills, they will naturally use some of those words in their writing—thus gaining more practice in applying the new skill. (Plus, the words in the book provide support for struggling writers.) Using a new skill when

writing connected text is essential to master the skill and should be a regular part of weekly instruction. This writing can occur during independent work time or be used as a great homework assignment. Note that for English learners and struggling writers, you might wish to provide sentence stems to support their early writing attempts (e.g., *The frog _____. Ben went ____.*).

4. Dictation often starts too late. It should be started as soon as we teach students letter–sound relationships, then grow and build in length and complexity as students' abilities develop. I previously showed examples of how dictation can build throughout kindergarten. Likewise, in Grade 1, the dictation lines can grow in complexity (e.g., more difficult words and sentences). However, this is not an activity that should dominate instructional time. The length of the dictation lists should remain fairly brief (much shorter than blending lines), and only one or two sentences is sufficient, especially if you are doing dictation multiple times a week.

Examine Your Practices

Now it's your turn. Ask yourself the following questions to examine your instructional practices and materials as they relate to dictation.

1. Am I doing dictation each week? If so, how many times?

2. Which words am I choosing? How many words am I choosing? Am I including review words from previous weeks?

3. Do I regularly evaluate students' writing (e.g., at least once a week in journals or more formal writing assignments) for transfer of phonics skills? Do I use that information to adjust instruction (both small and whole group)?

4. Am I extending students' reading through writing activities, including summarizing or retelling in writing what they read, writing a new adventure with the same characters, creating a list of facts learned, extending the story to show "what happens next," and other ideas?

Note that for all these writing exercises, it is beneficial for students to begin by expressing these ideas orally first. This can be accomplished through the use of partners. Once students express their ideas orally and get help clarifying them, they will be better equipped to express them in writing. As James Britton (1983) says, "reading and writing float on a sea of talk." For example, I have seen teachers, before retelling a story in writing, draw a "retelling path" on chart paper and place it on the floor. The pathway includes the words *beginning*, *middle*, and *end* at varying points to show the major parts of the story. Students can work together to add words or pictures at each point to help them remember key events in the story. Then, one at a time, the students "walk" the story pathway as they orally retell it. You or classmates can assist the student walking the path to fill in key missing events or details. Then the student writes the retelling. This generally results in richer, more robust retellings.

Create dictation lines for the skills listed below. I have added one line for review words (I will detail their importance in the next section).

Dictation Line 1 (Kindergarten)

Focus Skill: Short *o*

Review Skills: All consonants, short *a*, short *i*

Line 1 (letter sounds)   _____   _____   _____

Line 2 (words with new skill)   _____   _____   _____

Line 3 (words with review skills)   _____   _____   _____

Line 4 (sentence)   _____

Dictation Line 2 (Grade 1)

Focus Skill: Long *o*

Review Skills: All consonants, consonant blends, consonant digraphs; all short vowels; long vowels *a* and *e*

Line 1 (words with new skill)   _____   _____   _____

Line 2 (words with review skills)   _____   _____   _____

Line 3 (sentence)   _____

Line 4 (sentence)   _____

Now list places in your weekly schedule in which you could include dictation. Consider replacing or modifying existing activities (e.g., modifying the spelling pretest, replacing a phonemic awareness activity with a Sound Box activity in which students orally segment a word using counters, then replace each counter with a letter or spelling).

Changes to My Weekly Phonics/Spelling Instructional Cycle

Monday: _____
_____
_____

Tuesday: _____
_____
_____

Wednesday: _____
_____
_____

Thursday: _____
_____
_____

Friday: _____
_____
_____

Next Steps to Leap Forward

If you have a fairly strong dictation routine in place, there are several ways to take it to the next level and ensure all students are benefiting from this valuable instructional practice.

1. Add review skills to dictation work each week to extend the review and repetition cycle. I recommend that, after you do dictation with a few words focusing on the target skill, you quickly add a few words with skills from the previous four to six weeks. Since you should do dictation more than once a week, you can focus on two or three review skills at a time. See the example below.

Dictation Line (Grade 1)

Focus Skill: Short *o*

Review Skills: All consonants, consonant blends, short vowels *a* and *i*

Line 1 (words with new skill)	*mop*	*not*	*fox*
Line 2 (words with review skills)	*clap*	*stick*	*lift*
Line 3 (sentence)	*The frog can hop.*		
Line 4 (sentence)	*The frog hops on top of the rock.*		

2. Add writing follow-up work whenever reading a decodable story or book. Since students will draw from the words in the stories to write about it—whether a retelling, an extension, or a new adventure with the characters—they will have practice applying the new skill to writing and have a support tool (the actual text in the story) as needed. This is a natural way to extend that practice and offers better follow-up work to the reading of a story than a worksheet. It also provides great assignments for independent work time (while you meet with small groups) or for homework or can be used as a journal prompt.

3. Include technology, such as apps and interactive whiteboard activities, in your dictation work. Whiteboard activities, such as the one shown on the next page, are easy to create yourself and can be one of the centers students visit during independent work time. Many apps exist that focus on spelling. These include, but are not limited to, *Montessori Crosswords*, *Magnetic Alphabet*, *Word Wall HD*, and *ABC Writing*.

From *Teaching Phonics* by Wiley Blevins (2011b), the following is an easy white-board activity you can create using simple graphics and boxes.

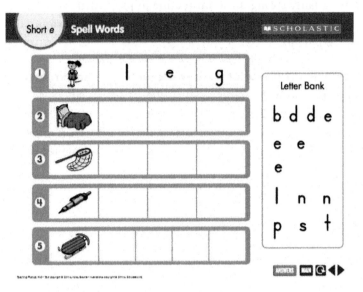

Source: Blevins (2011b).

Montessori Crosswords offers support in breaking apart a word by sound and letter and provides corrective feedback, as needed.

Source: Courtesy of Montessori Crosswords.

Magnetic Alphabet is one of those generic apps that can be used for a wide variety of activities. I like having this app in a learning center. I then create an activity card students use with the app. For example, I might list a word family, such as *-at*, and ask students to make words in this family. Or, I might have them build their spelling words for the week.

Source: Courtesy of Magnetic Alphabet.

4 BEST EFFECT

Selecting Apps

- Select apps with a wide range of scope (many skills and levels).

- Look for apps with instructional supports (e.g., feedback). Make a mistake when testing out the app; if you hear feedback (rather than a "ding"), then the app is more appropriate for classroom use.

- Create a central location (e.g., on your school or district website) for teachers to provide app reviews and recommendations. It is the easiest way to quickly learn about a wide range of tried-and-true apps.

- Ask your school's Parent–Teacher Association for funds to purchase apps. A small amount of money can go a long way.

Word Wall HD has great modeling of sounding out words and loads of practice writing words with high-utility phonograms. Plus, these words are then applied to simple connected text stories. It is an app with a wide range of skills, so it can be used for extended periods of time throughout the year to match what you are teaching in phonics and spelling.

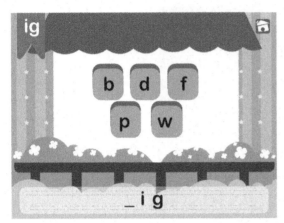 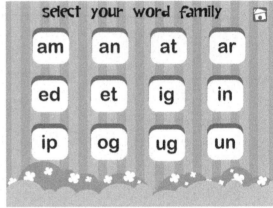

Source: Courtesy of Word Wall HD.

4. Differentiate spelling in small groups through the use of leveled word lists (based on your weekly lists) and using adaptive phonics technology programs that offer a spelling component. Many publishers are now developing these programs, and they are the best way to meet students exactly where they are in terms of their instructional needs. Adaptive technology programs quickly assess students' abilities, place them in a phonics and spelling continuum, and offer the right amount of support and practice based on how they respond to the activities provided. If students need a ton of practice, the program can provide that. If they master a skill quickly, students are moved forward in the scope and sequence. These programs are still in their infancy stage in terms of the promise of adaptive technology. However, the promise is great, and I see steady improvements in these individualized learning programs each year. It's very exciting! You want to find a program with a wide range of adaptive components and a strong back engine to support student movement through the program. Do your research on the programs publishers offer, ask *lots* of questions, and try out a few exercises (including making mistakes to see how the program responds) before selecting one that best suits your needs. In a truly adaptive technology, students do not all move through the content in the same linear pathway. Make sure that, whatever technology you use, the pathways are complex enough to meet the needs of all your students and deep enough to provide sufficient instruction and practice.

5. Establish a formal schedule for analyzing students' writing to adjust instruction. Like I mentioned earlier, we learn a lot about our students' understanding of how words work and their mastery of phonics skills through a careful analysis of their writing. On the next page is that quick assessment I gave at the beginning of the school year to a bunch of first graders in New York City. By asking them to write five simple words, I learned valuable information on Day 1 of school that helped me begin differentiated instruction on Day 2. Take a look again at some of the student samples. I was able to sort students into five groups according to instructional needs. See what you can figure out from these students' spellings. What are their instructional needs? How could you adjust instruction for them immediately?

Spelling Assessment: Day 1, First Grade

Evaluate each student's responses on the spelling assessment. Record your reflections on the next page. The five words stated were *sad*, *big*, *rake*, *coat*, and *flower*. Think about which sound spellings the students have mastered. Are they consistent? Are they overgeneralizing any skills? Are they avoiding certain sounds and spellings? Analyze the mistakes. Are the incorrect spellings similar to other spellings formed in the same way when spoken? Also, what does this tell you about the students' phonemic awareness skills? Are they representing words with more sounds with more letters? Do they have a clear sense of how words work?

Visit http://resources.corwin.com/blevinsphonics to see some example comments teachers have written about each student's assessment.

Student 1	Reflections
1. sad	
2. big	
3. rakce	
4. cote	
5. flower	

Student 2	Reflections
1. sad	
2. bag	
3. rak	
4. kot	
5. flar	

Student 3	Reflections
1. sd	
2. bg	
3. lk	
4. kt	
5. fw	

Student 4	Reflections
1. Seivrne	
2. Bog	
3. Rigvet	
4. Tetvai	
5. Levneia	

Student 5 (Student Name: Stephanie)	Reflections
1. ePraH	
2. PEBL	
3. eHPLn	
4. sieHgt	
5. cSeph	

Success Ingredient 4: Dictation

Background and Key Characteristics	Best Practices and Look-Fors for Success	Common Instructional Pitfalls	Day Clinic: Examine Your Practices	Next Steps to Leap Forward
Dictation is guided spelling; it connects reading to writing and accelerates the transition of skills.	• Use a strong dictation routine weekly. • Begin as early as kindergarten (first level with sound–letter matches, then slowly progressing to words and simple sentences). • Build on oral segmentation work during phonemic awareness (e.g., using Sound Boxes and counters). • Analyze student writing for evidence of transfer.	• Lack of formally teaching students how to transfer reading skills to writing through guided dictation early on (e.g., modeling thought process) • Teaching spelling in a haphazard manner • Need for increased opportunities to write words • Starting too late • Need to use sentence stems to build base of useful sentences with each word (e.g., for English learners)	Ask yourself: • Are you doing dictation each week? If so, how many times? Which words are you choosing? How many words are you choosing? Are you including review words from previous weeks? • Do you regularly evaluate students' writing (e.g., in journals or more formal writing assignments) for transfer of phonics skills? Do you use that information to adjust instruction (both small and whole group)? • Are you extending students' reading through writing activities? **Try it!** • Create dictation lines for the skills listed. • List changes to your weekly schedule to include the routine.	• Add review skills to dictation work to extend the review cycle for previous skills. • Add writing work to the reading of decodable texts and stories (a natural way to highlight the writing of words with target phonics patterns). • Include technology (apps and whiteboard activities). • Evaluate student writing on a regular basis with teacher teams and adjust instruction as needed.

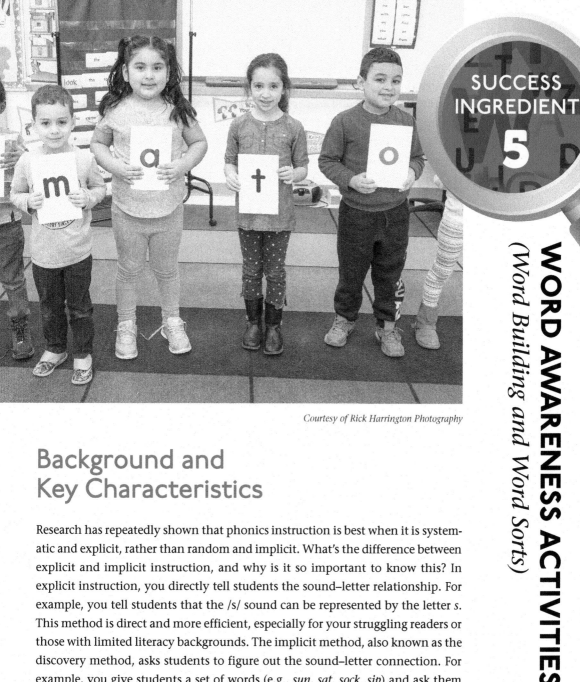

Courtesy of Rick Harrington Photography

Background and Key Characteristics

Research has repeatedly shown that phonics instruction is best when it is systematic and explicit, rather than random and implicit. What's the difference between explicit and implicit instruction, and why is it so important to know this? In explicit instruction, you directly tell students the sound–letter relationship. For example, you tell students that the /s/ sound can be represented by the letter *s*. This method is direct and more efficient, especially for your struggling readers or those with limited literacy backgrounds. The implicit method, also known as the discovery method, asks students to figure out the sound–letter connection. For example, you give students a set of words (e.g., *sun*, *sat*, *sock*, *sip*) and ask them what these words have in common. Through the course of your discussion, you guide students to notice that they all begin with the /s/ sound and this sound is represented by the letter *s*. Some believe that when students discover these connections on their own, they are more likely to remember them because of the cognitive processes it took to arrive at the information. While there is research support for the discovery method in other areas of learning, this approach fails for beginning readers learning phonics because too many children lack the prerequisite skills needed to arrive at the desired learning—that the /s/ sound is represented by the letter *s*. To arrive at this conclusion, a student needs sophisticated phonemic awareness skills in order to segment off the first sound of each word and note the similarity, as well as have multiple experiences with words to know the name of the letter *s* and its distinction from other letters. This is asking a lot of early readers. So it is not efficient to have a method that potentially leaves students out of the learning as their initial introduction to a skill. The explicit method is clear, simple, and efficient, and achieves the desired learning outcome.

While the initial introduction of phonics skills is best using an explicit approach, that does not mean there shouldn't be a time during the instructional cycle in which students play with and explore letter sounds. In fact, I think this exploration is *critical* for students to consolidate and solidify their learning of how words work. Yes, the initial introduction begins this learning efficiently, but it takes time and loads of experiences reading and writing words for that knowledge to be mastered. These types of "exploratory" activities provide essential "thinking" time for students as they incorporate new learning into already established learning. When phonics instruction fails, it often does so because it is rote, unthinking, and not applied to real reading and writing experiences.

Word Building and Word Sorts

The two best types of exploration exercises that increase a student's word awareness are *word building* and *word sorts*. Both should be an important part of the phonics instructional cycle for each skill introduced.

In **word building**, students are given a set of letter cards and asked to create a series of words in a specified sequence. This can occur during both whole and small group lessons. Generally, each new word varies by only one sound spelling from the previous word (there can be more variance as students progress in skills). For example, students might be asked to build, or make with letter cards, these words in sequence: *sat, mat, map, mop*. Notice how each word varies from the preceding word by only one sound spelling.

There are two types of word building, each with a clearly defined instructional purpose.

1. **Blending:** In this type of word building, students are asked to make a word, such as *sat*. They are then told to change the letter *s* to the letter *m* and read the new word formed. Thus, the primary goal is for them to blend, or sound out, the new word formed. This is the type of blending you might want to start out with at the beginning of an instructional cycle. It allows students time to decode many words with the new target phonics skills, while also reviewing previously taught skills.

2. **Word awareness:** In this type of word building, students are asked to make a word, such as *sat*. They are then told to change *sat* to *mat*. This is cognitively more demanding than the blending-focused word building. Why? Students have to consider how the words *sat* and *mat* vary (i.e., which sound is different), which letter must be removed from *sat*, which letter must be added to form *mat*, and in which position in the word it must be added. That's a lot of thinking about how words work! This is why word building is so beneficial. Students gain flexibility in how to use sound spellings in words. This type of word building is one you can do later in the week after students have had more exposure to the skill. And, by repeating the word-building sequences multiple times throughout the week with different instructional focuses, you only need to create one set of words and one set of letter cards—saving you valuable planning time.

4 BEST EFFECT

Managing Letter and Word Cards

- Store sets of letter (and word) cards in zip-up clear bags labeled for each student.

- Write the letters (or words) students will need for the daily lesson on the board. Students gather and organize the letter cards as part of their "get-ready-for-school" morning routine.

- Have students cut out letter and word cards during independent work time to save instructional time. Make copies of the cards on card stock, if available.

- Encourage students to work with the letter and word cards during independent work time, repeating word-building and -sort exercises independently or with partners, or just exploring the letters and words (e.g., seeing which words they can form on their own).

Word sorts also allow students time to think about how words work by drawing their attention to important and common spelling patterns. Generally, in word sorts, students are given a set of words that have something in common (e.g., all contain the same vowel sound, but with different spellings as in *-at* and *-an* words for short *a*). Students are asked to sort the words by their common feature.

There are many types of word sorts, each with a distinct instructional purpose. Below are three of the most common types.

1. Open sorts: In these sorts, students are not told how to sort the words. That is, students are given a set of words and allowed to sort them in any way they want. This is a good first sort with a set of words because it tells you a lot about how students are thinking about words and what aspects of words they notice. So, for example, if you gave the students these words—*boat, road, throw, grow, soap, show*—and they sorted them by first letter sound, that would indicate the students are noticing very simplistic aspects of words (initial letter sounds) and not noticing what is truly common among these words (they all contain the long *o* sound spelled *oa* or *ow*).

2. Closed sorts: In these sorts, students are told how to sort the words. So, for the long-*o* sort above, students are told to sort the words into two piles, each representing a different spelling for the long-*o* sound (*oa* or *ow*). These are fairly simple and direct sorts since students are visually scanning each word for a specified spelling pattern. The value in this type of sort is the conversation you have with students *following* the sort. For example, you should ask students questions like "What do you notice about these words?" "What do you notice about these spellings for long *o*?" and "Do you know other words with these spellings?" Then you guide students (if they don't notice on their own) to understand that the *oa* spelling for long *o* never appears at the end of the word. This is really valuable information about how words work that will have positive benefits for students' future reading and writing. That is, when students encounter a new word when writing (e.g., the word *snow*), what do they do? They think about each sound and the associated spelling. When they get to the long-*o* sound at the end of the word *snow*, they know they have two options that they've learned—*oa* or *ow*. Which is a better option? Well, if you've had the discussion during the sort, the students will know that the *ow* spelling is the only option since *oa* cannot appear at the end of a word. This is the kind of thinking and knowledge building we want to have happen as a result of word sorts. Word sorts are far more than a quick, visual, sorting task.

3. Timed sorts: In these sorts, students are told how to sort a set of words, but are given a limited amount of time to do so. This is an ideal type of sort to do with a set of words students have been working with all week (having already completed open and closed sorts). Adding the element of time creates a game-like feel to the task that students enjoy. However, even more, it provides an important benefit. Getting students to readily notice larger word chunks in words, such as these common spelling patterns, is essential to reading longer, multisyllabic words. As students progress up the grades, the words they encounter will increase in length. Instead of reading new words like *cat, soap,* and *barn,* they begin to encounter words like *unexpected, predetermined,* and *unhappily.* It becomes inefficient for students to attack these words letter by letter. Instead, larger chunks of these words need to visually "pop" out so the reader has fewer word parts to tackle, making the reading easier. Doing timed sorts helps to train the eye to see quickly these larger word chunks in new, unfamiliar words. Plus, it's a great way to extend the practice with the word card sets you have created for the week—giving you more bang for your time in creating and organizing the materials for these sorts. You can also set up these timed sorts on a whiteboard using simple word cards and a timer for students to practice during independent work time alone or with a partner.

This is the kind of thinking and knowledge building we want to have happen as a result of word sorts.

Other common sorts include sound sorts, pattern sorts, meaning sorts, buddy sorts, blind sorts, and writing sorts. For more information about these other types of sorts, I recommend *Words Their Way* (Bear, Templeton, Invernizzi, & Johnston, 2016).

Best Practices and Look-Fors for Success

Word building and word sorts should be a key component of each instructional cycle for every new phonics skill. Below are instructional routines for each.

WORD-BUILDING ROUTINE

See the "Sample Word-Building and Word-Sort Schedule" on page 122 for how to incorporate word building into your weekly instructional cycle.

Step 1: Introduce

Name the task and explain its purpose to students.

Say, "Today we will be building, or making, words using the letters and spellings we have learned."

Step 2: Model

Place letter cards in a pocket chart (or use letter cards on a whiteboard) to form the first word you are building. Model sounding out the word. Remember to (a) build words using the new, target sound spelling; (b) add words with review sound spellings as appropriate to extend the review and application of these skills to achieve mastery; and (c) use minimal contrasts to require students to fully analyze words and notice their unique differences (e.g., *sat* and *mat*, *pan* and *pen*, *rip* and *trip*, *hat* and *hate*, *cot* and *coat*).

Say, "Look at the word I've made. It is spelled *s–a–t*. Let's blend the sounds together to read the word: /sssaaat/, *sat*. The word is *sat*."

Step 3: Guided Practice/Practice

Continue by changing one (or more) letters in the word. Have students chorally blend the new word formed. Do a set of 8–10 words.

Say, "Change the letter *s* in *sat* to *m*. What is the new word?" Or, if students are more advanced in their understanding, say, "Change the first sound in *sat* to /m/."

If the focus on word building is word awareness (instead of blending like the above example), then tell students what the next word in the sequence is and give them time to form the new word. Circulate and provide assistance and corrective feedback (modeling your thinking process, modeling how to blend the word, etc.). Then build the new word in the pocket chart (or on the whiteboard), modeling aloud your thinking.

WORD-SORT ROUTINE

See the "Sample Word-Building and Word-Sort Schedule" on page 122 for how to incorporate the various types of sorts into your weekly instructional cycle.

Step 1: Introduce

Name the task and explain its purpose. Distribute the word cards and read each with students to make sure they know all the words. If you are doing a closed sort, introduce the categories in which students will be sorting the words.

Step 2: Sort

Have students sort the words. If you are doing a closed sort, model sorting one or two of the words. Then have students sort the remaining words. Circulate and ask students questions about why they are putting specific words into each category.

Step 3: Check and Discuss

Review the words in each sort category. Ask students what they learned about these words from doing the sort. Guide students to the word awareness aspect of each sort that will assist them in reading and writing. Have students store the word cards for future sorts (e.g., a timed sort using these words).

You know word building and word sorts are having a positive effect on students' word awareness when you see an increase in students' ability to comment on how words work and evidence that students are fully analyzing similar words and thereby avoiding common reading issues that result when only portions of a word are looked at in order to read it (e.g., using the beginning and perhaps ending letters, then guessing from those clues and the picture). Also, as students have regular weekly practice analyzing words in this way, you will start to see them noticing common spelling patterns and other aspects of words before you teach them. For example, I've had students point out sound spellings that we will study in upcoming weeks *before* I formally teach them because they have seen several words with this sound spelling in books we read together or I read aloud (e.g., the digraph *sh* in *she*, *should*, and *fish*).

These types of word awareness activities create students who become *word detectives*—curious about words and always on the lookout for what is common among words. This improved word awareness has generative effects as students progress through the grades and encounter words with prefixes, suffixes, spelling changes, and Greek and Latin roots.

Word building and word sorts are having a positive effect on students' word awareness when you see an increase in students' ability to comment on how words work and evidence that students are fully analyzing similar words.

Common Instructional Pitfalls

Many common pitfalls regarding word building and word sorts exist. These include the following:

1. Word building and word sorts require the use of materials—often lots of small pieces of paper, letter cards, or word cards for each student to use throughout the activities. **Allowing the organization, distribution, and collection of these materials to gobble up too much instructional time is a common problem.** Instructional time is valuable, and time lost in transitioning from one activity to another (as in distributing and organizing sets of letter cards) is time you can't get back. I have observed teachers losing 10–15 minutes of instructional time distributing and collecting letter or word cards in a short 20- to 30-minute phonics lesson. This adds up quickly. In one week, it can be over an hour of instructional time lost. We can't let this happen.

There are many ways to avoid this. One is to recognize that these transitional times are important instructional moments and plan ahead for them. This can take many forms. For example, you can sing "The Alphabet Song," play a phonemic awareness game, review your action rhymes for each letter, call out words for students to chorally spell, and so on. The important point is that you use this time to review and reinforce important skills, while keeping students engaged and on task. This has the added benefit of diminishing student behavior issues.

Another effective tactic is to treat the organization of these materials as part of a student's "get ready for school" or "get ready for learning" procedures. For example, some teachers I've worked with write the letter cards that will be used for that day on the board. As students enter the room in the morning, part of organizing themselves for the day includes gathering and organizing these letter cards (in addition to putting away their coats, adding their names to the lunch count, writing in their journals, or whatever morning procedures are already in place). Therefore, when it's time to begin the word-building exercise, the students have their letter card sets on their desk and ready to go. No time wasted. For word cards used during word sorts, students might need to cut out their word cards prior to school beginning (or finish this task during center time).

2. **Too often, word sorts are treated as a simple task of rearranging word cards, and the follow-up discussion to better understand how words work never occurs.** Every word sort should end with a question, such

as "What did you notice about these words?" or "What did you learn about these spelling patterns?" Students need to verbalize their thinking about words. Use follow-up questions to guide students if they don't readily recognize important features of the spellings and patterns. For example, "Where does this spelling appear in all the words? How is it different from the other spellings for this sound?" You might include a couple "outlier" words in a sort to highlight a concept. For example, if you are sorting words with final *e* like *hope*, *rope*, *home*, *joke*, and *note*, you might want to add the words *come* and *some* and point out common words that break the rule or pattern.

Every word sort should end with a question, such as "What did you notice about these words?" or "What did you learn about these spelling patterns?"

3. Sometimes the words chosen for these activities aren't the right ones. That is, the words used in these activities should be primarily high utility—words students will frequently encounter in reading or use in writing. Too often, I see word sets with rare words. To spend all that instructional time on words with such low utility does not make sense. Maximize student learning by focusing your activity word sets on those power words students *really* need to master to gain access to wider texts and words they can easily draw upon when writing or analyzing new words with the same or similar patterns. Think about the words you use (e.g., when was the last time you said, read, or wrote *vat*?). If you don't use the words in regular speech and writing on a weekly basis, then your students won't either, and they shouldn't be included in the activity.

Examine Your Practices

Now it's your turn. Ask yourself the following questions to examine your instructional practices and materials as they relate to word building and word sorts.

1. Am I including word building and word sorts as part of my regular weekly instructional cycle?

2. Am I using word building for both a blending focus and a word awareness focus throughout the instructional cycle?

3. Am I using multiple types of sorts to achieve different instructional goals?

4. Have I selected words for word building and word sorts that students are likely to encounter in their readings or use in their writings?

5. Am I having discussions following the word sorts about student observations and providing time for the students to verbalize their growing thinking about how words work?

6. Have I tried various ways to decrease the amount of time I spend transitioning from one activity to the next in order to maximize my instructional time and minimize waste?

7. Have I created word-building sequences and word-sort lists for each week's target skills, plus included review words to build toward mastery?

Below is a sample weekly instruction cycle schedule in which word sorts and word building have been added. Use this as a model to create your own schedule.

Sample Word-Building and Word-Sort Schedule

Monday	Tuesday	Wednesday	Thursday	Friday
Open Word Sort (as follow-up to spelling lesson)	**Word Building** (blending focus, as part of phonics lesson) **Closed Word Sort**	Students **repeat Closed Word Sort with partners** during independent work time **Repeat Word Building** (blending focus) **in small groups** with students needing additional support	**Word Building** (word awareness focus, as part of phonics lesson)	**Timed Word Sort** **Repeat Word Building** (word awareness focus) **in small groups** with students needing additional support

My Schedule

Monday	Tuesday	Wednesday	Thursday	Friday

Use the skills and sample word sets below to create word-building and word-sort sets for your students. For word building, limit the amount of letter cards to 8–10 (fewer for kindergartners). Note that long-vowel, complex-vowel, r-controlled-vowel, and diphthong spellings can appear on one card (e.g., *oa*, *oo*, *ar*, *oi*). For word sorts, you can include a word or two that don't fit the pattern.

Word Building

Sample Word-Building Word Set (focus on short *o*, review short *a* and *i*):

mop, hop, hip, tip, top, mop, map, mat, hat, hot

Letter Cards: *o, a, i, h, m, p, t*

Word-Building Word Set (focus on short *e*, review all short vowels):

_____

Letter Cards: _____

Word-Building Word Set (focus on long *a*, review all short vowels and long *o*):

_____

Letter Cards: _____

Word Sorts

Sample Word-Sort Word Set (focus on short *o*):

Word Cards: *hop, mop, top, hot, not, lot*

Word-Sort Word Set (focus on short *e*):

Word Cards: _____

Word-Sort Word Set (focus on long *a*):

Word Cards: _____

More Word Building

Here is a set of letter cards. What words can your students build? In what sequence?

Letter Cards:

h	i	d
r	e	a
m	n	p

1.

2.

3.

4.

5.

More Word Sorts

Here are the top 37 phonograms that can be used to make nearly 500 primary-grade words. What word sorts could you make with these common spelling patterns? Where in your scope and sequence would you use them?

ail	ash	est	ing	ore
ain	ask	ice	ink	uck
ake	at	ick	ip	ug
ale	ate	ide	ir	ump
ame	aw	ight	ock	unk
an	ay	ill	oke	
ank	eat	in	op	
ap	ell	ine	or	

Sort 1
Words:
Student Outcome/Learning:

Sort 2
Words:
Student Outcome/Learning:

Sort 3
Words:
Student Outcome/Learning:

Word-Building Card Template

Next Steps to Leap Forward

If you have fairly strong word-building and word-sort routines in place, there are several ways to take them to the next level and ensure all students are benefiting.

1. Upgrade your work with word building by creating an additional activity each week called word ladders. What distinguishes word ladders from the typical word-building exercise is the added element of vocabulary. Instead of asking students to build a word like *top*, then change it to make the word *mop*, you ask the students to change "one letter in the word *top* to name something you use to clean a wet floor." This is a fun activity to do at the end of the week when students have had multiple exposures to the words and know their meanings. Students love figuring out the clues, then determining how to make the new word.

This is a fun activity to do at the end of the week when students have had multiple exposures to the words and know their meanings.

Following is an example of a word ladder I helped create with teachers from a large, urban school district. It was simple and fun to create. Published versions of word ladders also exist, most notably those created by Timothy Rasinski. I love his work (e.g., Rasinski, 2005), and these books are a great resource. I've also included a blank template for your reference. Additional word ladders I created can be found at http://resources.corwin.com/blevinsphonics.

2. If you are having difficulty creating word lists for word building, more information is available in *Making Sense of Phonics: The Hows and Whys* (Beck & Beck, 2013) or by visiting www.education.pitt.edu/EducationalResources/Teachers/LEADERS/TeachingStrategies/WordBuilding/WordBuildingSoundsSequence.aspx. These resources can serve as great starting points. Additional word-building lists I created can be found at http://resources.corwin.com/blevinsphonics.

3. If you are struggling with what to point out during your conversations with students following word-sort exercises, possible linguistic understandings that will help students in reading and writing can be found in *Spelling: Development, Disability, and Instruction* (Moats, 1995), *Speech to Print: Language Essentials for Teachers* (Moats, 2010), and *Words Their Way* (Bear et al., 2016). Additional information for sorts can be found at http://resources.corwin.com/blevinsphonics.

Name _____   Date _____

Short-*o* Word Ladder

Read the clues, then write the words.
Start at the bottom and climb to the top.

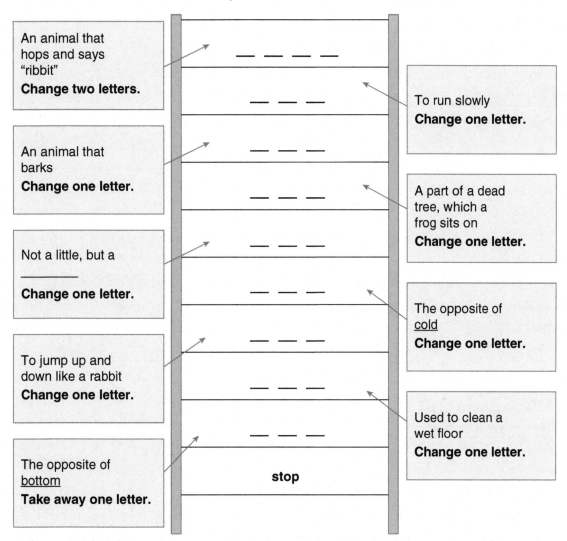

An animal that hops and says "ribbit"
Change two letters.
— — — —

To run slowly
Change one letter.
— — —

An animal that barks
Change one letter.
— — —

A part of a dead tree, which a frog sits on
Change one letter.
— — —

Not a little, but a _____
Change one letter.
— — —

The opposite of cold
Change one letter.
— — —

To jump up and down like a rabbit
Change one letter.
— — —

Used to clean a wet floor
Change one letter.
— — —

The opposite of bottom
Take away one letter.

stop

Source: The word ladder strategy was invented by Timothy Rasinski (2005) and is adapted here with the permission of the author.

Name _____ Date _____

_____ **Word Ladder**

Read the clues, then write the words.
Start at the bottom and climb to the top.

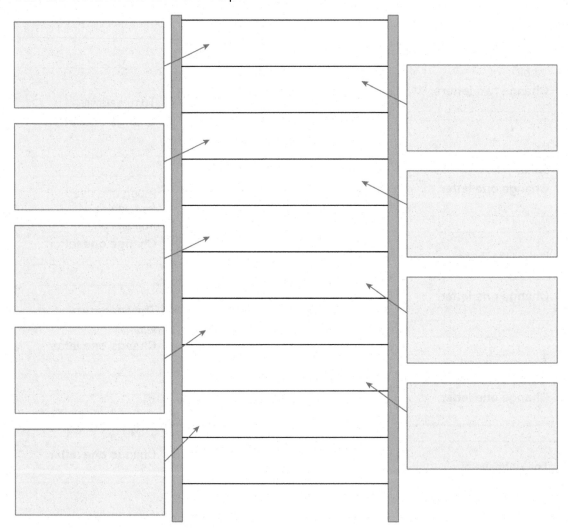

Source: The word ladder strategy was invented by Timothy Rasinski (2005) and is adapted here with the permission of the author.

Remember questions that guide students to note the position of specific spellings in words (e.g., the *oa* spelling for long *o* never appears at the end) and other generalizations about spelling usage (e.g., the *ck* spelling for /k/ as in *stick* or *luck* appears at the end of a one-syllable word and is preceded by a short vowel; you use the *k* spelling when the /k/ sound is preceded by a consonant as in *desk* or *milk*) are most beneficial.

4. To save time and effort, use the same word lists for all your word-building activities for one instructional cycle. This results in students only needing one set of letter cards for the week and ensuring multiple exposures to those all-important high-utility words. Do the same for your word-sort sets. The same series of words can be used for open sorts, closed sorts, and timed sorts. You can even create other activities using the cards, such as Living Words, a word-building activity in which five to seven students hold the letter cards for the word-building exercise in the front of the room and physically move to create the words in sequence, and Family Sort, in which all students are given a word card and asked to find other students in the class who belong to their "family." Students gather in corners of the room by family and explain to the class how they are related. Word cards can also be used by partners during independent work time to quiz each other (reading and spelling) or as aids for words to build on computer or app games.

Courtesy of Rick Harrington Photography

5. Many apps and whiteboard games exist for word building and word sorts. A few are shown below. These are arguably the easiest to create yourself as they require few elements—word cards, letter cards, sorting space. Adding a timer to the word sorts makes the activity fun and purposeful for review. The activities I showed earlier (pages 88–89) for word blending (e.g., those with spinners and spinning cubes) are also good for word building.

The following whiteboard activity is from *Teaching Phonics* by Wiley Blevins (2011b). It is easy to create these sorts for any skill you are teaching. Add a timer, and you have a fun practice activity students will enjoy during center time.

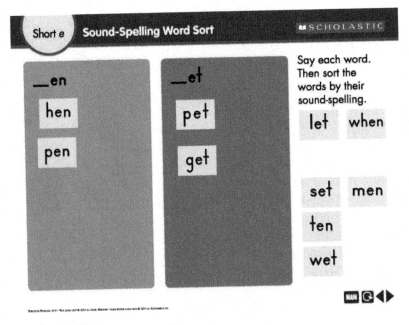

Source: Blevins (2011b).

The activities that follow are also from *Teaching Phonics*. Elements like spinners and spinning cubes make the activities fun, thought-provoking, and game-like.

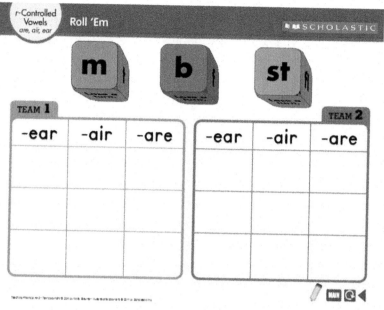

Source: Blevins (2011b).

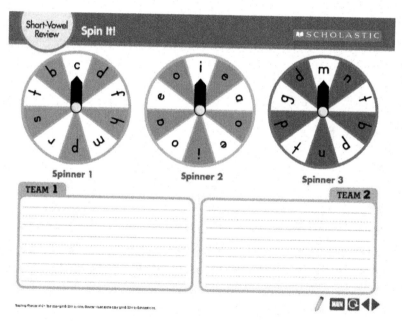

Source: Blevins (2011b).

Success Ingredient 5: Word Awareness Activities

Background and Key Characteristics	Best Practices and Look-Fors for Success	Common Instructional Pitfalls	Day Clinic: Examine Your Practices	Next Steps to Leap Forward
• Word building and word sorts are two great word awareness activities that should be a part of weekly instruction. • Word building has two main forms: blending focus and word awareness focus. • Word sorts can be varied for different instructional purposes (e.g., open, closed, timed). • These activities are used to consolidate and solidify learning. • It is necessary to provide time for students to explore how words work and play with key spelling patterns.	• Use the strong word-building and word-sort routines provided. • Notice how students talk about words and word parts.	• Too much time lost during transitions (e.g., distributing and collecting materials) • Lack of follow-up talk about how words work following activities, such as word sorts • Lack of focus on high-utility words in the activities	Ask yourself: • Am I including word building and word sorts as part of my regular weekly instructional cycle? • Am I using word building for both a blending focus and a word awareness focus throughout the instructional cycle? • Am I using multiple types of sorts to achieve different instructional goals? • Have I selected words for word building and word sorts that students are likely to encounter in their readings or use in their writings? • Am I having discussions following the word sorts about student observations and providing time for students to verbalize their growing thinking about how words work? • Have I tried various ways to decrease the amount of time I spend transitioning from one activity to the next in order to maximize my instructional time and minimize waste? • Have I created word-building sequences and word-sort lists for each week's target skills, plus included review words to build toward mastery? **Try it!** • Rearrange your weekly schedule to incorporate these activities. • Create word-building sets using the skills provided. • Create word sorts using the words provided.	• Add word ladders to weekly practice (adds element of vocabulary and fun). • Use the same word lists for different types of word sorts and word building to better utilize materials and scaffold learning. • Upgrade the conversations you are having about how English words work during the activities. • Include technology (apps and whiteboard activities).

Courtesy of Rick Harrington Photography

Background and Key Characteristics

High-frequency words are the words we see most often in printed English. While English has over 600,000 words, a relatively small number appear so frequently in print that they need to be addressed during instruction because a lack of mastery of these words will result in fluency issues. In addition, some of these words do not follow common sound-spelling generalizations (i.e., they are "irregular") or are needed to create early reading texts before they become decodable based on the phonics skills students have learned at that point in their instructional sequence.

The good news is that we know which words to target in our instruction. Surprisingly (to me, at least), only 13 words account for more than 25% of the words in print (Johns, 1980). These words include *a, and, for, he, is, in, it, of, that, the, to, was,* and *you.* And, 100 words account for approximately 50% of the words in print (Adams, 1990; Carroll, Davies, & Richman, 1971; Fry, Kress,

A relatively small number appear so frequently in print that they need to be addressed during instruction because a lack of mastery of these words will result in fluency issues.

& Fountoukidis, 1993). About 20% of the 250 words most frequently used by students in their writing (70%–75% of the words they use) are function words such as *a*, *the*, and *and* (Rinsland, 1945).

We know which words to teach.

What this means is that we know which words to teach. Several high-frequency word lists exist and are commonly used by teachers and publishers. These include the Dolch Basic Sight Vocabulary, which contains 220 words (no nouns); the Fry 100; and the *American Heritage Word Frequency Book* (Carroll, 1971) top 150 words. I have combined these three lists on the next page to give you the "power" high-frequency words to teach in kindergarten through Grade 2. Students should be fluent with these words by the end of Grade 2. I've marked with an asterisk (*) which words are "irregular," meaning they do not follow common sound-spelling generalizations, cannot be sounded out, and must therefore be taught in a different way. This is based on the standard skills taught in K–2 in most curriculum. Note that your curriculum might vary. These words should be assessed beginning in Grade 3, and words not mastered should be reviewed as they will negatively affect a student's fluency and comprehension of text. Fortunately, we know which words are most problematic and require greater review and practice. These include the following:

1. Reversals: *was* and *saw*, *on* and *no*

2. Visually similar words without concrete meanings: *of, for, from*

3. Words with *th* and *wh*: *there, then, them, that, this, their; where, when, what, with, were, why*

Fortunately, we know which words are most problematic and require greater review and practice.

I recommend in Grades 3 and up that you review 10 words a week with struggling readers to ensure mastery and assess students on these words every few months to check progress. If you don't have a mastery assessment or checklist, use the list I've provided. Circle each word students correctly identify rapidly. Underline each word students correctly, but not automatically, identify. Focus additional instruction on those words underlined and those incorrectly read.

High-Frequency Word List Top 248

1. a	26. better	51. don't*	76. give*	101. is
2. about	27. big	52. done*	77. go	102. it
3. after	28. black	53. down	78. goes	103. its
4. again*	29. blue	54. draw	79. going	104. jump
5. all	30. both*	55. drink	80. good	105. just
6. also	31. bring	56. each	81. got	106. keep
7. always	32. brown	57. eat	82. green	107. kind
8. am	33. but	58. eight*	83. grow	108. know
9. an	34. buy*	59. even	84. had	109. laugh*
10. and	35. by	60. every	85. has	110. let
11. another	36. call	61. fall	86. have*	111. light
12. any	37. called	62. far	87. he	112. like
13. are*	38. came	63. fast	88. help	113. little
14. around	39. can	64. find	89. her	114. live*
15. as	40. carry*	65. first	90. here	115. long
16. ask	41. clean	66. five	91. him	116. look
17. at	42. cold	67. fly	92. his	117. made
18. ate	43. come*	68. for	93. hold	118. make
19. away	44. could*	69. found	94. hot	119. man
20. back	45. cut	70. four*	95. how	120. many*
21. be	46. day	71. from*	96. hurt	121. may
22. because	47. did	72. full	97. I	122. me
23. been*	48. different	73. funny	98. if	123. more
24. before	49. do*	74. gave	99. in	124. most*
25. best	50. does*	75. get	100. into	125. much

(Continued)

(Continued)

126. must	151. pick	176. six	201. those	226. well
127. my	152. place	177. sleep	202. three	227. went
128. myself	153. play	178. small	203. through*	228. were*
129. never	154. please	179. so	204. time	229. what*
130. new	155. pretty*	180. some*	205. to*	230. when
131. no	156. pull	181. soon	206. today*	231. where*
132. not	157. put*	182. start	207. together*	232. which
133. now	158. ran	183. stop	208. too	233. white
134. number	159. read	184. such	209. try	234. who*
135. of*	160. red	185. take	210. two*	235. why
136. off	161. ride	186. tell	211. under	236. will
137. old	162. right	187. ten	212. up	237. wish
138. on	163. round	188. than	213. upon	238. with
139. once*	164. run	189. thank	214. us	239. word*
140. one*	165. said*	190. that	215. use	240. words*
141. only	166. same	191. the*	216. used	241. work*
142. open	167. saw	192. their*	217. very*	242. would*
143. or	168. say	193. them	218. walk	243. write
144. other*	169. see	194. then	219. want*	244. years
145. our	170. seven	195. there*	220. warm*	245. yellow
146. out	171. shall*	196. these	221. was*	246. yes
147. over	172. she	197. they*	222. wash*	247. you*
148. own	173. show	198. things	223. water*	248. your*
149. part	174. sing	199. think	224. way	
150. people*	175. sit	200. this	225. we	

Source: **Based on Fry Words: The First Hundred, Dolch Basic Sight Vocabulary 220, and** *American Heritage Word Frequency Book* Top 150.

Best Practices and Look-Fors for Success

The best instructional practices related to high-frequency words are those that accelerate learning and focus on mastery. Research shows that readers store "irregular" words in their memory in the same way they store "regular" words (Gough & Walsh, 1991; Lovett, 1987; Treiman & Baron, 1981). That is, readers pay attention to each letter and the pattern of letters in a word and associate these with the sounds that they represent (Ehri, 1992). More recent brain research has further confirmed this understanding.

Research shows that readers store "irregular" words in their memory in the same way they store "regular" words.

According to brain research, three parts of the brain must be activated in order for us to learn a word. These parts include where the sounds are stored, where the word's meaning is stored, and where the word's spelling (individual letters) is stored.

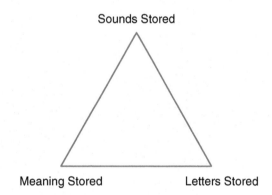

Sounds Stored

Meaning Stored   Letters Stored

Now think about that for a minute and what it means for your instruction. Are you teaching high-frequency words in a way that activates all three parts of the brain necessary to learn a word in your initial introduction of that word? I once heard Isabel Beck describe it as leaving a deep, dark imprint on the brain when students first learn a new word instead of a soft, gray imprint that could easily fade away. To do this during initial instruction, I use the Read–Spell–Write–Extend routine that follows.

Read-Spell-Write-Extend Routine

Read: Write the word in a context sentence and underline the word. Read aloud the sentence, then point to the target underlined word and read it aloud. Have students say the word.

Say, "I *see* a cat. [Point to the word *see*.] This is the word *see*. What is the word?"

Spell: Spell the word aloud and have students repeat. Briefly point out any letter sounds or spellings students might already know or that are the same as other words students have learned.

Say, "The word *see* is spelled *s–e–e*. Spell it with me: *s–e–e*. What is the first sound in the word *see*? What letter do we write for the /s/ sound? Does the word *see* begin with the letter *s*?"

Write: Ask students to write the word multiple times as they spell it aloud. This can be done in the air, on dry erase boards, or on paper.

Say, "Watch as I write the word. I will say each letter as I write it. [Model this.] Now it's your turn. Write the word three times. Say each letter as you write it."

Extend: Connect the word to other words students have learned. For example, if you have a word wall, work with students to place the word in the correct spot on the wall. Then ask students to generate oral sentences using the word. Have them work with a partner, and provide sentence frames as support, if needed. Then have students write their oral sentence. Build on these sentences as appropriate. These extension activities can be done on the days following the initial instruction when you have additional time to extend in this way.

Say, "Turn to a partner and finish this sentence: 'I see a ____.' [Provide time for partners to share.] Now, write on your paper the sentence you just said. [Wait for students to finish.] Let's expand our sentences. Tell your partner something about what you see. For example, if your sentence was 'I see a book,' you can build on it to say something like 'I see a big book' or 'I see a book about dinosaurs.' Tell your partner your expanded sentence. [Provide time for partners to share.] Now write your new sentence."

This routine offers a valuable tool for engaging all parts of the brain needed to learn a word, accelerates that learning, and aids in helping irregular words "stick." When you say the word, the "sound" part of the brain is activated. When you read the context sentence and discuss it, the "meaning" part of the brain is activated. And, when you spell the word, the "letters" part of the brain is activated. You know this routine is working when students quickly and automatically identify high-frequency words when reading connected text and easily distinguish visually similar words (e.g., *when* and *then*). To misread one of these words can have a serious impact on understanding.

Common Instructional Pitfalls

Many common pitfalls regarding the teaching of high-frequency words exist. These include the following:

1. The most common method of introducing high-frequency words is to provide them in a context sentence, read the sentence aloud, underline the word, pronounce it for students, and have them repeat. Students then get follow-up work, which might consist of writing a sentence for each word or using each to fill in the blank in a series of sentences. **This method does not activate all parts of the brain needed to learn the word and is not the best type of introduction.** Instead, replace it with the Read–Spell–Write–Extend routine.

2. **Certain types of high-frequency words are more challenging than others and require more instruction, practice, and assessment.** I listed these major types earlier: reversals (e.g., *was* and *saw*), visually related or confusing words with no clear meanings attached (e.g., *of, for, from*), and words with *th* and *wh* (e.g., *there, where, what, that*). Unfortunately, most programs treat all high-frequency words equally. As a result, the same amount of time is given to them for instruction and practice. You need to pull out the words we know cause students more difficulty, list these in the classroom and in students' journals, and do continued work with them throughout the year until students show mastery. This includes more frequently assessing them.

3. **High-frequency irregular words are often treated as "oddball" or "alien" words students just have to memorize. However, some of these words have something in common and actually form their own unique word families.** Learning them as families sharing a similar spelling pattern will help students better remember them. I recommend reorganizing the sequence in which you teach irregular sight words to take advantage of this. For example, teach the following irregular words as families: *come* and *some*; *to, do,* and *who*; *could, would,* and *should*; *there* and *where*; *give, live, have,* and *love*. Point out features of these words that will help students remember them, such as the fact that no English words end in the letter *v*. (I know you're all trying to think of one now. And yes, there are some names like *Liv* or *Tel Aviv*, but there are no pure English words that end in the letter *v*.) If a word ends in the /v/ sound, you must add an *e* to the end. This is a great tip for students to remember when writing—no more writing "hav" for *have*.

4 BEST EFFECT

Reorganize Your High-Frequency Words

- Teach "irregular words" that have something in common at or near the same time to take advantage of these spelling patterns. Reorder your curriculum's scope and sequence.

- Irregular word families include *come* and *some*; *to, do,* and *who*; *could, would,* and *should*; *there* and *where*; and *give, live, have,* and *love*.

- Address those words that are most confusing more consistently and for longer periods of time. These include reversals (e.g., *was* and *saw*), similar words with no clear meanings attached (e.g., *of, for, from*), and words with *th* and *wh* (e.g., *there* and *where, what* and *that*).

- Spend more time on instruction and practice of these words, assess them every two to three months, and focus on them more in reading and writing activities.

4. The amount of instruction and practice these words receive is often limited to the week of the initial instructional cycle. This is not sufficient. The belief is that these words will appear in enough future texts that students will have ample exposures to commit them to memory. Unfortunately, our young students are often reading controlled texts that focus on a particular week's skills without much attention to reviewing previously taught words. To resolve this, teachers can create cumulative phrase and sentence lists for students to practice regularly. That is, during each week of instruction, students create a phrase or sentence (with the teacher) using each new high-frequency word. This growing list can be at the back of their writing journals or in a separate (e.g., homework) folder. Throughout the week, students read these phrases and sentences as part of their normal instruction. This can include reading them to a partner during small group or independent work time, taking them home to read to a family member, or occasionally reading them to you (the teacher) as part of an informal check-in on their progress. Students read their growing phrase and sentence list from the beginning of the year each week. That's a lot of exposures

To resolve this, teachers can create cumulative phrase and sentence lists for students to practice regularly.

Keep in mind that most students need 8–12 exposures to a word to commit it to memory, but our struggling readers need 50 or more exposures.

to these words. Keep in mind that most students need 8–12 exposures to a word to commit it to memory, but our struggling readers need 50 or more exposures. These cumulative phrase and sentence lists can help a lot in achieving those repetitions. These phrases and sentences also assist English learners in understanding how these common, but sometimes irregular, words function in oral and written English. This is especially important for easily confused words like *of, for,* and *from* for which you can't easily define or explain their grammatical usage. Below is a student sample.

My Sentences

1. I am <u>from</u> New York.

2. I eat a lot <u>of</u> pizza.

3. Is that book <u>for</u> me?

Examine Your Practices

Now it's your turn. Ask yourself the following questions to examine your instructional practices and materials as they relate to high-frequency words.

1. How do I teach high-frequency words—both regular and irregular?

2. Am I organizing the words in a way that will benefit my students? If I'm using a packaged curriculum (e.g., a basal reading program), am I adding related words to help my students see common word families?

3. How much practice do I give my students for reading and writing these words? Are there ways I can add to my weekly practice activities to increase my students' work with and exposure to these all-important words?

4. How am I assessing these words? Am I assessing students reading them? Am I assessing students using them in writing? Is my assessment cumulative so I can look at progress over an extended period of time to check on mastery?

5. Am I doing more work with those words I know many students struggle with (e.g., reversals)?

Begin by creating a mini-lesson for three sight words. Write what you will say to students or ask them during the lesson. For example, what aspects of the word will you point out during the "Spell" portion of the lesson? (Think about what your students already know based on where they are in your curriculum.) What extension activities will provide the best oral and written practice?

Read–Spell–Write–Extend Routine: *where*

Read: _____

Spell: _____

Write: _____

Extend: _____

Read–Spell–Write–Extend Routine: *some*

Read: _____

Spell: _____

Write: _____

Extend: _____

Read–Spell–Write–Extend Routine: *from*

Read: _____

Spell: _____

Write: _____

Extend: _____

Next Steps to Leap Forward

If you have a fairly strong high-frequency word routine in place, there are several ways to take it to the next level and ensure all students are benefiting from it.

1. Add aspects of the Read–Spell–Write–Extend routine to your regular classroom practices and note their effects on student achievement. Modify your lesson routines as needed.

2. If you use flashcards, update their use to deepen students' understanding of the words. Most flashcards have the word on the front, and the back is blank. I recommend having students (themselves) write the word on the front, then work with you to create a meaningful phrase or sentence on the back. During practice time, students read the fronts of the cards as quickly as possible to practice recognizing the words, then repeatedly read the sentences on the backs to deepen their understanding of how these words function in English. This is especially important for our English learners. Students also review other words that are used in the sentences, thereby broadening their reading.

Especially for
**ENGLISH
LEARNERS**

Below are examples of flashcards I created with students I worked with in New York City. We created the sentences together, and they might tell you a little about our classroom! Note that, in some places, students used pictures instead of words if that is where they were in their reading development.

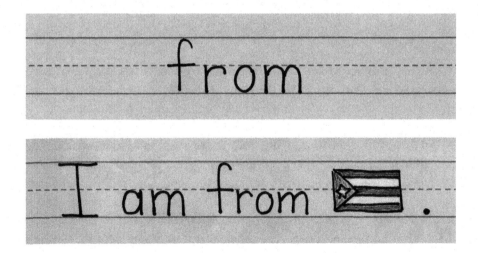

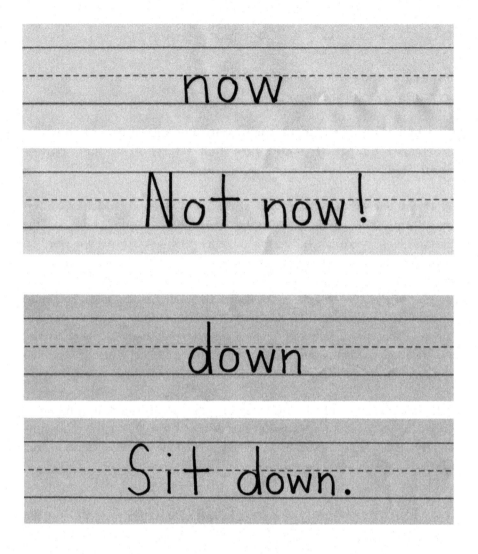

3. Revise your sequence of high-frequency words to take advantage of related words that can be taught as families, such as *could, would,* and *should; there* and *where; to, do,* and *who; give* and *live;* and *come* and *some.*

4. Add apps and whiteboard activities to your instruction. Both also provide great practice during independent work time. Students can practice at their level, focus on problematic words (e.g., you provide a list of words to practice spelling on an app like *Magnetic Alphabet*), or work with partners to review words. The best apps are those that provide a wide range of levels, like *Sight Words* shown on the next page. I recommend selecting apps with the broadest range of levels possible (e.g., multiple skills and age groups) and supports (e.g., specific and targeted corrective feedback rather than just a "ding" when students make errors). More apps are being created now with these features in mind as parents and teachers demand them and app creators become more informed and savvy. And, students need those supports when you aren't by their side.

I included *Sight Words* because of its multiple levels. It is one app that can be used throughout a large portion of the year, and students can be placed into it at the appropriate level.

Source: Courtesy of Sight Words.

Magnetic Alphabet is a generic app on which students make words that they want or from a list that you generate, such as their spelling or high-frequency words for the past four to six weeks.

Source: Courtesy of Magnetic Alphabet.

Success Ingredient 6: High-Frequency Words

Background and Key Characteristics	Best Practices and Look-Fors for Success	Common Instructional Pitfalls	Day Clinic: Examine Your Practices	Next Steps to Leap Forward
• Only 100 words account for 50% of the words in print (13 words account for 25%). • It is critical for reading fluency that high-frequency words (some of which are "irregular") are taught in a way that makes them "stick."	• Use an instructional routine that activates all parts of the brain needed to learn a word (e.g., Read–Spell–Write–Extend).	• Weak instructional routine and practice • Lack of understanding of which words are most problematic and, therefore, need more instruction and practice (e.g., reversals, words with *wh* and *th*) • Lack of focus on spelling patterns of irregular words and not connecting those that share a pattern (e.g., *come* and *some*, *there* and *where*) • No cumulative practice and application	Ask yourself: • How do I teach high-frequency words—both regular and irregular? • Am I organizing the words in a way that will benefit my students? If I'm using a packaged curriculum (e.g., a basal reading program), am I adding related words to help my students see common word families? • How much practice are my students getting reading and writing these words? Are there ways I can add to my weekly practice activities to increase my students' work with and exposure to these all-important words? • How am I assessing these words? Am I assessing students reading them? Am I assessing students using them in writing? Is my assessment cumulative so I can look at progress over an extended period of time to check on mastery? • Am I doing more work with those words I know many students struggle with (e.g., reversals)? **Try it!** • Write a mini-lesson for the words provided using the Read–Spell–Write–Extend routine.	• Use the Read–Spell–Write–Extend routine to accelerate learning. • Update use of flashcards (phrases and sentences on back, words on front). • Revise sequence to take advantage of common patterns. • Include technology (apps and whiteboard activities). • Have students create cumulative sentences in the back of their writing journals to reread each week.

Courtesy of Rick Harrington Photography

Background and Key Characteristics

Why do we teach phonics? The goal of phonics instruction is to develop students' ability to read connected text independently (Adams, 1990). That is, we teach phonics to give students access to words so that they can comprehend text. Let's look briefly at the connection between phonics and comprehension again.

Phonics instruction is designed to teach students how to map sounds onto spellings—to teach them that these strange squiggles and lines we call letters represent the sounds in our spoken words. This mapping of sound spellings enables students to **decode**, or sound out, words while reading. The more opportunities students have to decode words, the more their **word recognition** skills improve because they have worked through these words enough to commit them to memory. The more words a student recognizes on sight, the easier the reading task becomes. Therefore, phonics instruction develops word recognition skills by providing students with an important and useful way to

> *The goal of phonics instruction is to develop students' ability to read connected text independently.*

figure out unfamiliar words. As readers begin to recognize larger and larger numbers of words automatically, their reading **fluency** (the speed and accuracy with which they read) improves. The more times a student encounters a word in text, the more likely the student will recognize it by sight and avoid making reading errors. Reading fluency is linked to reading **comprehension**. Improvements in reading fluency improve understanding of text. Since students are no longer struggling with decoding words, they can devote their full mental energies to making meaning from text. This is critical as texts become more complex year after year in school. Students need to devote more of their mental energies to the vocabulary and ideas presented in these texts and less to the sounding out of individual words. If students have to devote too much attention to decoding words, their reading will be slow and labored. They will struggle getting through enough words fast enough to form meaningful units. As a result, they will experience comprehension breakdowns.

Many types of books exist for instruction, and teachers have choices in which ones they use during phonics lessons and/or as follow-up reading. Each type of book has a purpose and place in early reading instruction. The types of text most frequently encountered in primary-grade classrooms include the following:

1. Decodable text: This type of book is controlled based on taught phonics skills. That is, the majority of the words can be sounded out based on the sound–spelling relationships students have learned. Often, these books focus heavily on the target phonics skill for a specific week of instruction. For example, if the teacher is teaching long *o* spelled *oa* and *ow*, the students might read a book called *The Slow Boat*. This book would contain a lot of words with *oa* and *ow*, as well as words with previously taught phonics skills. It would also contain some sight words—words like *the*, *come*, and *was* that had been taught. It might even contain a couple vocabulary words that would be neither decodable nor sight words already taught, such as *river* (although these would be minimal and might not exist at all).

2. Predictable, or patterned, text: This type of book has a repeated pattern that students quickly pick up while reading. For example, the text might read something like this, with one sentence per page or spread: "I see a cat. I see a bat. I see a tree. I see a bee." The stories are often about familiar concepts, there is a tight match between the pictures and words, and the text might contain elements of rhyme or alliteration. Some of these books will have a familiar sequence or be a version of a familiar story. Students rely heavily on their sight word knowledge and picture and context clues to figure out words in these stories. Often, these books have few decodable words based on the phonics skills students have learned so far in the instructional year, but this is not the focus of the book. Guided reading levels A, B, and C generally have these types of books. These books are not ideal for developing students' decoding skills as students have to rely too much on sight word knowledge and guessing. I do, however, like to use these books with early learners before they have enough phonics skills to read a fully decodable text. For me, these books are highly motivating to beginning readers. They give these students a sense of how to read in English by developing key concepts of print (e.g., left-to-right progression) and some sight word knowledge that can be used when reading later, more complex texts. These beginning readers also learn the difference between text and illustrations and the importance of each in telling a story, as well as other early reading behaviors. The problem arises when these books are used as the sole source of reading when decoding instruction is in full swing and students have a large enough toolbox of skills to read text in which they can practice their sounding out of words. While some of these books are popular trade books by well-known authors and illustrators, most are written especially for beginning readers (such as the majority found in leveled collections for school libraries).

3. Trade books: These books are generally written by well-known authors, illustrated by popular artists, and published with high-quality paper and strong binding. They come in a wide range of genres and formats. These stories have no connection to the phonics or sight word skills students are learning. As such, they are not ideal for practicing these skills unless books can be found in which the majority of the words correlate highly to the instructional sequence. They do, however, often contain rich vocabulary, a great sense of story, and interesting concepts. They are ideal to be read to young students to develop their vocabularies and background knowledge, and to work on their general comprehension skills (including listening comprehension and retelling) while they develop their basic decoding skills. These books and decodable texts are equally as critical to the skills students need to develop. Generally, by mid–Grade 1, students have acquired enough phonics skills to begin accessing high-quality picture books.

A variety of texts is needed in early reading instruction, each with a specific purpose. One type of text cannot meet all the reading demands of our early readers.

What is essential to understand is that a variety of texts is needed in early reading instruction, each with a specific purpose. One type of text cannot meet all the reading demands of our early readers. Therefore, it is important to select texts that match your instructional goals. For example, if you have just completed a phonics lesson and want students to practice using their newly taught phonics skills, decodable text is the appropriate choice. Juel and Roper-Schneider

(1985) explained why text selection in lessons is so critical. When their study was conducted, formal reading instruction generally began in Grade 1, unlike now when students begin learning to decode words and read decodable texts in kindergarten.

> The selection of text used very early in first grade may, at least in part, determine the strategies and cues children learn to use, and persist in using, in subsequent word identification. . . . In particular, emphasis on a phonics method seems to make little sense if children are given initial texts to read where the words do not follow regular letter-sound correspondence generalizations. . . . [T]he types of words which appear in beginning reading texts may well exert a more powerful influence in shaping children's word identification strategies than the method of reading instruction.

Wow! Read that last sentence again. "[T]he types of words which appear in beginning reading texts may well exert a more powerful influence in shaping children's word identification strategies than the method of reading instruction." What this means is that we can teach an award-winning phonics lesson, but if we follow that up (day after day, week after week) with texts to apply the phonics skills containing few decodable words, our efforts might be in vain. That's because students gravitate toward the word-reading strategies that work most frequently for them. If they are given texts in which they have to rely on sight words, context, and picture clues to figure out or even guess words, that's what they think reading is. This might work for them for a while, especially through about mid–Grade 1 when the texts are short and simple and there is a close picture–text match. However, as soon as these supports are taken away, the students' reading falls apart.

We can teach an award-winning phonics lesson, but if we follow that up (day after day, week after week) with texts to apply the phonics skills containing few decodable words, our efforts might be in vain.

Let's assume you've just taught students that the letter *s* stands for the /s/ sound. It is early in the year, and you've taught only a handful of other sound spellings. If you then give students a story in which a lot of words begin with *s*, such as *sand*, *sister*, *sandwich*, and *silly* (common to patterned texts such as those in guided reading levels A–C), yet none of these words is decodable based on the sound–spelling relationships you've previously taught, how will students read these words? Well, they'll use context clues and picture clues—not their phonics knowledge—to try to figure out the words. Over time, because they aren't using their phonics skills, students will undervalue their knowledge of sound–spelling relationships and over-rely on context and pictures. Most poor readers over-rely on these types of clues, which quickly become less sufficient as the text demands increase and the picture clues decrease (Stanovich, 1986). If you want to teach students how to use all three cueing systems effectively (graphophonic, syntactic, semantic), you must ensure they are getting quality practice applying all three when reading connected text.

A direct connection between phonics instruction and what students read is essential. "Like arithmetic without application, phonics without connected reading amounts to useless mechanics. And like arithmetic that we never did understand well enough to do the word problems, it is easily forgotten altogether" (Adams, 1990). I liken it to teaching a child chords for playing a guitar, then sitting him at a piano to practice. Unfortunately, too much of the text students are given to read in today's classrooms has too little connection to the phonics skills they have been taught.

> *A direct connection between phonics instruction and what students read is essential.*

Give it a try. Imagine you are a kindergartner and these are the skills I have taught you:

High-Frequency Words: *I, see*

Phonics Skills: ◆ = /a/   ■ = /t/

Now read this sentence. Imagine a picture of a cat above the sentence:

I see ◆ c◆■.

That's right! The sentence is "I see a cat." It was easy for you to read because I taught you most of the skills needed to recognize or sound out the words. You confirmed the last word by looking at the picture and thinking about context.

Now try a sentence that is a bit harder. I've added one word. What does this sentence say?

⊙◆□ c◆❖ see ◆ §◆★★O■.

(Continued)

(Continued)

This is a very simple sentence. But can you read it? How do you feel right now? Frustrated? Have you given up? Do you want to stop reading? Well, this sentence reads "Pam can see a rabbit," but you couldn't figure it out because I hadn't taught you enough skills to access the text. Now consider the stories you have your students read versus the skills you have taught them (phonics and high-frequency words). Is this the type of text they are encountering every day?

In 1985, the government document *Becoming a Nation of Readers* (Anderson, Hiebert, Scott, & Wilkinson, 1985) provided a set of criteria for creating controlled, decodable text. This type of text should include the following three criteria:

1. Comprehensible: Vocabulary must be understandable. Words must be derived from students' speaking and listening vocabularies. The stories should make sense and follow natural-sounding English spoken and written patterns. No sentences should be in these stories that you, as a proficient speaker and reader of English, have not uttered, written, or read.

2. Instructive: The majority of the words must be decodable based on the sound spellings previously taught. A strong connection between instruction and text must exist.

3. Engaging: Connected text must be engaging enough for students to want to read it again and again, like a good trade book. Just because this is an instructional tool doesn't mean we should throw our standards out the window. Students need to revisit this text to develop fluency and increase reading rate. The text should be worth revisiting (and talking about). In early texts, some of the engagement and discussion will be derived from the photos and illustrations, but the text must support them.

These criteria came with the following warning. I cannot overemphasize the importance of this warning as it has been universally ignored to the detriment of students all over the country.

> **WARNING:** The important point is that a high proportion of the words in the earliest selections children read should conform to the phonics they have already been taught. Otherwise, they will not have enough opportunities to practice, extend, and refine their knowledge of letter–sound relationships. However, a rigid criterion is a poor idea. Requiring that, say, 90% of the words used in a primer must conform would destroy the flexibility needed to write interesting, meaningful stories.

Where and why has this warning been ignored? In the 1990s, when whole language was at its height in popularity with publishers of reading materials, beginning readers were given trade books to learn to read that had little connection to their skill base. In the early 2000s, after far too many students failed to learn to read on grade level, states began enacting policies to attempt to correct this. One policy was the requiring of decodable text for students in kindergarten through Grade 2 or 3 (depending on the state). California and Texas went further and outlined the amount of text required at each grade (e.g., two books per phonics skill) and the degree of decodability. In California, it was 75% decodability per book; in Texas, it was 80%. The thinking was that not only would students now have a valuable instructional tool, but this tool would afford them a great deal of decoding practice—the type of practice they had been missing during the use of whole language instructional materials.

I applauded the inclusion of this text in early reading materials and conducted a study in 2000 to show its potential impact on early reading and spelling growth as well as motivation to read. (You can read about this study, in an excerpt from Blevins [2006], a bit later in the chapter.) However, like many things in education, a good idea can sometimes be applied in ways it was never intended and without consideration of its limitations. Likewise, all practices in education need to be continually studied, evaluated, and modified as new information arises. This has not been the case for these state mandates regarding decodable text, and they have resulted in some unwanted consequences.

Like many things in education, a good idea can sometimes be applied in ways it was never intended and without consideration of its limitations.

These mandates require that publishers create text that first and foremost is judged by the percentage of decodable words it includes. I have seen editors pushed to include a certain number of words with the target skill in each book so that all the books in the series have what marketing departments feel is an "acceptable" number of words (with no regard to the story needs or usability of the specific spelling patterns). This forcing of words into a story often results in awkward and nonsensical sentences. The "more is better" mantra is common. I have witnessed sales representatives from publishing houses boasting that their decodable text is more decodable than another company's in an attempt to win sales. Let me be very clear: Relying solely on numbers to determine or evaluate text quality and appropriateness is dangerous at best, educational malpractice at worst. Even the Common Core State Standards have recognized the need to be more global in our evaluation and selection of text for our students. Now, selecting appropriate texts for any grade level and student is done after considering three important factors: **quantitative features of the text** (e.g., readability and Lexile scores), **qualitative features of the text** (e.g., structure, levels of meaning, and knowledge demands, à la guided reading levels), **and the matching of the reader to the text by the teacher** (e.g., considering interests, knowledge base, and purpose). In addition, treating a text like a number doesn't take into consideration the issues our struggling readers and English learners will face—where concrete language and common sentence structures are even more important.

It is time that we correct this problem and work to create a greater awareness with state departments of education and educational publishers on this issue and the need to fix it. Imagine you are a struggling reader or an English learner, and you are presented with texts like these (from actual published sources):

Lin bit the hot rib. Let Lin dab a lip.

The pup is up on the hut in the sun.

We can't allow this to happen. Instead of stopping the use of an incredibly important instructional tool (decodable text), we need to improve the tool by going back to the three requirements outlined by *Becoming a Nation of Readers*—instructive, comprehensible, and engaging (Anderson et al., 1985). We also have to work together to modify state policies that force publishers to create texts that are not at an acceptable standard for our students. I concur that the majority of words should be decodable, but a story that is 65% decodable and makes sense is far more valuable as an instructional tool than one that is 80% decodable and nonsense. We have to do better.

Decodable Text Study

In 2000, I conducted a study to examine the effectiveness of decodable text in promoting word identification skills, phonics, and spelling abilities, as well as positive reading attitudes in early readers. Previous research on the influence of basal readers had indicated that the types of words that appear in beginning reading texts exert a powerful influence in shaping children's word identification strategies (Juel & Roper-Schneider, 1985). However, there had been no research on the direct effects of decodable texts on early reading growth. In my study, I hypothesized that students receiving reading practice with decodable texts would achieve greater mastery in early reading skills than students who continued reading with standard classroom literature as follow-up reading to phonics instruction.

Research Questions

My research questions included:

- Does practice with decodable text in conjunction with a systematic phonics program accelerate word identification skills for first-grade students?

- Do first graders who use decodable text demonstrate significantly greater gains in word identification skills than a comparison group of students who use trade literature?

Sample

Two New York City Public Schools participated in my study from September of 1999 to February of 2000. There were two first-grade classrooms selected at each school—one experimental classroom using decodable text and one control classroom using trade literature. A total of 101 children in first grade participated in this research. The selected schools were in the lowest third of the district based on achievement scores. Ninety percent of the students in this district qualify for free or reduced lunch. Sixty-two percent of the students

(Continued)

(Continued)

were classified as below grade level and 80% of the students were identified as Latino. Both schools used the same systematic and explicit phonics instruction covering the identical phonics scope and sequence. The only difference between the experimental and control classrooms was the type of text used for reading practice: the decodable text or the standard trade literature series.

Program Background

The decodable texts used in this study were written to directly address the requirements outlined in *Becoming a Nation of Readers* (Anderson et al., 1985). Students in both groups read a major piece of literature for the week and received phonics lessons follow-up practice five days a week. First graders in the experimental group practiced reading with decodable (controlled) text for their phonics lessons follow-up. The controlled texts were 100% controlled for phonics and sight words (for example, *Sam sat. Sam sat in the sand. Sam sat and sat.*). The major reading text was 80% controlled for phonics and sight words, as well as being specially written and illustrated.

In comparison, the control group's phonics lessons follow-up included patterned and predictable text (for example, *Sam sees a sandwich. Sam sees a snake. Sam sees a sailor. Sam sees a lot!*). For their major reading text the control group used popular first-grade books written by well-known authors. Many of these texts were approximately 35% decodable.

Controlled text percentages were determined through a decodability analysis I did based on a clear scope and sequence of phonics skills. In addition, a review of Marcy Stein's study "Analyzing Beginning Reading Programs: The Relationship Between Decoding Instruction and Text" (Stein, Johnson, & Gutlohn, 1999) confirmed controlled text percentages for both the experimental and control groups of students.

Professional Development

I conducted an initial training session with experimental group teachers on how to incorporate the decodable text into their comprehensive reading program.

Each participating classroom was visited and observed four days per week—two days by me and two days by my research assistant. This method ensured that all teachers stayed on pace, taught the phonics lessons as intended, and read the required books. Detailed anecdotal notes on these sessions were kept. In addition, each classroom was formally observed for two weeks to develop classroom profiles.

Assessment Measures

This study included four assessment measures:

- The Woodcock Reading Mastery Test (WRMT)—Word Identification sub-test: Required children to look at printed words and read them aloud.

- The Blevins Phonics–Phonemic Awareness Quick Assessment: A simple 5-word spelling test administered at the start of school. Students fall into three categories—below level, on level, and above level. This test quickly identifies students in need of intervention and provided information about students' phonemic awareness and phonics proficiency.

- Decoding Assessment: A phonics mastery assessment developed specially for the study. It consisted of 20 words, all decodable based on the phonics scope and sequence. Ten of the words presented on the assessment appeared multiple times (four or more) in the reading selections by both groups of students. The other ten words never appeared in the stories read by both groups, or they appeared only once. Ability to decode 75% of the words or more was necessary to receive a "passing" score. All words were real words, not pseudowords.

  Note: I don't have a problem with assessments in which students are asked to read pseudowords, or nonsense words, if and only if students are familiar with creating and reading nonsense words in general, such as in regular, fun classroom activities. One example is the whiteboard activity below that I created. Students spin the spinner then string together the letters to make a word. If it is a real word, they record it and earn a point. If it is a nonsense word, the next student gets a turn at the spinner.

(Continued)

(Continued)

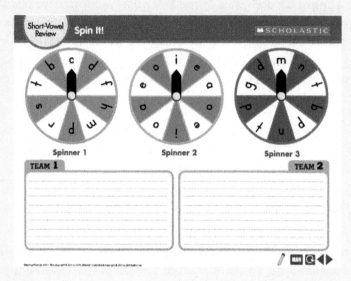

Source: Blevins (2011b).

> If students haven't had this kind of regular classroom practice, then a nonsense-word assessment can be disastrous. I have worked with many first graders who, no matter how many times you tell them this is a silly nonsense word, will try to make it a real word 'cause that's what they're supposed to do while reading.

- Reading Attitudes Survey: An informal interview-style assessment, which evaluates how children feel about learning to read, as well as how they perceive themselves as readers.

The study included a pre- and posttest design for the WRMT, the Blevins Phonics–Phonemic Awareness Quick Assessment, and the Reading Attitudes Survey. Pretesting was conducted in September 1999, and post-testing was conducted in February 2000. The Decoding Assessment was only administered at the end of the study, in February of 2000.

Data Analysis

WRMT—Word Identification Sub-Test Results

Results revealed that students in the experimental group significantly outperformed students in the control group on the WRMT. Analysis determined that W-score differences were statistically significant at $F(1.69) = 12.954$, $p < .001$. The Effect Size was determined to be $E = 0.16$.

Furthermore, results revealed that a significantly greater number of students using the decodable text for their reading practice achieved on-level WRMT mastery: 72% decodable text students vs. 54% trade literature students. The decodable controlled text group made a significant leap from 28% on-level mastery at the beginning of the year to 72% mastery in February. In contrast, the trade literature group only increased WRMT mastery from 40% in September to 54% in February. Some students in the decodable controlled text group achieved as much as two years' growth during one half of the school year.

Phonics–Phonemic Awareness Quick Assessment Results

Findings revealed that a significantly greater number of decodable text students vs. trade literature students achieved mastery on the Phonics–Phonemic Awareness Quick Assessment: 92% decodable text students vs. 66% trade literature students. Ninety-two percent of decodable controlled text students were able to spell all five words correctly.

Decodable (Phonics Mastery) Assessment Results

Results revealed that 87% of the students using the decodable text achieved mastery (75% or higher score) on the Decoding Assessment as compared with only 54% of the students in the trade literature group.

Reading Attitudes Assessment Results

Findings revealed that significantly fewer students reading decodable text vs. trade literature reported a dislike of reading or identified themselves as poor readers. Only 3% of decodable text students reported that they didn't enjoy reading vs. 11% of trade literature students. The percentage of students in the decodable controlled text group who reported a dislike of reading decreased during the study from 14% in September to only 3% in February. I attribute this to their growing sense of confidence and control in their reading. In comparison, the percentage of students in the trade literature group who reported a dislike of reading actually increased during the study from 6% in September to 11% in

(Continued)

(Continued)

February. This is a very troubling number to me. Already students realize something isn't working and we are beginning to lose them.

Classroom Observation Results

Classroom observations revealed that working with decodable controlled text carried over to other important areas of teaching, such as read-aloud modeling and writing activities. In general, teachers were observed over time to pay more attention to words and specifically how words work.

As further evidence of the power of decodable controlled text, classroom observations also revealed that children in the decodable controlled text group were more confident in tackling difficult books for their read-at-home reading choices. It was observed that children in the experimental (decodable controlled text) group would examine the words in books before selecting a story to take home. Conversely, children in the control group were observed to have difficulty choosing books with appropriate text for their level.

Discussion

Overall, students in the decodable controlled-text group were more prepared to transfer their phonics skills to new words presented to them in formal assessments. In addition, these results reinforce what previous research by motivation experts has revealed: reading success breeds reading self-confidence and enjoyment of reading. This study also reinforces that the type of text for beginning readers does matter. Students who use decodable controlled text in their early reading instruction get off to a stronger start in their reading development.

Source: Excerpt from Blevins (2006, pp. 127–130).

Interestingly, before I began my study, I had a conversation with Jeanne Chall, my former Harvard professor and author of *Learning to Read: The Great Debate* (1967). I went to visit her to ask about the research California and Texas were using to support their policies of decodable text with 75% or 80% decodability. She replied that there were no such studies. I then asked how each state (e.g., its department of education) arrived at these numbers. She looked into my eyes and dryly stated, "They made it up." We went on to discuss what, based on her incredible wealth of experiences, she thought I would discover in my study. She suggested I would discover that the amount of decodability needed for students and the amount of time students needed receiving this type of text would vary based on student needs. She was, of course, right. By mid–Grade 1, many students in my study were ready to tackle texts with less controls. They had a sense of comfort and confidence in their growing reading abilities. We still provided decodable text for the remainder of the year as follow-up to our phonics lessons, but moved children into richer trade books with fewer controls earlier. Other students relied heavily on the controlled text to develop their skills and struggled with text containing less control. This has implications for our policies. We need to take our cues from our students in terms of when they are ready for fewer controls, and we need to continue to monitor the level of support they need so that the best foundation in early reading can be built.

We need to take our cues from our students in terms of when they are ready for fewer controls, and we need to continue to monitor the level of support they need so that the best foundation in early reading can be built.

Best Practices and Look-Fors for Success

Comprehension should be as important an aspect of reading these texts as the actual decoding practice.

Having a strong routine for reading and interacting with decodable passages, stories, and books will be essential to your phonics instructional success. Reading these books should involve far more than just calling out the words on the page. Applying one's phonics skills to connected text (with a wide range of previously taught skills included) can be challenging for students. It forces them to access all their skills in a way that aids in learning. Also, the goal of all reading is understanding. Therefore, comprehension should be as important an aspect of reading these texts as the actual decoding practice. I recommend the following routine for reading decodable texts. Students should read (or reread a previously read text) every day to achieve sufficient practice for mastery.

READING A DECODABLE BOOK ROUTINE

Step 1: Preview and Predict

Read the title. Have students repeat. Describe the cover illustration using key words to frontload vocabulary. Ask students to tell what they think the story will be about and why (noting details in the art and title).

Step 2: First Read (Read Together)

Have students point to each word as they chorally read it aloud. If students have difficulty with any word, stop and provide corrective feedback (e.g., model how to sound it out using the corrective feedback model earlier presented). Then have students reread the sentence with the corrected word. Confirm that the word is correct by asking students to use other cues. For example, ask, "Does the word make sense in the sentence? Is it the kind of word that would fit [e.g., noun, verb]? Is it the right word?"

Step 3: Check Comprehension

Ask questions about the story. Allow students to discuss answers with a partner before you call on a volunteer to answer. Prompt students to answer in complete sentences and find details in the text or art to support their answers.

Step 4: Second Read (Develop Fluency)

Have students reread the book to a partner. Circulate, listen in, and provide corrective feedback.

Step 5: Retell and Write

Have students retell the story to a partner in their own words. They can use the illustrations as cues to their retellings. Then have students write about the story. They can write their retelling, a story extension, a new story with the same characters, or what they learned from the book (if nonfiction). For extra support, use sentence starters and allow drawings.

You know you are using those "just right" texts for decoding practice when students have multiple opportunities to read words with the new target skill. For example, if you are reading a story after teaching short *a* and the only word with this phonics element that students encounter is *cat* (a word they might already know by sight), you aren't providing your students the type of practice needed to achieve mastery. If, however, the story contains many words with short *a*, such as *cat*, *man*, *map*, *at*, *am*, and *pan*, then it's a good indicator of application opportunities. Of course, one story doesn't have to carry the burden of all the practice. Examine everything students will read for the week (instructional cycle) and take note of the number and variety of words with the target skill as well as the number of opportunities students have to read these words in context (including repeated readings of the same stories). The goal is to encounter these words enough times that students begin to recognize them automatically and can easily sound out new words with the target skill because of their comfort with the new skill.

One story doesn't have to carry the burden of all the practice.

Keep in mind that decodable stories for beginning readers are instructional tools and, as such, should be a key part of each phonics lesson. Students need to be reading daily text they can handle based on their phonics and sight word skills. But this type of text will not be the only text students encounter. While decodable stories are ideal for building decoding skills, they are not sufficient for developing vocabulary or deep sense of story structure. Other texts, generally presented through read-alouds, are better suited for those instructional needs.

Keep in mind that decodable stories for beginning readers are instructional tools and, as such, should be a key part of each phonics lesson.

If you are using a guided reading leveling system, then the decodable texts during the phonics lessons are even more critical. The texts in

4 BEST EFFECT

How to Use Decodable Text

- Must be read daily, with attention to both decoding and comprehension

- Must have a close match to the phonics skills taught up to that point in the phonics scope and sequence

- Multiple texts (minimum of two) needed for each skill to ensure ample practice

- Should be reread to build fluency, be used as springboards for writing exercises, and *not* be the only text students are exposed to each day (e.g., they also need read-alouds to build vocabulary)

these leveled collections are not created using decoding as a major criterion and might contain few or no words linked to the week's phonics skill. Certainly, you can preselect books in a given level that more closely align to these instructional goals. And you can use the decodables as a scaffold to these leveled texts. That is, students read a highly controlled decodable text during the phonics lesson, then read (with your support) a somewhat less controlled text during the guided reading lesson. If carefully chosen, these texts can be organized to create small stepping-stones in which less control is afforded students as they develop their overall reading skills. (See the Guided Reading Level/Recommended Phonics Skill chart on pages 45–46.)

While decodable texts are not ideal for developing vocabulary skills, since the word choices are limited and often basic, vocabulary can be built via discussion about the text and its illustrations or photographs. For example, imagine that your students will read a decodable text called *Hop* during their phonics lesson this week. *Hop* is a simple photo book that features frogs. It shows frogs in various places and at various stages of a frog's life cycle. The text might read something like "I see a frog. It can hop. It hops to the pond. Hop, hop, hop! Frogs hop a lot!" Yes, there's not much to work with here in terms of new vocabulary. However, if you read a trade book like *Red-Eyed Tree Frog* (Cowley, 2006) or a page or two from your science book about frogs, their body parts, habitats, survival needs, and/or life cycle *before* students read the simple decodable, now imagine the conversation you could have using the photos. You could ask questions about frogs—their habitats and life cycle—using sophisticated vocabulary and engage students in a conversation about the photos in which they have opportunities to use these words. If we are more careful about our selection of read-alouds and link them to our early texts, we can get so much more out of them. Remember, whatever you frontload before reading a simple decodable text, you can then reinforce it during and after the reading through conversation and writing. Blow open the door in terms of all the ways you can use these simple early texts!

4 BEST EFFECT

Vocabulary and Decodable Text

- Decodable texts do not contain the amount or types of words students need to build robust vocabularies.

- Daily read-alouds are needed for building vocabulary (both fiction and informational text).

- Vocabulary can be built with decodable texts using the illustrations or photographs and concepts of the stories. Introduce and define new terms when talking about the stories with students.

- For informational decodable texts, use read-alouds on the same concept (article, book, video, or part of a book) to frontload vocabulary. Then reinforce the more sophisticated vocabulary when talking with students about the text or when they write about the text.

Common Instructional Pitfalls

Many common pitfalls regarding reading connected text exist. These include the following:

1. Two common issues with the use of decodable texts are (1) not using them in the phonics instruction as a daily practice tool and (2) using weak decodable texts that lack comprehensibility or don't follow common English speaking and writing patterns. Both are serious issues that affect learning.

The bulk of the time in any given phonics lesson should be devoted to applying the skill to real reading and writing situations.

Sometimes I see teachers treating the decodable text as the reward for a week of study on a specific skill. That means the bulk of the instruction during the week was in isolated skill work, probably skill and drill. This type of instruction has its place in the instructional cycle, but it should only be a small portion of the work. The bulk of the time in any given phonics lesson should be devoted to applying the skill to real reading and writing situations. That's when learning occurs as students have guided experiences in applying their skills in ways that consolidate and solidify their learning. Look at these two phonics schedules. Which teacher's students do you think have a greater likelihood to progress rapidly in the development of their phonics skills? Why? That's right. The teacher who follows Schedule B spends at least half of the instructional time applying phonics skills to authentic reading and writing experiences. Fifty percent should be the minimum amount of time in each phonics lesson devoted to application.

Schedule A

10 minutes: Action rhyme review

10 minutes: Phonemic awareness (rhyme)

5 minutes: Introduce letter sound

5 minutes: Read story

Schedule B

5 minutes: Review warm-up (cumulative)

5 minutes: Phonemic awareness (oral segmentation)

5 minutes: Introduce letter sound and model blending

10 minutes: Read story

5 minutes: Writing follow-up

The second issue is more problematic. Let's be honest: Many decodable texts are poorly written, and you might be stuck with a set of books that vary in their quality. Too many publishers assume that cramming increasing numbers of words with the target skill into a text makes it a better practice tool. The opposite is true if the text doesn't make sense or reinforce common English speaking and writing patterns. If a text reads like a tongue twister, as some of these stories do, it is difficult to make meaning from, and we know that the goal of all reading is comprehension. We should never compromise on that. Also, when students are beginning to learn to read, they are attempting to transform their spoken sentences into print. The stories they read, as a result, often contain simple words and sentence constructions. That aids in early reading growth. Unfortunately, too many decodable texts break those rules. This is especially problematic for our English learners. Imagine learning to speak, read, and write in a new language, and the first stories you are given to practice contain sentences like "The kid did hit it" (which uses a sentence structure not common in English) or "Pop had the tan cat. Len can lug the cat with the rug" (which uses low-utility and confusing words and makes little sense). No sentences should exist in these early books that do not follow common English language constructions. None! Zero. Zilch. If you see a sentence that you have never uttered (or one following the same pattern), it needs to be fixed. Teachers, as consumers of these materials, need to apply more pressure to the publishers creating these stories to fix them. Set higher standards, and don't settle for less. When I work with teachers stuck with faulty decodable texts, we either look for better texts (when monies become available), rewrite problematic sentences (literally pasting patches over text), or write our own little stories. It can be a lot of work, but the payoff in student growth is worth it.

Especially for
**ENGLISH
LEARNERS**

What If Your Decodable Texts Are Bad?

- Sentences in decodable texts should use high-utility English words (e.g., words students will commonly and regularly encounter when reading books or use when writing) and not be tongue twisters filled with lots of words with the target phonics skill, but lacking in "sense."

- Sentences in decodable texts should *all* follow normal English language speech and writing patterns. This is especially critical for our English learners.

- If your decodable texts break the above rules, then purchase new texts or find replacements in your curriculum or online.

- If new texts are not available or feasible, rewrite the most problematic sentences in the decodable texts (e.g., tape over replacement sentences).

The most common issues in these texts that must be fixed include

a. The use of low-utility words to try to squeeze in more words with the target skill (e.g., "I can lug the cat with the rug," "Let Lin dab a lip," "Put it in the vat.")

b. The use of nonstandard English sentence structures (e.g., "Ron did hit it," "The pup did run at Kit.")

c. The use of nonsensical sentences or tongue twisters (e.g., "Slim Stan did spin, splat, stop," "Fun Fran flips, flaps, flops.")

d. The use of too many referents or pronouns (because they are easier words) instead of specific concrete words, making the meaning difficult to figure out (e.g., "She did not see it, but she did put it in.")

e. Using too simple language to explain scientific concepts due to phonics constraints (e.g., "The sun will make plants rise.")

f. Using odd names to get more decodable words in the story (e.g., "Ben had Mem. Tam had the pup.")

g. Avoiding using the word *the*, the most common word in the English language (Because *the* is *not* counted as decodable until students are taught the digraph *th* and the long-*e* sound spelled *e*—as in *we*, *he*, and *be*, since it can also be pronounced this way—most writers of decodable text avoid using *the* or replace it with the word *a*. This often results in stilted sentences. Also, the words *the* and *a* have different uses in English. For example, "I see *a* cat" can refer to any cat. "I see *the* cat" refers to a specific cat. Therefore, interchanging the two words can also affect understanding. Unfortunately, in most scopes and sequences, the word *the* doesn't become decodable until around mid–Grade 1. That's a long time to avoid or use sparingly the most common word in English!)

2. In many balanced literacy classrooms, I see each part of reading instruction segmented, with little connection across the lessons—phonics, guided reading, writing workshop. What happens in one part of the reading instructional block often has no clear connection to another part. This disjointed instruction makes it more difficult for students to rapidly master skills. They don't get the concentrated practice and application needed. Nowhere is this more evident than in the disconnect between the phonics lessons and the leveled books students are reading. I've already discussed this at length. To help, I've provided a suggested scope and sequence (see the Guided Reading Level/Recommended Phonics Skill chart on pages 45–46) that connects to each guided reading level as a possible starting point. It offers a systematic and sequential look at building phonics skills. It is not meant to be limiting. That is, if a book offers multiple opportunities to work on a phonics skill not suggested, by all means introduce it if it is critical to students reading that specific book. I've also offered some guidance on making more-informed choices when selecting books for guided reading lessons—examining them prior to reading to not only look at key aspects to teach and reinforce, but identify which phonics skills can be practiced. Doing your best to have links between your students' growing phonics and sight word abilities and the leveled books they read will greatly benefit them. If you are limited in your leveled book choices, then using decodable texts in the phonics levels is even more essential.

3. Too often, there is a lack of emphasis on comprehension and missed opportunities to build vocabulary when reading decodable stories. Yes, these stories have limited vocabulary, and that is not their instructional purpose. However, while students read this type of text, they should be engaged in rich language read-alouds throughout the day that immerse them in vocabulary, and any connections that can be made between these read-alouds and decodable stories should be taken advantage of (e.g., using the read-aloud to frontload concepts and vocabulary that can be reinforced through the photos and illustrations in a decodable text). Also, you can introduce more sophisticated language when talking *about* the stories. That is, you can identify important conceptual words (e.g., *friendship*, *habitat*, *conflict*, *solution*) and prompt students to respond using the new words.

Courtesy of Rick Harrington Photography

4. I rarely see the **decodable books being used as springboards to writing**. When we ask our students to write about a decodable story, they will, by the very nature of the task, need to use words from the story—many of which will contain the target phonics skill. Plus, the book offers struggling students scaffolded support in selecting and writing words. These writing extensions can include the following and more! One caveat to these writing activities is that they should always be preceded by talk. Talking about what students will write before they pick up their pencil gives them an opportunity to clarify and refine their ideas before expressing them in print.

    a. Have students write a retelling of the story (if fiction). One fun activity to do before students write a retelling is having them "walk and talk" a story path. To do this, you draw a story pathway on a long sheet of bulletin board or butcher paper. Write "beginning," "middle," and "end" on the pathway. Students can then write key words or draw simple pictures on small slips of paper and place them along the pathway at the appropriate location to help them remember key story events. Students then take turns walking the pathway as they orally retell the story. You or student partners can offer corrective feedback and model "look-backs" into the story to add missing details.

b. Have students create a list of new facts learned (if informational). Suggest that they add an illustration to accompany the list and record any new words learned associated with these facts or concepts (some possibly coming from your discussion rather than the text).

c. Have students write a story extension answering the question, "What happens next?"

d. Have students write a new story using the main characters, putting them in a new setting or creating a new story problem.

e. Have students write a dialogue between two characters that they first act out with a partner. It can be a dialogue in which the characters discuss a key event or problem in the book or a new problem the characters must solve.

f. Have students write a letter to the author or illustrator explaining why they liked the book, giving two or three details.

g. Have students write a letter to one of the story characters.

h. List 5–10 words from the story, including several with the target phonics skill. Ask students to use some of the words to create a story.

i. List sample words with the target skill in columns based on spelling pattern (e.g., _at, _an, _ap, _ack, _ad). Have students generate lists of words with each pattern (real words only). Ask them to write fun story titles using some of the words, such as "The Very Bad Cat."

Examine Your Practices

Now it's your turn. Ask yourself the following questions to examine your instructional practices and materials as they relate to reading connected text.

1. Do I have a sufficient amount of decodable text to use with my phonics lessons (at least two different texts per skill)?

2. How strong are the decodable texts I have? What are their weaknesses? Can these be easily fixed? How might I be able to obtain more decodable texts?

3. What instructional routine do I use when reading these texts? Am I providing modeling and self-correction based on student attempts?

4. Are students reading the decodable texts multiple times to build fluency (each book should be read at least twice)?

5. Am I extending the decodable texts through associated writing activities?

6. Am I monitoring comprehension during and after reading the decodable texts?

7. What is the content and quality of the discussion I am having around these decodable texts? Have I tried ways to enhance these conversations to build vocabulary and conceptual knowledge (using read-alouds to frontload vocabulary, using graphic organizers to record and examine story structure, etc.)?

Try the following activities to deepen your exploration of decodable text and its use in phonics instruction.

1. Look at the three texts that follow. Examine the words used, compare your findings to your phonics scope and sequence, and determine the best instructional use for each one.

Sample 1	Instructional Use
We like to play. We like to run. We like to eat. We like to sleep. We like to laugh. We like to read. We like to do a lot!	

Sample 2	Instructional Use
The frog can hop. It can hop on a log. It can sit on top of the log. The frog can hop on a rock, too. That is a good spot to sit. If it is hot, the frog can hop in the pond.	

Sample 3	Instructional Use
A shark's sleek body is built for finding food. That's because sharks have super senses! A shark's nose can smell a drop of blood a mile away. Its inner ears can hear people thrash in the water. Its beady eyes can see in dim light.	

2. Create a decodable passage for your students to practice reading. Following is the target phonics skill and a list of the previously taught phonics skills. You can use whatever sight words you have already taught your students. Write a passage that contains at least 25 words.

Target Phonics Skill: Short *e*

Previously Taught Phonics Skills: Short *a*, *i*, *o*; consonant blends (*s* blends, *l* blends, *r* blends)

```



```

Now let's see how decodable your text is.

a. Count the number of words in your passage. _____

b. Put a box around all the short-*e* words in the story. How many have you included?
    _____

c. Circle all the words that can be sounded out using *only* those phonics skills you have previously taught, including any short-*e* words. If a word contains even one letter sound not taught, you can't count it. For example, if a word contains a digraph like *sh*, *ch*, *th*, or *wh*, you can't count it. You also cannot count any sight words (with irregular spellings like *the* or *was*) or any multisyllabic words.

d. Count the number of circled words. _____

e. Divide the number of circled words by the total number of words. Write the percentage here. _____

f. Is your text over 50% decodable? _____ Over 75%? _____ Over 80%? _____

g. How many *different* nondecodable words are in your text?
    _____

h. How will students figure out these words? _____

3. Ever had a bad decodable text—one that didn't make sense or that read like a tongue twister? Following are sentences from actual decodable texts that need to be fixed. Fix each one and write the corrected text below. I've corrected one as a sample. Remember, it is often better to replace a vague or imprecise word (e.g., a pronoun) with the name or noun it refers to in order to clarify meaning. When we overload sentences with these referents, it increases the propositional density of a text, or the amount of meaning connections a reader must make in order to understand

the sentences. As a result, a very simple sentence like "He hit it" requires a lot of thought and meaning connections on the part of the reader—for example, who is "he"? What did he hit? Is that what the "it" refers to?

Sample: He did hit it.

Correction: Sam hit the ball.

a.   Sam did pat the dog.

Correction: _____

b.   Lin bit the hot rib. Let Lin dab a lip.

Correction: _____

c.   The pup is up on the hut in the sun.

Correction: _____

d.   Jim and Jen had Kit. Ben had Mem. Pam and Tam had the pup. (picture of kids with different pets)

Correction: _____

e.   "Can I hit it?" said Ron. Ron did hit it. It went and went.

Correction: _____

f.   Look at this. I got it for me. (picture of a boy with a baseball bat)

Correction: _____

g.   The fat tan cat saw Kit. The tan cat ran at Kit. Kit, the tan cat, the pup, and Jen and Ben ran.

Correction: _____

Which Decodable Text Is Best?

Examine the three decodable texts on the next page. Complete the chart for each one. Determine which text is best to practice the focus skill and record any corrections or modifications you would make to the text to improve its use and quality.

Sample 1	Unique Words With Target Skill
In the forest, there lived a snake and an ape. The snake's name was Jake. The ape's name was Kate.	**Other Criteria** **Evaluation/Possible Fixes**

Sample 2	Unique Words With Target Skill
Jane's frog got away! Where did Wade end up? He jumped in the fish tank. What a way to have fun!	**Other Criteria** **Evaluation/Possible Fixes**

Sample 3	Unique Words With Target Skill
In the forest, there lived a snake, an ape, and a bat. The snake's name was Mac. The ape's name was Pat. The bat's name was Dale. The animals came to a big lake to talk.	**Other Criteria** **Evaluation/Possible Fixes**

Source: Text samples from Beck & Beck (2013).

For example answers to these and other activities, go to http://resources.corwin.com/blevinsphonics for completed charts.

Next Steps to Leap Forward

If you have a fairly strong reading-connected text routine in place, there are several ways to take it to the next level and ensure all students are benefiting from it.

1. **Add cumulative rereading of previously read stories to extend students' practice of skills over time and build toward mastery.** In one school district I worked with, we used the following procedure.

   a. After students read a decodable text, we typed the story to fit on one page. The page was numbered to indicate the sequence, then a copy was made for each student. The story was placed in students' independent reading folders, which students used during independent work time while the teacher met with small groups.

   b. Each day, the teacher wrote the numbers of two or three stories for students to read aloud to a partner during independent work time. Their partner listened, offered corrective feedback, and signed the back of the story as an accountability measure. For example, let's say we were reading stories 20 and 21 this week. If so, we would focus on rereading stories from the previous four to six weeks to build fluency. On Monday, students would reread stories 10 and 11, on Tuesday stories 12 and 13, on Wednesday stories 14 and 15, on Thursday stories 16 and 17, and on Friday stories 18 and 19. Since the stories are numbered and collected in one folder, students have easy access. And since their partner must sign and date the back after hearing each story read aloud, there is a strong accountability piece in place.

   Note: If you have access to additional stories focusing on the same target skill, this is even better. Number these stories in the same manner. Have students read these new texts focusing on previously taught skills each week as part of their independent work time routine.

2. **Include writing about the decodable stories as regular follow-up work two or three times per week.** This writing can be a part of the lesson time or be used as a great application assignment during independent work time or for homework. Possible writing extension ideas can be found in the previous section.

3. Many apps and whiteboard activities contain decodable texts.
Select apps that have a wide range of text levels and built-in supports, such as sounding out words for students when they need assistance. Find whiteboard activities that are interactive (i.e., students are marking up the text as they search for specific phonics patterns) and that have comprehension follow-up to check understanding. You can also post decodable texts on a whiteboard for students to mark up during independent or partner work (e.g., finding all the words with specific spelling patterns). Below are some examples.

The simple, black-and-white *Bob Books* have been transformed into a really good app with decoding support and student motivation built in.

Source: Courtesy of Bob Books.

Rock 'N Learn has lots of simple texts and some built-in supports for young readers.

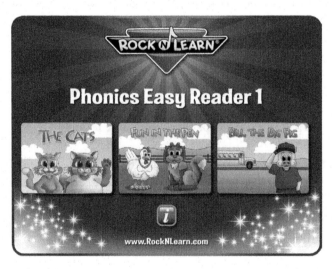

Source: Courtesy of Rock 'N Learn.

In *Teaching Phonics* by Wiley Blevins (2011b), students mark up decodable texts after they read them to locate words with specific spelling patterns that are the focus of the week's instruction.

Source: Blevins (2011b).

Success Ingredient 7: Reading Connected Text

Background and Key Characteristics	Best Practices and Look-Fors for Success	Common Instructional Pitfalls	Day Clinic: Examine Your Practices	Next Steps to Leap Forward
• Use controlled, decodable text at the beginning level to develop a sense of control and comfort in reading. • Decodable text is a primary practice tool in early phonics instruction. • Key characteristics of this text are outlined in *Becoming a Nation of Readers* (Anderson et al., 1985): instructive, comprehensible, engaging. • Two key studies on decodable text have detailed their importance (see Blevins, 2006; Juel & Roper-Schneider, 1985).	• Use the decodable text routine to engage students while reading in decoding, vocabulary, and comprehension work. • Examine the texts you are using and compare the words included to what students have learned (phonics and sight words).	• Not using decodable texts as key instructional tools • Using weak books that impede understanding • Not replacing or revising poor-quality texts • Focusing more on decodability count than comprehensibility • Not focusing on decoding *and* comprehension • Not frontloading vocabulary to build language during text conversations and not extending the books to writing	Ask yourself: • Do you have a sufficient amount of decodable text to use with your phonics lessons (at least two different texts per skill)? • How strong are the decodable texts you have? What are their weaknesses? Can these be easily fixed? • What instructional routine do you use when reading these texts? Are you providing modeling and self-correction based on student attempts? • Are students reading the decodable texts multiple times to build fluency? • Are you extending the decodable texts through associated writing activities? • Are you monitoring comprehension during and after reading the decodable texts? • What is the content and quality of discussion you are having around these decodable texts? Have you tried ways to enhance these conversations to build vocabulary and conceptual knowledge (using read-alouds to frontload vocabulary, using graphic organizers to record and examine story structure, etc.)? **Try it!** • Examine a series of texts and evaluate their use during phonics instruction. • Create and evaluate your own phonics text given a set of skills. • Revise weak texts provided. • Determine the instructional use of a range of texts.	• Add cumulative rereading of previously read stories to ensure mastery over time (e.g., numbered story sheets). • Include writing about stories as follow-up and application of key words. • Include technology (apps and whiteboard activities).

Courtesy of Rick Harrington Photography

No matter how strong our instructional materials, routines, and resources are, without a skilled and informed teacher to implement them well, they will fall flat. A teacher's background knowledge of phonics and linguistics and attitudes about and expertise in specific phonics practices (e.g., instructional routines, using decodable text, error analysis) play a crucial role in instructional success.

The more you know about phonics and linguistics, the better prepared you are to understand and respond to student errors. For example, **a teacher who knows how sounds are formed in the mouth has a better understanding of why students use certain spellings to represent similarly formed sounds.** An experienced teacher knows that when a student writes *tran* for *chain*, that makes sense because of how the /tr/ sounds and the /ch/ sound are made in the mouth.

Likewise, **a teacher with this expertise improves the language of instruction to avoid student confusion.** A classic example of this is the teaching of rhyme. I frequently hear teachers working with young learners explain that two words rhyme because "they sound the same at the end." To us—skilled readers and writers—we know what that means. When we see the words *mat* and *sat*, we know that they rhyme. However, a beginning reader who

> *The more you know about phonics and linguistics, the better prepared you are to understand and respond to student errors.*

learns the above definition of rhyme might think that *mat* and *bit* rhyme since they both "sound the same at the end." That is, both end in the /t/ sound. What we need to explain to our early learners is why words rhyme in terms that are simple and concrete.

So, why do words *really* rhyme? Let's look at *mat* and *sat* again. They rhyme because they both end in /at/. In order for a teacher to explain rhyme in way that avoids possible student confusion, the language of instruction has to change and be more explicit, such as "The words *mat* and *sat* rhyme because they both end in /at/. Listen, /m/ . . . /at/, *mat*. /s/ . . . /at/, *sat*. Do you hear /at/ at the end of *mat* and *sat*? Yes. The two words rhyme because they both end in the /at/ sounds."

Knowing more about phonics and linguistics also helps a teacher better evaluate a student's writing for possible areas of strength and weaknesses. Previously (see page 108), I showed you a five-word spelling test I administered to first graders and how their spellings provided me with a great deal of information regarding the sound spellings they had mastered, their level of phonemic awareness, and their understanding of how words work.

Periodically reviewing student writing samples (something I recommend you do at least once a month with your colleagues to get a fresh eye on your students' work) is a great way to assess student growth over time, form small groups for differentiated instruction, and make grade-level course corrections as needed.

When it comes to helping teachers with their developing phonics knowledge, I like to meet with teachers when district administrators aren't present. (Sorry, principals and reading coordinators.) This allows teachers opportunities to freely express their thoughts and feelings about their instructional tools, materials, practices, and policies. I've found that only when I can dig deeply into these attitudes and beliefs can they be addressed in measured and respectful ways. During one conversation I had with a group of teachers, I discovered that they weren't using their decodable texts because, as one teacher put it, "they're boring and stupid." I then did some staff development on the importance of these texts as an instructional tool and their proper place in a phonics lesson and overall reading curriculum, and found better texts for these teachers to use. A lot can be accomplished by openly exploring our strengths and weaknesses, likes and dislikes, and overall attitudes regarding our work with our students and the resources we use.

Unfortunately, today's teachers face many challenges that can stand in the way of achieving instructional success. I encounter far too many teachers who are forced to use materials they know aren't meeting the needs of their students, are in situations in which their modifications or creativity are punished, or feel like the fun in teaching has been sapped away. These are serious concerns to me. While issues with personnel and district policies can be challenging to solve, below are some anecdotes to illustrate my experiences with some of these issues and how schools have addressed them. I offer them only as ways to spark discussion about what might work in your school or district. Be courageous. Think outside the box and work for change that can improve your experiences as a teacher and your students' overall success as early learners.

Today's teachers face many challenges that can stand in the way of achieving instructional success.

1. Bringing back some teacher control to reading instruction: The most alarming thing I see when visiting classrooms are teachers who have shut down due to the pressures and constraints placed upon them. As teachers, we know our students better than anyone else. Yet in some schools, teachers are given curriculum and told to follow it with fidelity—to do exactly what the guide says and never veer. To compound this issue, principals and district personnel visit these teachers, observe their teaching, and criticize or punish them when the lesson hasn't been followed verbatim.

This happens for a variety of reasons that are important to understand. A district reading coordinator, for example, is responsible for the academic growth of all the students in the school system. She purchases a packaged curriculum with research data to support its efficacy and believes that this program will have a strong, positive impact on student growth. She devotes a great deal of time and money to select, purchase, and train on the use of these new instructional materials and practices. So, it makes sense that the district administrator would want these materials used properly and implemented well. When principals and district-level personnel visit classrooms for observations, some have reading expertise; others do not. So what do they do? They pick up the lesson and follow along as the teacher teaches. Of course, any deviation from that plan will be noticed. Over time, teachers begin feeling like these observations are increasingly punitive and decide it's best to just "follow the plan." In some instances, the result is teachers who are going through the motions, not thinking about their students' needs to the level they can and should be. It's fear-based teaching, and it's the most disheartening thing I see in classrooms. So what do you do?

In some school districts I've worked with, I've recommended using an 80–20 principle of instruction.

In some school districts I've worked with, I've recommended using an 80–20 principle of instruction. I didn't make this up (I wish I had); it was something used by one of my principals back in the '80s and is common to high-tech companies today. Here are the basics behind the 80–20 principle. Workers devote 80% of their time to the assignments given them by their managers. The other 20% of their time is theirs, time in which they can innovate to create new product ideas and grow and develop. This creates a situation in which the company is getting the work it needs from its employees, and the employees are respected and highly engaged because they have time to be creative, use their training, and possibly create breakthrough ideas.

Eighty percent of the time, teachers use the district-approved materials and resources. Twenty percent of the time, teachers examine their student needs and use their own creative ideas and best practices to meet those needs.

How does this apply to the teaching of reading? It means that 80% of the time teachers use the district-approved materials and resources; 20% of the time, teachers examine their student needs and use their own creative ideas and best practices to meet those needs. This can occur in many different forms.

In one school, teachers followed the curriculum four days a week (80% of the time). The fifth day was called a "flex day." The teachers could meet the stated learning objectives in any way they saw fit. Some teachers would "bank" their flex days for a month and have a "flex week" in which they would do an author study, book study, or larger project-based learning mini-unit.

In another school in which the curriculum was written by the district, we built in places in the actual lesson plans each day where teachers had choices. Some were simple places, such as the selection of the daily read-aloud. The district's curriculum only provided a read-aloud for one day each week, yet students need to be read to every day. So, the district created a list of books from collections it had purchased, books available in the school library, and other recommended titles that the teachers could choose from related to the unit's theme. The teachers could also choose any book of their own that they liked. The teachers were given a generic read-aloud protocol (routine for selecting a book, identifying vocabulary words to highlight, writing text-based questions, etc.) to use with the books they chose. Teachers loved this freedom, and the amount of reading aloud increased in the classrooms. That's a simple fix.

We built in places in the actual lesson plans each day where teachers had choices.

In other places of the lesson, teachers were asked to think about the formative assessment data they had collected throughout the lesson or week and make decisions about what to do next based on their students' needs, rather than what the curriculum suggested. For example, on the last day of an instructional cycle in any reading program (generally Day 5), teachers are given a series of review activities, one per main skill taught that week. In classrooms where teachers felt punished for not following the curriculum, they would simply march through these (often simple and boring) activities without regard to whether or not their students needed them. In an 80–20 situation, teachers instead look at which skills their students need reinforcement on (and which students need what), then select from the activities provided; choose from a list of additional, more engaging activities provided by the district; or create their own activities to use. This is so much more fun for teachers and more purposeful for students! For teachers who don't have the time (or desire) to create their own engaging activities, many options are provided. For teachers who do, they can really run with it. If a district observer entered the classroom and picked up the lesson plan, he would know this was a place the teacher was thinking about her students' needs and innovating using her wealth of experience, resources, and expertise.

We need to put systems in place in which teachers are respected, highly engaged, thinking professionals with the necessary support tools.

Another example of bigger choice involved the use of novel studies. For the last unit of the year (in which we really wanted to reinforce the skills taught during the year in a longer text than those provided in basal reading anthologies), teachers could choose to do the unit provided in the basal or replace it with a novel study. The specific novel used was selected by the teachers after several were distributed for review and a vote was taken. (Teachers must have a say in some of these decisions.) A few master teachers then worked together at the district level to create a lesson guide including some support for vocabulary selection and instruction, text-dependent questions, writing experiences, and so on. However, teachers were asked to evaluate their students' growth on all the major standards for the year and focus on those that students still needed work on. That means teachers could innovate on the plan provided. Additional support readings were provided to supplement the novel. These were often short, informational text pieces so those skills could be addressed, too.

The point I'm trying to make is that we need to put systems in place in which teachers are respected, highly engaged, thinking professionals with the necessary support tools. This involves a system in which district-level administrators also know that their efforts (time, money, expertise) are being utilized and publishers are comfortable that their materials are being implemented with enough efficacy to ensure their success. Let me be clear—I do not define *efficacy* as "blindly following" as many in the educational world do. Efficacy with respect to instructional materials is important to publishers. If you purchase their materials and use them poorly (e.g., pick and choose activities, modify greatly) and your test scores go down, it reflects poorly on the publishers and can negatively impact their sales. No one knows that you didn't adhere closely to the lessons and materials provided; they only see the weak test scores. That is why publishers push for efficacy in the use of their materials. But remember, a textbook or instructional resource is only a tool. A *tool*. You want to find and use the best tools possible for your students. But you and only you can take each tool to the next level by adjusting it to your students and their specific needs. No one tool will be perfect.

You don't have to wait to read a study or go to a conference to improve your daily instruction. Think. Try. Assess. Adjust.

2. Becoming teacher-researchers: You don't have to wait for research to be published in a professional journal or magazine to test instructional routines and practices in your classroom. Even in my early years of teaching, I was conducting mini-studies to examine the effect certain practices would have on my students if I felt a modification to what I was doing was needed and I wanted to find the best practices to meet those needs. For example, one year, I was teaching a Grade 2–3 combo class. I was given the 30 lowest-performing second and third graders (4 of whom had severe behavioral issues). In the district in which I was teaching, formal spelling instruction did not begin until students were reading at the second-grade level. I don't remember the rationale for that (and it still doesn't make sense to me). Regardless, a large group of my Grade 2 students were reading at a Grade 1 level, so I was not allowed to teach spelling. These students observed their other classmates and friends from other Grade 2 classrooms practicing their spelling lists and doing fun activities with the words. It developed into a motivational issue, with these students wondering each week, "Why?" So I set up a small study to last six weeks. I showed my principal how I would collect data (pretests, posttests, student writing samples) as well as attitude surveys. I showed how I would teach and incorporate spelling into the existing lessons and, once I got my principal's sign-off, began my mini-study. The results supported the inclusion of spelling for these students even though their reading level was a bit low. My mini-study paid off. You might be facing similar questions or concerns in your classroom. My recommendation is to get support from your principal or district reading coordinator if the resource or practice you want to implement will dramatically change your curriculum and formally plan how you will collect and analyze the data. If it is something smaller (e.g., a modification to an existing routine such as the Read–Spell–Write–Extend routine I outlined in the section on high-frequency words), then try it out and closely monitor student growth. Take note of the impact the adjusted routine has on your students and with which students (some routines work better with some students than others, and it is always good to have a repertoire of techniques and strategies in your teaching toolbox). You don't have to wait to read a study or go to a conference to improve your daily instruction. Think. Try. Assess. Adjust.

3. Group planning for instruction: When it comes to phonics, group planning with grade-level teacher teams can be an effective tool. I recommend meeting regularly (at least once a month) to evaluate student writing samples, review cumulative phonics assessments, discuss strengths and weaknesses in existing curriculum, and make course corrections as needed. It is better to do this frequently rather than wait for issues to build or curriculum weaknesses to get too firmly rooted in your practices. Ongoing critical evaluation with everyone offering advice, expertise, and viewpoints can sometimes lead to creative and useful solutions. In addition, use what you discover about teacher knowledge base and student performance to plan your own professional development as a grade-level team.

We spend so much time differentiating our instruction for our students and are so attuned to their wide range of needs, but when it comes to our professional learning, it is almost always treated as a "one size fits all" proposition.

4. Restructuring professional development: School- and district-level professional development has always baffled me to a certain degree. Why? Well, we spend so much time differentiating our instruction for our students and are so attuned to their wide range of needs, but when it comes to our professional learning, it is almost always treated as a "one size fits all" proposition. It's like we throw out everything we know about teaching and learning when it comes to our own personal growth. We have to do better.

I highly recommend differentiated professional development. Let me provide a very basic example of this. Let's say that your district is holding an all-day staff development workshop. The students get the day off, and everyone meets at some central location. Let's say that the main focus of this professional development is on the implementation of a new phonics assessment system your district has purchased. Let's say that your district also wants to spend part of the day addressing phonics instructional practices that have been observed to be district-wide weaknesses. What generally happens is that all teachers sit through a day in which they all hear the same material in the same way—even school personnel who might not be teaching phonics or who do so quite effectively. You might have other teachers who are new to the district or to teaching and have had little previous training on phonics basics. Yet, they all receive the same material.

Now imagine if we developed our professional development the way we teach our students. Instead of one size fits all, we would rearrange our day. In the morning, we might have all teachers together to hear the ins and outs of this new phonics assessment system since it is new content for all of them (much like we do with our whole group instruction in our classrooms). Then, in the afternoon, we would ask our principals and reading coordinators to assign teachers to different groups for "phonics intensive" work based on their level of need.

There might be one group for teachers who need the basics to start developing a strong foundational understanding. There might be another group for teachers who have the basics in place, but for whom there are places in their instruction in which some fine-tuning would really make a difference in their students' growth. You might have a small third group of master teachers with whom you discuss how to implement and monitor this training (follow up to ensure application, support, and additional training as needed). These master teachers might also assist in the training of the first two groups. Now doesn't this sound more like what we do in our classrooms during our small group differentiation time?

Imagine if we developed our professional development the way we teach our students.

And, to take it a step further, I would recommend offering an additional training session that afternoon (spend only half of the afternoon on the phonics issue). This time would be devoted to addressing areas of development that teachers in the district are concerned about. For example, a quick survey could be given to teachers in which they identify areas for which they would like (or feel they need) additional training. A few of the biggest issues would be selected and sessions offered on them, much like if the teachers went to a professional conference. In this way, teachers would be respected and have some say in their own personal growth. Thus, at the end of the day, the district would have trained everyone on a new assessment tool, teachers would have received tailored training in phonics based on their assessed needs and levels of expertise, and teachers would have been able to choose one area that they wanted to learn more about. It's a win-win.

The other thing about professional development that always surprises me is the inability to use the best practices by the strongest teachers in a district. Whenever I visit a district, I'm shown teachers doing exciting and innovative things. My first question is always "Why aren't all your teachers trained in this?" Why districts aren't scaling up the techniques, strategies, resources, and ideas of their best teachers remains a mystery to me. Providing differentiated professional development days like the one I described above is one way to give these teachers opportunities to do just that. Try it!

4 BEST EFFECT

Differentiated Professional Development

- Part of the day, focus on the district's needs in a whole group session.
- Part of the day, focus on teachers' needs as assessed by principals and district administrators in small group sessions.
- Part of the day, provide "teacher choice" sessions based on a survey of district teachers as to the curricular areas in which they desire or need additional professional development.
- Brainstorm other ways to differentiate professional development throughout the year (e.g., online videos of key instructional routines or procedures on the district or school website).

The last aspect of professional development that must be addressed is the need for everyone to acknowledge that phonics or word study is specialized learning and that learning varies based on what grade band you teach: K–2, 3–5, or 6–8. What you teach and how you teach phonics and word study as a K–2 teacher is quite different from that for a 3–5 teacher, for example. This becomes an issue when teachers move from one grade band to another (e.g., a fourth-grade teacher moving down the grades to become a first-grade teacher). Often, these teachers are experienced, perhaps having spent many years in the grade they just left. As a result, schools and districts rarely provide the kinds of basic professional development they might need to address the specific learning needs of the students in their new grade band. I've seen too many teachers apply instructional routines and practices from one grade band to another, with limited success. Any teacher moving across grade bands should have the opportunity for specialized training in the area of phonics and word study.

5. **Videotape. Videotape. Videotape:** As painful as it is to see ourselves on film, I highly recommend occasionally videotaping your lessons (or pieces of a lesson you are concerned about) and analyzing them. You might set up the camera so that it is focused on the students, for example. Monitor time on task, use of every-pupil-response techniques, lesson time wasted, use of corrective feedback, success of a specific strategy, or any other aspect of your teaching. Ask a colleague to watch the video and offer feedback, too. These mini-evaluations when you are "faced with the truth" can go a long way to opening up your eyes to issues you might not easily see otherwise.

Plus One More Essential Success Ingredient: You!

Background and Key Characteristics	Day Clinic: Examine Your Practices	Next Steps to Leap Forward
Teacher attitudes and background knowledge or phonics expertise play a crucial role in instructional success.	• In grade-level teacher teams, explore attitudes and knowledge base of teachers in your school (and how this affects instructional practices). • Examine ways to (a) bring back some teacher control to early reading, (b) become teacher-researchers, (c) group-plan for instruction, and (d) restructure professional development.	• Plan professional development around assessed weaknesses in knowledge or research-based routines and linguistics (as well as focusing on areas of concern or dislikes in current materials and practices). • Group-analyze reading and writing work (including assessments) to adjust instruction and classroom practices. • Videotape lessons and evaluate your practices.

10 Common Causes of Phonics Instruction Failure

and How to Avoid Them

Courtesy of Rick Harrington Photography

My work with teachers, publishers, and school district administrators has offered me an interesting view of three discrete and sometimes competing perspectives on what is best for phonics classroom practice. Add into this mix of ideas our country's odd fascination with chasing the next "shiny new thing" in education, and it highlights our need to stop, take a breath, reexamine the research data, and be more objective (and brutally honest with ourselves) about how well our practices are really working for our students (including those practices we really love).

Novelists frequently talk about "killing their darlings" when editing their books. I know that sounds harsh, but what it means is that they painfully delete or modify those sentences, paragraphs, and even chapters that they thought were "brilliant" when writing that first draft, but really don't service the story and are unnecessary. We need to take that same approach to our instructional practices— taking a step back to reevaluate what we do. This is essential if we are going to maximize our instructional practices and materials to benefit our students. It's tough work. It has been painful for me to find flaws in my own practices and beliefs, but that's what new information and data will do: open our eyes and push us to revise, fine-tune, and improve. Our students are the benefactors of our efforts, and they certainly deserve it.

This next section highlights 10 of the most common causes of phonics failure in our classrooms. While there are others, I selected these 10 because they are the most prevalent, and all of them can be readily fixed. Some of the content in this section will be familiar. I've revisited and expanded upon some of the ideas I presented earlier. I hope that this repetition will aid in your continual thinking about and retention of these issues.

Phonics is detailed, can be difficult at times, and takes years to master. So, don't worry if some of these principles seem overwhelming at first. Select one or two to attack each month or semester of the school year, and keep working through them as needed. Use your school and district resources to help you—both people and print. And don't give up! The ideas presented here reflect over 20 years of my constant research and exploration on the topic. And, as I finish this book, I continue that exploration. Who knows? In 20 years, I'll probably have much more to say!

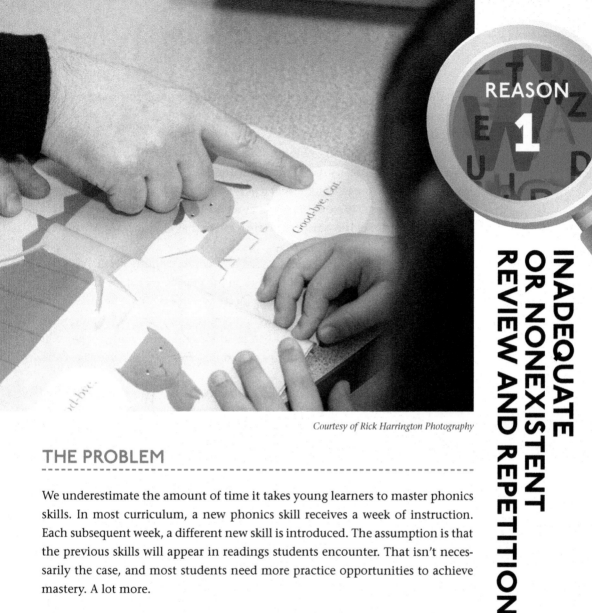

REASON

1

INADEQUATE
OR NONEXISTENT
REVIEW AND REPETITION

THE PROBLEM

We underestimate the amount of time it takes young learners to master phonics skills. In most curriculum, a new phonics skill receives a week of instruction. Each subsequent week, a different new skill is introduced. The assumption is that the previous skills will appear in readings students encounter. That isn't necessarily the case, and most students need more practice opportunities to achieve mastery. A lot more.

When a new skill is introduced, it should be systematically and purposefully reviewed for the next four to six weeks. That means there should be significant instructional and practice opportunities for students. Our goal must be to teach to mastery rather than just exposure. Although we all agree with this statement, when we look at our curriculum objectively, we see that it too often has an "exposure focus." When you adopt a "mastery focus," it changes the way you teach, write lessons, and assess a skill. Once a skill is introduced, you are "in it for the long haul" and don't give up until all your students can successfully apply the skill to authentic reading and writing experiences weeks or months after the initial introduction.

HOW TO FIX IT

Our goal must be to teach to mastery rather than just exposure.

With the fast pacing of most curriculum, a more substantial review and repetition cycle must often be added. Look at the skill you are teaching this week, then mark all the instances it is reviewed in the upcoming four to six weeks. These should be substantial—not one or two words in a story here or there. With that information, determine places in the instructional cycle to increase practice through additional words in blending lines, dictation, and repeated readings of previously read decodable stories. Below are some of the **ways you can build in a more systematic and purposeful review and repetition cycle** that I have previously shared.

1. Blending work: During blending, you list words with the new target phonics skill as well as words with skills taught in the prior four to six weeks. See the example in which the teacher is focusing on words with short *u*. The teacher has added lines (Lines 5 and 6) with words containing review skills (the previously taught short vowels). In this way, she can continue to provide guided practice in reading these words for an extended period of time (many weeks after the skill's initial introduction).

Blending Lines

up	cup	pup	but	cut	hut (vary by beginning sound)
cup	cut	bug	bun	hug	hum (vary by ending sound)
cap	cup	pop	pup	bug	bag (vary by medial sound)
sun	rub	dug	fun	gum	jug (mixed set, target skill)
map	led	hip	rock	dot	rip (mixed review sets)
fell	tap	fog	beg	tan	lid (mixed review sets)
cups	hugs	buns	bugs	(challenge lines)	
cutting	hugging	bugging	humming	(challenge lines)	

2. Dictation: During dictation, you model how to transfer phonics skills to spelling, then provide practice for students to apply the skill. You can add words with review skills to this weekly activity. While the activity is focused on spelling words with short *u*, the list also contains a few words with previously taught short vowels.

up, run, cut, bugs

map, fix, lock, red

We had fun in the sun!

3. Rereading decodable stories: The rereading of previously read books and stories is a great way to build fluency. It is also ideal for extending practice of skills over multiple weeks. Most programs have students revisit books read only during the initial instructional cycle, which is generally one week. However, to ensure practice with skills previously taught, I work with teachers to create a system in which students systematically reread stories. This can be accomplished in many ways. In one school district I visited, once students read a decodable story, they were given a one-page story sheet (just the text of the story—not the pictures) to put in their reading folder, which students kept at their desks. These stories were numbered in sequence. The reason the teachers gave a story sheet was that distributing and managing a large number of little books was difficult. So, the teacher typed in the text of each story read and made copies for the students. Most stories fit on one page. Then, during small group instructional time when students were working independently or with partners (i.e., not meeting with the teacher), the students were assigned specific stories to reread each day. The teacher would list on the board the number or numbers of the stories to reread. So, for example, on Monday, the students might reread Story Sheets 4 and 5. On Tuesday, they might reread Story Sheets 6 and 7, and so on. In this way, the teacher could easily cycle through the stories from the previous four to six weeks. To hold students accountable for the rereadings, the students had to reread the stories to a partner. The partner followed along, then signed and dated the story on the back (which the teacher periodically checked). Not only did students have extended practice reading stories with review skills, but reading with partners during independent work time is far better than doing worksheets or other similar types of activities. The students interacted with, supported, and assisted their partner in any way necessary. Some teachers also send these story sheets home for students to reread with families. This helps parents see their child's growing reading skills. Teachers with a wider range of resources created story sheets for

Create a system in which students systematically reread stories.

new stories focusing on each previously taught skill instead of having students reread the same story so many times. Other teachers added follow-up discussion questions and prompts for the partners to use following the rereading, including retelling the story in their own words, answering basic comprehension questions, finding details in the story, extending the story through writing, circling all the words with a specific phonics pattern, and so on.

4. Word building and word sorts: In word building, the teacher has students use a limited set of letter cards to build a series of words that generally vary by only one or two letters. For example, a word-building set for short *u* might include the following letter cards (*u, b, c, g, p, r,* and *t*) and series of words to be built in this sequence (*up, cup, cut, but, bug,* and *rug*). To build in review and repetition, a teacher would modify the sequence of words to include a few with review skills, such as *up, cup, cap, cat, cut, but, bat, bag, bug, big, rig, rag,* and *rug.* The new set of letter cards only adds the short vowels *a* and *i*.

In word sorts, students are given word cards and asked to sort them by related sounds or spellings. For example, for short *u*, students might be given the following word cards: *but, cut, hut, bug, dug,* and *rug.* They would then sort the words by phonogram -*ut* and -*ug.* To build in review and repetition, the words *bag, tag,* and *rag* or *big, dig,* and *rig* could be added. In this way, words with previously taught skills could be included. These words also require students to fully analyze and carefully distinguish them from the -*ut* and -*ug* words as they are quite similar in spelling (*ug, ag, ig*).

In these and other ways, you can easily add a systematic and purposeful review and repetition cycle to your basic instruction where it might be lacking *without* significantly increasing instructional time. In addition to these simple fixes, make sure you have at your fingertips review lessons and small group activities for the skills taught during the previous four to six weeks so you can pull over a group of students at any time to work on these skills as you notice needs based on their reading and writing progress. Collect these from your published curriculum (e.g., create a folder for each skill or skill set, such as short vowels), find great lessons and materials online, or design your own. This is a great activity to co-create with other teachers on your grade-level team.

Sample Grade 1 Weekly Instructional Cycle (with built-in review and repetition cycle)

Day	Instructional Sequence
1	**Phonemic Awareness** (5 minutes) Students engage in one of the "power" phonemic awareness skills: oral blending. **Introduce Sound Spelling/Blending** (5 minutes) Students are introduced to the new skill using an action rhyme, then practice blending differentiated word lists to apply the skill with teacher guidance. These word lists contain review skills from the previous four to six weeks. **High-Frequency Words** (5 minutes) Students are introduced to the week's sight words using the Read–Spell–Write–Extend routine. They only complete the Read–Spell–Write portion. **Read Connected Text** (10 minutes) Students read and interact with a decodable text (the first for the week) applying the new skill in context. Review words are built into the text. (If good texts don't exist, the teacher creates sentences with new and review skills for students to read.) **Word Sort** (5 minutes) Students engage in open and closed word sorts using the new skill and discuss what they learn about how words work. **Teacher Table and Independent Work** **Sound Spelling/Blending** (small group teacher table) The teacher works with English learners to address vocabulary issues in blending lines and in decodable texts. This continues throughout the week. **Learning Center** (independent work time) Students work with partners using weekly learning centers and technology. Students reread two previously read decodable texts with a partner.
2	**Phonemic Awareness** (5 minutes) Students engage in one of the "power" phonemic awareness skills: oral segmentation. **Review Sound Spelling/Blending** (5 minutes) Students review the target skill and the blending lines—interacting with them in a new way. This includes a cumulative review of previous sound spellings (last four to six weeks). **High-Frequency Words** (5 minutes) Students review the week's sight words using the Read–Spell–Write–Extend routine. They complete the Extend portion. Students reread the week's decodable text to a partner during this time or independent work time to build fluency with phonics words and high-frequency words. **Dictation** (5 minutes) Students engage in a guided spelling activity to begin transferring their new reading skill to writing. This includes some words with skills from the previous four to six weeks.

(Continued)

(Continued)

Day	Instructional Sequence
2 (cont.)	**Word Building** (10 minutes) Students use letter cards to build words to increase their word awareness and flexibility with the new and previously taught skills. Words with previous skills are folded into the word list. **Teacher Table and Independent Work** **Read Connected Text** (independent work time) Students reread two previously read decodable texts with a partner. **Dictation** (small group teacher table) The teacher repeats the dictation exercise with students who struggle and continues with other words. (Includes review words.)
3	**Phonemic Awareness** (5 minutes) Students engage in one of the other Common Core State Standards (or state standards) phonemic awareness skills. **Review Sound Spelling/Blending and Word Study** (10 minutes) Students review the target skill and learn the week's word study skill. This includes a quick cumulative review of all previous skills (e.g., show letter cards, and students chorally say the corresponding sound). **High-Frequency Words** (5 minutes) Students review the week's sight words using the Read–Spell–Write–Extend routine. They then apply the words to a writing exercise. A quick review of previous words, such as chorally reading word cards or simple sentences with words, occurs. There is a focus on the most problematic words. **Read Connected Text** (10 minutes) Students read a decodable story for the week (the second for the target skill) and focus on comprehension. Review words are built into the text. **Teacher Table and Independent Work** **Word Sort** (independent work time) Students repeat the closed word sort with a partner during independent work time. Students reread two previously read decodable texts with a partner. **Word Building** (small group teacher table) The teacher repeats the word-building exercise (from Day 2) in small groups with students needing more practice.
4	**Phonemic Awareness** (5 minutes) Students engage in one of the "power" phonemic awareness skills: oral blending. **Review Sound Spelling/Word Study** (5 minutes) Students review the week's target skill and word study skill. This includes a quick cumulative review of all previous skills (e.g., show letter cards, and students chorally say the corresponding sound). **High-Frequency Words** (5 minutes) Students review the week's sight words, then work on adding sentences with the new words to their creative cumulative sentences in their writing journals.

Day	Instructional Sequence
4 (cont.)	**Dictation** (5 minutes) Students engage in a guided spelling activity to continue transferring their new reading skill to writing. (Includes review words.) **Read Connected Text** (10 minutes) Students reread a decodable story (the second for the week) with teacher (and partner) support to build fluency and interact with the text. **Teacher Table and Independent Work** **Word Building** (independent work time) Students work with partners to build words that the teacher lists and to make other words with the letter set. Words with previous skills are built into the word list. Students reread two previously read decodable texts with a partner. **Word Study** (small group teacher table) The teacher revisits the word study skill with students who struggled during the lesson.
5	**Phonemic Awareness** (5 minutes) Students engage in one of the "power" phonemic awareness skills: oral segmentation. **Review Sound Spelling/Blending and Word Study** (5 minutes) Students review the week's target skill and word study skill. **High-Frequency Words** (5 minutes) Students review the week's sight words using the cumulative sentence in their writing journals. **Word Building/Word Ladder** (10 minutes) Students complete the word ladder (combines word building and vocabulary). **Read Connected Text: Write About It** (10 minutes) Students revisit a decodable story and complete a writing extension. **Teacher Table and Independent Work** **Cumulative Assessment** (small group teacher table/independent work time) The teacher uses cumulative assessment to assess a small group of students' mastery (and will cycle through all students throughout the month). Other students work with partners to reread two previous decodable texts.

Courtesy of Rick Harrington Photography

THE PROBLEM

Students progress at a much faster rate in phonics when the bulk of instructional
time is spent on applying the skills to authentic reading and writing experiences,
rather than isolated skill-and-drill work. It is through application that learning
is solidified and consolidated. I can't stress enough the importance of increasing
application time—portions of the lesson in which students apply their growing
phonics skills to reading and writing connected text. At least 50% of a phonics
lesson should be devoted to these application exercises for all students, but especially for struggling readers. Unfortunately, the instruction we provide our struggling readers is usually dominated by isolated skill work when in fact what these
students need is even more application work. Regardless of their level, students
must be thinking about their toolbox of phonics skills in ways that are useful to
becoming skilled readers and writers.

HOW TO FIX IT

At least 50% of
a phonics lesson
should be devoted to
application exercises.

Evaluate the average amount of time your students spend on reading and writing during your phonics lessons. Below are two schedules from actual teachers that we discussed earlier. Note how much time in each lesson is devoted to application. Consider the cumulative effects of this over time. If week after week I taught you chords on the guitar, how well would you play at the end of a month if you rarely got to pick up a real guitar and try out the chords? Now imagine that each day I let you pick up that guitar. You might struggle at first, and I might initially assign very short songs or portions of songs. But, over time, those chords would become automatic, and we would move on to more complex songs.

Schedule A

10 minutes: Action rhyme review

10 minutes: Phonemic awareness (rhyme)

5 minutes: Introduce letter sound

5 minutes: Read story

Schedule B

5 minutes: Review warm-up (cumulative)

5 minutes: Phonemic awareness (oral segmentation)

5 minutes: Introduce letter sound and model blending

10 minutes: Read story

5 minutes: Writing follow-up

So, what can you do? Begin by timing each portion of your phonics lessons for a week. Record each major part of the lesson (phonemic awareness activity, skill introduction, modeling blending, word building, reading decodable text, etc.) and write the amount of time you spend on each. Add up the application activities (reading connected text and writing) to see if they consume at least 50% of your lesson. Make adjustments to your lessons for the next week and experiment with ways to increase the application portions of the lesson. Ask yourself, "Does this activity really connect to my goal this week of helping my students read and write using the new phonics skill?" Continue throughout the upcoming month to adjust your lessons to maximize application time. It might be easier to videotape your phonics lessons for the week, then review them back to back to monitor application and student engagement. Remember that each portion of a phonics lesson should be fast-paced and robust. Be critical with yourself. Are you belaboring an activity that could be sped up? Are there moments in the lesson that would best be delivered during small group time? Can you extend application to small group and independent work time?

One of the easiest ways to increase application time (in addition to speeding up portions of the lesson in which you introduce and model skills in isolation) **is to add daily writing work.** This can include dictation (where you also dictate a sentence or two) and writing extensions to decodable stories read. I rarely see students write about the decodable texts they read. Instead of racing through them, use them as springboards to discussions about story content or structure and assign writing to take advantage of the links between the words in the stories and the phonics skills you are teaching and reviewing. **Make sure the writing exercises are thought-provoking and engaging.** I'm not talking about having students write three sentences about the story. I'm talking about having them write a detailed retelling in their own words (adding rich descriptions), extend the story by putting the characters in new situations, or (if nonfiction) explain what they learned and how it adds to all they know about the book's topic.

REASON

3

INAPPROPRIATE
READING MATERIALS
TO PRACTICE SKILLS

THE PROBLEM

The connection between what we teach and what we have young learners read has a powerful effect on their word-reading strategies (Juel & Roper-Schneider, 1985) and their phonics and spelling skills (Blevins, 2006). It also affects their motivation to read. I discussed this in depth in the section on reading connected text. Unfortunately, far too many students receive phonics instruction followed up by text that has a limited relationship to their growing skills or opportunities to practice the new target skill.

The type of text that is ideal for this practice is decodable text. This text is controlled based on the phonics skills taught up to that point in the scope and sequence, with an emphasis on the new target skill for that instructional cycle (e.g., week of instruction). That is, the majority of the words in this text can be sounded out based on the sound–spelling relationships students have learned—giving them loads of opportunities to apply those skills to real reading experiences. For example, if the teacher is teaching long *o* spelled *oa* and *ow*, the students might read a book called *The Slow Boat*. This book would contain a lot of words with *oa* and *ow*, as well as words with previously taught phonics skills. It would also contain some sight words—words like *the*, *come*, and *was* that had been taught. It might even contain a couple vocabulary words that would be neither decodable nor sight words already taught, such as *river* (although these would be minimal and might not exist at all).

As Juel and Roper-Schneider (1985) explained,

> The selection of text used very early in first grade may, at least in part, determine the strategies and cues children learn to use, and persist in using, in subsequent word identification. . . . In particular, emphasis on a phonics method seems to make little sense if children are given initial texts to read where the words do no follow regular letter-sound correspondence generalizations. . . . [T]he types of words which appear in beginning reading texts may well exert a more powerful influence in shaping children's word identification strategies than the method of reading instruction.

In 1985, the government document *Becoming a Nation of Readers* (Anderson, Hiebert, Scott, & Wilkinson, 1985) provided a set of criteria for creating controlled, decodable text. This type of text should include the following three criteria:

1. Comprehensible: Vocabulary must be understandable. Words must be derived from students' speaking and listening vocabularies. The stories should make sense and follow natural-sounding English spoken and written patterns. No sentences should be in these stories that you, as a proficient speaker and reader of English, have not uttered, written, or read.

2. Instructive: The majority of the words must be decodable based on the sound spellings previously taught. A strong connection between instruction and text must exist.

3. Engaging: Connected text must be engaging enough for students to want to read it again and again, like a good trade book. Just because this is an instructional tool doesn't mean we should throw our standards out the window. Students need to revisit this text to develop fluency and increase reading rate. The text should be worth revisiting (and talking about). In early texts, some of the engagement and discussion will be derived from the photos and illustrations, but the text must support them.

HOW TO FIX IT

How do you know if you have the right kinds of text for your students to practice their growing decoding skills? **Examine a few pages from the books you give your students to read** (especially in K–1). Using your phonics scope and sequence, mark all the words that can be sounded out using those and *only those* skills. Add up the total and divide it by the total number of words in the passage. Students should be able to sound out over 50% of these words based on the phonics skills you have taught them up to that point for the text to be a strong phonics practice tool. (If you are short for time, a quick look at the vowel patterns in the words as compared to those you have taught will give you a snapshot of the text's general decodability.) If the text is less than 50% decodable, more controlled text will be needed until students learn additional phonics skills and develop a sense of comfort or control in their reading. This generally happens for most students around mid–Grade 1, although decodable text is an essential phonics practice tool for most students for all of kindergarten and Grade 1, and should be used for struggling readers in Grades 2 and up who have not mastered the basic phonics skills.

You can **purchase texts that align with your phonics scope and sequence, search for texts online, or create your own passages.** Whichever path you choose, make sure that students have daily opportunities to practice their decoding skills and build fluency.

SKILL–SEQUENCE MATCH: THE BEST FIT

Look at the three passages below. Which skills in your scope and sequence would you use each passage to reinforce?

Passage 1

The black horse runs in the grass.

Clip! Clop!

Is it fast? You bet!

The green frog hops into the pond.

Flip! Flop!

Where did it go?

Skill Focus: _____

Passage 2

Lee is a farmer. He plants seeds in his field each year. Lee grows three things to eat. He grows peas, beets, and corn. These vegetables will feed a lot of people.

Skill Focus: _____

Passage 3

I could've painted a picture. But, I can't find my paint set.

My friend would've lent me hers. But, she isn't home yet.

I should've called her in the morning. But, she sleeps late.

I could've, would've, should've. Oh, well.

I'll think of something else to do tomorrow. I won't worry!

Skill Focus: _____

Source: Passages from Blevins (2011b).

Courtesy of Rick Harrington Photography

THE PROBLEM

Teachers of struggling readers often spend too much instructional time doing the "heavy lifting," such as overmodeling and having students simply repeat. I think it's natural for us teachers to want to support our students and guard them from too much frustration. Unfortunately, when it comes to our lower-level readers, we often go overboard without realizing it.

Effective instruction is based on the gradual release model: I Do, We Do, You Do (Pearson & Gallagher, 1983). In this model, the teacher provides a brief intro-duction to the skill while the students watch and listen (I Do). Then the teacher models the skill as students join in during guided practice. The teacher slowly turns over the responsibility of the practice to the students (We Do). This is a large portion of the lesson. Finally, students practice the skill on their own (You Do). This practice can occur during the lesson (e.g., with a partner) and as fol-low-up (e.g., during independent work time). This is also a large portion of the

Effective instruction is based on the gradual release model: I Do, We Do, You Do.

lesson and will extend over multiple days. Below is a graphic showing the gradual release model. Notice that the "I Do" portion of the lesson is quite small. In many classrooms with struggling readers, this model is turned upside down, and the majority of time is spent in "I Do" activities with students passively sitting and listening or parroting the teacher.

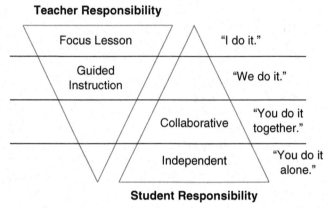

Teacher Responsibility

Focus Lesson — "I do it."

Guided Instruction — "We do it."

Collaborative — "You do it together."

Independent — "You do it alone."

Student Responsibility

A Structure for Instruction That Works

Source: Fisher & Frey (2014).

Sometimes I videotape teachers to show them examples of when and how this is happening. During the lesson, we are so aware of providing support, scaffolding, and corrective feedback. But, when we take a step back and watch what is really happening, it can be surprising how little work our students are actually doing. Remember that whoever does the thinking in a lesson does the learning. Students might struggle, but you are there to provide corrective feedback and support—only after they have made a serious attempt at working through the word or sentence. Always keep what I call "parrot" activities to a minimum. These are activities in which you model a skill, then have students simply repeat what you did (e.g., you model how to sound out or orally segment a word, then have the students sound out or orally segment the same word).

Whoever does the thinking in a lesson does the learning.

HOW TO FIX IT

Don't overdo the modeling. For example, model only a word or two in the blending lines, then have the students do the heavy lifting by sounding out the remaining words. Provide corrective feedback after students have made their attempts. Apply this principle to all aspects of your phonics instruction—blending, dictation, word building, word sorts, reading connected text. Prompt students with questions that help them verbalize their thinking, and model your own thinking through activities.

In addition, **videotape some of your phonics lesson.** Monitor the amount of opportunities students have to "think, interact, try, apply." Post these words around your classroom as reminders of the types of learning experiences your students need every day. Take note of how much wait time you provide students before you jump in with support. Stretch out that time if you find yourself offering support too quickly. Also, take note of which students you provide with lengthier amounts of time to attempt to read a word or sentence (versus jumping in right away). Is there a pattern?

Monitor the amount of opportunities students have to "think, interact, try, apply."

Courtesy of Rick Harrington Photography

THE PROBLEM

Phonics lessons tend to require a lot of manipulatives such as big books, letter cards, photo cards, magnetic letters, or other small pieces. Often, too much time is lost during a lesson distributing, organizing, and collecting these materials. Instructional time is valuable, and time lost in transitioning from one activity to another (as in distributing and organizing sets of letter cards) is time you can't get back. I have observed teachers losing 10–15 minutes of instructional time distributing and collecting letter or word cards in a short 20- to 30-minute phonics lesson. This adds up quickly. In one week, it can be over an hour of instructional time lost. We can't let this happen.

Transitional times, when materials are distributed or collected, should be viewed as valuable instructional moments. As such, they must be planned in advance. We can't afford to waste even a minute of instructional time in our already over-crowded instructional day.

HOW TO FIX IT

Allowing the organization, distribution, and collection of phonics materials (e.g., during word-building or word-sort activities) to gobble up too much instructional time is a common problem. And most teachers aren't even aware of how much time they are losing. The good news is there are many ways to avoid this.

One approach is to **recognize these transitional times as important instructional moments and insert into our lesson plans specific transitional activities.** The best activities are centered on skills we want or need to review. And this can take many forms. For example, you can sing "The Alphabet Song," play a phonemic awareness game, review your action rhymes for each letter, call out words for students to chorally spell, and so on. Whatever you decide to do, plan these transitions at the beginning of each week by selecting three or four great transitions. The important point is that you use this time to review and reinforce important skills, while keeping students engaged and on task. This has the added benefit of diminishing student behavior issues.

Another effective tactic is to **treat the organization of these materials as part of a student's "get ready for school" or "get ready for learning" procedure.** For example, some teachers I've worked with write the letter cards that will be used for that day on the board. As students enter the room in the morning, part of organizing themselves for the day includes gathering and organizing these letter cards (in addition to putting away their coats, adding their names to the lunch count, writing in their journals, or whatever morning procedures are already in place). Therefore, when it's time to begin the word-building exercise, the students have their letter card sets on their desk and ready to go. No time wasted. For word cards used during word sorts, students might need to cut out their word cards prior to school beginning (or finish this task during center time).

Look at the lesson outlines that follow. Record how you will transition from one activity to the next. Are there things your students could do at the beginning of the day or during independent work time to prepare for these activities?

Kindergarten Lesson Outline

1. Play a phonemic awareness game using picture cards (stored in a box in your reading center).

Transition: _____

2. Read aloud a rhyme from a big book of rhymes to highlight a spelling pattern (stored on an easel beside the rug where you gather students for whole group readings).

Transition: _____

3. Introduce a new letter sound using an action rhyme and an Alphabet Card.

Transition: _____

4. Model blending words using the new letter sound.

Transition: _____

5. Read a little book (decodable text) to practice the skill in context.

Transition: _____

6. Have students record words (from the story) in their writing journals with the new phonics skill.

Transition: _____

1. Do an oral segmentation exercise with Sound Boxes and counters.

Transition: _____

2. Review blending words with the new target skill using blending lines recorded on a whiteboard from a previous day.

Transition: _____

3. Do a word-building activity in which each student has his or her own set of letter cards.

Transition: _____

4. Reread a decodable book to build fluency.

Transition: _____

5. Students write a retelling of their decodable book in their journals.

Transition: _____

Courtesy of Rick Harrington Photography

THE PROBLEM

We all know that the more knowledge we have regarding how our students learn to read, the better prepared we are to meet their diverse instructional needs. Teacher expertise and attitudes about various aspects of phonics instruction matter. For example, teachers with a background in phonics or linguistics are better equipped to make meaningful instructional decisions, analyze student errors, and improve the language and delivery of instruction. Also, teacher attitudes toward phonics instructional materials (e.g., decodable text) and routines (e.g., sorts, word building, blending) have a significant effect on the use and effectiveness of these resources.

Our phonics knowledge base, beliefs, and feelings about phonics need to be explored within grade-level teacher teams. Professional development can then be tailored to our specific needs and wants after this exploration. For example, if teachers in a school or district don't use their basal-provided decodable texts (a powerful phonics instructional tool) because they don't like the stories, that can be addressed (e.g., examine these resources and edit or rewrite the stories or urge the principal to purchase better ones).

Teacher expertise and attitudes about various aspects of phonics instruction matter.

HOW TO FIX IT

Below are some of my recommendations for examining and enhancing your and your grade-level team's phonics expertise.

Evaluate (as a grade-level team) your overall phonics knowledge base. I suggest taking the quick test in "The Missing Foundation in Teacher Education: Knowledge of the Structure of Spoken and Written Language" (Moats, 1994). Then create a mini-course of self-study for you and your teacher team based on areas of need. Below are a few sample questions from the assessment. Answers are provided in the article.

1. For each word, determine the number of syllables and the number of morphemes: *salamander, crocodile, attached, unbelievable, finger, pies, gardener, psychometrics.*

2. How many speech sounds are in the following words? *ox, boil, king, thank, straight, shout, though, precious.*

3. When is a *ck* used in spelling?

4. What are the six common syllable types in English?

5. Account for the double *m* in *comment* or *commitment.*

Moats's article goes on to detail how this knowledge affects teaching and learning. She recommends that aspects of linguistics be taught to students to help them better understand how English words work. This knowledge also assists a teacher in being able to (1) interpret and respond to student errors, (2) pick the best examples for teaching decoding and spelling, (3) organize and sequence information for instruction, (4) use morphology to explain spelling, and (5) interpret the components of language arts instruction. I highly recommend this article as a starting point for any professional development work on phonics. A copy of it can be found at http://resources.corwin.com/blevinsphonics.

Another great source of support in your school or district is your speech therapist. These professionals receive a great deal of training in linguistics. Use them as a resource and plan professional development with them. There are also targeted phonics courses available for intensive study by your teacher team. Be selective. Review the materials and the credentials of the authors. In addition, many of the books in the reference list will serve as great source materials for in-depth exploration of phonics and its role in early reading instruction (e.g., Adams, 1990; Beck & Beck, 2013; Beck & Juel, 1995; Chall, 1967, 1983, 1996; Snow, Burns, & Griffin, 1998). You don't have to wait for your district to plan a special day around phonics to begin your study to maximize your teaching. Plus, phonics is a complex topic that needs to be explored over extended periods of time, with space to experiment and test out routines and practices with your students.

Courtesy of Pixabay (Unsplash)

THE PROBLEM

Teachers often spend too much time on activities they enjoy or that are easier for students and less time on the more challenging or "meaty" activities that increase learning. This can create an imbalance of activities within the phonics instructional cycle and result in too little time devoted to applying the skills to reading and writing.

Keep lessons fast-paced and rigorous. Phonics should be fun with students active and engaged the entire lesson. The bulk of time should be devoted to "real reading and writing" experiences and activities directly linked to these goals.

HOW TO FIX IT

Activities such as blending (using minimal contrasts), dictation, word building, and reading decodable text should be a significant part of

your weekly lesson routine. These activities should take precedence over others because they have the most direct link to reading and writing growth as well as overall word awareness. Revisit your weekly lesson plans and carve out more time for these activities. Experiment with speeding up other activities (such as phonemic awareness tasks) or using some of these activities as transitional activities (e.g., singing action rhymes for letter sounds introduced during transitional moments instead of using large portions of the phonics lesson).

The bulk of time should be devoted to "real reading and writing" experiences and activities directly linked to these goals.

Below are suggested time frames for each activity type. These are only provided as guidelines, not written in stone. The goal is to fine-tune the use of these practices so that they are quick and efficient.

1. Cumulative review of previously taught phonics skills (using letter cards): 1–2 minutes

2. Phonemic awareness task: 3–5 minutes

3. Introduction of new skill and blending practice: 5 minutes

4. Reading of decodable text: 10–15 minutes

5. Dictation: 5 minutes

6. Word building: 5–7 minutes

7. Word sorts (with follow-up discussion): 5 minutes

8. Writing extensions (following decodable text reading): 5–7 minutes (can also be completed during independent work time)

Weekly Schedule

Use the chart below to create a weekly schedule that takes advantage of these powerful activities. Record suggested times beside each activity. Create enough activities to fill the time, and focus on reading and writing (50% of the time minimum). Then experiment with this schedule. It might take weeks to fine-tune each activity type to get it at its most efficient. Keep timing yourself during the phonics lessons and improving on efficiency.

Monday	Tuesday	Wednesday	Thursday	Friday
Activity:	Activity:	Activity:	Activity:	Activity:
Time: _____	Time: _____	Time: _____	Time: _____	Time: _____
Activity:	Activity:	Activity:	Activity:	Activity:
Time: _____	Time: _____	Time: _____	Time: _____	Time: _____
Activity:	Activity:	Activity:	Activity:	Activity:
Time: _____	Time: _____	Time: _____	Time: _____	Time: _____
Activity:	Activity:	Activity:	Activity:	Activity:
Time: _____	Time: _____	Time: _____	Time: _____	Time: _____
Activity:	Activity:	Activity:	Activity:	Activity:
Time: _____	Time: _____	Time: _____	Time: _____	Time: _____

Courtesy of Rick Harrington Photography

THE PROBLEM

Assessment of phonics skills must be done over an extended period of time to ensure mastery. Weekly assessments focusing on one skill often give "false positives." That is, they show movement toward learning, but not mastery. If the skill isn't worked on for subsequent weeks, learning can decay. Cumulative assessments help you determine which skills have truly been mastered. All skills should be evaluated based on two factors: accuracy and speed.

HOW TO FIX IT

If you don't have cumulative weekly phonics assessments, they are easy to create. Following are guidelines, examples, and templates. Additional models are available at http://resources.corwin.com/blevinsphonics.

Creating Cumulative Assessments

Use these tips for creating a cumulative weekly assessment to monitor student mastery. Note that the assessment will change each week. Therefore, you will have over 30 weekly assessments for the year, each with skills from previous assessments *plus* the new target skill for that week.

1. Select three or four words from each week of instruction to create your cumulative word list.

2. Choose words that are less common (e.g., *vat* instead of *cat*) to avoid sight word issues. Nonsense words can also be used if your students are comfortable reading them.

3. Make a separate list for each week of instruction. This list should include the words from the current week and the previous five weeks. (See the sample on the next page.)

4. Assess six to eight students each week. This test should be administered one-on-one. You will monitor both accuracy and rate. This will allow you to cycle through your entire class in a month, yet not tax your time on any given day in a week.

5. Form differentiated instructional groups based on assessment results. Also address large issues, such as skills many students are struggling with, during whole group lessons. Add review and maintenance lessons and practice for these skills.

Unit 2, Week 2

Unit 1		Accuracy	Speed
Week 2	bag		
	vat		
	ham		
	lack		
Week 3	dim		
	jig		
	quiz		
	wax		
Week 4	grin		
	crack		
	trim		
	bran		
Week 5	fast		
	wink		
	mint		
	band		

Unit 2		Accuracy	Speed
Week 1	cot		
	pod		
	dock		
	jog		
Week 2	fed		
	yet		
	test		
	rent		

Number Accurate: _____ / 24

Number Automatic: _____ / 24

REASON 8: **No Comprehensive or Cumulative Mastery Assessment Tools** | 237

Directions for Administration

1. Make a copy of the assessment form for each student you are assessing in a given week. Assess six to eight students per week so that each student is assessed at least once per month.

2. Make a copy of the assessment for the student to read. Ask the student to read each word in order. The word list for each week includes words with the week's target phonics skills and words with skills from the previous five weeks to monitor mastery over time.

3. Put a check mark in the first box if the student accurately reads the word.

4. Put a check mark in the second box if the student automatically reads the word (fast—not slow or labored decoding).

5. If the student makes an error, record the error beside the word. Analyze the student errors for patterns that can inform small group instruction.

6. Score the assessment. The number or percentage read accurately indicates progress in learning the assessed phonics skills. The number or percentage read automatically indicates mastery (fluency).

Optional Administration

Pull together the words for each week to create a large, cumulative assessment for the year. (See the template that follows. Put words in each unit and week based on your curriculum's scope and sequence.) Administer the entire Cumulative Phonics Mastery Assessment at the beginning of the year and after each quarter or semester to check students' mastery of all the grade-level skills. Adjust instruction and reorganize small groups based on these results. Since you are assessing a large set of skills (some of which haven't been formally introduced), stop the assessment if a student misreads more than four words in a row (to avoid frustration early in the year). Monitor those skills students have mastered (i.e., those they can automatically and accurately decode over an *extended* period of time). Take note of those skills further in the sequence that students have an awareness of or can easily decode. Form differentiated instruction groups accordingly.

Grade — Cumulative Phonics Mastery Assessment

Unit 1		Accuracy	Speed
1 Week 1			
2			
3			
4			
5 Week 2			
6			
7			
8			
9 Week 3			
10			
11			
12			
13 Week 4			
14			
15			
16			
17 Week 5			
18			
19			
20			

Unit 2		Accuracy	Speed
1 Week 1			
2			
3			
4			
5 Week 2			
6			
7			
8			
9 Week 3			
10			
11			
12			
13 Week 4			
14			
15			
16			
17 Week 5			
18			
19			
20			

(Continued)

(Continued)

Unit 3		Accuracy	Speed
1 Week 1			
2			
3			
4			
5 Week 2			
6			
7			
8			
9 Week 3			
10			
11			
12			
13 Week 4			
14			
15			
16			
17 Week 5			
18			
19			
20			

Unit 4		Accuracy	Speed
1 Week 1			
2			
3			
4			
5 Week 2			
6			
7			
8			
9 Week 3			
10			
11			
12			
13 Week 4			
14			
15			
16			
17 Week 5			
18			
19			
20			

(Continued)

(Continued)

Unit 5		Accuracy	Speed
1 Week 1			
2			
3			
4			
5 Week 2			
6			
7			
8			
9 Week 3			
10			
11			
12			
13 Week 4			
14			
15			
16			
17 Week 5			
18			
19			
20			

Unit 6		Accuracy	Speed
1 Week 1			
2			
3			
4			
5 Week 2			
6			
7			
8			
9 Week 3			
10			
11			
12			
13 Week 4			
14			
15			
16			
17 Week 5			
18			
19			
20			

Number Accurate: _____ / 120

Number Automatic: _____ / 120

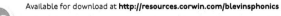
REASON 8: **No Comprehensive or Cumulative Mastery Assessment Tools** | 241

Courtesy of Rick Harrington Photography

When assessing students' knowledge of the alphabet, you need to assess both letter names and letter sounds. In addition, you need to assess both accuracy and speed. Following are two assessments. One is for monitoring mastery of letter names (both uppercase and lowercase). The other is for mastery of letter sounds. The sequence of the letters for each is based on the typical order in which letters and sounds are acquired (Phillips, Piasta, Anthony, Lonigan, & Francis, 2012; Piasta, 2014). I created it so that each assessment progresses from simple to complex. In that way, you can use the assessment results to modify your whole group lessons (e.g., spend less time on letters your students already know and more on those they don't) and form small groups based on specific letter-knowledge needs.

Letter-Name Assessment

	Uppercase	Accuracy	Speed			Uppercase	Accuracy	Speed
1	O				13	R		
2	B				14	K		
3	A				15	D		
4	C				16	F		
5	X				17	L		
6	P				18	Y		
7	S				19	Z		
8	E				20	G		
9	H				21	J		
10	T				22	N		
11	W				23	I		
12	M				24	Q		
					25	U		
					26	V		

Accuracy: _____ / 26

Speed: _____ / 26

Letters Mastered: _____

Focus Letters for Next Instructional Cycle: _____

Letter-Name Assessment

	lowercase	Accuracy	Speed
1	o		
2	b		
3	a		
4	c		
5	x		
6	p		
7	s		
8	e		
9	h		
10	t		
11	w		
12	m		

	lowercase	Accuracy	Speed
13	r		
14	k		
15	d		
16	f		
17	l		
18	y		
19	z		
20	g		
21	j		
22	n		
23	i		
24	q		
25	u		
26	v		

Accuracy: _____ / 26

Speed: _____ / 26

Letters Mastered: _____

Focus Letters for Next Instructional Cycle: _____

Letter-Sound Assessment

		Accuracy	Speed
1	c		
2	a		
3	b		
4	t		
5	p		
6	s		
7	k		
8	o		
9	j		
10	z		
11	f		
12	d		

		Accuracy	Speed
13	m		
14	v		
15	e		
16	g		
17	l		
18	h		
19	n		
20	r		
21	q		
22	i		
23	w		
24	x		
25	u		
26	y		

Accuracy: _____ / 26

Speed: _____ / 26

Letter Sounds Mastered: _____

Focus Letter Sounds for Next Instructional Cycle: _____

Courtesy of Rick Harrington Photography

REASON
9
TRANSITIONING TO MULTISYLLABIC WORDS TOO LATE

THE PROBLEM

Most curriculum focuses on one-syllable words for a large portion of Grade 2, yet the stories students read at that grade level are filled with more challenging, multisyllabic words. This mismatch between instruction and text poses challenges to many students who don't have the tools to effectively transition to reading these longer, more complex words. As a result, more emphasis needs to be given to transitioning to longer words at this grade level (e.g., going from known to new words like *can* to *candle* and teaching the six major syllable types).

In Grade 2, there is often some multisyllabic work, but too much occurs at or near the end of the year. Our second graders need to transition to multisyllabic words at a much faster rate than is provided in most curriculum because they will encounter these words in increasing numbers in the books and stories they read. So, for example, if you are reviewing short-vowel consonant–vowel–consonant (CVC) words at the *beginning* of the year, then add challenge words for *all* students that focus on a multisyllabic skill, such as "consonant + *le*." As a result, students will read words like *can, candle, bat, battle, rat,* and *rattle.* This easy transition using known words to build new words is a simple and scaffolded first step to students reading longer words without becoming overwhelmed. I recommend beginning this transition to longer words (and adding blending lines for all students) in late Grade 1. Add this "transition to longer words" work to your weekly lessons from the beginning of the year on in Grade 2.

This mismatch between instruction and text poses challenges to many students who don't have the tools to effectively transition to reading these longer, more complex words.

HOW TO FIX IT

Start by modifying your blending instruction to incorporate multisyllabic words. Below is an example of a blending line for Grade 2 that does this. Teach this lesson in the first week of school when students are reviewing short vowels. Notice that Column 1 goes from known words to multisyllabic words using the known word. Column 2 goes from closed syllables (one syllable) to multisyllabic words. Column 3 goes from open syllables (one syllable) to multisyllabic words. This lesson builds from the simple to the complex and gives the teacher an opportunity to review or introduce several syllable types (closed, open, consonant + *le*).

Column 1		Column 2		Column 3	
can	candle	drib	dribble	ta	table
bat	battle	peb	pebble	bu	bugle
scram	scramble	puz	puzzle	bri	bridle
jig	jiggle	un	uncle	fa	fable
bun	bundle	stum	stumble	ma	maple
sad	saddle	jun	jungle	ti	title
rid	riddle	ped	peddle	a	able
pick	pickle	tum	tumble	bi	bible

Directly teach the six syllable types in English to students in late Grade 1 and up. You might wish to only introduce a couple syllable types in Grade 1, then cover all of them beginning in Grade 2. The six syllable types include the following. Closed and open syllables are the most common and should be taught first. I've provided suggestions for which syllable types can be taught with which skills in Grade 2 in the suggested scope and sequence earlier in the book.

1. **Closed:** These syllables end in a consonant. The vowel sound is generally short (e.g., *rabbit, napkin*).

2. **Open:** These syllables end in a vowel. The vowel sound is generally long (e.g., *tiger, pilot*).

3. **Consonant + *le* (final stable syllable):** Usually when *le* appears at the end of a word and is preceded by a consonant, the consonant + *le* forms the final syllable (e.g., *table, little*). Other final stable syllables include *tion, sure,* and *ture.*

4. **Vowel team:** Many vowel sounds are spelled with vowel digraphs (teams) such as *ai, ay, ea, ee, oa, ow, oo, oi, oy, ie,* and *ei*. The vowel teams appear in the same syllable (e.g., *explain, rainbow*).

5. **r-Controlled:** When a vowel is followed by *r*, the letter *r* affects the sound of the vowel. The vowel and the *r* appear in the same syllable, acting as a team that can't be separated (e.g., *turtle, marble*).

6. **Final *e* (vowel–silent *e*):** These syllables generally represent long-vowel sounds, and even though the vowel and *e* don't appear side by side in a word, they act as a team and cannot be separated over syllable boundaries (e.g., *compete, decide*).

Just like you focus instruction in Grades K–1 on the many spellings for each of the 44 sounds in English, beginning in Grade 2 or 3, you can redirect some of that attention to the most common syllables in English so that students visually recognize them in longer words automatically. Edward Fry, Elizabeth Sakiey, Albert Goss, and Barry Loigman published a list of the 322 most common syllables in the 5,000 most frequent English words in the journal *Visible Language* (1980), and it's a highly useful list upon which to develop instruction. Research has shown that 92% of the syllables found in primary-grade readers have no more than two pronunciations, while 66% have only one pronunciation (Fry, Sakiey, Goss, & Loigman, 1980). This makes them highly reliable to teach. Numerous weekly activities can be created around these syllables (Blevins, 2011c).

Several other activities can help young learners gain flexibility with syllable parts in words. Use these and others to transition your students from reading one-syllable to multisyllabic words.

1. **Separated-Syllables Read:** Write words syllable by syllable, leaving enough space between the word parts to see the syllable divisions. Have students use their knowledge of syllable types to pronounce each syllable, then string the parts together to read the whole word. This reinforces syllable types and helps students verbalize their understanding. Point out how the final word will be an approximation of its syllable parts, since unaccented syllables generally take on the schwa sound.

fa ble   ad ven ture   fan tas tic

2. **Related-Syllables Read:** Write a series of related syllables. Have students use their knowledge of syllable types to correctly pronounce them. This reinforces students' understanding.

re rem em   bo bot ot

3. **Multisyllabic-Words Manipulation:** Divide words into syllables. Write each syllable on a note card. Display the syllables in jumbled order (e.g., *tas fan tic*). Have students rearrange the syllables to form the word.

4. **Syllable Scoop:** Write words from upcoming stories. Draw an arc (or scoop with your finger) under each syllable as students pronounce the word piece by piece. Extend the activity by having students code the words (open syllables, closed syllables, prefixes, suffixes, etc.).

5. **Speed Drills:** Create timed drills using a small set of syllables or words with a specific syllable type for students to practice. Students read the words on the speed drill multiple times over a week or more. After each drill, they are timed to see how long it takes to read the entire list, or how many words they can read in one minute. The goal is to become automatic with a small set of words with each syllable type that can be used to analyze other new words with the same syllables or syllable types. Following is an example of a speed drill. I took 20 words and repeated them multiple times throughout the drill. The same can be done with isolated syllables.

Sample Speed Drill

able	bubble	marble	eagle	handle	riddle	jungle	apple	single	puzzle
beetle	table	turtle	bubble	turtle	trouble	riddle	single	able	marble
puzzle	beetle	trouble	puzzle	single	handle	eagle	apple	jungle	table
marble	turtle	table	bubble	handle	able	apple	trouble	riddle	puzzle
eagle	handle	able	single	apple	eagle	jungle	puzzle	table	beetle
trouble	apple	beetle	marble	jungle	bubble	turtle	able	beetle	riddle
table	jungle	marble	single	trouble	riddle	handle	bubble	turtle	eagle
fable	puddle	bible	little	middle	settle	uncle	giggle	scramble	whistle
little	scramble	fable	whistle	puddle	scramble	giggle	settle	uncle	bible
settle	giggle	middle	uncle	puddle	middle	whistle	bible	little	fable

6. Reading Big Words: Lastly, teach a flexible way for students to attack any longer, more complex words. I recommend the following strategy:

   a. Look for the word parts (prefixes) at the beginning of the word.

   b. Look for the word parts (suffixes) at the end of the word.

   c. In the base word, look for familiar spelling patterns. Think about the six syllable spelling patterns you have learned.

   d. Sound out and blend together the word parts.

   e. Say the word parts fast. Adjust your pronunciation as needed. Ask yourself, "Is it a real word? Does it make sense in the sentence?"

REASON

10

OVERDOING IT

(Especially Isolated Skill Work)

THE PROBLEM

Some curriculum overemphasizes phonics (especially the isolated skill type of exercises) while ignoring other key aspects of early reading (e.g., vocabulary development and background knowledge building) that are essential to long-term reading growth. Modify your reading time to provide better balance, especially small group or Response-to-Intervention (RTI) time for struggling readers.

HOW TO FIX IT

The most important way to fix this issue is the most direct: Stop it! I am disheartened whenever I observe RTI time for our struggling readers and see the entire time devoted to phonics. There is such a focus on phonics instruction that students' vocabulary, background knowledge, and general comprehension needs are not being met. I get it. Students lack phonics skills, their development is easily measured, and progress can be shown more readily than the

> *Modify your reading time to provide better balance.*

development of vocabulary or background knowledge. However, *all* these students need *tons* of vocabulary and background knowledge building in order to continue to progress as readers and meet the increasing reading demands as they go from grade to grade. This is what plants the seeds of comprehension, especially in the later grades. To not have a more balanced approach with these students is a serious flaw that will perpetuate many of the reading issues they face. The vocabulary and background knowledge deficits might not be as evident until students reach Grade 3 and beyond, but what we've done is lost three years (kindergarten through Grade 2) in which we could have been aggressively building those skills to avoid the issues we know they will face in these upper grades otherwise. To overemphasize phonics in the early grades at the detriment of other critical skills is very shortsighted. So what do you do?

All these students need tons of vocabulary and background knowledge building in order to continue to progress as readers and meet the increasing reading demands as they go from grade to grade.

Devote at least half of your extra time with struggling readers to mastery of the basic phonics elements as long as this time is heavily focused on application of these skills (as opposed to mindless skill-and-drill activities or worksheets). Then develop a robust read-aloud and vocabulary strand. Commercial products for this are available (e.g., Beck's *Text Talk*; see http://teacher.scholastic.com/products/texttalk/research.htm) or you can create your own using read-alouds in your curriculum as well as books in your school or classroom library. Link those books to stories your students are reading, and their power will be increased. I discussed earlier in this book how a meaty read-aloud prior to students reading a decodable text can transform the discussion and inclusion of more sophisticated language you and students use with these books.

A meaty read-aloud prior to students reading a decodable text can transform the discussion and inclusion of more sophisticated language you and students use with these books.

For example, imagine that your students will read a decodable text called *Hop* during their phonics lesson this week. *Hop* is a simple photo book that features frogs. It shows frogs in various places and at various stages of a frog's life cycle. The text might read something like "I see a frog. It can hop. It hops to the pond. Hop, hop, hop! Frogs hop a lot!" Yes, there's not much to work with here in terms of new vocabulary. However, if you read a trade book like *Red-Eyed Tree Frog* (Cowley, 2006) or a page or two from your science book about frogs, their body parts, habitats, survival needs, and/or life cycle *before* students read the simple decodable, now imagine the conversation you could have using the photos. You could ask questions about frogs—their habitats and life cycle—using sophisticated vocabulary and engage students in a conversation about the photos in which they have opportunities to use these words. If we are more careful about our selection of read-alouds and link them to our early texts, we can get so much more out of them. Remember, whatever you frontload before reading a simple decodable text, you can then reinforce it during and after the reading through conversation and writing. Blow open the door in terms of all the ways you can use these simple early texts!

Carve time into each school day for reading aloud. I know many teachers who say they don't have time or who feel like this is wasting time. You do have time, and it isn't wasteful. If you have interactive conversations about these books with students, highlighting new vocabulary and concepts and giving students opportunities to express these ideas with new words, the benefits will be great. I recommend reading aloud 15 minutes in the morning (e.g., before going to lunch or recess) and 15 minutes in the afternoon (e.g., after returning from lunch or before going home). Aim for a 50/50 split between fiction and informational read-alouds. Select a fiction book for the morning, perhaps a longer chapter book that you and your students can sink into. Select an informational book for the afternoon. Keep in mind that informational read-alouds don't have to be entire books. They can be a chapter or even a few pages from a book, followed by an engaging conversation. They can even be a video on a topic, followed by word work and discussion. The more systematic you can be and the more you can link these read-alouds to student readings in your curriculum, the greater the benefits.

Aim for a 50/50 split between fiction and informational read-alouds.

Becoming more focused in your phonics instruction (e.g., adopting a faster pace to the instruction and activities, removing activities with less impact on reading and writing, balancing which activities receive more attention) will allow you to create the time needed for vocabulary and read-aloud work.

Also, **using adaptive technology (where available) can greatly assist you in meeting students' needs.** These programs create individualized pathways for each student based solely on that student's strengths and weaknesses, including varying degrees of support throughout the activities. Having students spend time each day on a phonics adaptive program can lessen the time needed to focus on these skills during differentiated small group instruction.

Courtesy of Rick Harrington Photography

My hope when writing this book was that the information, practical classroom ideas, and resources would encourage you to think about your phonics instruction in a *fresh* way. Many assume that since we have phonics lessons and instructional materials in place, our students are getting from this content what they need. As you have read, I believe that this isn't always the case. With new things for us to focus on in education—addressing text complexity, teaching students to find text evidence and write critically about what they read, implementing new standards, providing RTI time and instruction—phonics has faded in our consciousness. That doesn't mean we've mastered the teaching and assessing of this critical foundational skill and that it can or should be ignored. There's still more for us to do to fine-tune our instruction and practice to best meet our students' needs. As I said earlier, the best teachers I've worked with over the years are never satisfied. They are always questioning, always searching, always striving to improve their practices. That is why, I believe, you read this book. That is why, I believe, you will challenge yourself and everyone who comes in contact with your students to push their instruction to its highest level. Your students deserve that, and I thank you for your hard work and dedication to opening the door to reading, books, and a world of knowledge for each and every student who passes through your classroom.

References

Adams, M. J. (1990). *Beginning to read: Thinking and learning about print.* Cambridge: Massachusetts Institute of Technology.

Anderson, R. C., Hiebert, E. H., Scott, J. A., & Wilkinson, I. A. G. (1985). *Becoming a nation of readers: The report of the Commission on Reading.* Champaign, IL: Center for the Study of Reading and National Academy of Education.

Bear, D. R., Templeton, S., Invernizzi, M., & Johnston, F. (2016). *Words their way: Word study for phonics, vocabulary, and spelling instruction* (6th ed.). Upper Saddle River, NJ: Pearson.

Bear, D. R., Templeton, S., Invernizzi, M., & Johnston, F. (1996). *Words their way: Word study for phonics, vocabulary, and spelling instruction.* Englewood Cliffs, NJ: Merrill/Prentice-Hall.

Beck, I., & Beck, M. E. (2013). *Making sense of phonics: The hows and whys* (2nd ed.). New York, NY: Guilford Press.

Beck, I., & Juel, C. (1995, Summer). The role of decoding in learning to read. *American Education, 19*(2).

Blevins, W. (2011a). *Teaching the alphabet: A flexible, systematic approach to building early phonics skills.* New York, NY: Scholastic.

Blevins, W. (2011b). *Teaching phonics: A flexible, systematic approach to building early reading skills.* New York, NY: Scholastic.

Blevins, W. (2011c). *Week-by-week phonics and word study activities for the intermediate grades.* New York, NY: Scholastic.

Blevins, W. (2006). *Phonics from A to Z: A practical guide.* New York, NY: Scholastic.

Blevins, W. (2001). *Teaching phonics and word study in the intermediate grades.* New York, NY: Scholastic.

Britton, J. (1983). Writing and the story world. In B. M. Kroll & C. G. Wells (Eds.), *Explorations in the development of writing: Theory, research, and practice* (pp. 3–30). New York, NY: Wiley.

Carroll, J. B. (1971). *The American Heritage word frequency book.* Boston, MA: Houghton Mifflin.

Carroll, J. B., Davies, P., & Richman, B. (1971). *Word frequency book.* Boston, MA: Houghton Mifflin.

Chall, J. S. (1996). *Stages of reading development* (2nd ed.). Fort Worth, TX: Harcourt.

Chall, J. S. (1983). *Stages of reading development.* New York, NY: McGraw-Hill.

Chall, J. S. (1967). *Learning to read: The great debate.* New York, NY: McGraw-Hill.

Cowley, J. (2006). *Red-eyed tree frog.* New York, NY: Scholastic.

Dolch, E. W. (1948). *Problems in reading.* Champaign, IL: Garrard Press.

Ehri, L. C. (1992). Reconceptualizing the development of sight word reading and its relationship to recoding. In P. Gough, L. Ehri, & R. Treiman (Eds.), *Reading acquisition* (pp. 107–143). Hillsdale, NJ: Erlbaum.

Ehri, L. C., Nunes, S. R., Stahl, S. A., & Willows, D. M. (2001). Systematic phonics instruction helps students learn to read: Evidence from the National Reading Panel's meta-analysis. *Review of Educational Research, 71,* 393–447.

Ehri, L. C., & Roberts, T. (2006). The roots of learning to read and write: Acquisition of letters and phonemic awareness. In D. K. Dickinson & S. B. Neuman (Eds.), *Handbook of early literacy research* (Vol. 2, pp. 113–131). New York, NY: Guilford.

Fisher, D., & Frey, N. (2014). *Better learning through structured teaching* (2nd ed.). Alexandria, VA: ASCD.

Fry, E. (2000). *1000 instant words.* Garden Grove, CA: Teacher Created Resources.

Fry, E. B., Kress, E., & Fountoukidis, D. L. (1993). *The new reading teacher's book of lists.* Englewood Cliffs, NJ: Prentice-Hall.

Fry, E., Sakiey, E., Goss, A., & Loigman, B. (1980). A syllable frequency count. *Visible Language, 14*(2), 137–150.

Gough, P. B., & Walsh, M. A. (1991). Chinese, Phoenicians, and the orthographic cipher of English. In S. A. Brady & D. P. Shankweiler (Eds.), *Phonological process in literacy: A tribute to Isabelle Y. Liberman* (pp. 199–209). Hillsdale, NJ: Erlbaum.

Haddock, M. (1978). Teaching blending in beginning reading instruction is important. *The Reading Teacher, 31,* 654–658.

Hanna, P. R., Hodges, R. E., Hanna, J. L., & Rudolph, E. H. (1966). *Phoneme-grapheme correspondences as cues to spelling improvement.* Washington, DC: U.S. Office of Education.

Hattie, J. (2012). *Visible learning for teachers: Maximizing impact on learning.* New York, NY: Routledge.

Hattie, J. (2009). *Visible learning: A synthesis of meta-analyses relating to achievement.* New York, NY: Routledge.

Honig, B. (1995). *How should we teach our children to read?* Center for Systemic School Reform, San Francisco State University.

Johns, J. L. (1980). First graders' concepts about print. *Reading Research Quarterly, 15,* 529–549.

Juel, C., & Roper-Schneider, D. (1985). The influence of basal readers on first-grade reading. *Reading Research Quarterly, 20*(2), 134–152.

Lovett, M. W. (1987). A developmental approach to reading disability: Accuracy and speed criteria of normal and deficient reading skill. *Child Development, 58*(1), 234–260.

Manzo, A., & Manzo, U. (1993). *Literacy disorders: Holistic diagnosis and remediation.* New York, NY: Harcourt.

McGee, L. M., Kim, H., Nelson, K. S., & Fried, M. D. (2015). Change over time in first graders' strategic use of information at point of difficulty in reading. *Reading Research Quarterly, 50*(3), 263–291.

Moats, L. C. (2010). *Speech to print: Language essentials for teachers* (2nd ed.). Baltimore, MD: Brookes.

Moats, L. C. (2000). *Speech to print: Language essentials for teachers.* Baltimore, MD: Brookes.

Moats, L. C. (1995). *Spelling: Development, disability, and instruction.* Timonium, MD: York Press.

Moats, L. C. (1994). The missing foundation in teacher education: Knowledge of the structure of spoken and written language. *Annals of Dyslexia, 44*(1), 81–102.

National Institute of Child Health and Human Development. (2000). *Report of the National Reading Panel: Teaching children to read: An evidence-based assessment of the scientific literature on reading and its implications for reading instruction* (NIH Publication No. 00–4769). Washington, DC: U.S. Government Printing Office.

Pearson, P. D., & Gallagher, M. C. (1983). The instruction of reading comprehension. *Contemporary Educational Psychology, 8*, 317–344.

Phillips, B. M., Piasta, S. B., Anthony, J. L., Lonigan, C. J., & Francis, D. J. (2012). IRTs of the ABCs: Children's letter name acquisition. *Journal of School Psychology, 50*(4), 461–481.

Piasta, S. B. (2014). Moving to assessment-guided differentiated instruction to support young children's alphabet knowledge. *The Reading Teacher, 68*(3), 202–211.

Pinnell, G. S., & Fountas, I. C. (2003). *Phonics lessons: Letters, words, and how they work.* Portsmouth, NH: FirstHand.

Popp, H. M. (1964). Visual discrimination of alphabet letters. *The Reading Teacher, 17*, 221–226.

Rasinski, T. (2005). *Daily word ladders.* New York, NY: Scholastic.

Resnick, L., & Beck, I. (1976). Designing instruction in reading: Initial reading. In A. J. Harris & E. R. Sipay (Eds.), *Readings on reading instruction.* New York, NY: Longman.

Reutzel, D. R. (2015). Early literacy research: Findings primary-grade teachers will want to know. *The Reading Teacher, 69*(1), 14–24. doi:10.1002/trtr.1387

Rinsland, H. D. (1945). *A basic vocabulary of elementary school children.* New York, NY: Macmillan.

Rosenshine, B., & Stevens, R. (1984). Classroom instruction in reading. In P. D. Pearson, R. Barr. M. L. Kamil, & P. Mosenthal (Eds.), *Handbook of reading* (pp. 745–798). New York, NY: Longman.

Shankweiler, D., & Liberman, I. (1989). *Phonology and reading disability: Solving the reading puzzle.* Ann Arbor: University of Michigan Press.

Snow, C. E., Burns, M. S., & Griffin, E. (Eds.). (1998). *Preventing reading difficulties in young children.* Washington, DC: National Academy Press.

Stanovich, K. E. (1992). Speculations on the causes and consequences of individual differences in early reading acquisition. In P. B. Gough, L. C. Ehri, & R. Treiman (Eds.), *Reading acquisition* (pp. 307–342). Hillsdale, NJ: Erlbaum.

Stanovich, K. E. (1986). Matthew effects in reading: Some consequences of individual differences in the acquisition of literacy. *Reading Research Quarterly, 21,* 360–407.

Stein, M., Johnson, B., & Gutlohn, L. (1999). Analyzing beginning reading programs: The relationship between decoding instruction and text. *Remedial and Special Education, 20*(5), 275–287.

Torgeson, J. K., & Bryant, B. (1994). *Phonological awareness training for reading.* Austin, TX: Pro-Ed.

Treiman, R., & Baron, J. (1981). Segmental analysis ability: Development and relation to reading ability. In G. E. MacKinnon & T. G. Waller (Eds.), *Reading research: Advances in theory and practice* (Vol. 3, pp. 159–198). New York, NY: Academic Press.

Wong, M. (2015, May 29). Brain wave study shows how different teaching methods affect reading development. *Medical Xpress.* Retrieved from medicalxpress.com/news/2015-05-brain-methods-affect.html

Yoncheva, Y. N., Wise, J., & McCandliss, B. (2015, June–July). Hemispheric specialization for visual words is shaped by attention to sublexical units during initial learning. *Brain and Language, 145–146,* 22–33.

Index

definition of, xi–xii

effective instruction, key characteristics of, xviii–xx

explicit instruction and, xxv

failures in, xx–xxi

guided reading, phonics sequence for, 45–50

language/meaning, access to, xv, xvi, 28–29

phonics-comprehension flowchart and, xxvi

phonics vs. whole language debate and, xv, xviii

planned/purposeful instruction and, xiii

research/literature on, xii–xiii, xv, xxiii–xxv

skill-and-drill reputation of, xvi, xxv

sound-spelling patterns and, xix, xxvii

systematic approach to, xxv

See also Blending strategy; Connected texts; High-frequency words; Literacy learning; Phonemic awareness; Phonics instruction problems; Readiness skills; Scope/sequence issues; Teaching practices; Word awareness activities

Phonics instruction problems, xx–xxi, 201–220

comprehensive/cumulative mastery assessments, lack of, 235–245

curriculum imbalance and, 253–255

gradual release model, ineffective use of, 219–222

inappropriate lesson pacing and, 231–233

inappropriate reading materials and, 215–218

multisyllabic words, late transition to, 247–251

real reading/writing experiences, lack of, 211–213

review/repetition opportunities, inadequacies with, 203–209

teacher phonics/linguistics knowledge, limitations on, 227–229

transitions, time lost during, 223–226

See also Phonics instruction; Professional development; Teaching practices

Phonics/linguistics knowledge limitations, 52–53, 227

grade-level teacher teams and, 227, 228, 229

linguistics, utility of, 228

phonics knowledge base, evaluation of, 228

professional development opportunities and, 227–228

self-study mini-course, development of, 228

speech therapists, linguistics knowledge of, 229

targeted phonics courses and, 229

See also Phonics instruction problems

Phonics-Phonemic Awareness Quick Assessment, 163, 164, 165

Phonological awareness, 4

Picture-sound sort, 22

Pinnell, G. S., 47

Prior knowledge, 27–28, 53

Problems. *See* Phonics instruction problems

Professional development:

best practices, exploration of, 194

blending routines, enhanced teacher knowledge of, 78–79

decodable text, use of, 162–163

differentiated professional development and, xix, 193–194

linguistics background and, 52–53, 188, 227–229

phonics knowledge, enhancement of, 188–189, 227–229

restructuring of, 193–195

teacher capacity building and, xix, 188–189

See also Phonics instruction problems; Teaching practices

Proficient readers, xii

Pseudowords, 163–164

efficacious materials/tools and, 191–192

80–20 principle of instruction and, 190, 191

formative assessment data and, 36, 92, 107, 190–191

high-frequency words and, 135–141

high-frequency words self-assessment and, 145–146, 151

instructional leap forward and, 196

linguistics background and, 52–53, 188, 227–229

novels, study of, 191

phonemic awareness instruction and, 8–19

phonics knowledge, enhancement of, 188–189

phonics/word study, specialized learning activity of, 195

professional development, restructuring of, 193–195

readiness skills instruction, 17–25

readiness skills self-assessment and, 17–19, 20, 25

research-based phonics routines and, 227–229

rhyme activities and, 187–188

scaffolded instruction and, 9, 13, 47, 247–248

scope/sequence issues and, 37–50

scope/sequence self-assessment and, 56–58, 67–68

skill review, instructional transitions and, 21

summary of, 196

systematic instruction and, xxv, 51, 203–204, 206

teacher-controlled reading instruction and, 189–192

teacher-researcher role and, 192

teaching practices self-assessment, 196

team teaching/group planning and, 193

videotaped lessons and, 195

word awareness activities and, 111–118

word awareness self-assessment and, 121–127, 134

See also Apps; Phonics instruction; Phonics instruction problems; Professional development; Whiteboard activities

Templeton, S., 4, 115

Text alignment. *See* Connected texts; Inappropriate reading materials; Real reading/writing experiences

Trade books, 155, 167

Transitions, 223

grade 1/grade 2 lesson outline and, 226

instructional transitions and, 21, 224

kindergarten lesson outline and, 225

manipulatives, distribution/collection of, 223, 224

readiness for learning procedure and, 224

skill review, instructional transitions and, 21

student misbehavior and, 224

time lost during, 223–226

See also Multisyllabic words; Phonics instruction problems

Vocabulary development, xxiv, 53, 169–171, 175–176, 253

Vowel-consonant (VC) words, 28, 39

Vowel teams, 27–28

Whiteboard activities:

blending strategy and, 87–89

decodable texts activities and, 184, 185

decoding assessment activity, 163–164

dictation exercises and, 103, 104

phonemic awareness activities and, 22

word building/word sort activities and, 131–133

Whole language approach, xi, xv, xviii

Whole-word method, xviii

Wilkinson, I. A. G., xxiv, 158, 160, 162, 216

Willows, D. M., xi

Wong, M., xviii
Woodcock Reading Mastery Test
    (WRMT), 163, 164–165
Word awareness activities, xix,
    111–112
  apps for, 132
  benefits of, 118
  best instructional practices and,
      116–118, 134
  blending strategy, use of, 86,
      113, 116
  explicit instruction and, 111
  follow-up questioning and,
      119–120, 128, 131
  high-utility words and, 120
  implicit/discovery method and,
      111–112
  instructional leap forward and,
      128–133, 134
  instructional pitfalls and, 119–120
  letter/word cards, management of,
      113, 119, 124, 132
  leveled word lists and, 106–107
  materials, management of, 119
  modeling word building and, 116
  phonogram list word sort activity
      and, 125–126
  phonological awareness and, 4
  rote learning and, 114
  sound-spelling patterns and, 118
  summary for, 134
  teacher self-assessment and,
      121–127, 134
  whiteboard activities for, 131–133
  word-building card template
      and, 127
  word-building procedure and,
      116–117
  word-building schedule and, 122
  word building, types of, 112–113
  word ladder activity and, 128,
      129–130
  word sets, creation of, 123, 128, 131
  word-sort procedure and, 117
  word-sort schedule and, 122

word sorts, types of, 114–115
words, selection of, 120, 123, 131
  See also Phonemic awareness;
      Readiness skills
Word building, xix, 15, 28–29, 61–62,
    86, 112
  blending strategy and, 113, 116
  materials, management of, 119
  modeling of, 116
  procedure for, 116–117
  review opportunities and, 206
  schedule for, 122
  summary for, 134
  word awareness and, 113, 117
  word-building card template
      and, 127
  word sets, creation of, 123, 128
  See also Word awareness activities
Word families, 142, 143, 148
Word ladder activity, 128, 129–130
Word sorts, xix, 61–62, 86, 112, 114
  closed sorts and, 114
  common word sorts and, 115
  knowledge building and, 115
  materials, management of, 119
  open sorts and, 114
  phonogram list word sort activity
      and, 125–126
  procedure for, 117
  review opportunities and, 206
  schedule for, 122
  summary for, 134
  timed sorts and, 115
  word sets, creation of, 123
  See also Word awareness activities
Word Wall HD app, 103, 106
Writing practice:
  connected texts and, 169,
      176–177, 183
  phonics growth and, 57–58, 92,
      98–99, 103
  reading decodable texts and, 169,
      176–177
  See also Dictation; Real reading/
      writing experiences

CORWIN LITERACY

Nancy Boyles

On classroom-ready resources to get close reading right in grades 3–6

Nancy Boyles

On ready-to-go units and planning tools to ramp up close reading for grades K–2 and 3–6

Douglas Fisher, Nancy Frey, & Diane Lapp

On how to use complexity as a dynamic, powerful tool for using right text at just the right time

Douglas Fisher, Nancy Frey, & John Hattie

On identifying the instructional routines that have the biggest impact on student learning

Douglas Fisher & Nancy Frey

On how text-dependent questions can inspire close and critical thinking

Douglas Fisher & Nancy Frey

On five access points for seriously stretching students' capacity to comprehend complex text